Saving
Bliss

Zanne Sweeney

This for you, Jude - Lone Wolf.
You saved the best for last! Miss you. RIP

Thank you to our Armed Forces. Stay safe.

Acknowledgements:
Jude Paine
Maureen Sanchelli
Elm Street Design Studio
Rick Schroeppel
Cover photo by: Iordani

Chapter 1

Eighteen-year-old Bliss Allan turned the worn brass doorknob and leaned her shoulder against her homes front door to push it open. Her attention was focused on what her best friend Caitlyn was jabbering away about. Tonight, was their Senior Talent Show and Caitlyn was sharing with Bliss all the gossip that she had heard about tonight's acts. It was tradition at their high school that the Seniors put on a show. Most of the students and many parents attended the variety show that was completely run by the Senior class. It was also tradition that one of the skits, entitled, 'This Really Happened' was based on some poor, unsuspecting students high school drama. Last year's victim was Tommy Lee, who had been dating his girlfriend Andrea for a year. He made the grave error of drunkenly hooking up with a sophomore after Andrea had left a party. Somehow, Andrea had never found out about it until last spring's show, when two Seniors decided to out Tommy Lee in the skit. Andrea had taken one look at Tommy Lee, realized the skit was true, and had fled the auditorium crying. Bliss thought it was mean and had silently worried that she might be the butt of the skit this year.

Caitlyn continued to prattle "It could be about Brook and Liam's break up, or how Peter told Harvey he was gay and then the next day denied it."

Bliss opened the door and turned back towards Caitlyn, "or it could be about you and how you were dating three guys at the same time and none of them knew about the other." she told her best friend with a chuckle.

"Oh no, you're the only one who knew about that. You didn't tell anyone did you?" Caitlyn was momentarily silent as she followed Bliss into her living room, but deep down she knew there was no way Bliss would ever betray her.

"No, of course not." Bliss said slightly exasperated that her one friend would even consider that she would tell her secret. Bliss came to an abrupt stop and Caitlyn ran into the back of her, causing her to grunt.

"What the hell Bliss?" Caitlyn said as she moved to stand alongside of Bliss. What Caitlyn saw caused her to gasp.

Bliss' mother lay unmoving on the wooded floor in the living room, A large pool of dark liquid fanned out from her misshaped head. The smell of copper hung in the air.

Caitlyn stood frozen in her tracks. Her hand slapped over her open mouth in horror. "Mom!" Bliss screeched in an almost inhuman voice. Bliss ran to her mother's side and fought back the vomit threatening to come up. Bliss heard Caitlyn crying hysterically as she gave the 9-1-1 operators her homes address. Years later, when Bliss looked back on that horrific moment, she gave Caitlyn major creds for not running out of the house. Bliss knew her mom was gone as she knelt down next to her. Her beautiful face was colorless and the sickening wound to her head had left her skull partially collapsed. Bliss felt for a pulse knowing she wouldn't find one. She even tried to shake her, praying the injury wasn't as bad as it looked. Tears spilled down Bliss' face, distorting the lenses in her glasses. She took off her thick lensed, heavy framed glasses and burrowed her face into her mom's chest and sobbed.

Within minutes the police arrived, followed by an ambulance, and then finally Caitlyn's parents came. Rose, Caitlyn's mom wrapped Bliss in an afghan, that she took from the couch. She gently coaxed Bliss to unclasp her mother's cold body, and she walked Bliss and her daughter out of the house. The coroner arrived as they traversed the now busy front walkway. Behind the coroner two young men wheeled an empty gurney. Bliss shivered and gulped back bile, knowing her mom's lifeless body would soon be placed in the neatly folded, ominous black bag that lay strapped on the wheeled stretcher. The General, Caitlyn's father, his name was Liam, but everyone called him General, referring to his elite status in the Army, pulled up behind his wife's SUV and gathered Caitlyn into his loving arms. He then ushered the two girls and his wife into his wife's car and hurriedly dismissed the solider that had driven him to the horrific crime scene with a salute.

In the car, being held maternally by Rose, Bliss thought of Jax, her brother, who was five years older than herself. Jax had been recruited by the Drug Enforcement Agency (DEA) after graduating college. After he had successfully completed his training, he had been given his first undercover assignment. Bliss and her mom rarely heard from him, and there was no way to get in touch with him directly. Bliss' mom had the number of someone they could contact in case of an emergency, but Bliss had no idea where that number even was. She whispered to Rose that she wanted her brother and Rose nodded as she looked towards her husband who was watching them in the rearview mirror of the car.

When they got to Caitlyn's house, Bliss and Caitlyn were seen by a doctor who gave them both sedatives. Caitlyn fell off to sleep, but Bliss remained awake. The police arrived, two in uniforms and two plain clothed detectives. They questioned her but she couldn't tell them anything. It was unfathomable to her that someone would want to hurt her mom. Her mom was sweet and kind and had worked hard to give her and Jax a good home. She had no enemies; everyone loved her.

Bliss explained to the detectives that she and Caitlyn had stopped by her house to pick up clothes for tonight's Senior show. Then they were going to Caitlyn's house to get ready. Rose confirmed all this t the detectives. Then Rose added that, Bliss' mom, Fran, the General, and she were planning to attend to the show as well..

They questioned the General, since Bliss' mom worked for him on the nearby Army base, but he too had no idea who would want Fran Allen dead. The General told them he wasn't working on anything that would warrant Fran's death. The General then called the Military Police, (MP's) from his base, since Fran had worked for him. They sent over two men and a Criminal Investigator. Bliss sat on the couch, still wrapped in the afghan and half listened while the men around her talked in hushed tones.

Her entire world had just been upended. She was a Senior in high school and two short weeks away from graduating. In the fall she would be attending the University of Maryland Baltimore County, (UMBC) an honors college in Maryland that had become nationally known for their cutting-edge courses in technology. Bliss had been given a decent scholarship, but it wasn't a full ride. Her Mom assured her she could handle the extra expenses, but to make sure Bliss was going to join Reserve Officers' Training Corp (ROTC). That scholarship money wouldn't kick in for a year though. A profound sense of loneliness assaulted Bliss. She was essentially on her own now. Jax was so off the grid it was daunting. Bliss knew he would be devastated when he found out. Their father had left when she had been a baby and Jax had been only 5 years old. It had had destroyed him and she knew her mom had never gotten over his leaving either. Her mom had rarely spoken of her father. She remembered the one time she had

asked her mom about the lack of photos of her dad. Her mom had grown sullen making Bliss instantly regret the question, so Bliss never brought him up again.

Her brother Jax had carried around a major chip on his shoulder for a long time. He had gotten into fights in school, which prompted her mom to move their family from Colorado, to Ohio. The only time Bliss had heard her mom and Jax argue was when her mom had told Jax they were moving. Jax did not want to move. She remembered how he begged their mom to stay, telling her that if they moved, their dad would never be able to find them. It hadn't mattered; two weeks later they moved to Ohio. Whenever anyone asked where their father was their automatic response was that he had died. It was just easier that way. After Jax graduated from college and joined the DEA, Bliss' mom once again moved them, this time it was to Pemberton, New Jersey Her mom wasn't in the Army, yet she had always worked for someone on a base. The very first week her mom started working for the General, they had been invited to the Doherty's house for a barbecue. That's how Bliss met Caitlyn. They would have eventually met each other when school started in the Fall, they were both going into the 8th grade, but even Bliss had to admit that it was pretty nice going to a new school and already knowing someone, especially since that someone was as popular as Caitlyn. Caitlyn was pretty, outgoing, and was the middle school fashionista. She also had a ton of friends. She was the polar opposite of Bliss. Bliss wasn't considered to be pretty; she was shy and reserved, and with no desire to dress to impress; her normal attire consisted of sweat pants and sweat shirts. Bliss had a decent figure, but because it was hidden under her baggy sports clothes no one even knew. There were a few things Bliss excelled at. For one she was a good athlete. She loved field hockey and lacrosse but wearing goggles proved problematic during games, so she ended up switching to cross country and track. She was a straight 'A' student, a computer guru, and put others to shame with the amount of Community Service hours she acquired. The one personal hell that Bliss suffered was her severe farsightedness that had plagued her since she was three years old. She wore thick framed, heavy glasses that hid much of her face and left red indentation marks on her nose and. Her vision worsened with age and in accordance with her diminishing vision her ugly lenses became thicker When they had attended their first dance Caitlyn had encouraged her to wear mascara, but Bliss was farsighted so she couldn't see when she took her glasses off, making it impossible to put the mascara on. Caitlyn had applied it and had even helped her with lip-gloss. The makeup had not made any difference though. Bliss was still snickered at. The teasing that she looked like Mr. Magoo was one she'd heard so often that it didn't even faze her anymore. The first time she had heard it, she had to look up who Mr. Magoo was.

Rose walked into the living room and handed her a cup of tea, which jolted Bliss back to the present. She politely said thank you, placing the cup and saucer on the nearby end table. Bliss was still feeling overwhelmed. How could her mom be dead?

The front door burst open and Collin, Caitlyn's middle brother burst through it. He took one look at all the officers in the room and seeing the pain etched on everyone's faces knew he had been called home from college because of a tragedy. He immediately sought out his parents and after seeing they were fine, he looked for Caitlyn. He didn't see her, but before he could freak out his mother grasped his arm and pointed up the stairs. He then mouthed, 'Connor?' to his mom and after she shook her head his eyes then locked on Bliss, his sister's best friend. He saw the

grief stamped on her face and watched helplessly as she kept lifting her heavy glasses to wipe the tears from her
eyes.
Rose led him back into the kitchen and Bliss followed them with her eyes. Collin kept looking back at her as Rose walked him through the men that stood in the living room, talking quietly. Bliss knew he was about to hear the gruesome details of how she and Caitlyn had discovered her mother.
The day of the funeral came, and Bliss knew she would have never survived it without the support from Caitlyn's family. She had been staying at the Doherty's since the tragedy. Rose and the General had been instrumental helping her plan her the funeral. Caitlyn was an emotional rock. Collin rarely left her side during the wake and funeral. Caitlyn had held one of her hands and Collin had stood guard over the two of them. After the funeral the guests went back to the Doherty's for the repast. Rose and the General had food catered in and Bliss and Caitlyn sat side by side on the couch, Caitlyn still held Bliss' hand as she received condolences from her mom's work friends, her friends, their parents, teachers and people Bliss did not even know. It was distressing, exhausting, and overwhelming.
Caitlyn was quietly chatting with one of their classmates as Bliss numbly stared out the front window. She watched as the front door opened thinking she would see another guest, but instead Connor, Caitlyn's oldest brother walked in. Caitlyn jumped off the couch and ran into her big brother's arms. Connor dropped his green duffel bag and

scooped up his little sister. Collin was the next one to greet him and then Rose flew out of the kitchen to hug her son. Connor was six years older than Bliss and Caitlyn and he was a Green Beret, Special Forces. He was never home, and Bliss wondered if the General had pulled some strings to get home. After shaking his father's hand Connor headed towards Bliss. His face was so serious as he approached her, and she willed back the tears that threatened to rain down her face. Connor knelt down next to the couch and touched her knee.

"Hey kid, I'm sorry about your mom."

Bliss nodded and tried to think of something intelligent to say back to him, but her mouth was dry, and she knew whatever she said would come out garbled, so she remained quiet.

"Mom says you're staying here." Bliss looked up from examining his hand on her knee and nodded.

"I think that's a good idea. Now when I come home, I won't have to track down my favorite gamer." That brought a tiny smile to Bliss' face and she watched as Connor smiled back at her. Along with being a natural athlete Bliss was a total geek in the world of video games, Call of Duty, Grand Theft Auto; she was good at all of them. Caitlyn always thought Bliss would grow tired of playing them, but if anything, she had become even more hooked. Bliss played on line and had established a good rep in the gaming communities she participated in. Collin gave up trying to beat her years ago, but Connor had always been able to hold his own against her, and they had developed a habit of playing a few games, when he was stateside, and at least one whenever he had come home to Pemberton. Through the years they had developed a unique bond. Partially over their mutual love of gaming, but Connor was military, and Bliss knew she would one day be military too, although no one but her knew that. Connor was six years older than herself, but he had never treated her like a little kid and Bliss appreciated that.

The General approached them, and Connor stood up as the General sat down next to Bliss on the couch. "Bliss, your mom's lawyer is here. Can you handle this now?"

Bliss let out a long breath and stood up. "Might as well get it over with, right?" She answered. The General gave her a fatherly pat and Connor stepped aside as Bliss followed the General towards his study. Outside of the closed door the General stopped and turned to her, "Bliss you are 18, of legal age, you can meet with the lawyer alone, but if you'd like, I can come in with you?"

Bliss did not even have to think about her response. The General and Rose had been such a constant in her life for the last five years that it was inconceivable that she would ever purposely shut them out of her life. She had a fleeting moment of despair thinking that it was just as inconceivable that she had buried her mother today and she would never see her again. "No, General, please come in with me. I'd actually appreciate it."

The General smiled gently at her. Bliss could see he too was feeling the loss of her mother. She had been his administrative assistant for the last five years and they had formed a bond not only at work but also as parents of two girls that had become best friends.

The General opened the door to his study and she saw a woman who Bliss had never seen before sitting in one of the chairs near the Generals desk. The woman, dressed in a business suit, stood as they walked in and extended her hand.

"Bliss, my name is Carla Peterson. I'm your mom's lawyer." Bliss shook her hand and then shook her head back and forth.

"I didn't even know she had a lawyer." she expressed quietly.

Carla motioned towards a vacant seat indicating that Bliss should sit and the General took a seat behind his desk.

"I'm so sorry about your mom. She was a wonderful person."

"Thank you." The response was now rote.

"I have your mom's will here and I just want you to know what it says. I think it will help answer some questions you probably have."

"Shouldn't we wait for Jax? I mean, am I even allowed to hear the will without him here?"

The General spoke softly. "Bliss, Honey, I called his contact. They are trying to reach him."

"Oh, I didn't know. Thank you."

"Bliss your mom owned her home, but the bank owns a good part of it too. If you sell it, at current market price, you and Jax would get about 50 thousand dollars each. The furniture is all yours to do with what you want. The car is paid off and is yours as well. Your mom owned a few pieces of jewelry that she wanted to make sure you received." Bliss nodded remembering her mom wearing a few special pieces. The General reached into his top drawer and brought out her mom's bracelet. A bracelet that Bliss knew her father had given her and one that she had never, ever taken off. She gasped when she saw it and cupped her hand so the General could place it in her palm. Tears formed in her eyes again and she lifted her glasses to wipe them away.

"My mom never took this off. I can't believe I forgot about it."

"Your mom wrote in her will that she would like for you to wear it." Bliss nodded and

Carla helped her fasten it to her wrist.

The bracelet was silver and had two small discs attached to the delicate chain. One disc had an 'X' etched into it and the other 'O'. Bliss knew one was for a hug, and one was for a kiss. The clasp was a square piece that had an intricate and beautiful etching of a mountain and a sun. These represented Bliss, Colorado where Bliss was born and Jacksonville, Florida where Jax was born. It was where their names came from. Her mom had told her that her father had given her the bracelet after she had been born and he had asked that she never take it off. The square clasp had a rectangle shaped thin opening in which a two pronged catch was inserted to hold the bracelet together and it also had a small chain which attached on either side of the clasp that would prevent the bracelet from falling off the wrist if the clasp were to break.

Bliss had once asked why she had continued to wear the bracelet, after all her father had just abandoned them. Her mother had gotten a sentimental look in her eyes and told Bliss that her father had given her the bracelet out of love, and that although he had left them, he had loved her Bliss and Jax with all of his heart. When Bliss tried to question her as to why he would leave if he loved them, her mother had quickly changed the subject.

Bliss did not have any pictures of her father, which she thought was odd. Jax remembered him somewhat but with whatever memory a five-year old can retain. Bliss often wondered if her mother was still in contact with her dad. Every once in a while, maybe twice a year, her mom would get a call on her cell and when she answered it, she would quickly move to a more private place in the house. After receiving those calls, her mom had always seemed somewhat sad and on more than one occasion she had pleaded a headache and gone into her bedroom. The trip down memory lane was broken as Carla said her name for the second time.

"Bliss, your mom has a few stocks that will be divided between you and Jax, you can keep them or sell them, just let me know what you want to do. Something I know you didn't know about was that your mom has saved over two hundred thousand dollars and that is to be used for your college tuition and after you graduate the remaining amount will be split between you and Jax."

"No way." Bliss said in a hushed voice. "She didn't have that kind of money. I think there's been a mistake."

Carla chuckled and handed Bliss a printed copy of a bank statement. The total was two hundred and two thousand dollars.

"I can't believe it. She worked so hard. She was always saying we needed the money. I don't understand?"

"Well here's all you need to know. The funds are available for you to use for college. She made the General the trustee so he can pay for all your college bills and anything else you will need for school. After you finish school or when you turn twenty-five, whichever comes first, whatever is left will be transferred into yours and Jax's personal accounts."

"So Jax can't have his part of the money until I graduate or turn twenty-five?"

"That's correct." Carla acknowledged.

"What if he needs money?"

"Well that's where the General comes in. If Jax needs money and you are okay with it, the General can draw against the account. The General understands that you must have your college paid for though, your mom was insistent upon that. Bliss, she paid for Jax's college and she said it's only right that she pays for yours as well"

Bliss looked at the General and he nodded. "Believe it or not we discussed this Bliss. Neither of us expected this tragedy to occur, but when your mom made the appointment with Carla, she came to me first and we discussed this. She made the will two years ago."

"General, the money though. Where did she get that money?"

"I have no idea, Honey. The amount was a surprise to me as well."

"Okay, this is all so surreal." Bliss said sadly. "What happens next?"

Carla smoothed down her skirt. "Well, I think you should take a few days to think about everything. You need to think about the house and I'm afraid without

Jax you will need to make these decisions on your own. The will states that both you and Jax can make decisions separately regarding these things. She trusted that you would take care of each other, no matter what."

Bliss nodded, her head was spinning with all the new information. She was elated that she could still go to college; then she chastised herself for feeling happy about school when her mom would never get to share that experience with her.

"Bliss, it's a lot to take in. We just wanted you to know about all of this so you wouldn't worry about anything financially. Your mom left you well provided for."

"She did. I know and thank you for trying to put me at ease. I just wish Jax were here." The General stood and stepped around his large desk then knelt by Bliss' chair. "Sweetie, do not underestimate yourself. Your mom knew how self-reliant and smart you are. You are special Bliss. It's going to be hard, but my family is going to help you get through this. You'll never get over the loss, I'll share that with you, but the pain eventually lessens."

Bliss knew he was referring to her 'gift', as her mom liked to call it. Her father had the same 'gift'. Bliss had a photographic memory, especially when it came to words and numbers that she saw. She was terrible with faces and she couldn't remember the names of people she met, but you put a page of numbers, letters, and even squiggly random lines in front of her for a minute and she could make an exact duplicate of the page from memory.

Her gift had come in handy for school purposes and

only her mom, Jax, Rose, the General, and Caitlyn knew about it. Caitlyn would often tease her and try to get her to memorize fashion magazine articles before they went shopping, but Bliss hated reading the fluff magazines and Caitlyn finally gave up.

"Well, I guess that about covers it Bliss. I will handle whatever you decide to do with the house, and I will transfer the stocks into your name as well. There is a buildup of cash from the stock dividends totaling a little over one thousand dollars that I will send over to the General's house in your name."

"Thank you." Bliss said softly, it was all so final. The trio stood and Bliss left the office leaving the General and Carla to discuss logistics.

Bliss walked into the living room to find everyone was gone. She was glad they were. Her head was pounding, and her chest was heavy with a sensation that was actually painful. She knew it had to be grief that she was feeling and she knew then; without a doubt that people could probably die from a broken heart, because Bliss felt like her heart was shredded and would never be whole again.

She heard voices coming from the kitchen so she headed that way. Rose was loading the dishwasher with the glasses that had been used and Caitlyn, Collin, and Connor
were sitting on the stools around the kitchen island. All conversation ceased as she walked in making her feel very self-conscious. Bliss took a deep breath and adjusted the glasses on her face that hadn't needed adjusting.

"Hey" Caitlyn said, hopping of her stool. "Is everything all right?"

Bliss looked to Rose and Rose told her, "I know Honey, but I didn't share any information, that's up to you."

Caitlyn and Collin looked so concerned about what possible information a lawyer would have had to say to their friend that their faces were almost comically revealing. Connor was stoic; he was so hard to read. His only tell were his eyes and in them Bliss saw a flicker of concern.

"No, actually, it's all good. My mom left me enough money so I can go to college." "Yay!" Caitlyn hugged her causing Bliss to grunt from the tight bear hug she was lovingly embraced in. Bliss had confided in Caitlyn her very real fear that she would not be able to go to college right away. Bliss knew, no matter what, she was going to put herself through school, but her fear of not having the finances had been looming over her since her mom's death.

"You thought you weren't going to be able to go to school?" Connor asked in a steely voice. Everyone in the kitchen turned towards him. His tone was that commanding. Bliss stepped out of Caitlyn's hug.

"Yes, I was worried." She answered truthfully.

She could see Connor's eyes turn a shade darker. He was seriously worried about her. "Connor, it's going to be okay." Bliss told him. Caitlyn, Rose, and Collin looked on in disbelief that Bliss was actually trying to comfort Connor.

Connor took a deep breath, exhaled and crossed his muscled arms over his thick chest. "You should not have been worrying about that." He spoke softly but authoritatively. "Yes, I agree, no one should have too, but the fact of the matter is I had thought about it and now, after meeting with my mom's lawyer I know that I can go to college and not have to worry about how I'm going to pay for it."

The General walked into the kitchen. "Carla just left," he announced to no one in particular. "Why's everyone so quiet?" he asked opening the refrigerator and taking out a beer.

No one answered him and that clued him in that something was off. His wife finally spoke up.

"Connor was concerned that Bliss had been worried about going to college." The General smiled at his oldest son. Connor was a bad ass Green Beret, nerves of steel, battalion leader, yet he was the most empathetic of all his children.

"Your mom and I had discussed this the night it happened. Bliss was going to school no matter what." Bliss looked uncomfortable. She was only a family friend, yet the General basically just announced to his children that she would have been supported by their parents so she could go to school.

"Bliss, Honey we love you." Rose said coming to her side. "You are part of the family; of course, we would take care of you."

Once again tears filled Bliss' eyes and she removed her glasses to wipe them away.

"I don't want to be a burden to anyone." She told them honestly. She placed the glasses back on her face. "You have all been so kind and I could have never gotten through these last few days without your support, but like Carla said, I need to make some decisions and I guess I should start that now."

"What are you talking about?" Caitlyn asked nervously.

"Well for starters, tonight I'm going to sleep at my house." The family looked at each other and then back to Bliss.

"Sweetie we want you to stay here." Rose told her gently.

"I can't stay here forever."

"Yes, yes you can." Caitlyn said, her voice creaking nervously.

"Bliss, the General and I want you to move in with us."

Bliss teared up again but this time she didn't take her glasses off, instead she poked her index finger underneath the thick frames to wipe the tears away.

"That's nice and truly I appreciate the offer but." The General moved to stand in front of her. "Bliss your mom would have wanted you to stay with us. I understand you are having mixed feelings and you have been through so much. Take some time to think it over. Honestly, it would just be for summers and vacations if you really think about it. You are off to school in August."

Bliss did not answer him right away. He was right she needed to think about this and everything else that had been thrown into her lap.

"Thank you for the offer, I appreciate it, really I do, and I will think about it. Tonight though, I would like to sleep home." She spoke softly but with determination. There was no malice or harshness in her tone and the General recognized that Bliss needed some space.

"Okay, Honey, but will you come have breakfast with us tomorrow morning please?"

The next morning was Sunday and Bliss knew after

Church the family liked to have a large breakfast together.

"That would be great. Thank you." Bliss turned and headed upstairs to Caitlyn's room to gather the few things she had brought with her. When she came back downstairs with her bag Collin was waiting for her with his knapsack slung over his shoulder.

"I'm driving." he told her.

Bliss went back into the kitchen and hugged everyone good-bye and thanked them again. Connor was quieter than usual, and Rose looked like she was going to start crying. Caitlyn and the General walked her to the front door where Collin stood waiting.

"Bliss, think about what I said, seriously. You are already part of the family." Bliss thanked him again, Caitlyn gave her a big hug, and Bliss knew Caitlyn was about to ask her to stay with her, so Bliss put her hand on her best friends shoulder.

"Caitlyn, I'm okay. I need to spend some time alone to think. So much has happened. You need time too. You were with me. Thank you for everything. I'll see you at 11:15am." That's when they got back from church.

"Okay, if you're sure, but keep your cell phone with you. If you get lonely," Caitlyn started to choke up as tears formed in her eyes. "or you get scared, just call, I'll be there."

"Like the song." Bliss said weakly.

"Like the song." Caitlyn repeated giving her another hug.

When Collin pulled into her driveway, Bliss was already second guessing her decision to stay there for the night alone. She hadn't gone into the house since the murder, which had been over a week ago. Collin started to get out of the car and Bliss told him she could go in alone.

"Bliss I'm coming in and I'm sleeping over. You are not staying here by yourself."

"Collin, really I..."

"Don't bother Bliss, I'm staying. I'll sleep in the living room on the couch."

Bliss blanched, "Uh, Collin the living room, is, ah, where."

"I know, it's been cleaned up and I'm not taking no for an answer."

Bliss smiled gently, "Thank you."

They headed inside and Collin held her arm at her elbow as they looked into the living room. He knew coming home would be tough on her. Heck, most girls would have never wanted to step foot into the place again, but Bliss was different.

This time only the smell of lemon cleaner was in the air. The living room looked remarkably normally.

Bliss looked at the floor and saw there wasn't even a stain. The image of her mother lying there caused her to shudder and Collin took her by the arm and led her upstairs.

When they reached her bedroom door, he pulled out a can of Fresca from his pack. "This is from Connor."

Bliss took the can and grinned.

"I love Fresca."

"Yeah, he knew you might want it."

Bliss actually giggled. "That was sweet of him."

Collin guffawed. "Bliss my brother cannot be defined as sweet." He laughed.

"Yeah, well, this was sweet."

Collin rolled his eyes, "Whatever." He chuckled good-naturedly.

"Good night Collin and thank you."

Collin gave her a grin. "No problem. Yell if you need me."

Bliss closed her bedroom door and looked around her bedroom. Everything was exactly the same except it wasn't. Everything was changed, out of whack, different, and with that somber thought, Bliss curled up on her bed and cried. She had cried before, but she had always restrained herself because people had been around her. The nights had been the hardest. Her heart was broken, she was beside herself with grief and the uncertainty about what lay ahead for her had been over whelming, but because Caitlyn was in the bed next to her, she had cried softly, not wanting to upset her friend. Now, alone she let out all the emotion she had been holding back and the torrent of tears and anguished poured out of her until she literally cried herself to sleep.

The next morning when she opened her door she saw that Collin was curled up on the hallway floor using his jacket as a pillow and a blanket from Jax's room as a cover.

He stirred and opened his eyes then he quickly sat up. "Hey, morning." He mumbled sleepily.

"I thought you were going to sleep on the couch?" She said trying to act tough.

"I was, I tried, and then I just decided to camp here." Bliss nodded. "Thanks Collin that was sweet."

"Ha, we're back to sweet. Well, at least this time, I'm the sweet one." He teased her. Bliss laughed out loud as she walked down the hall towards the bathroom.

Chapter 2 Five Years Later

The years had flown by and Bliss had accepted the General and Rose's offer to stay with them. Bliss wasn't with them very often though. She was with them that first summer. Jax had finally gotten a call through to her. He couldn't come in from his job and Bliss could hear the sorrow in his voice. He agreed they should sell the house, so

Bliss took on that job. Any furniture or household belongings they wanted, which really weren't much, were stored in the Doherty's basement.

The General hired a moving company to take the furniture they didn't want to a consignment shop. Other items were given to the local Veteran's Association. Bliss kept her mom's car, a white, gas efficient Toyota Corolla.

Cleaning out her mom's room had been achingly difficult. Thankfully Rose had helped her. Bliss kept a few remembrances; her mom's bible, a scarf, a quilt, that had been hand made by her great - great - grandmother, and a few other sentimental items.

Bliss' room had been packed and moved to the Doherty's. Caitlyn and Bliss were to share a room and Caitlyn moved all her things to one side of her large room, giving Bliss the other side. It was a little cramped, but both girls were happy.

The Doherty's had a few family traditions that Bliss soon became a part of. One was Rose's birthday. It was always celebrated the day after Thanksgiving no matter what the actual date was; unless you were deployed or on your death bed, you were expected to be there. The other no-nonsense date was Christmas. The first Thanksgiving that Bliss attended at the Doherty's, she had actually tried to stay at school. Caitlyn, who was at Columbia, tried in vain to talk her into coming home and even Collin, who was at William and Mary, tried to convince her she needed to come home. Bliss, however, did not want to intrude on the family get together, so she got permission from the college to stay in her dorm room and she planned to simply study throughout the long weekend.

That did not happen. The Tuesday before Thanksgiving there was a knock on her dorm room door, outside the door stood the General.

"Get your gear Bliss, you're coming home." He announced in a very authoritative but tender voice. Bliss didn't even bother arguing. She hurriedly packed and the warmth of spending Thanksgiving with people she loved and who loved her put a huge smile on her face. After that Bliss always went home for Thanksgiving, Rose's birthday and Christmas. Summers were a different story though. Bliss was completing a two-degree program, so she took extra classes in the summer. She was getting her degrees in Computer Economics/Programming and in Computer Science. UMBC which was well known for their cutting-edge technology courses and Bliss was soaking in the education.

Bliss didn't date and she never partook in the keg parties or bar crawls her classmates were always so gung - ho about. Her free time was consumed with things that she liked to do. She spent two nights a week with her Computer Club, on Sunday mornings she volunteered at a Soup Kitchen, she took a martial arts class on Friday nights, and in her Sophomore year she joined ROTC.

Her mother would have flipped, but Bliss liked the regimentation and she liked that she would come out of school as an Officer. It also was a relief that she had a job waiting for her when she graduated. Her skills with computers were just what the Army was looking for and because she was a woman, she had been heavily recruited. She had, of course, tested off the charts in logistics and information because of her 'gift', and she had already been told she would be going to Afghanistan after she completed a six- week boot camp in the summer right after she graduated. Bliss told the family during that second Thanksgiving that she had spent with them that she was ROTC and although Caitlyn was stunned into silence, the General and Rose smiled approvingly.

Connor never made it home for either of those first two Thanksgivings or Christmas'. Bliss knew they worried for Connor. If he wasn't able to get home, he was most likely on a mission and that worried even her.

Connor stayed safe though and emailed the family, with Bliss being included in the emails that he was well, and although he could not tell the family where he was or where he was going, it was enough that he wrote to give the family peace of mind.

It was Thanksgiving of Bliss' Senior year and Caitlyn had been sending daily emails to Bliss for the past week about Thanksgiving Eve. They were both 22 and Caitlyn was excited to go to the bars the night before Thanksgiving Day to party with all their old high school classmates. This was a town tradition. Bliss was not as motivated about the evening as Caitlyn was, but since Bliss had made an appearance the year before and had stayed for all of a half an hour before pleading a headache and leaving, Caitlyn was persistent and annoyingly insistent in her emails, phone calls, and text messages that she was expecting Bliss to go out with her and stay out with her. Thanksgiving Eve night arrived, and Bliss was unenthusiastically getting dressed. Caitlyn was looking very grown up and sexy in a knit sleeveless dress and ankle boots. Bliss was at a complete loss as to what to wear. This was so out of her element. Finally, Caitlyn pushed her into a shimmery gold dress that fell almost obscenely just below her behind. Next, Caitlyn straightened Bliss' hair. Bliss had been blessed, or cursed depending on the day, with hair that fell naturally down her back in twirls and ringlets in all shades all gold. By the time Caitlyn finished straightening her hair, it reached almost to her backside. Next, the makeup, Bliss really didn't like wearing makeup. She often hid her face behind her mass of hair hoping to hide the fact that she wore ugly thick glasses.

There was an operation that Bliss had been researching that she could get to correct her vision, but she couldn't afford it until after she received her inheritance, which was now only six months away. Her glasses were heavy and made her self-conscious, the heavy frames hurt her nose and she was so tired of the hushed comments about them. Caitlyn applied Bliss' makeup and since Bliss couldn't see anything close up unless her glasses were on, Caitlyn had to keep reassuring her that she looked awesome. One thing Bliss could not wait for was to see what she looked like when she wasn't wearing glasses. She could imagine, but the fact was her eyesight was so poor that without her glasses on, her face was a total blur when she looked in the mirror. Caitlyn kept up the positive endorsements regarding how awesome Bliss looked and this bolstered Bliss' confidence. Soon Caitlyn's enthusiasm for their Thanksgiving Eve started to rub off on Bliss.

Collin was waiting in the living room for his sister and Bliss to finish getting ready. He was their designated driver. Already in the work force, Collin had already passed his bar and was working at a prestigious law firm in New York City. He and a friend lived in the city and Bliss admired how stable and put together his life was. He seemed so much older now, too. Two years ago, he would have been just as excited to go out and whoop it up, but now he was taking on the role of designated driver and he didn't even mind.

When Bliss walked down the steps Collin stood up from the couch. Bliss saw surprise register on his face and then he composed himself quickly. The General put his newspaper down and Rose stood up to stand with Collin.

"Holy smokes Bliss, you look great." Collin blurted out. Bliss smiled genuinely pleased that he had noticed.

"Hey! What about me?" Caitlyn quipped, but she was just as happy that her work on Bliss had garnered the effect it had. Collin was open-mouthed floored, and he couldn't take his eyes off of her. "You look beautiful, both of you." Rose said diplomatically. Bliss blushed with the compliments. She knew how the dress looked on her. It was skintight and hugged her curves perfectly. Her hair was so long and soft from the straightening that Caitlyn administered that when she moved her head, it swished softly on the open back of the daring dress. Bliss was 5'6" but the heels Caitlyn had strapped on her put her at 5'9" and she prayed she wouldn't topple over. She did love how long they made her legs look and with her strict work out regime, her legs were well toned and even she thought they looked good. It was her face that gave her pause. Caitlyn had done her makeup, but the glasses still hid her features and when Bliss looked in the mirror, she just saw a face with big ugly glasses. She wondered if that's what others saw, too.

"Well ladies let's get this party started." Collin said as he sprinted to open the front door for them. Caitlyn followed Collin but Bliss held back for a second.

"Any word from Connor?"

"No, we are hoping he gets in, but we haven't heard from him in weeks." Rose said somberly.

"He'll get here if he can." Bliss grinned. "You know he loves Thanksgiving." "He does. I even made a pumpkin chiffon pie, his favorite."

"Well, fingers crossed." Bliss told them as she left the room.

"Have fun Honey." Rose said giving her a maternal hug.

"I'll try." She laughed. The General and Rose knew that it was only their daughters pestering that had made Bliss go out.

Bliss sent a small prayer up to God that if Connor was

able, to please send him home. Bliss hadn't seen him for two years, but they stayed in touch with emails and they even played on-line video games together and against each other. The last time he'd been home was last Christmas and Bliss knew his parents really wanted to see him. The emails were great and reassuring but seeing him in person would be the best birthday present Rose could receive.

The place was packed and there were no tables or even seats at the long wooden bar. Bliss and Caitlyn stood at the corner of the dance floor where they could place their drinks on a small ledge provided by a decorative plant stand. Collin was at the bar, standing between two gorgeous girls who occupied bar stools. He was flirting wickedly with them and Bliss couldn't help but notice how handsome he was. She knew Collin was a lady's man, he had been a notorious heartbreaker in high school, but she had never actually seen him in action. She watched as he smiled and laughed and gave each girl special attention. Sometimes he would brush his fingers against their bare skin and then retreat. It was all a game to him, and Bliss knew he was winning.

A pensive sigh escaped Bliss observing Collin as he seduced the two beauties. Bliss had a momentary mini pity party wondering if any man would ever look at her the way Collin was looking at them. Even if it were a game to Collin, if she were to be flirted with like that would be so validating.

"Hey." Caitlyn shouted above the music. "We need to dance. You've had your two

drinks, you have got to be ready now!" Bliss had never really danced in front of people before. Sure, she had be-bopped around her room when she was alone, but this was a whole new ball game. She had told Caitlyn she needed to be alcohol induced fortification before getting on the dance floor. So, Caitlyn had plied her with two mai-tai's and was now calling her out.

"Okay, next good song, I promise."

The next song was one of Bliss' favorites and she put her drink down and clapped her hands.

"Now or never," she yelled leading Caitlyn onto the packed floor. Caitlyn was laughing and they moved to an open spot and began dancing. Caitlyn was a good dancer and after a few hesitant seconds Bliss relaxed and began to move trying to replicate some moves she had seen on television.

"Bliss! You're good!" Caitlyn shouted in her ear. The two girls stayed on the floor for the next three songs. Bliss was actually enjoying herself. The dance floor was crowded but no one was even looking at her or Caitlyn, which Bliss loved so she lost some of her inhibitions and just relaxed.

Back at the bar a large hand clamped down on Collins shoulder. He turned quickly prepared to knock someone down and saw Connor standing behind him grinning. Collin grabbed him into a bear hug. "Oh man, I am so glad to see you. Does mom know you're home?"

"Yeah, I stopped there first. She told me where you were. Where are the girls?" Collin pointed at the dance floor. Connor saw Caitlyn but didn't see Bliss. "Where's Bliss?"

"Right in front of Caitlyn." Collin told him as he watched his brother's face for the moment it registered that the girl with the long blond hair in the tight sexy dress was Bliss. Collin grinned watching the same shocked look that he had when he had first seen Bliss in the racy dress, now was on Connor's. Connor looked at the girl dancing by his sister and his heart thudded. "Holy crap." He muttered.

Collin laughed, "Yeah, that's what I said."

One of the beauties sitting next to Collin pulled on his sleeve. "Want us to make room for your handsome friend?" She said gesturing to Connor.

Connor shook his head and Collin gave him a knowing look. He then told the girls that his friend wasn't interested and then he must have said something funny because both girls giggled. Connor barely heard them. His eyes were glued on Bliss. He turned back to Collin and asked him to get him a beer. When the beer came Connor told Collin that he was just making the rounds. Which to normal people meant they were going to talk to friends that were in the bar, but Collin knew Connor hated being with too many people, so when Connor said he was making the rounds, it meant he needed to move around and find some space.

Connor couldn't take his eyes off of Bliss. Her body was moving seductively with every song that was being played. Her dress was so short he wanted to pull the damn thing down every time it shimmied up an inch. The only thing he didn't like was her hair. Bliss had great hair; all cork screwy crazy with every color of gold woven through.

He watched them from a short distance not wanting to interrupt their obvious glee as they enjoyed the

evening. He kept his eye on Collin too. The kid was four years
younger than him but light years older when it came to handling woman. Connor had his fair share of women, but he wasn't smooth with them the way Collin was. Fact was, most women picked him up and he just followed their lead.

Connor walked back towards Collin to get another beer and watched as two young men approached Caitlyn and Bliss. Bliss had her back to them, and her ass swished provocatively. The one man facing Caitlyn took her hands and placed them on his shoulders encouraging her to continue dancing as he held her hips. The big brother in him wasn't happy, but it seemed harmless enough. The second man took hold of Bliss' hips and pushed up behind her encouraging her to continue moving.

Connor saw Bliss freeze momentarily, but the guy started moving with the music so Bliss began dancing again. The guy was whispering something in her ear and when she turned to look at him, he froze and his hands fell away from her.

Connor put his beer down on the bar knowing what was about to happen.

The man backed away from Bliss and started laughing. His friend saw what he was laughing at and gave Bliss a sad smile.

"Girl you are Magoo with a banging body." The idiot man said out loud.

Bliss was stunned with the meanness of the comment and she tilted her face downwards embarrassed by the scene he was making. Other couples on the dance floor had stopped dancing and were now staring at her. The look of pity they had in their eyes for her was her undoing.

Bliss turned from the asshole, but before she could leave, a hand latched on to her shoulder.

"Honey, are these ass wipes bothering you?" Connor said in a deep voice that echoed his mood.

"Connor!" Caitlyn yelled flinging herself into his arms. The two guys stood back watching as the very large, and intimidating man glared at them.

"Hey sis," he said hugging Caitlyn.

Connor pulled Bliss towards him. "You okay?"

She reached under her glasses and nodded. "Yeah, just dandy," she replied cheekily. Connor chuckled. The man that had been dancing with Bliss was smart enough to leave the dance floor quickly. Connor was thinking that was too bad because he would have loved to have punched the little bastard into next week.

Caitlyn saw that Bliss was okay, so she left the dance floor to retrieve her drink.

"How about dancing with me?" He said to Bliss who was attempting to leave the dance floor too.

"Connor, I appreciate you stepping in, but you don't like to dance."

"Who says?" He said as he swiveled his hips causing Bliss to laugh.

"Well, maybe you do like to dance, but you don't have to dance with me. I'm okay; been there done that." She said tiredly referring to the Magoo comment that she'd heard a thousand times before. This time though was especially mean. The guy said it out loud and to her face. Her ugly face. Well, at least he thought her body was banging. Bliss sighed.

"Maybe I want to dance with you."

Bliss smiled at him. Connor was a good guy. If he wanted to dance, she was going to dance with him.

"Okay then Connor Doherty, show me what you got."

Bliss was wonderfully surprised because Connor was a great dancer. He moved his large frame so easily that he looked incredibly sexy. Bliss watched the other women staring at him and then she noticed how they looked at her. She knew they were all wondering what he saw in her. Bliss decided to forget the mean comment and the quizzical looks from other dancers and just enjoy dancing. She actually liked shaking her body to the music.

Bliss saw Caitlyn and Collin watching them from the bar and both she and Connor waved to them at the same time causing them both to laugh. The next song that came on was a slow tempo tune. Bliss naturally assumed Connor would want to leave the floor, but instead he turned her back towards him and when he put his arms around her, he encouraged her to sway with him. Bliss had never danced slowly with anyone before and she liked how it made her feel. Wanted.

"I'm glad you're home Connor. Rose was worried." She told him looking up into his handsome face.

"I know. I stopped there first. We just flew in."

"How long are you home for?"

"Just for the weekend."

They didn't speak for the rest of the song and when it had ended, Bliss knew nothing that night would be better than that dance with Connor. He had held her tenderly against his body and she even thought she felt his thumb rubbing her bare back. It had been like a fairy tale dream and Bliss shook off the crazy notion. This was Connor Doherty.

The song ended so they walked off the floor and found Caitlyn and Collin.

"You guys dance great together." Caitlyn said enthusiastically. Bliss smiled sheepishly. Collin was looking at them with a sly smirk on his face and it made her feel like she'd done something evil.

"Caitlyn, can we leave now? I'm pretty much done." Bliss said wearily.

"It's just getting good Bliss. Those jerks won't bother us again, I promise. You'll watch out for them right Collin?"

Collin nodded but his eyes remained on Connor.

"Caitlyn, I'm sorry but I'm beat. You stay and have fun. All your friends are here and I'm just holding you back."

"Don't you dare say that Bliss Allen. I want you to stay."

"I know you do, but really, I'm exhausted and my feet are screaming in these heels. I'm just going to head home."

"I'll take you home Bliss." Connor offered.

"Connor really I can UBER, you stay and have fun. I'm good."

"No, really, I just came to see you guys. I'm beat too. Collin you got Caitlyn?"

Again Collin nodded without talking and Bliss wished she could read his mind.

Bliss followed Connor out the front door and to his Jeep. He opened the door for her and helped her inside.

When he slid into the driver's seat, Bliss was already taking off her heels.

"Oh my gosh this feels great." She said wiggling her toes.

"Not much for heels Bliss?"

"I guess not."

"Too bad, they look great on you."

"Ugh, Connor really?" He laughed, shrugged his shoulders, and they headed home.

"Are you going to bed?" Connor asked as they quietly made their way inside. They knew Rose and the General would be in bed, it was after 11:00pm.

"I could unless you want to play a little Grand Theft Auto. I got the new version." "How did you get it? I didn't think it was out yet."

"It's not, I got a test market version."

"How did you pull that off?"

They walked into the kitchen.

"I'm friends with someone who works in the company. He got it for me." Connor opened the fridge and pulled out two Fresca's, handing one to Bliss. "Thanks."

"He got it for you?" Connor said exaggerating he. Bliss slapped his arm playfully. "Yes, he, and he is just a friend."

They headed down to the basement where the game box was set up and Bliss set the game up explaining a few of the new features to Connor.

They played for two straight hours pausing once for a bathroom break, which included grabbing a bag of chips and more Fresca. Bliss couldn't remember the last time she had laughed so hard. Connor was so fun to play with. When they played long distance, it had always been entertaining, but being with him, watching his face, hearing his silly jokes was something different. When they finished playing, they sat on the couch side by side, feet up on the table and talked.

Bliss told him about school. That she was President of the Computer Club, and that she was still serving food at the Food Kitchen. Bliss told Connor about ROTC and that she really enjoyed the training. She explained how her martial arts class was also keeping her in shape, and she conveyed how excited she was to graduate in May. Finally, she told him a secret she had been bursting to share, but just hadn't found the right person to share it with. She confided to him that she had already been given an assignment overseas after she graduated. She hadn't disclosed that news to anyone else yet, but with Connor it just kind of tumbled out of her mouth.

Connor was concerned about her being in a war zone, but he didn't voice any chauvinistic views. He just asked simple, but tough questions. Bliss had an answer for all of them. ROTC had trained her well and Connor knew they were lucky to have her. Connor, in turn told her about some of his missions. Bliss knew being an elite member of a highly trained Special Forces group was hard to attain. They were based out of Fort Bragg when they weren't overseas, but most of the time they were deployed and waiting for assignments or training for one. Connor disclosed to Bliss that most of the assignments were Dark Ops, which meant it was a secretive well-guarded assignment and was often pulled off without many people knowing about it until after it happened. Connor assured her that they were all so well planned out that the percentage for success was high. He described his townhome that he shared with a team member, near the base.

Their conversation flowed, and both felt completely at ease with each other. Their chat turned to family and how proud they were of Collin, and how Caitlyn was hoping to land a job in France that she was beyond excited about. She had yet to tell her parents and Connor commented that he didn't think they'd be thrilled. Connor asked about her brother Jax and Connor knew, just from the pained expression she tried to disguise in her face and the wistfulness in her tone, that not having her one family member accessible for Holiday's or simply to talk with, weighed on her heavily.

Bliss told Connor that she and Jax had worked out a way to talk on the phone without putting him in danger. It involved using her gift, but Bliss didn't tell Connor about that. In reality, Jax would text Bliss using a series of nonsensical numbers and letters which Bliss easily memorized. She then converted the numbers and letters using a code that she and Jax had come up with two years earlier when they had seen each other. Bliss explained to Connor that the message Jax sent her was simply a phone number and a time. She left out the whole 'Gift thing'. Bliss explained to Connor that she would call the number, if she could, at that time, and that's how they kept in touch with each other. The last time she had seen Jax had been two years ago, when he was pulled from one undercover assignment and before he was sent to another.

Connor could feel the sadness Bliss felt missing her brother and he took her hand in his without saying a word and they sat quietly next to each other, each thinking their own private thoughts. Bliss thought about Jax, and like she did countless times a day, she prayed he was staying safe. She thought about her future, that in six months her life would change, and she hoped it would be awesome. She was excited to graduate, but what she couldn't wait for was the operation on her eyes. Would she feel differently? Would guys like her? She even wondered what Connor would think about her if she didn't wear glasses.

She felt so close to Connor, but she knew he only thought of her like a little sister. He was so handsome, so kind, and so damn sexy. Maybe when she didn't have to wear her glasses anymore some gorgeous and nice guy like Connor would want her. She could dream, couldn't she?

Connor was staring down at Bliss' feet that were sitting on the worn coffee table. He was remembering her wiggling her toes after taking off those sexy as sin heels. God, she had a great body, her mind was incredible, and she was pretty, even if most of her face was hidden behind those hideous glasses. He knew she couldn't see without them, and that she couldn't wear contacts because of the severity of her eyesight. Connor was picturing her in her in her martial arts class taking people down and knew she was in great shape. Crap just looking at her body in that clingy dress, he had noticed that her legs were toned and went on forever.

Spending time with her tonight, playing Grand Theft Auto and then just talking, Connor realized that they had so much in common, but also how much he admired her. She was going to be full military, like he was. She had survived losing her mom, and he appreciated how strong her character was, and like him, she hid her emotions. She was scary smart, had a great sense of humor, was athletic, and she played a mean video game. It hit him like a sledgehammer how much he enjoyed her company, how easy she was to be with, and that for the last few hours he had actually relaxed. He gazed at her, and although distorted because of the thick prescription lenses, he saw that her eyes were closed. She looked so peaceful, and damn, just looking at her made his heart squeeze a little. He couldn't believe the knuckleheads that she knew hadn't tried to claim her for themselves; or had they?

"Bliss?"

Her head was laid back and her eyes remained closed, "Hmmm?" she replied sleepily. "Do you have a boyfriend?"

Bliss kept her head back on the couch, as she spoke in barely more than a whisper. "No, too much work, too immature, and I'm Magoo."

"Bliss you're not Magoo." He paused and looked down at their hands comfortable intertwined between them. "You're beautiful."

Connor couldn't believe he said that out loud. What the hell was wrong with him, she was his little sister's best friend. He looked at her hoping she wasn't getting ready to bolt off the couch, and much to his relief he realized she was sound asleep. Her mouth was open slightly and Connor had to refrain from rubbing his thumb over her pink, desirable lips. He laid his head back on the couch, still holding Bliss' small hand in his and before long he too, was fast asleep.

Bliss recalled feeling cold and uncomfortable, but now she was warm and cozy. She snuggled into the heat and continued to sleep. Connor too remembered feeling a chill, but he too remained asleep feeling content and warm.

Connor woke first feeling remarkably relaxed, until he realized he was lying next to Bliss on the couch. He was wrapped around her body, holding her small body to his. Her dress had risen to bunch around her waist, and he looked down between them to see her small naked ass pressing against his morning hard on, causing him to still. Every fiber in his body wanted to grind up against her backside and he called upon all his restraint not to do just that. Bliss was wearing a thong, a very little lace one, and Connor was so glad he hadn't known that last night. He would have lost every round of Grand Theft Auto thinking about what lay under that barely their dress.

Bliss was nestled in his arms and looked so peaceful that he didn't want to wake her. Her glasses must have come off and realized he'd never seen her without them. Geez, she was gorgeous. He noticed the red marks alongside of her nose and knew her glasses had to be heavy to leave those imprints.

As much as Connor wanted to continue lying on the couch holding Bliss in his arms there was no way he wanted anyone in his family to see how they were cuddled up and he'd probably shoot Collin if he saw her sweet ass. Immediately after having that jealous thought it was as if a light bulb flickered on in his Neanderthal brain. Shit! He liked Bliss. Not like a big brother liked a sister, he actually liked her. What was he? Six years older than her? Was that creepy?

Bliss stirred in his arms and when she slowly opened her eyes, she rubbed them, squinted and then felt around the couch until she located her glasses. When she put them on, she thought she must have still been dreaming. She was prone, on the couch, lying in Connor's strong arms with her back snug against his warm chest with her rear pressed against his hard length. It was such a sensuous feeling that her nipples hardened, and she felt liquid warmth gather between her legs. Connor was holding her gently and she saw that he was watching her almost nervously.

"Don't scream." He whispered.

"Why would I scream?" She answered quietly, still wondering how they had ended up laying together on the couch and wishing she could rub herself against his male hardness.

"We fell asleep and we must have sought out each other for warmth."

Bliss nodded. "Okay I'll buy that." She grinned apprehensively.

Hating that she was going to lose the feeling of their intimate contact Bliss rolled over, so she was on her back. Her head was perched on his bicep and she studied Connor's handsome face as he looked down on her.

"You're so pretty." He said touching her cheek. She could hear regret in his voice and wondered why. Bliss was afraid to breath. She didn't want the magical moment to end. His lips were so close to hers. If she picked her head up, she knew she'd feel his breath on her lips.

"Hey," Collin called from the top of the stairs. "Are you guys still down there?" They heard him walking down the steps and they quickly sat up. It was then Bliss realized her dress was bunched up, but she didn't have time to be embarrassed. Connor helped her tug it down just as Collin came into view.

"What happened? Did you guys fall asleep down here?" Collin said as he reached the floor.

"Yeah, we were playing Grand Theft Auto. We didn't hear you guys come in." Connor replied.

"Well, we heard you." Collin answered mischievously.

Connor laughed. "We probably woke the General. We were pretty loud." He said looking at Bliss remembering how hard they had laughed.

"Nope, I don't think so. We just heard you when we got home. I couldn't hear you when I got upstairs."

"Why didn't you come down?" Bliss asked.

"Cause, we were exhausted, and Caitlyn was pretty fried. I wanted to get her to bed before mom saw her precious baby girl all sloppy drunk." Like the night before, Collin kept looking at them with a funny lopsided smirk on his face.

"Anyway you guys better get up. I heard the General moving around."

Bliss stood up quickly and almost toppled over. Connor steadied her and Collin watched as his brother's hand lingered on her hips.

Bliss grabbed her heels from the floor and scampered up the steps leaving the two brothers alone. Connor stood and stretched, hoping his hard on had died down enough not to be noticeable. He caught the look Collin was giving him.

"What?"

"You and Bliss, is there something you want to tell me?"

"Let it be Collin, okay?"

"She's too young for you bro."

Connor shook his head. "I keep telling myself that too, but we fit. I can't explain it." "There is no way this can end good Connor. Think about it."

Connor stood and headed towards the steps. He clamped his hand on Collins shoulder affectionately. "Yeah, I will. Come on let's make breakfast like the old days, mom will love that."

Chapter 3

Bliss took the steps up to her room two at a time hoping she didn't run into the General or Rose. How would it look if they saw she was still wearing her dress from last night? She giggled thinking she was doing the walk of shame in her own house. She made it to her room and quietly slipped inside.

Caitlyn was snoring softly from her bed. She was still wearing her dress from last night and her makeup was smeared giving her raccoon eyes. Collin must have just dumped her in bed and covered her. Bliss thought about getting into bed, but she wasn't tired, in fact she was feeling well rested. A smile broke out on her face and she chastised herself for feeling so good about waking up in Connor's wonderful arms. She needed a hard reality check if she thought Connor Doherty had feelings for her.

Bliss changed into her running clothes. She gathered her long hair that had begun to curl again and braided it. It was cold outside, so she wore her long running pants, her combat boots, a long-sleeved cold gear shirt, then she put her bulletproof vest over that shirt, and finally she threw on her ROTC sweatshirt. The first weekend that she spent training with ROTC she had learned that she needed to stay in shape and combat ready. That meant she had to work out wearing what she would wear in the field. They issued her combat boots and a bulletproof vest just last month, when she had received her assignment and ever since she wore them dutifully when she worked out. She knew some of the guys even wore their cargo fatigues, and on occasion so did she, but

Bliss didn't want to draw attention to herself running in the small neighborhood. The boots alone drew stares, thankfully most people had no idea she had the vest on.

She stepped out of her room and ran right into the General.

"Good morning, did you have fun last night?" He whispered not wanting to wake anyone that was still asleep.

"Yes, actually I did." Bliss answered knowing he was talking about the bar. She hadn't lied, but she was only referring to afterwards, when she had been with Connor.

"Going for a run?" He said noticing her boots. He then poked a finger into her chest and smiled feeling the hard-protective vest.

"Maybe later we should have a chat?" he said with a knowing grin.

Bliss nodded. "Yes, I do have something I should share with you." She knew the General already had guessed she'd been given an assignment. He was too military not to know that when you trained wearing boots and vest you were getting yourself ready for deployment.

Bliss followed the General downstairs and at the bottom of the steps Connor stood holding the Generals morning paper, which he must have retrieved, from the driveway. "Good morning, son," The General said. "Thanks." He took the paper from Connor and walked into the kitchen.

Connor was looking at what Bliss was wearing. 'Like father, like son.' Bliss thought. "Going for a run?"

"Yes, I want to run off those two drinks." She said

with a grin.

"If you wait a second, I'll go with you."

"Connor, really, you don't have too. I run by myself all the time."

Connor put his hand on her arm.

"Bliss I need a run, too. Just wait a second okay?"

She nodded and watched as Connor did just as she had done a few minutes earlier and took the steps upstairs two at a time.

When he came back down he was dressed similarly to her but he had on baggy sweats that said ARMY on the leg. She poked his side and found that he was wearing his flak jacket and he in turned poked her and they both chuckled.

"The General knows." She told him.

"Yeah, you'll have to tell Rose though." Bliss nodded in agreement.

Connor told her he would be right back and walked into the kitchen. Bliss heard him tell the General and Collin that he and Bliss were going for a run. She heard Collin tease him about backing out of cooking breakfast and Connor said he'd clean up if Collin cooked, which Collin readily agreed to.

Bliss and Connor stretched for a few minutes in the driveway before starting to jog down the quiet street.

"Where are you headed?" He asked as they jogged side by side.

"I usually go to the park on Headly. They have a fitness trail. It's a mile there, a two-mile fitness trail, and then the mile back. Do you want to do more or less?" She asked referring to the mileage.

"No, that's good."

They ran at a comfortable pace. Bliss was pretty sure

Connor was not running at his usual speed, but she enjoyed running with someone even though they weren't talking. They entered the wooded park and stopped at the first fitness station, which were step-ups. Three square wooden box obstacles were situated in a small clearing. A white sign was attached to a wooden post explaining how to safely perform the exercise.

Bliss did 20 step-ups on the mid-sized box and Connor did the same using the higher platform. As they jogged towards the next station Connor asked her about her classes and if she knew what she was going to be doing overseas. She told him what she knew.

She explained that she would be working with a small unit in charge of relaying information to various battalions and bases that were stationed in Afghanistan. As Connor listened to her, he heard the unmistakable excitement in her voice, in her tone. It made him remember when he got his first assignment and he understood that she was feeling that kick rush of adrenalin. He still experienced it before he went out on an assignment, but now his were tempered from experience, some of it good; some missions were not so good.

They finished the circuit of ten fitness stations and headed out of the park towards home. They were both sweating, and he hated that Bliss had to keep lifting her glasses to wipe the sweat from her eyes. Bliss noticed that he was watching her, and she almost told him about the operation that she was having the day after graduation, but something made her remain quiet. She had not told anyone about it, not even Jax.

The operation required a night's stay in the hospital and was done using a laser, but because her eyes would be bandaged for 24 hours afterwards, she had opted to stay overnight in the hospital instead of asking someone to take care of her. She hated being reliant upon people and this operation was so personal that she wanted to have it done without any fanfare. She knew Caitlyn would be mad that she hadn't confided in her and she figured Rose would be hurt, and she hated that after all that woman had done for her, she might upset her, but Bliss couldn't bring herself to divulge her secret. When they reached the driveway, they both stopped and began stretching to warm down. Although it was in the low 30's, droplets of sweat poured off Bliss' forehead and ran down only to disappear beneath the thick frames. Connor saw her breathing begin to return to normal quickly and realized she was in really good shape, maybe even in better shape than he was since he was still breathing heavily.

As they turned to go inside, Connor reached out to stop her before she pushed the door open.

"I had a good time last night." He said rubbing the back of his neck as if he was rubbing out a kink.

Bliss' stomach got that zippy feeling in it again, like she had when she felt Connor's arms around her this morning. Her mouth went dry and she felt her heart pounding against her chest. She felt something for Connor, something special, but she knew he couldn't be feeling the same way. Could he?

"You liked the game?" She asked meaning the video game.

Connor hesitated, looking at her with his head slightly

cocked. "No."

"No?" she echoed quickly.

"I mean yes, I liked the game." Again, he paused. "I liked spending time with you." He said quietly.

The sensation in her stomach became an all spasm and her heart felt like it was going to break out of her chest.

"I liked that too, Connor, but."

The front door opened suddenly and Collin stood there still wearing his flannel bottoms and a worn tee shirt from high school.

"I thought I heard voices." He said stepping aside so they could enter.

Bliss walked through the door and Collin put his hand on Connor's arm holding him back.

"Don't do it Connor. You'll hurt her."

Connor watched as Bliss headed towards laughter coming from the kitchen.

"Maybe she'll hurt me." He said solemnly before pushing Collin aside and heading towards the kitchen.

Bliss entered the kitchen to see a much-disheveled Caitlyn sitting at the counter with a big glass of orange juice in front of her and a bottle of Advil. The General was grinning, and Rose was lovingly, but sternly telling Caitlyn that nice girls didn't get drunk.

Caitlyn looked at Bliss and pointed at her.

"It's your fault you know." She said without any malice in her voice, so Bliss knew she was about to get teased.

"If you hadn't left with Connor..." Connor chose that moment to walk into the kitchen and he halted when both his parents looked at him like he had some explaining to do. He put his hands up, palms out, like he was surrendering.

"Oh no you don't kiddo." He said mocking his hung-over sibling.

"Bliss was done and so was I. We came home and played video games."

Collin walked in and snickered. "Yeah, all night long."

Rose and the General swung their heads back to Connor and Connor glared at Collin. Bliss could see he was pissed.

"Collin we didn't play all night." Bliss tried to diffuse the obvious attempt to get Connor in trouble. "We talked too." Bliss knew how to take the heat off Connor.

She had all the attention focused on her now so she decided it was the best time to tell the family about her deployment and it would get Connor out of any scrutiny. Bliss took off her sweatshirt and showed everyone her bulletproof vest.

"You're wearing a bulletproof vest?" Caitlyn said incredulously.

"Yes, I have to when I exercise."

"Why?" Caitlyn asked still not understanding.

"Because I got my assignment. I've been assigned to a communications analyst team and after I do the training in June and July I'm being deployed. I talked to Connor about it last night." There she had gotten him out of hot water.

Caitlyn was still not getting it. "But?"

The General placed his hand on his daughters' shoulder. "Soldiers train with their boots and their vest on to simulate what they will be wearing in combat."

It finally dawned on Caitlyn what was happening, and Bliss saw tears fill her best friend's eyes.

"You're going overseas? First Connor and now you?"

Bliss stepped to Caitlyn, "You know I'm ROTC, you know it's what I've been working towards, why the tears." Bliss asked gently.

Caitlyn wiped her eyes. "Well, I just thought, I don't know. I just hoped you would work here, on the base like dad does and we could still hang out."

Bliss chuckled giving Caitlyn a big hug. "Uh, you want me to stay in Pemberton and work on the base while you are where?"

Caitlyn started laughing too. "Yeah, well I won't be in Paris forever."

"Yes, and I won't be overseas forever!"

"Paris?" Rose said looking at her daughter prompting Connor and Collin to laugh. Caitlyn explained that she was hoping to go to Paris to study abroad and she animatedly launched into all the reasons why it would be so good for her career. While she was talking, Connor stared at Bliss over his cup of coffee and winked at her setting off the butterflies again in her chest. Bliss knew it was just a thank-you gesture for putting his parent's attention elsewhere.

The tension in the room had dissipated amid the smiles and teasing that Caitlyn's announcement had triggered. Breakfast was wonderful. Collin had made eggs, pancakes, bacon, rolls and hash browns. The entire Doherty family was together making it a significant occasion. Bliss loved that she was included in the family dynamics. Collin was in his glory retelling funny stories about how he had saved Caitlyn from the countless men that had flocked to her while she was in her inebriated state. Caitlyn kept interjecting, 'two Collin, there were two men,' and then she gave up, obviously still feeling hung-over. Prompted by the General, Bliss elaborated on what she had been told regarding her deployment. Connor told the family that he would be in D.C. for a few months. He and his friend Andy were in pistol competitions and they were also interviewing a new recruit for their team. Then he was heading to Fort Brag to train. He thought they were probably deploying again in August; he wasn't sure though. His family knew he could be stateside one day and off on a mission the next.

After breakfast Connor cleaned up like he had promised then Rose shooed everyone from the kitchen so she could get started on the Thanksgiving meal. Bliss tried to help her, but Rose really enjoyed cooking for her family and she just asked Bliss to sit and chat with her while she worked.

Rose asked all the questions Bliss' mother would have asked about school, boys, and her deployment. Rose also asked about graduation and Bliss told her that she wouldn't be walking. Caitlyn chose that moment to walk into the kitchen and before Bliss could say anything, Caitlyn told her mom that she and Bliss' graduation days were the same. "Bliss, you need to walk. One of us will come to your graduation and one of us will go to Caitlyn's."

Bliss shook her head no. "No, I've already sent in my paperwork. I've tested out of all my exams, so I'm done with school two weeks earlier. I'm not walking.

I want to get ready for camp."

Rose looked at her trying to decide whether to fight her on it and then shrugged her shoulders. "Okay, Honey but I want you to come home before camp. I want to see you."

"I'll try, really I will." Bliss was already lost in thought. The day after she finished her last class she was going in for the operation. She had planned to have all her stuff packed and then drive herself to the hospital and hopefully, 24 hours later she'd be able to drive home without wearing her glasses.

"Bliss did you hear me?" Rose broke through her thoughts.

"No sorry what?"

"Can you send me a list of everything you need for training?"

"I don't have it yet, but I think it's pretty minimal and I'll just get it myself, but thank you." "Where is your training?" Caitlyn asked.

"San Francisco."

"Really? Wow, that's cool."

"Yes, I've never been there. Part of my training is completing the physical tests, but the other part is learning what my job will entail and how to do it, and I'm really excited to start that."

Rose smiled at her gently. "Your mom would be so proud of you."

Bliss teared up and she had to lift her glasses to wipe away the tears, and that's when Connor stepped into the kitchen.

"What's the matter?" He said quickly stepping to Bliss' side.

Caitlyn giggled, and Bliss smiled up at him thinking

what a great guy he was. "No, I'm good Connor. I just got a little nostalgic."

Rose was watching her eldest as he stood next to Bliss. The concern on his face for Bliss was evident and the look of relief that washed over his face that she saw when he heard she was okay was gratifying. Connor and Bliss? Rose realized this was why Collin had teased them about playing video games all night. Rose wasn't sure how she would feel if they were a couple. She loved Bliss like a daughter anyway. Connor was older, but Bliss had always been more mature than girls her age. She'd have to talk to her husband about this.

"So mom, the General wants to know what time we're eating." Connor asked.

Rose smiled and snapped her dishtowel at her big son. "You tell your father..."

Caitlyn, Bliss, and Connor finished her sentence for her. "It will be ready when it's ready." They recited one of Rose's favorite sayings, as all four of them began laughing out loud.

The weekend was one of the best family weekends the Doherty's had in a while. With the entire family being home they went to a movie one night, out to dinner another, and spent lots of time in front of the television just relaxing. Bliss and Connor cajoled Collin and Caitlyn into trying to play video games with them, but neither of them enjoyed playing and they weren't good at them, so the two times they played, Bliss found herself alone with Connor again. Bliss did not miss the small touches Connor would give her. Her imagination was in total overdrive wondering if it meant what she hoped it meant.

Connor and Bliss worked out every morning together and Connor even helped her with her pull ups, which Bliss had trouble with. He helped her position her hands better and now she was able to squeak out ten, whereas before she could only do seven.

Sunday afternoon Bliss was getting ready to leave and so were Connor and Collin. Caitlyn was going to stay another night. The family was in the driveway everyone hugging each other good-bye and Connor approached Bliss.

He gave her a brotherly hugged and whispered in her ear. "Meet me at the elementary school."

Bliss nodded and then after hugging the General and Rose one last time she left, with Connor behind her and Collin behind him. At the end of the street Bliss turned right followed by Connor and Collin turned left. Connor could see his brother giving him a concerned look as he turned toward the highway. The same way Bliss and Connor should have turned.

When they got to the elementary school Bliss got out of her car and Connor did the same. He wasn't wearing a coat and as he walked towards her Bliss could not help but notice how handsome he was. He was dressed in faded blue jeans that stretched across his firm thighs and a khaki tee shirt that accentuated his strong arms by filling out the normally loose short sleeved shirt. His chest and shoulders were thickly muscled and wide, tapering into a trim hard waist and tight athletic hips that sported an Army issued belt. When Connor reached Bliss, he put one hand behind her neck and pulled her towards him. The move was so unexpected that Bliss faltered almost tripping. She felt like such a klutz.

Connor stopped short of kissing her. His face was close to hers and she could see he was breathing heavily.

"I have wanted to do this all damn weekend." He said, his lips almost touching hers, but not quite. "Please, tell me I can."

Bliss had latched on to his waist. Was he actually asking if he could kiss her? Connor did not move any closer to her. He was waiting for her answer.

"Bliss," he pleaded softly.

"Please kiss me Connor." Bliss whispered against his soft lips.

Connor lowered his mouth to hers and they both moaned upon contact. The kiss was tender and sweet, but it wasn't what Bliss wanted. She stepped closer to Connor, fitting her body up against his. Her body responded as did his and she soon felt his hard length against her stomach and an ache between her legs that she knew would remain there without some relief. Bliss had only kissed a few men, but it had not even compared to this kiss. Connor bracketed her head with his hands and kissed her with so much passion that Bliss couldn't help pressing herself against him. She lifted her thigh, so it hugged his hip bringing her ache closer to his prominent bulge and Connor's hand held it there, lifting her against her car, moving his hard length against her.

Connor had to get a hold of himself. He was ready to spill in his jeans like a teenager and Bliss was starting to shake.

He lifted his head from the kiss and let her leg fall slowly until she found her footing on the pavement. He still held her, and he watched her carefully as he continued to press against her.

Bliss was numb. Connor had just kissed her. He kissed her like he really liked her and it was heavenly. Bliss was breathing hard and she laid her forehead on his chest affording Connor the chance to rub his hands up and down her back affectionately.

"I knew it would be like that." He murmured.

Bliss picked her head up and pushed her glasses that had fallen slightly down her nose back up again. She gave him a smile he knew he would always remember. "I had no idea." She whispered.

"No idea?" Connor asked perplexed.

"No idea a kiss could be... could be that," she faltered for the appropriate word. "Hot?" Connor said smiling. "Yes, hot, wow," she said grinning up at him.

"It was good because we were kissing each other." Connor told her swiping his thumb over her kiss swollen lower lip.

Bliss nodded agreeing with him. She did not even want to try to speak. It was enough that Connor had kissed her, and he had even said that he had been dying to do that all weekend. She sighed thinking that this had better not be a dream.

"I guess we better get going." Connor admitted reluctantly.

"Yes, I hate the traffic on 95."

"Bliss, will you text me when you get back?"

"Sure. Stay safe Connor." It's what she always said to him when they parted ways. "You too." He gave her one more tender kiss and then opened her car door for her. He watched as she drove away, and his heart felt heavy as he watched her car turn from the lot out of sight. When he got into his car his phone was ringing.

He didn't even need to look at the Bluetooth above his stereo to know it was Collin.

Chapter 4 Six Months Later

Bliss had no idea how to categorize her and Connor's relationship. It was something more than friendship, but since they didn't see each other, and the one and only physical encounter they had experienced was a hot as hell kiss in an elementary school parking lot she didn't think they were boyfriend-girlfriend. It didn't really matter to her though; what she had with Connor was good, better than good, it was great. They spoke and texted each other every day, sometimes multiple times. They attempted to Face Time once a week, but the Wi-Fi on Connor's base was sketchy, and he could only use the Wi-Fi in the Officers game room so when there were other men around, it got a little loud.

Bliss had finished her classes and had undergone a successful eye operation; no more glasses. She couldn't believe how light her face felt.

The first time that she used Face Time to call Connor without her glasses on she was so nervous she was actually nauseous. Bliss was at the Doherty's home spending the week with them. She had planned to go to Caitlyn's graduation and then she was heading to boot camp.

Connor had texted and said he could Face Time if she was free. She texted back that she was and then opened up her computer waiting for the telltale ring. When Connor's face came up on the screen she watched as his face registered the surprise of her not wearing her glasses.

"Bliss? Where are your glasses? Did they break? Can you see?"

Bliss started laughing and pushed her curly hair back off her shoulders casually leaning her chin on her hand.

"Connor I had an operation. I don't need them anymore."

Connor didn't speak right away. "You had an operation? Who was with you?"

Bliss realized he was more concerned that she had had surgery with no one around.

"Connor, listen, I've been planning to have this operation for years. Years upon years I've planned this. I knew in December the date I was having it. It was a simple procedure."

"Bliss you shouldn't have been alone. I would have..." Bliss cut him off. "You would have what Captain?" She said using his rank.

"I would have tried to get there. I would have asked my mom."

"Connor stop, please. It's done. I'm happy. I feel great. I can see. Please just be happy for me, please." She pleaded.

"Honey, I am happy for you. I just don't like you doing things like this alone. You have a family; we care about you. I care about you."

Bliss smiled at the screen. It was the first time Connor had ever voiced his feelings out loud.

"I care about you too, Connor." She said successfully shutting his mouth. He then grinned and her heart once again pitty patted recklessly.

"Can you get home for Caitlyn's graduation?" She asked hoping he'd say yes.

"I don't know. I've put in for the leave, but Mike's wife is supposed to have a baby and if she has the baby, we both can't be off base."

"I hope you can. I'd really like to see you before I leave."

"Are you nervous?" He asked seriously.

"Not really, I'm actually excited. I'm driving to San Francisco on Saturday. Caitlyn graduates on Friday and that will give me one day with her."

"We won't be able to talk much when you leave." Connor told her.

"I figured. Will they let me keep my phone?"

"Yes, you're an Officer so you'll have the better bunks, your own recreation room and you'll be allowed to keep your phone as long as it's locked in your trunk during training times."

"What about you? Any more word on when you're leaving?"

"No, the time frame is the same. We're probably heading out some time in August." "How's Fort Bragg, NC?"

"Hotter than hell." He answered with a laugh.

A few men walked past the screen and one of them cat whistled forcing Connor to tell him to 'shut it'. Bliss could hear the men snickering in the background.

"I have to go." She told him knowing he was about to say that to her.

"Okay, Bliss, listen." He paused. "I miss you."

"I miss you too. Stay safe."

"You stay safe too." Then they logged off.

The next few days Bliss spent with Rose and the General. She had put the stuff from her dorm room in their basement and the General had taken her to the bank and now she was officially in charge of her money. Rose had given her a day at a spa for a graduation gift and Bliss had been waxed and polished and styled and blown dry, but the end results were worth it.

Bliss had never known it before, but she thought she had pretty eyes. They were a bright blue and her eyelashes were long and dark enhancing them even more. The lady at the spa shaped her eyebrows and the stylist gave her a cut that was so easy to take care of Bliss wished she had gone to the spa years ago. She could easily pull her hair up in a bun for working out, but when she wanted a sexier look, she blew it dry with a

diffuser and her natural curls swirled softly around her face making her appear almost angelic.

The day of Caitlyn's graduation Bliss packed her car. She kept her computer out in case Connor was able to Face Time again. She had really hoped he would fly in for Caitlyn's graduation, but more so because she really wanted to see him. She went with the family; Rose, the General, and Collin and watched as Caitlyn graduated with honors. When the family arrived home that night, her and Caitlyn, in Caitlyn's packed- to- the -roof car, and Collin, Rose and the General in the Generals sedan they stooped in town and ate dinner. Caitlyn wanted to go out and celebrate and both she and Collin were groaning knowing how Caitlyn could not handle her liquor.

That night at the bar was a far different story than the last time Bliss had been there. She had men offering to buy her drinks and one guy had to be forcibly nudged away by Collin.

"Sheesh Bliss you're really attracting attention here." He teased her.

"Sorry, I don't really notice it." She admitted.

"You are very pretty you know." Collin told her honestly playing awkwardly with his beer napkin.

"Thank you Collin."

Caitlyn danced up to them and dragged them both on the dance floor and Bliss had to admit her timing was perfect. She had a feeling Collin was going to say something, maybe even about her and Connor and Bliss honestly would not know how to respond.

The next day, Collin, Caitlyn, who was of course hung over, Rose and the General all said good-bye to Bliss as she began her cross-country trek to the base in San Francisco. Rose was trying not to cry; Caitlyn was holding back tears and the General even looked upset.

"Guys I'll be back before I deploy." Bliss told everyone happily. "I'm happy! Be happy for me!"

That got the family smiling and Bliss headed her car west.

Chapter 5

Boot camp wasn't as bad as Bliss thought it would be. Luckily, she had come to camp in the best shape of her life. The full gear jogs were hard because she had to carry 50 pounds in her pack, on her body, but she never quit or complained. She was able to surpass twelve pull ups, and even though some of the men could do twenty, she was pleased with herself. What

Bliss loved the most though was working with the computers.

The Officers teaching her were amazed at how quickly she had learned the program she would be in charge of. She had, of course, read the journals and manuals cover to cover, and all that material was now locked away in her brain for when she needed it. Bliss learned that in Afghanistan, she would be sent information that was coded and her job was to decode it, give it to whomever it was intended for and then make sure all evidence of the message or information was erased

She would be traveling to different bases with a team of four Marines, who were basically guarding her and the other Analyst, which was their technical title. One of

them would be at the computer at all times.

The other Analyst was an ROTC grad like herself, out of Virginia Tech. He was a geek at heart like her, but he didn't have the gift of memorization that Bliss had, so for him, memorizing the different codes and IP addresses that they had to use was proving difficult. Sometimes Bliss pretended she was having trouble remembering a code sequence just to make him feel better. The guy was nice enough, but he complained constantly.

Bliss found out through the grapevine that some of the information that they would be relaying was as mundane as what rations were coming in and when, but she also heard that they would be delivering serious information as well, such as strike targets, drone routes, and where certain battalions were. It was a little intimidating that she would be privy to that kind of information and she was very well aware that lives were on the line. Connor had gotten through to her a few times, but she hadn't heard from him in over a week and she worried that he'd already deployed. He had promised he'd at least send her a text and she was pretty sure he would, so she kept checking her phone when she able. The times they had gotten to talk they were both so tired that the conversations were stalled. Connor always ended the conversation with 'Miss you,' and she always ended it with 'Stay safe.'

The week before Boot Camp ended Bliss made arrangements to have her car shipped back home. She knew that she would have to fly back to North Carolina and wouldn't have time to drive her car back. When Boot camp ended, Bliss was physically and mentally fatigued, but giddy with excitement. She and the other Analyst were flying out of San Francisco on Monday morning. They would pit stop in Charlotte, North Carolina and then head overseas. Bliss booked herself on the first plane she could back to New Jersey. She had promised Rose that she would try to get home before leaving and she was not going to let the woman down.

While she waited to get on the plane she texted Connor and told him that she was heading home until Monday and that she missed him. She hadn't spoken with him in two weeks, just a few short texts and she hated that she was feeling a little needy.

When Bliss' plane landed in Atlantic City, Collin, Caitlyn, Rose and the General were all there to greet her. She asked if anyone had heard from Connor but like her, no one had. Caitlyn was once again insistent that they make a night of it and on cue Bliss and Collin groaned good-naturedly.

The General drove them right to a restaurant; Bliss' favorite and the warm feeling of being loved and wanted surrounded Bliss. She knew she had been so lucky that the Doherty's had taken her in like they had. She couldn't imagine life without them. Her thoughts turned to Connor and she felt an ache in her chest that she knew was there because she missed him.

Bliss' phone buzzed inside her purse indicating that she had received a text message and when she saw the random numbers and letters pop up on the screen she quickly excused herself from the table.

When she got back to the family she was so excited that even the General knew the phone call had been special. He should, he had a hand in making it happen, although he'd never tell Bliss.

"Jax is coming!" Bliss announced bouncing up and down, clutching the phone to her chest.

Caitlyn hugged Bliss knowing this was huge. Bliss saw Jax every couple of years and Caitlyn knew that Bliss had wanted to see him before she headed out. Bliss never saw the General wink at his wife.

"When's he coming?" Collin asked.

"Tonight, I'm meeting him at the bar."

"Is that safe?" Caitlyn asked knowing Jax was undercover and had always stayed away from Bliss so as to not put her in harm's way.

"Yes, he says he's between assignments now. I guess I'll find out more tonight."

"Bliss I'm so happy for you." Rose said as Bliss sat

back down.

"I can't believe it." Bliss whispered happily to no one in particular. "I had prayed that I'd get to see him before I left. I can't believe it."

When she looked up, she saw all four Doherty's grinning at her. She was so lucky, she thought.

The family finished dinner and headed home. Caitlyn was trying to talk Bliss into wearing a sexy little black dress, but Bliss refused. She had a dress that she'd been saving for a special occasion and this certainly qualified as a very special occasion. When Bliss walked down the steps into the living room, she saw Collin gape at her with an open mouth.

"Sheesh Bliss, I'll be needing a stick to beat the guys off of you."

"Hey!" Caitlyn whined. "What about me?"

"You look good too. Okay, I better carry two sticks." He joked good-naturedly, but his eyes never left Bliss.

With Collin, once again volunteering to be the designated driver, the trio set out for the bar.

Bliss hadn't seen Jax in years. She had not told him about the operation, and she wanted to surprise him. He knew she was in the Army and was going to be deployed, but the last time they had even spoken to each other was last March and that chat had been brief.

The bar was crowded, but not as crazy as it had been Thanksgiving Eve. Collin bought the girls their first drink and then found a seat at the bar. Bliss refused to dance with Caitlyn because she didn't want to be sweaty when she saw Jax. She and Caitlyn found a table in the corner where Bliss could see the front door. Her hands were sweating she was so nervous. Around 10:00pm the front door opened and in walked Jax. Bliss knew it was him immediately even though she hadn't seen him in years. He wore a man bun and he was so much taller and bigger than she remembered. His face looked hardened, but he had the same eyes as she did. He was good looking, and she saw the way some of the girls were glancing at him. He was wearing a tee shirt sporting a Clemson logo and she wondered where he'd gotten that.

Bliss stood up and smoothed down her dress. Her heart was pounding. Jax moved off to the side of the room and looked around. When his eyes landed on Bliss, they stalled and then his face broke out into a huge smile. He strode quickly towards her and when he reached her he lifted her off her heels and gave her a gigantic hug. Caitlyn had also stood up. She'd never met Jax.

"God, I've missed you." Jax said as he continued to hug his little sister.

"I've missed you, too." Bliss squeaked out; he was hugging her so tightly.

Jax heard the squeak in her voice and laughed knowing he was being overzealous and put her down, but he kept his hands on her upper arms and looked Bliss over head to toe and back again.

"Shit, girl you look great." He said appreciating the woman that stood before him.

Bliss blushed and then pointed at Caitlyn who had been standing quietly nearby. The Doherty's had never met Jax, so Bliss made the introductions.

"Jax, this is Caitlyn."

Jax shook her hand and then Collin came over.

"And this is Collin."

"I'm glad you were able to make it." Collin said shaking Jax's hand.

"Me too," Jax said looking back to Bliss. "Little sis we have tons to talk about I see."

He said pointing to her eyes.

"Come on Caitlyn, let's give these two some privacy." Caitlyn followed Collin back to the bar and Bliss sat down at the table with Jax sitting across from her. The waitress came and Jax ordered a beer. "So what's been going on?" He asked with a chuckle. Bliss laughed, they could probably talk for a week and still not get caught up.

Jax and Bliss talked for hours. Jax had reached over and was holding Bliss' hand marveling at how beautiful she looked, how strong she sounded. He was so happy that she was doing something that she loved. She told him everything, everything except that she really cared for Connor Doherty.

Jax told Bliss that he was between assignments. He couldn't tell her too much, but he shared that he had gotten the evidence he needed to bring down two high-level drug runners and a Mexican drug lord. The DEA got him safely out of his assignment by helping to fake his death in a motorcycle accident.

He was free for four months, which he totally planned to use relaxing on a beach. He then would probably be given another assignment. They spoke about their mother and Jax noticed that Bliss was wearing their mom's bracelet. She told him she never took it off. The General had given her a magnetic fake medical medallion, which she wore over the pretty clasp so she wouldn't have to take it off. She wasn't allowed to wear any jewelry when she was on base and she knew she wouldn't be allowed to wear anything metal, other than a medical bracelet overseas either.

When the General had given her the disc, she was actually very surprised. The General was very much a by the book man and helping her to break regulation was baffling, but she didn't question it and she accepted his gift.

Connor had busted his ass to catch the last flight out of Charlotte, so he could get home and see Bliss before she left. He had been told that he was being deployed next week too, so it was his last chance to see her. He'd been out on a training mission with his team and when he got back, he grabbed his duffel, jumped in his car and made it just in time for the flight. He had to pay for a First-Class ticket, but he didn't care. He was going to see his girl. He chuckled thinking about him calling her his girl. He hoped she knew he felt that way.

Connor arrived home just as the General was turning out the living room lights. "Hey son," The General said hugging his oldest to him. "We didn't know you were coming home."

"I wanted to surprise Bliss."

The General paused, "That's nice of you. She's at the bar with your brother and sister." "Crap, of course they are." Connor said hating that he'd have to go there.

"I'll tell your mom your home."

"Thanks dad." Connor said as he walked back out the front door.

Connor walked into the dimly lit, loud bar. The band was playing a country hip-hop song and the dance floor was packed. He stood off to the side and saw Caitlyn was on the dance floor with some meathead. Collin was at the bar, but where was Bliss?

Finally he spotted her at a table. She took his breath away. She was beautiful and he watched knowing she had no idea how fantastic she looked. He loved that about her, she was so unassuming. The waitress was standing at the table and Bliss was smiling and he realized that she was talking with someone. Who the hell was putting that smile on her face? Connor started to walk over to the table and when the waitress moved away, Connor saw Bliss was holding hands with a man. A man he'd never seen before. He was close enough that he could hear her laughing and then he heard the man say, "Baby girl, I have missed you so much."

Connor did an about-face and turned into the hallway leading to the restrooms, hoping she hadn't seen him. What the hell? His chest ached and he was steaming mad. He should have known that she'd have men flocking to her now. She was gorgeous. Her body was dream worthy and she was fun to be with. The idiot men she'd met before had never paid any attention to her when she was wearing her glasses, not like he had. When had she met this guy? She had never spoken about any other guys. There was no way he was from Boot Camp. That laugh, that was his laugh. The one he liked to hear. The one he had worked so hard to give her when others had been unkind. Had he totally misinterpreted how she felt about him? He could have sworn she cared about him.

Connor punched open the emergency exit door hoping no alarm would sound and left. He got back in his rental car, drove to his parent's house, picked up his duffel, which was still by the front door, and left. Thankfully, there was midnight flight back to Fort Bragg, NC. He was able to trade his return ticket in and get on that flight.

He called his dad while he was waiting to board and when the General answered groggily, he hastily explained that he had been called back. He asked that he not tell the family, meaning Caitlyn, Collin, and Bliss, that he'd come home. Before the General could even ask why, Connor had already hung up. The General knew his son pretty well and he realized something must have happened at the bar. There was no way he would have been called back to base like that.

The next morning at breakfast Bliss was telling Rose all about Jax. She was positively glowing and the General now had a feeling what had made his oldest leave town. He pulled Collin into his study.

"Did you three have fun last night?' He asked cautiously.

Collin was a lawyer and he knew when someone was hedging for information. "What's up dad?"

The General smiled and sat down behind his desk. "Connor came home last night. He wanted to say good-bye to Bliss. I told him you were all at the bar. The next thing I know I get a call from him and he said he'd gotten called back to the base, which I'm pretty sure was a lie."

"He was at the bar? I didn't see him."

"Collin what was Bliss doing at the bar?"

"You know what she was doing, Sir. She was talking with her... shit!"

"Yeah, that's what I thought. Connor had no idea the guy she was talking to had been her brother."

"They were holding hands. Not like weird holding hands. They were sitting across from each other holding hands on top of the table."

"Connor must have seen that," the General surmised.

"You know about them?" Collin asked.

"Yes, your mom and I had a feeling."

"Should I call Connor? He's probably pissed."

"No, we better let this alone. Bliss is headed to Afghanistan and Connor is leaving next week. Maybe it will work out. He asked me not to tell anyone he was home and I don't want him knowing I told you."

Collin nodded. "Crap, Bliss has no idea."

"Yes, I feel bad about that, but she's so happy right now after spending time with her brother. That girl's been through so much. Let's let her enjoy herself."

"Okay dad."

Collin didn't agree with the General. He knew his big brother really liked Bliss and that they had been talking for the last eight months often. He also knew Connor didn't fall for just any girl. Connor had to be hurting thinking Bliss had been with another guy. Maybe Caitlyn will tell him if he calls before he leaves. He hoped so. He hated the thought that Connor was hurting, and that Bliss had no idea she was probably being cussed out, poor kid. Then on the other hand maybe it was for the best. Collin still felt strongly that the two of them should not be together. It would break the family up. He was sure of it.

Chapter 6

Seeing Jax, even for that short time had been like drinking a magic energy potion for Bliss. When she returned to base on Sunday, she was happy and ready for her deployment. The other Analyst, Mike, was all doom and gloom and gave her crap about how happy she was. She didn't care, she had seen Jax. He was going on a four-month vacation, he looked awesome, and although she knew he had changed, the change agreed with him. He was quieter, more thoughtful now.

Bliss tried to call Connor, but it went right to voice mail. She wished she could talk to him before she left, but it was looking more and more like that wasn't going to happen. She sent him a long text telling him that she had seen her brother, Jax and he was good and safe. She felt so much better now that she had seen Jax before she left. She wrote that missed Connor and hoped they would be able to talk once in a while. She sent him a kissy emoticon and brazenly wrote that she wished she could kiss him again before she left.

Bliss had a hard time sleeping the night before she and Mike were flying out. She hadn't heard from Connor and she was anxious about being in Afghanistan. Mike was so nervous; she had heard that he had puked. They packed their gear, including their combat ready gear, night goggles, and an extra set of clothes, it left very little room for anything else. They weren't allowed to bring their cell phones, but Bliss squeezed in her Kindle that she had to disable the internet on. She had uploaded a ton of books onto it and she also had filled her iPod shuffle.

She and Mike walked nervously up the back entrance of the transport plane. There were six other military persons inside, five men and one woman. Bliss sat down next to the woman who introduced herself as Sally. The big plane took off and Bliss felt a combination of excitement, tempered with anxiousness slide through her.

Their first stop was Seymour Johnson Air Force Base, in North Carolina, where they would spend the night on base before leaving the next morning on their final leg of their journey that would drop them in Afghanistan.

Bliss knew from there she and Mike would meet up with the two Analysts that they were replacing and they would also meet the four Marines that would be with them 24/7 for security purposes. She and Mike would shadow the two Analysts persons for four days. When they left, Bliss would be in charge of their team. She was the higher-ranking officer and she knew this irked Mike, but she didn't care. She deserved it. She had placed higher than him in almost every physical test, except those darn pull ups, and she had totally aced the computer tests they had been given.

Bliss settled down next to Sally for the five-hour trip to North Carolina. The two chatted for a little bit and then they both brought out their e-readers. Sally ended up falling asleep, but Bliss couldn't shut her mind off. She wondered where Jax was relaxing and hoped he was having fun. She thought about the Doherty's, she had sent them a selfie before she turned her phone off of her dressed and packed. In the text she sent a thumbs-up. Lastly, she thought about Connor.

Whoever said that absence makes the heart grow fonder was spot on. She really missed him. She wanted to tell him about Jax. She wished she could tell him what she had packed. He would have reassured her that she'd been trained well. He was the only one who talked to her about her deployment logically. He didn't get misty eyes like Caitlyn or look at her like she was odd for wanting the Army life, like Collin. No, Connor accepted her choices because he knew it was what she wanted, and he respected her for it. She did think it was pretty strange that Connor had not even been able to get a text off to her. Even if he had shipped out already, he would have had a least a second to text or call her. Maybe she had read too much into their relationship?

The plane touched down and Bliss and Mike hauled off their packs and the three heavy computer cases. A military transport picked them up and they were taken to a mess hall where they ate alone since it was late and then they were shown their sleeping quarters. Sally and Bliss were the lone occupants of the woman's quarters and Bliss promptly picked out a bunk and fell asleep. Tomorrow she'd be leaving the United States and starting her twelve months in war torn Afghanistan.

The next morning Bliss and Sally entered the mess hall to find it packed. They grabbed trays and then their breakfast. Bliss was too nervous to eat so her tray consisted of yogurt and a granola bar. Sally on the other hand had loaded up. They sat down and Bliss looked at the clock on the wall. They had forty-five minutes before their plane left. Just enough time to eat, brush her teeth, pack, and get to the airfield. Sally was chatting away about her family. She was from Iowa and she had six brothers. Three were military and, three ran the family farm. Bliss was halfway listening when she spotted a familiar face. Connor sat at a table across the room. He hadn't seen her. She couldn't believe her luck. Bliss excused herself from the table and shyly headed towards him. Her brain imploded with questions. Why was he here? Why hadn't he called her? If he had been here, he could have called her. Her stomach pitched nervously.

As Bliss approached the table, she saw that a pretty redhead was sitting next to him and damn if she wasn't smiling at him like he was her everything. The woman's hand was wrapped possessively around Connor's bicep and she leaned into Connor as she whispered something into his ear. Bliss felt her heart practically leap out of her chest and her face warmed with embarrassment. Now she knew why she had not heard from him. She abruptly turned away from his table hoping to disappear before Connor spotted her, but she ran into a big guy carrying a tray, and although he didn't drop the tray, he made a few loud comments regarding her running into him 'anytime she wanted,' which drew the attention of the entire mess hall, including Connor.

Bliss mumbled an apology and fled the mess hall. She reached the steps to the woman's quarters and heard

Connor calling her name. Shit! She might as well get it over with she thought glumly. Just seeing him had her heart racing and the immense sadness that squeezed her heart was so painful it actually hurt to draw air into her lungs.

Connor reached her and stopped short. His hands remained at his side and she noticed his fists open and close nervously.

"What are you doing here?" He asked sounding miffed.

"I'm being deployed this morning." She refused to show him how much she was hurting.

"What are you doing here?" She threw back at him.

"I'm leaving this morning, too."

They both remained silent, making for an awkward moment. She had so many questions, but she swallowed them. They stood looking at each other uncomfortably. Connor drew his hands behind his head and massaged his neck. Bliss knew that was his tell that he was worried about something. She decided to be the bigger person.

"It's okay Connor. I know."

He looked at her like she had sprouted another head. "You know what?" He asked cautiously.

She sighed heavily. She couldn't believe he was going to make her say it. "I know you haven't called me because you have a girl."

The look on his face was one of genuine surprise. "Bliss, I don't have a girl."

"The girl in the mess hall, I saw how she looked at you. It's okay Connor. I get it."

"You get it!" His voice had risen, and he looked around to make sure they were still alone.

"You get nothing Bliss." He said viciously. Bliss was so taken a back that she stepped back from him.

"I saw you Bliss. Last weekend, I came home to see you and I saw you with your guy." He emphasized the word guy loudly.

"What?"

"So don't make it sound like I'm the bad guy here." He spit out.

"Connor wait, stop, I don't have a 'guy,'" she said using her fingers to air italicize 'guy'.

"I was at the bar Bliss. You two were holding hands, so no, you don't get it. I got it, loud and clear!"

Bliss realized he must have seen her with Jax. She placed her hand on his forearm. She could feel how tense he was.

"Connor," she said softly, making sure he was listening before she continued. "That was my brother, my brother, Jax."

Connor was stunned into silence. He watched as it registered on Bliss' beautiful face that he had been in Pemberton and left without talking to her.

"Shit." He swore softly as he watched her eyes fill with tears. He knew she rarely showed emotion like this and he felt terrible.

"You left?" She sniffed, wiping her hand across her eyes.

Connor's shoulders slumped realizing what a grave error he had made. "Bliss I thought you were with him."

"Why? Why would you think that? Why would you just leave?"

Connor put his hand on her shoulder and guided her to the side of the building for more privacy.

"I saw you holding hands." He admitted sheepishly. "I heard him call you 'baby girl' and said that he missed you."

Bliss wasn't ready to talk yet. She was still floored that he had been in Pemberton and hadn't stayed to see her.

"Bliss it killed me to see you with another guy, all right? I left. I couldn't handle seeing you with someone else."

"But I wasn't." Her reply was meek.

"I know. I know now. I'm so sorry."

Bliss dropped her face to the ground and nodded. Her arms were crossed protectively over her chest. She stood waiting, knowing what was coming next, and he knew it would probably wreck them.

"So you left, went back to base, and to make yourself feel better you hooked up with Red?" She said referring to the redhead he'd been sitting with in the dining hall.

Damn, if she wasn't right on the money. He had hooked up with Teresa, the redhead, and now she was following him everywhere. He and his unit had flown up to Seymour two nights ago and immediately hit the town. Teresa was ready, willing, and accessible. They had rented a room at the local motel and were back on base in two hours. Since then, she had followed him around whenever possible. It was annoying and he'd been kicking himself for his lapse in judgment. Not because he was feeling anything for Bliss, he thought she had dumped him, but Connor usually found women that he wouldn't see again.

The look on Connor's face told her everything she needed to know. The guilt reached his eyes and he didn't even offer an excuse.

"Well, okay then, that about wraps this up." She said sarcastically as she walked away from him. Connor remained standing against the tin house.

"Bliss," he tried to make her stop walking, "Bliss, please."

Bliss turned at the top of the steps. Her heart was shredded but she was trying to get through her first ever break up with dignity. He needed to leave her alone.

"Connor please, I need to focus. I can't do my job and handle this," She said pointing at her heart.

"I'm sorry Bliss. I thought we were done."

"We are." She said and she walked into the room. Bliss lay down on her bunk and realized she had about twenty minutes to get her shit together. She went into the bathroom and showered for a second time that morning, because that was the only place, she knew she could cry without anyone seeing her. Twenty minutes later, tears shed, eyes cleared with the help of Visine, Bliss and Sally stepped on to the tarmac of the airstrip.

Connor was outside the hanger with eight guys around him. Bliss realized they were his team. They were all talking, and some were even laughing, but not Connor. He watched as Bliss lugged her stuffed pack and two large metal cases towards the plane. He observed another soldier following behind her, carrying one case similar to the two Bliss had. Connor knew the plane ride was long and he knew he had that time and only that time to fix the mess he had made. He homed in on what one of his guys were saying, "Her ass is fine, and I've got an entire day to meet it." Connor looked at what his men were looking at and realized they were all watching Bliss, his Bliss. Connor pulled Andy, his best friend, out of the group. Andy was the team's pilot and one of Connor's oldest friends. They'd been on the same team for years and been through so much together that they could finish each other's sentences.

"That's Bliss," he told Andy.

"That girl is Bliss? Your Bliss?"

"Yeah."

"Shit, Cap. Did you know she was coming here?" Andy said using Connor's rank. Connor was a Captain and the team's leader, but his men often referred to him as Cap. When other Officers were around, they addressed him appropriately, but they used Cap most of the time and Connor was fine with it.

Connor shook his head. "I screwed up Andy." He admitted watching Bliss as she struggled with the two heavy cases.

"You mean you screwed Teresa and she knows."

Connor frowned, "Yeah."

"Well, this plane ride just got a whole lot more interesting."

"I'm going to try to explain things to her. Can you keep the guys from making it worse?" "Connor, they all know you did Teresa. I'll do my best, but I can't guarantee they'll play nice."

"Just try okay?"

"Okay, good luck." Andy slapped him on his back sympathetically.

Connor saw the copilot wave at him and knew he had to get his team on the plane. They'd been on so many long trips that they knew to wait for the last second before boarding. The transport plane held enough fuel that it would make it to Kuwait without a stop to refuel. They were riding on a C-17 Globe master 111. The plane was big and held cargo in the back. It had side jump seats, which the guys had to be strapped into when they took off, but for most of the trip they'd sprawl where ever they found space. The trip took about 28 hours barring bad weather. There were no stewardess', like on commercial flight. Food and drinks were stored in a small kitchen space near the front and the guys fended for themselves. In the back of the plane was where the cargo was stored.

Connor followed his men onto the plane. Their packs were deposited under the bench seats they were belted into. There were forty military personnel on the C-17 and as he watched his men settle into the seats, he looked for Bliss.

He saw that she was near the back and the guy that had followed her on was sitting next to her. Bliss caught his eye for a brief second and then pretended to adjust her seatbelt. Connor sat down next to Andy making sure his team members had stowed their gear properly and were buckled in.

"What are you planning on doing?" Andy asked him quietly.

"I don't know. She was really upset, and honestly, I'm not good with this stuff."

"Do you need to do anything?"

"What do you mean?"

Andy grinned at his friend. "I mean, is she worth it? Maybe it's better this way."

Connor thought about that for a nano second and then shook his head.

"No, she's worth it. I like her, a lot. This was my screw up. I already owned it. I just need to fix it."

"What if you can't?"

"I don't know man. I sure as hell don't want to start a tour with this hanging over my head."

"Yeah, this first mission is going to be a doozy."

Connor nodded. "I'm still trying to figure out another exit route, but I just don't see one that's viable."

"We need you focused Connor. Get your girl back or get over her, and then get your head in the game."

Connor knew Andy was worried that if Connor was distracted, even the slightest bit, that it could affect the mission. He didn't like this first mission when he was told about it and he liked it even less after he had reviewed the logistics. His men had been training for it for a solid month now and he still was worried. After this mission his team would be sent to a base in Afghanistan and they would receive their next assignment and train for that. His team was top notch, but he had two new members. One man was a total rookie and the other had been a replacement for one of his guys that had been wounded last year and was still recovering. Connor had vetted them himself, but until they were actually under fire, he wouldn't know how they would react.

The big plane rumbled down the long tarmac and after it had leveled off, the Captain spoke over the intercom telling his passengers they could move about the cabin.

Most of the service men unhooked their seatbelts and got settled in for the long ride. Men were laying on the seats or the floor napping. A bunch of guys had out iPads watching movies they had downloaded. A few people had e-readers. Most of Connor's team settled into a circle to play poker.

Bliss remained in her seat with her seatbelt on. She was tired but laying on the bench seat or on the floor seemed so wrong; too relaxed for where they were going.

The plane had been in the air for ten hours of the 28-hour trip. Bliss had finally relented to lie down on the skinny bench seat that she and Mike had been sitting on. He had claimed a piece of the floor and had fallen asleep across from her.

When Bliss woke up, she found Connor sitting near her head reading an e-reader. She sat up and he put his tablet down.

"Sleep okay?"

She stretched, finding her muscles to be sore. She wished she could go for a run and work out. She always thought better after a run. She folded her hands on her lap feeling the hurt she had shoved aside pummel her again.

"Bliss it's a long ride. You can't shut me out forever, we're family."

Bliss gasped, appalled that he'd pull the family card, and he watched as her quick mind thought of remarks that he knew she would never say out loud because she just wasn't wired to be mean.

Bliss turned her back to him so she was looking out the window. She didn't know how to handle this problem she had. She was hurt, mad and jealous.

Connor leaned towards her. "Ready to talk?"

Bliss finally turned towards him and the pain he saw on her face was like a punch to his gut.

"I'm sorry." He said softly. "I'm really sorry."

Bliss was looking at her hands that were still folded tightly in her lap. She was willing her tears to stay away and once she composed herself, she looked up at him.

"I don't know what you want from me?"

"I want us to go back to being us." He said gently. Bliss shook her head no and she heard him sigh. "I fucked up Bliss. I thought you were with someone else. I left without talking to you. I hooked up with someone else." Bliss looked back out the window and Connor took her chin into his hand and moved her face so she was looking at him again.

"Do I get any points for flying home to see you?" Bliss sighed and put her head so it was resting near the window. He could see that she was trying to remain in control.

"Why couldn't you have come up to me or spoken with your family? They all knew I was with Jax." Connor rested his elbows on his knees but tilted his head towards her. "I should have. God, I wish I had." He paused and Bliss looked at him.

"Bliss I was out of my mind that you were with someone else. I was ready to kill the guy. I was hurt and."

"So you know how I feel." She said solemnly.

He nodded. "I'm sorry. I'm so sorry."

"Do you love her?"

"Teresa?"

"The redhead?"

"God no, I was drunk; I was so hurt thinking that you had moved on. She was all over me. I just took what she offered."

Bliss closed her eyes and turned her head back

towards the window.

"I'd never knowingly hurt you like that. You have to know that," he said in a hushed voice.

"I don't know what to think. I only know how I feel, and I've got to tell you; how I feel sucks."

Connor moved closer. "I felt that way, too. I know I messed up. I screwed someone who meant absolutely nothing to me because I couldn't have you!" His tone was harsh and he spoke louder than he should have.

"Connor, shush!" she reprimanded him quietly.

Connor placed one hand on the edge of the bench seat and rubbed the back of his neck with his other hand.

"We have to fix this," he mumbled to her.

"Why? What do we need to fix? We were friends, good friends. We played video
games together, shared a few laughs."

"You know damn well it was more than that." He whispered tersely touching her thigh with his hand. Bliss looked down where his index finger rubbed the side of her leg. She looked back up into his face. Could she forgive him? He had made a monumental effort coming home to see her and he had thought she was with someone else. Why did he have to hook up with Red?

"I missed you Connor. I missed talking to you, seeing you. I understand you misinterpreted what you saw, and I also know I don't have any right to think you were not going to date other women. It just..."

"Stop Bliss, you do have that right. I never even thought about being with someone else after last Thanksgiving."

Bliss blew out a long breath. "But you were," she said so sadly that Connor felt like a heel.

Connor took her hand in his hoping that no one on the plane would notice. "Don't push me away. I've missed you too. I miss talking with you."

Connor looked around the plane. He and Bliss were in the last seats on the right and no one was sitting next to them. He wanted to kiss her so badly. He needed to. He had to make sure they were okay. He hadn't released her hand and Bliss was feeling uncomfortable with the physical display of affection. They were on their way into a war. They were both their team leaders, she needed to act professionally. She took her hand out of his. "Connor listen, why don't we just forget this happened and be friends again?"

"Friends?"

"Aren't we friends?"

"We are more than damn friends."

"Why don't we just start over at being friends?" She looked at her watch. "In fourteen hours, we will be touching down and we both need to keep our minds clear. I'm nervous and want to do well. I don't want to fight with you."

"I don't want to fight either, but you know we are more than friends."

"Right now you're the highest-ranking officer on this plane. You need to act like the CO that I know you are and set a good example."

Connor grinned at her and she couldn't help but smile back.

"You've always been so logical, so responsible. It's one of the things I really like about you."

"Well, thank you Captain." Bliss said giving him a mock salute.

Connor relaxed a little, at least she was talking to him now, and he'd gotten a smile out of her. He had fourteen hours to make sure she understood that she was his girl. He was feeling confident.

Connor stood from the seat and went up front where his team was sitting. He had gotten up with the intent of getting Bliss a Fresca, he'd seen they were stocked when he had boarded, but he saw how his men were looking at him, so he stopped near them. "Hey Cap," one of his men said.

"Roy, everything okay?" Connor noticed his men were looking at him and he could see they wanted to talk to him. He knelt down so he was eye to eye with them.

"Okay guys, spill. What's up?"

The guys looked at each other and then one of his men, Tippy, who had been on his team for years, spoke for the group.

"Cap, it's none of our business, but you had Red this weekend, and now you're moving in on the hot Lieutenant. What gives? It's a little out of character for you is all." Connor smiled and hoped what he was about to say would only reach his teams ears. "I guess you all deserve to know the truth."

They all nodded, and he knew some were thinking he was going to tell them some juicy dirty tidbit.

"That Lieutenant back there," he waited until he saw them all nodding, "that's my girl." There were a series of hushed, 'no ways' and 'get out of here,' so Connor held up his hand silencing them.

"It's a coincidence that she is on the same plane as me. Neither of us knew." "That's the girl from home?" Roy asked.

"Yup."

"That's the girl who would whoop our ass in video games?"

Connor chuckled, "That's her."

"Shit Cap, she's hot." One of his men said causing Connor to grin.

"She is," he agreed.

"Does she know about Teresa?" Tippy asked.

"Yeah, we had a major misunderstanding and I fucked up. She knows and I'm trying to work my way back into her good graces."

A few lewd comments were tossed back regarding him 'getting back in' and Connor stopped them from talking with his hand.

"So guys, I'm asking as a friend, please don't bring up Teresa, okay?"

"Sure Cap, we get it." Tippy said and the rest of his team nodded.

Connor left his men and grabbed two Fresca's. When he got back to Bliss, he found the one other woman on board sitting next to her. Connor looked at Bliss and then the woman.

Sally grinned at him from her seat. "Sir, I guess I'm in your seat?" she said as she started to rise.

Bliss grabbed her arm. "Sally you can stay. I'm sure Captain Doherty wants to sit with his men."

Connor's entire mood deflated. He thought he'd been making headway.

"Sure, I'll sit with my men." He said curtly. He gently tossed the Fresca to Bliss and walked away.

"Bliss, are you nuts? That man is A-1 prime and you'd rather sit with me?"

Bliss cracked her Fresca. "It's a long story."

"Are you gay?" Sally asked cautiously.

"No, I actually know him, and I really like him. Well, I used to like him. He just threw me a little and now he's got me discombobulated. I need to be ready for when we land and."

Sally cut her off, "and with that hunk sitting next to you, you would be thinking of nothing but jumping his bones." Sally started laughing hysterically and Bliss laughed but quickly slapped a hand over her mouth.

Two hours later, Bliss got up to use the restroom and when she opened the door to leave, she was gently pushed back inside the large stall.

"Connor, what the heck?" Bliss said nervously.

"I thought we were going to work on being friends again?" He said sarcastically.

"We are," she said slowly.

"Is that why you made that woman sit with you?"

"Connor really, I don't know what you want from me right now?"

"Right now I want to kiss the shit out of you so you know how I feel about you."

Bliss rolled her eyes at him.

"What?" He asked. He was totally frustrated.

"You can't just expect me to forget that your mouth has been elsewhere, recently, I might add."

"You're kidding, right?"

"No, I'm serious. I can't get the image of you and Red out of my mind."

"I'm done apologizing." Connor told her. "I told you it meant nothing. I was an idiot" He paused and sighed deeply. "If you're really not going to forgive me, I'll leave you alone." Connor had finally had it. He turned to open the door and she grabbed his arm turning him around towards her. He could see that she had tears in her eyes. Connor took her hands in his and held them against his chest. Bliss felt his heart beating through his tee shirt. Her emotions were frayed. She hated fighting with him. She was so jealous about Red that she couldn't even think straight. She still cared for him though. She cared for him a lot. Bliss leaned against his chest allowing the tears fall.

Connor held her against him and pushed his fingers up through the back of her hair loving how her curls felt as they slid through his fingers.

"It's going to be all right Bliss. I'll make it all right." Bliss held him tightly. "I hate that you made love to that woman."

"I didn't make love to her. I took what she offered and tried to make myself feel better. I know I sound like a jerk, but I was hurting."

"Did it work?"

"No, it didn't help at all." He said so softly bracketing her face with his hands. He was staring into her eyes and the heated look he gave her was panty melting.

"Connor, I'm scared," she admitted softly. "I'm afraid of messing up in Afghanistan. I'm afraid that I'm not good enough and I'll let my fellow soldiers down." She sniffed and raised her face towards him. "But I'm so scared of losing you that I think I'm losing my mind."

Connor put two fingers under her trembling chin and guided her mouth to his.

The gentle kiss turned more frenzied and when he lifted her against the wall, Bliss was pulling him closer and whimpering softly as he pressed himself against her.

She lifted her mouth from his and he buried his mouth into her soft neck.

"Connor, we have to stop," she murmured breathlessly.

Connor pulled out of her delicious neck. He knew she was right. He was surprised no one had knocked to use the bathroom yet.

With her cheek against his tee shirt she whispered, "I really have missed you Connor." "I missed you, too." He said rubbing her back.

"I had so many things I wanted to run past you and you never answered my calls."

"I know, Honey, we were training and there was no service where we were, then I wanted to surprise you by coming home, so I didn't call when I could. Later, after I saw you with Jax, I was so pissed. I couldn't believe you had moved on to another guy so quickly,"

"I wouldn't do that to you. I can't believe you wouldn't know that."

She lifted from the embrace and looked at him.

"Bliss you are so beautiful and I guess I just figured that guys were now seeing what I've always seen." "What do you mean?"

"I've always thought you were beautiful; your face, your body, but especially your mind.

I just thought that guy."

"Jax."

"Yes, Jax, was just one of probably many, that were now wanting you."

"But the fact that you thought I'd be with someone else bothers me."

"I guess I didn't have enough faith in you. I know that

sounds awful."

"I don't have a lot of experience dating Connor, but what I do know is how I feel. Why would I want to be with another guy when I have you?"

A knock sounded at the door and Bliss and Connor heard Mike. "Cap if you come out now, no one will see you."

Connor opened the door to hear singing. He looked towards the front of the plane and saw that Jeb had pulled out his guitar and was singing. Many of the service men had formed a circle around him to listen and the others were sleeping. Connor led Bliss from the bathroom and mouthed thank you to Adam. He knew his team had just pulled off a perfect distraction. He owed them.

Bliss sat back down on her seat and Connor moved to the front of the plane to sit with his men. Jeb had a great voice and he played for a full hour.

The flight was achingly long, yet Bliss and Connor were able to grab a few more moments alone. They sat next to each other and Connor wanted to hold her hand, but he knew that was out of the question. Bliss was starting to look nervous and he remembered what she had said right before they kissed.

Connor sat as close to her as possible without drawing attention. He assured her that what she was feeling was normal. If she wasn't afraid, she probably wouldn't be a good soldier. He told her she had been trained for whatever she would come up against. He did tell her to never go anyplace alone and to not trust anyone. He said she should use her instincts and to never let her firearm be more than an arm's length away from her. Bliss asked where he was headed, and he told her he didn't know. He and his team were being picked up in Kabul and transported someplace for their next mission. Bliss didn't even bother asking what it was. He asked her where she was headed, and she told him what she knew; that she and Mike were to be given their first assignment in Bagram. They were meeting their Marine guards in Kabul, when they landed and then they were to drive to Bagram.

"Bliss how well do you know this Mike guy?" Connor asked quietly.

"Not very well, just from boot camp and computer class, we didn't mix socially."

"I don't trust him." Connor admitted.

"You don't even know him." She laughed softly.

"I know guys like him." Connor said thoughtfully.

"He's probably pissed that you are the team leader."

"He is," she admitted reluctantly.

"And he will make things difficult for you." "Like how?"

"He'll do the minimum and try to make it appear as if you're lacking as the leader. He'll make friends with the Marines and make you feel like an outsider."

"Sheesh that would suck."

"Just be careful, okay?"

"I will."

The pilot came over the speaker and told everyone to strap in. Connor strapped in next to her and when they were touching down, he reached over and covertly held her hand. Bliss was so anxious that she didn't even try to pull away. She was flat out scared. Once they left the plane, she would be on her own. Connor would be off getting shot at and she'd be dealing with Mike, who Connor had pegged, and the four Marines.

When the plane stopped taxiing the pilot said they could unbuckle and the service members were eerily quiet as they grabbed their gear and walked down the steps. On the ground Bliss looked for the General that was supposed to meet them. She watched as a man in full combat gear climbed out of a Jeep. He wore a silver eagle on his fatigue cap and Bliss guessed he was their contact.

Bliss and Mike headed towards him and when they were standing in front of him, they both dropped what they were carrying and formally saluted him.

"First Lieutenant Allen and Second Lieutenant Marks reporting in Sir." Bliss recited formally.

"At ease," the General commanded.

Bliss and Mike put their hands behind their backs and spread their legs in the formal 'at ease' position and waited.

"No, really, you two, at ease." The General chuckled. Bliss smiled liking the man immediately. "I'm General Leonard Paine. I'll be your direct CO. I've got your first set of orders here." He patted his jacket, "I'll be taking you to the four Marines that will be guarding you."

They followed the General back towards his Jeep. Bliss took a moment to see if she could see Connor one last time. She spotted him and noticed that that he was watching her while he stood with his men. He broke from the group and jogged towards her.

"Captain?" The General said when Connor got close. "Something I can do for you?" "No Sir just want to say good luck to Lieutenant Allen here. We're from the same town in New Jersey."

"Go right ahead. We'll just get these cases onto the Jeep, won't we Marks?"

Mike looked pissed and Bliss sighed knowing Connor was right about him. She'd have to watch her back. Connor guided Bliss a few steps away from the Jeep so that they could talk privately. "Bliss, please stay safe." She could see the worry lines creasing his forehead and she wished she could smooth them away with her fingers.

"Hey, that's my line," she teased him, making him smile.

"I'll email you when I can. Don't take any shit from anyone and for God sakes, stay alive."

"I will Connor. You stay safe, too."

Bliss knew he wanted to say something else just from how he was looking at her.

He leaned and speaking softly, "I'll miss you."

Connor reached into his jacket pocket and pulled out a thin leather strand. He placed the leather piece around her wrist and secured it with a knot that she'd never seen before. Just wearing it made her feel closer to him. He then covertly kissed her wrist right on top of the knot he had tied. Their eyes locked and Bliss felt her heart pitty patter.

"I'll miss you too." She said whispered back to him. The General beeped the horn on the Jeep and Bliss smiled nervously at Connor. "Gotta run."

"Keep your head down kid," he called after her. As he watched her drive away, he felt las if a piece of him was being torn away. It was at that exact moment that he knew he was falling in love with her.

Unfortunately, they would probably not see each other for over a year. Connor was a seasoned military man; he knew a lot could happen in a year.

Chapter 7

The General drove the Jeep off the airstrip and through Kuwait. He followed a cobblestone road that took them to an area totally fenced in with barbwire. The Jeep was stopped at the perimeter and a guard checked all three of their credentials, while another man used a mirror attached to a pole to look under the Jeep and yet another man walked a large German Shepherd around their vehicle. Satisfied that they were who they said they were and that the Jeep was clear they were allowed to pass onto the base.

The General drove to a large tent and indicated to them that they should get out of the Jeep, which they did.

When they got inside, there were two military officers, both Lieutenants and four Marines.

"Lt. Felix Brant and Lt. Henry Russ, I'd like to introduce you to Lt. Allen and Sec. Lt. Marks, your replacements."

The four shook hands and Bliss couldn't help but feel like she was a prime rib dinner the way the men were ogling her.

Brant and Russ were grinning ear to ear. "So glad you guys finally got here." Brant said.

"We've been waiting for you for a month now." Russ informed them.

"I'm sorry we just finished training last week."

"Yeah, that's what brass told us." Brant said.

"Well, you're here now, that's all that matters." Russ finished.

Bliss and Mike weren't quite sure what came next. They had been told they would be shadowing the men they'd be replacing, but these men were standing next to packed bags.

"Colonel," Brant said stepping to him and shaking his hand. "It's been an honor Sir." "Go home and hug that wife of yours Felix, you've been a good soldier." The General said shaking his hand, he then turned to Russ. "Henry, I'm sorry your tour has been so difficult. I hope you can patch things up with the Mrs."

"Thank you Sir, it's been an honor."

"Ducky," the General said to man wearing a Privates First Class patch. "Take these men to the airstrip. That C-17 is refueling and leaving in an hour and I want these men on it."

Ducky saluted the General and Brant and Russ followed him out to the Jeep.

Bliss and Mike kept their mouths shut. Mike had started to say something but Bliss shot him a look that kept him quiet.

"Okay you two. Your Marine team is in the next tent." He reached into his pocket and extracted an envelope. "You are to head to Bagram." He handed Bliss the envelope. "You'll set up on the Bagram Airbase. You'll receive your next instructions in an email." "Yes, Sir." They said as they saluted him before he walked out the door.

Mike looked questioningly at Bliss but before she could say anything the General popped his head back in the door and said, "Are you coming?"

They both hurried after him.

The General led them to another tent where there were about 20 Marines sitting at tables, some were watching a television; others were playing cards or just talking. When the General walked in, they all jumped up and saluted him. "At ease guys." He commanded and they all resumed what they had been doing.

"Bo." The General said when a hulk of a man walked up to him.

"Sir," Bo greeted him.

"Bo, this is Lt. Allen and Second Lt. Marks, your new charges. Where's your team, son?"

Three other men appeared at Bo's side.

"Good men," the General said looking at the four leathernecks. He proceeded to introduce Bliss and Marks and once again Bliss was a little intimidated by the looks the men gave her. She noticed one of them wore a wedding band and that made her feel better for some reason. The four marines, the General and Bliss and Mike left the tented area and the General shook hands with Bliss and Mike.

"I'm sure you'll be back this way. Any trouble let me know." Then he left them with the Marines.

Bliss saw that the men were waiting for instructions from her.

"We need to go to Bagram." She informed them. They didn't wait for further instructions, the three men took off while Bo, who was also a Lieutenant, remained behind. "A word, Ma'am," he said motioning to Bliss.

Bo and Bliss moved away from Mike.

"Listen Lieutenant, I know you just got off the plane but you're looking a little shell shocked, what's up?"

"May I speak frankly, Sir?" She said addressing him formally as he had her.

"Yes."

"We were told that we would be shadowing the men we replaced, but they have headed home."

"Those guys were chomping at the bit to get home. I don't think they knew they were supposed to hang around. I know for a fact that Russ' tour was over last month, and Braggs' was over two months ago. Russ has had a rough go of it. I'm not too sure of what happened, but he got a "Dear John letter" from his wife last month and he kind of closed up after that. I guess you've been kind of thrown for a loop." Bo said, with his country boy accent coming through.

Bliss smiled. "Yeah, you could say that."

"Well, I can steer you a little. My team has been with Russ and Brant for the last four months."

"Great, so my first question is, am I supposed to requisition the vehicles, or do you do that?"

Bo gave her a big smile. "It's done, Ma'am. We ride with a Jeep and truck. Two Marines in each vehicle, you and the Second Loo can ride in which ever vehicle you choose."

"Okay then, let's get to Bagram." Bliss said feeling slightly better. "Would you mind if I ride with you and pick your brain along the way?"

"No Ma'am, I don't mind one bit." She noticed that he looked down at her ring finger and when he realized that she had noticed where his gaze had strayed, the big man actually blushed.

Bliss chuckled, "I guess I better get used to that, huh?" She laughed good-naturedly and that got a laugh out of Bo.

"Yes, Ma'am," He answered, relieved that she wasn't going to be a hard ass. He already liked her. The fact that she was gorgeous didn't even factor in. He appreciated that she was a straight shooter and instead of bluffing her way around her job had asked for some guidance. She also had a good sense of humor. Yup, he and the Lieutenant were going to get on just fine.

A few minutes later an Army Jeep pulled up and a truck with a canvas back pulled up behind that. Bliss went back into the tent where she had left the Computer cases and she lugged two of them out along with her pack. She hoisted the two cases up into the back of the truck along with her pack and after Mike hoisted up the one remaining case and his pack, she told Mike to ride with the truck. Mike looked put out being told what to do in front of the Marines and Bliss thought smugly that he better gets used to taking her orders. Bliss climbed into the Jeep and into the back. Bo was in the passenger seat while another Marine drove.

Along the way to Bagram Bliss learned the other Marine was First Sergeant Billy Ness. She learned Bo's last name was Pike and the other two Marines were Master Sergeant Harry Glen and Lance Corporal Phil Decklin. It took all of twenty minutes for them to stop using the Sir's and Ma'am's. Bliss realized they were formal when they needed to be. Usually they used their last names, but she didn't care if the men called her Bliss and she told them so, which sat really well with the two Marines she was driving with. She found out Lt. Bo Pike was from Mississippi and had played ball at Mississippi State until he'd blown out his shoulder. He graduated and went right into the Marines. First Sergeant Billy Ness was from

Michigan, and he'd only been over for a few weeks. He had already done a tour, and this was his second tour. He had a fiancé back home, and he probably would have talked about her the whole trip if Bo hadn't cut him off, which made Bliss laugh. Master Sergeant Harry Glen who was driving the truck behind them was well into his first tour and according to Bo, he was not going to re-up. He missed his wife and family and he couldn't wait for his final day. Lance Corporal Phil Decklin was the baby of the group. He signed on to be a Marine right out of high school and right after boot camp he'd been shipped over. The kid was young and still sported pimples on his chin.

Bo told Bliss that she and Mike would receive their orders through emails; which is what the General had said, too. The orders would tell them where they were to go and then when they were there, they'd receive a message to be given to whoever it was intended for. She learned that sometimes they didn't sleep on a base and those were the scary times because they would make camp on a road or in a village and they really had to be on their toes then.

When they reached the Bagram Air Force Base, Bliss took her cues from Bo. He told them to set up their computers in the truck and he showed them the small table that pulled down from the side wall of the truck bed. He then showed them how to fasten a small antenna to the top of the truck and he threw a canvas blanket off of a large machine, which Bliss recognized as a generator.

Mike set up the computer and Bliss set up the server. When they were done, they had a small little office space ready to relay information.

Once they were set up, Bo said he would show them where they could eat. Bliss declined because she knew someone always had to stay with the computers, so she asked Mike to bring her back something. Two hours later Mike still hadn't returned, and Bo slipped his head through the canvas partition. "He never brought you dinner, did he?" Bo said shaking his head.

"No, but I'm all right."

"Listen, Bliss. I don't want to tell you your business, but my guys told me he's already telling stories about you. You're going to have to put him in his place."

Bliss heaved a sigh, "Yeah, I know."

Her stomach was rumbling and Bo laughed, "Especially if you ever want to eat."

"The mess halls closed, right?"

"Yup."

"Shit."

Bo dug into his pocket and produced a granola bar. "I knew he'd leave you hanging. I'll try to rustle you up something more substantial." He tossed her the granola bar and she thanked him.

Bliss decided to make a schedule and a list of a few chores and rules that she and Mike would share. She typed them up and emailed a copy to Mike and to Commander Paine. This way she covered her back. When Mike returned, he apologized profusely but Bliss knew he didn't mean it. She left the truck telling him she'd be back in an hour. She knew he'd have to check his email. When she returned, he was pissed. "What's with the list of chores and rules?" He said hotly.

"Just making sure we're on the same page." She said easily.

He grumbled and sat back down in his chair. Bliss climbed up into the bed of the truck. "So, listen up Mike. If I ever hear that you're talking about me behind my back, I'll put a red flag in your jacket so fast it will make your head spin. I don't care that you got a bug up your butt that I'm your CO deal with it. We have a job to do and I can't be worried about you pulling shit to make yourself look better. I won't put up with it, so cut the crap. Tomorrow night, you don't eat."

"What the hell?"

"You heard me. You don't have to like me, but you damn well will obey my orders. I told you to bring me back dinner and you purposely didn't. Tomorrow night you don't eat." "You..." she knew the word bitch was just itching to come out, but luckily for him he held his tongue.

She waited for him to calm down. "I'm always going to take the night shift." She told him. You can bunk with the men. I want you back here at 06:00 for your shift. I will eat breakfast Mike, you hear me?"

"Yes, Ma'am." he mumbled as he grabbed his pack and left the truck. A few seconds later Bo stuck his head through the partition. "Nicely done, Loo." He said giving her a little salute.

"Thanks."

"Why are you taking the night shifts?"

"I'm going to sleep in the truck. If my computer pings, I'll hear it. I'm a light sleeper." "There are bunks for women folk." Bo said mildly.

"Yeah, but I'm not great with people. I've learned that

women can be to meaner than men; so really, I'm good here. Do you guys have shifts?" She asked.

"Yeah, it depends where we are. When we are in a safe place like the base here, we take four hour shifts only one man on at a time. When we are off base, there are two men on."

"Well, I'm always on the night shift and I'll probably always sleep in the truck. You okay with that?"

"It's pretty smart really. No scorpions or snakes sneaking into your bed."

"Cripes Bo, really?"

He laughed, "Well sure, especially when we're on our own."

"Will we be on our own a lot?"

"Yeah, usually we are." Bo shoved a bag through the curtain. "I got you a sandwich, PBJ and an apple."

"Oh man, you are my new favorite person." She said biting immediately into the sandwich. Bo was beaming.

Chapter 8

The team of six settled into a routine. Mike continued to be prickly, but Bliss pretended not to even notice, which she was sure annoyed him further. The four Marines turned out to be great guys and at night when they were off base, they'd build a fire and Bliss loved hearing stories about their lives in the States. They had tried to get her open up and Billy asked if she had a boyfriend, which she replied no.

"Then who gave you that bracelet?" He said pointing at her leather strands around her wrist.

"Um, a good friend of mine." She replied thinking about Connor and hoping he was safe. Really, he wasn't her boyfriend. They had something, but what they were didn't fall into any category.

"Well, Loo," if they didn't call her Bliss, they called her Loo, which was fine. "That bracelet is tied with a knot called a 'Love Knot.'"

Bliss looked at the intricate knot. "You're kidding right?"

"Nope, looks like someone is sweet on you." Bo said making her blush.

They spent most of their days on the road. They'd receive messages at all hours and as soon as they got one it had to be decoded and delivered. They'd been to a bunch of camps already like: Camp KAIA, Phoenix, Eggers, Ghanzi, and Arian, to name a few. The US troops were sequestered all over Afghanistan and it was Bliss' team's job to deliver messages to them that could not be trusted over the normal internet routes. Bliss was good at what she did, especially since her memory was a fortress of information. Mike had to keep referring to the manuals they'd packed, and he detested the fact that Bliss never had to look at any of them. Many messages they'd delivered were for the CO of a base. Using a series of numbers meant the CO was to be given the information, in person, no writing it down. The way it usually worked was that they would receive the coded message, decode it, and then it had to be hand deliver it. Bliss never wrote any of the messages she received down. She urged Mike not to either. She was worried the information would fall into the wrong hands.

Bliss had been in Afghanistan for two months and she hadn't heard from Connor. She knew he would email her if he could and the fact that he hadn't, had her worried. The General and Rose wrote her every couple of days. Caitlyn was in Paris and she emailed her once a week and so did Collin. When Bliss sent out an email it went through a firewall that scrubbed most of what she said out. No dates, times, names of persons or places were allowed. Bliss realized that what she said really wasn't important anyway. It was the fact that she was okay that her family was more interested in. She had heard from Jax a few times. He had already been given another undercover assignment, but he wasn't scheduled to start it for another two months.

During the first few months their team of six had skirted a few skirmishes and encountered two lone sniper attacks. The first attack happened when they were near a small mountain range while they rode along a dirt road. Bliss had heard a pinging sound hit the side of the Jeep that she was riding in and the next second Bo was yelling for her to get down as he slammed on the brakes and jumped out his side door. Billy followed Bo out his side door and Bliss jumped into the front seat and then out Bo's door landing between the two men. She saw that Mike and the other two Marines were also hunkered down. All six of them had their weapons drawn.

She watched Phil army crawl under the truck with a rifle that had a scope and a mounted tripod attached to the barrel. He positioned his body behind one of the tires and Bliss saw Bo watching him closely. Phil scanned the nearby mountain range and then she saw him lift his hand and hold up one finger.

"One man." Bo said quietly.

Bo gave Phil a hand signal and she watched as Phil made adjustments to the scope and then to his rifle. She saw him look through the scope, take a deep breath, and pull the trigger. The sound boomed harshly from under the truck and echoed back from the range loudly. Bo was still watching as Phil flipped the tripod legs closed and then wiggled out from under the truck.

He looked at Bo and held one finger up.

The six got back into their vehicles and no one spoke. Phil had just killed someone, and it served to bring the harsh reality of war back into focus. Bliss learned later that whenever possible, Phil would mask the sound of his sniper rifle by using other sounds in the area to cover his. In this case he hadn't been able to. Bliss also found out later that Bo had been worried that the sound would have signaled others as to where they were. She realized she was still such a rookie when it came to warfare.

Another month went by and Bliss' team was working their way to a base 100 miles away. They had stopped for the night, but Bo wouldn't let them make a fire because he didn't like the area and he wanted camp to remain black. Bliss made her bed up and slipped into her sleeping bag. She was almost out when her computer dinged. She got out of her sack and saw she had an email from Connor. Thank goodness she thought as she hastily opened it.

B, miss you tons. Wrote the family. Wish we would cross paths, but that's doubtful. I really miss you. CD. She wrote back immediately hoping that he was still on line.

C., Miss you tons, too. Lonely. I've got a good team. Wish I could see you. Stay safe. BA

She waited, hoping he'd respond but he didn't. Well, now she at least knew he was safe.

Two more months went by and the weather had turned cold. Now, Bliss was really glad she slept in the truck because even though the men slept in tents and were protected by the elements, the ground was cold. The sound the wind made as it whipped around the truck's canvas covered back was spooky eerie. She slept in a knit cap and mittens and her wool socks stayed on too.

They got to camp Phoenix and delivered a message to the head of a Marine battalion. After seeing her message safely received Bliss headed to the Post Exchange, (PX), which was luckily well stocked. She purchased long underwear, another set of gloves, and personal hygiene products. She also bought a hand-woven blanket from a villager. While she was gone, Mike had received an email that needed to be delivered to a small battalion of Marines encamped near a village that had been deemed friendly, but, of course, one never knew. The team loaded up with a week's supply of rations before heading out.

The snow was making it dangerous to drive. The white out conditions had completely severed the Global Positioning System (GPS) and internet connections. Bo made the decision to stop. He was hoping they hadn't driven down the wrong road. All the roads they were supposed to be on were checked regularly for Improvised Explosive Devices (IAD)'s, but the storm was so blinding that Bo was concerned they would miss a turn. The snowstorm lasted for four days. Bo had not even attempted to put up the large tent, so the bed of the truck became camp for the six of them. Bliss was actually glad the men were with her because it was warmer with more of them in there. The generator was used to power up the small space heater and they used a 24,000 BTU two burner camping stove to heat their meals and to make coffee on. With no messages coming through the six of them passed their time playing cards and napping. Bo and his team worked in two man shifts guarding the site, but Bliss couldn't believe that anyone would willingly be out in the blizzard. She could not have been more wrong.

It was on the final night of the blizzard that Bliss had first fired her weapon. Five of them were in the truck bed. Harry was on duty but had stopped in to refill the thermos for himself and Billy, who was in the Jeep. They used the Jeep to sit in between patrolling the camp on foot. With the weather being so harsh Bo had changed the shifts, so they were one hour on and three hours off.

Inside the truck Bliss had been dozing when she heard a gun fire. The Marines were up, weapons drawn in mere seconds. Bo motioned for Phil to slip into the front of the truck and then Harry stealthily and quickly drew back the canvas flap allowing Bo to jump out of the truck. She and Mike heard more gunfire and Bliss quickly packed the computer and server into the cases and locked them. She saw that Mike had his gun drawn so she took her gun from its holster and cautiously jumped out the back of the truck.

Bo was squatting behind the back tire and practically dragged her by the back of her pants behind him as bullets sprayed the deep snow around her feet and pinged off the truck bed. Bo gave her a slightly exasperated look and then focused on the gunfire. He pointed in two directions to indicate where the guns were being fired from. Harry jogged to where they were crouched down and with hand signals gestured to Bo what he was about to do. Bo gave him the thumbs up, and then he touched Bliss' shoulder silently mouthing for her to stay put. Bliss nodded. Phil took off in one direction and Bo took off in another. Bliss heard gunfire erupt and she thought her heart was going to beat out of her chest. She had never been more afraid in her entire life.

A bullet ricocheted near where she was hiding, so even though Bo had told her to stay put she knew she'd been seen, and her gut told her to move. Mike was still in the truck and part of her was glad because he could at least guard the computers. Not that there was any information on it, but if the computer or mobile server got damaged, their entire operation would be halted.

Bliss dove for a mound of snow nearby and banged her shoulder against a hidden snow-covered boulder. She crawled around the large rock wishing she had thought to put her helmet and vest on. Although Connor should have been the furthest thing from her mind, she thought that if he knew she was out without her protective gear on, he'd really give her an earful. Bliss heard more gunfire to her left and the sound of movement, but she was so hyper alert it could have been a bunny hopping and she knew she would have heard it. A lone figure appeared off to her left, the snow was blinding so she couldn't tell if it was someone on her team or not. She watched as he crept towards the truck. Her gun was trained on the person moving, but she didn't want to shoot someone on her team, so she held her aim and her breath. The person was close enough now that she could see the white puffs of breaths coming from the mouth. Her heart was pounding, and she shifted slightly causing snow to slide down the boulder hiding her. The man spun towards her and she knew she'd been seen. He was dressed in fatigues but sported a Taliban turban. She fired off two quick shots as did he. She heard the shots that he fired ricochet off the rock and drive into the ground near her spraying white snow into her face. She wiped the snow from her eyes and when she chanced a peek, she saw that the man was lying face down about fifteen feet away from her.

Her heart was beating so hard she thought she might pass out. She stayed on her knees with her gun drawn waiting to see if the man would move. He did not. Bo ran through the snow and got to her first. He stopped short when he saw that she was okay. Then he saw the man lying on the ground. The snow was swirling around them and it seemed surreal. She had just killed someone, and it wasn't in a video game.

Bo cautiously walked over to the man in the snow and took the gun he from his hand. He then felt for the man's pulse. When he didn't find one, he turned his attention to Bliss. Billy came running from the other direction and then Phil and Harry appeared running from the other direction. Bo knelt next to Bliss and took her gun from her hand gently.

"They're gone Loo." Phil told Bo.

Phil raised one finger and so did Harry and Billy. Bo answered by raising two. Bliss knew there had been six kills, one of them by her hand.

He told his men to do a thorough search of the area just to make sure they had not missed anyone.

"Bliss come on, you're freezing, and let's get you inside." Bo helped her to her feet and Bliss started to walk towards the truck.

"They're gone right?" She whispered to Bo.

"Yeah, they're gone, for now."

The harsh reality of war and the fact that she had just killed someone sank in. "I need a minute Bo."

Bo stopped walking and watched as she headed towards the Jeep. Bo told the guys to fan out and double check the perimeter. He waited for five minutes outside the Jeep giving Bliss a few minutes of privacy before he got into the Jeep with her. He didn't talk, he just sat there.

Bliss broke the silence. "That was almost surreal." She said quietly.

"Yeah, your first kill is usually tough."

"I know I'm not supposed to dwell on it."

"Bliss it was you or him, you know that."

Bliss smiled weakly at him. "I know."

"Come on let's get you back to the truck. Your lips are blue."

Bliss touched her lips and realized she had no feeling in her fingers. She started to get out of the Jeep, but Bo stopped her by placing his hand on her shoulder. He leaned in close to talk since the wind was making it hard to hear anything.

"You scared the shit out of me, woman."

Bliss shrugged and made a bit of a grimace with her face. "Sorry, I thought I could help."

"You did well. You probably saved yours and Mike's lives Bliss. That guy was going to ambush the truck and he would have gotten a few good shots off." Bo took his hand off her shoulder and Bliss saw him look at it. His palm was red with blood. Bliss saw his face change from soft to hard and he turned her so he could look at her back.

"Bliss you were shot."

Bliss felt something stinging near her back near her shoulder, but she had honestly thought it was the cold.

He moved her quickly to the truck and helped her inside. Mike was kneeling in one corner and when he saw Bo helping Bliss in, he knew right away that something was wrong. He jumped up and took her from Bo. When Bo got himself into the truck, he told Mike to turn around and he told Bliss to take her jacket off. Bliss didn't hesitate and she quickly took her jacket off letting it drop to the floor. She saw blood had discolored the top of the jacket near her shoulder.

Bo pulled off her two shirts and she grimaced with pain.

"Ouch," she hissed. Then she immediately said, "Sorry." She did not want to appear wimpy, but the wound was starting do a bit more than just sting now that she was getting warmer.

Bo looked at her wound and she heard him say, "Thank God."

"What is it?" She asked.

"You were grazed. There's no bullet embedded. It's a pretty deep groove, but we can steri strip it and you should be fine."

"Purple heart?" Bliss joked finally getting a smile out of Bo.

"No, sorry, not this time," he joked back.

The guys came back to the truck and told Bo they had tracked two more men west, but then they had stopped, not wanting to travel too far from camp. Bo told the group they needed to stay ready in case they were revisited. Bliss knew he was worried, and she couldn't help but think what a great soldier Bo was. She also knew if she didn't care for Connor so much, she would have been attracted to the big Marine.

No one slept that night and thankfully the snow let up just as daylight cracked orange ribbons over the snow-covered mountain tops. Bo used his GPS and discovered that they were slightly off course. He drove them back onto the correct road and not until they hit that road did the server sputter to life.

CO Paine had been worried about them when they hadn't checked in. They had to check in every twelve hours. They had almost been declared Missing In Action (MIA). Bliss knew the Doherty's would have lost it. Bo took the phone from Bliss who had been the one to call in said they'd exchange fire with a group of eight, telling him that they took out six. He gave the CO the approximate location. Bliss took Advil to keep the pain away from her cut and Bo made sure she kept applying antibiotic ointment and keeping it clean. That day Bo pushed them until well after midnight, until they reached a secure military camp. He checked them in with the CO and ordered his men and Bliss into separate small structures complete with cots and working showers. Bliss wanted to stay in the truck, but Bo put his foot down and helped her to rig the server near her bunk. Being on the Army base allowed the team of Marines the luxury of all six of them being able to get some real rest.

Chapter 9

Another month went by with no word from Connor. She and her team worked like a well-oiled machine now. She became good friends with Bo, and she knew if she gave him any encouragement, they would be more than friends. She knew that military personnel were not supposed to fraternize, but she also knew it was done all the time. They'd been on plenty of bases and camps, and she'd watch men and women sneak off all the time. No one ever said anything or called them on it. It was hard enough just being overseas, and Bo had told her that sometimes they just needed a little loving to remind them that they were human. Bliss didn't have to ask what that meant. She had heard horror stories from the men who had been fighting.

The team drove into Bagram and Bliss delivered a non-urgent message to General Paine regarding personnel that were flying in on the next C-17. The General thanked her and then told her and Bo to let the team relax for a day. Bo dismissed his men and Mike fled as soon as he knew he was free. The General then stopped Bliss and told her that she had just missed her hometown friend. Bliss knew he was talking about Connor. "He and his team were here for a few days. One of his men was wounded and they brought him to our hospital. They just pulled out this morning."

Bliss feigned indifference and simply said she was sorry she had missed him. She had hoped her face didn't give away the intense sadness she felt knowing she could have seen Connor if they had gotten to Bagram earlier. The General pulled out an envelope and handed it to her.

"He knew you were coming here. I told him; hope you don't mind. He gave me this to give to you." Bliss took the envelope and thanked the General before walking out.

"You want to open that in private?" Bo asked pointing at the envelope.

"Yeah, maybe. Let's eat, I'm starving for real food." Bo chuckled. "Now that's when you know you are not a rookie anymore, when you start referring to base food as real food."

Bliss laughed with him and they headed for the mess tent.

Inside there were chairs scattered around tables and many of the tables were filled.

The men and women were all watching a large flat screen television, which was showing video clips of what looked like a party.

They got their trays and sat down watching the video like the others. Bliss could see the video was of a party and it looked like it had been shot right there in the mess hall. There was music and dancing and many of the men and women held red solo cups. The person taking the video did a good job of keeping the camera angle wide so almost everyone there was visible, especially the persons dancing. Every so often the camera would zoom in on someone who was an especially good dancer, both men and women. The viewers in the mess hall were enjoying watching the recorded festivities on the big screen. Once in a while, one of them would throw out a funny comment about someone on the screen causing the room to laugh good-naturedly.

"What's this of?" Bo asked a man at another table.

"We had a bit of an impromptu celebration last night. The General unlocked the beer. The Green Berets had just come in from a mission, so we celebrated with them and had a good time. We always video our parties, it gives us all a good laugh. It also keeps the men from getting too shit faced, since it's all captured on film." This made Bo chuckle.

"Guess we missed out." He said looking at Bliss.

Bliss didn't hear him; she was staring at the large screen in disbelief. The camera was homed in on the people dancing, but in the background, Bliss saw Connor. He was standing off to the side with a few of his men and drinking from a cup. She was once again struck by how handsome he was and her heart pitty pattered just seeing him. As quick as her heart had pitty pattered, it splintered, as she watched a woman with a long red hair strutting towards him, Red. Bliss saw his men disperse, leaving the two of them alone. Bliss watched as they stood talking for quite a while. They were laughing and smiling at each other and the overt touches Red shared with Connor were a clear indication of what the beautiful woman wanted. Bliss fought down the emotional lump forming in her throat.

The camera moved so she couldn't see them anymore, but she continued to scan the video hoping to see Connor again, hopefully without Red. The camera panned back to the dance floor and once again Bliss saw Connor and Red in the background. Red was plastered against his side and Connor was whispering in her ear. He said something to her, and Bliss watched in utter disbelief and horror as Red smiled up at Connor and they walked out the exit they were standing near.

"Bliss? Bliss?" Bliss realized Bo was talking to her. "What's the matter?"

Bliss stood from the table leaving her full tray of food untouched and left the tent. She got to the truck, gathered her gear, and went to find the showers. Her heart ached and she knew then, that she and Connor were over. She was holding off the tears until she got into the shower. She thought sadly, that they never really had a chance. She couldn't believe that her luck was so bad that she just happened to one, miss Connor by less than a day, and two, that she had witnessed his reunion with Red through a video playing on the mess hall television. Bliss sighed as the gloomy sense of loss she felt began to make her physically ill. She walked faster towards the showers hoping she wouldn't embarrass herself by barfing in public. Well, message received she thought miserably. We were never meant to be.

Bliss entered the shower area, and of course, who did she run into; Red.

"Well, hey there." Red said with a sexy southern cheerful accent. Bliss flinched adding adorable accent to her growing list of attributes. "I saw you back in Charlotte."

Bliss nodded, "Yes, hello. Are you stationed here?"

"Yes, I'm a nurse. I got here a couple months ago."

Red was gathering her belongings. Bliss nodded and headed towards a stall. Well, Fudge My Luck, Bliss thought. Red was a nurse; a smart, military, beautiful nurse.

Bliss turned on her shower and heard Red say, "You missed a great party last night." "Yes, I saw the video, it looked fun."

"It was one of the best!" Red said happily. "Well, see you around." Bliss peered over the curtain-rigged stall and saw that Red had left.

She slumped against the wall and let the tears slide down her face. After allowing herself to wallow in self-pity for a good five minutes Bliss got herself together. She scrubbed her body as if she was washing Connor out of her system, slipped off the leather bracelet, and then gave herself a stern mental pep talk. When Bliss left the shower, she was in control of her emotions and hoped that she was not showing signs that her heart had just been ripped out of her chest.

She walked back to the truck to deposit her stuff and found Bo waiting for her.

"Where did you go?"

"Uh, I had to shower." She said meekly.

"Bliss, it's me." His tone was gentle, and she could see the concern he had for her in his brown eyes as he looked at her. "What's the matter?"

Bliss thought about it and decided to tell him about Connor. He had proven to be a good friend. She took him back to the mess hall and pointed out Connor to him on the television screen. Bo watched and saw the big Green Beret flirting with the gorgeous Redhead, and then he watched as they left the mess hall together. He took one look at Bliss and knew that he was the guy she was hung up on, the 'love knot' guy.

Bo wasn't a womanizer. He'd been brought up to respect women and care for them. He wasn't a saint either. He'd had his fair share of dating and one-night stands, but he always made sure the women knew where they stood. There had been very few women that Bo had ever become friendly with and Bliss fell into that category. In fact, he felt that if given the chance, he and Bliss could be a great couple. They had a lot in common and she was just flat out special. There were no other words to describe her. He felt bad for her and he wished the Green Beret was still around because he would kick his sorry ass.

"I'm sorry Bliss. That has to sting." He told her shaking his head.

"Yeah, well, I guess we really never had a chance."

"Did you read the letter?" Bo said. He figured out that the Green Beret was the one who had left it. Bliss had actually forgotten all about it.

She paused dreading the thought of what it contained. "No."

"Maybe you better read it, before you jump to any conclusions." Bo hated that he was defending the jerk.

"Bo you saw the video. He left with her. They have history." She told him.

"Really?"

"Yeah, long story, not worth getting into."

"You still need to read the letter."

Bliss took out the envelope and leaned against the truck tire. She looked back to Bo who was watching her. "I'm going to be okay Bo; you don't need to stay here."

"I know, but I'm going to." Bliss smiled at him. He was a good guy.

The letter was only a short paragraph, but it spoke volumes.

Bliss heard you were coming in, sorry we had to leave. I've been thinking about you, about us for a while now. Things have been crazy. We had to leave one of my men here in the hospital. He's going to be okay, and I know he's being well cared for. You and I need to talk, and I want it to be face to face. I hope you are staying safe. Love, Connor.

Bliss guffawed when she saw that he wrote, 'Love, Connor'. She handed the letter to Bo and watched as he read it.

"It's not exactly a Dear John." He said handing it back to her. "It's pretty close." She said glumly.

"He signed it, Love, Connor."

"We're practically family, that doesn't count."

"Practically family?"

Bliss decided to explain everything to Bo. Maybe she needed a different perspective. They walked around the base and Bliss told him what equated to her life story. She began with losing her mom and how the Doherty's had taken her in. She then told him how she and Connor had become closer. She explained what happened with Connor mistaking Jax for a boyfriend and then how he had hooked up with Red. She then explained how they had patched things up on the flight over and that he had given her the bracelet before she left.

"Have you heard from him?"

"A couple of times."

Bo took her hand in his and lifted her sleeve to find

that she had taken off the bracelet. "Yeah, took it off. Guess it wasn't really a love knot," she joked sadly. Bo couldn't understand how Connor could do what he had done to Bliss. He thought the redhead was great looking, but Bliss was beautiful, inside and out, she was intelligent, with a great sense of humor and a body that provoked wet dreams. She was also funny and brave and really good at her job. Bo knew he needed to tread lightly with her. She was on the rebound and now, maybe he had a shot with her, but he didn't want to scare her off by coming on too strong. Right now, he was going to be her friend, because that's what she needed.

Chapter 10

Bliss slept in the woman's quarters that night. She needed a good night's sleep and just because she was worried that she might run into Red again, she wasn't going to miss the opportunity to sleep on a real mattress. She giggled to herself remembering how she had slept in the truck that first month even when they had come to a camp. Yeah, she thought with a grin, she wasn't a rookie anymore. Bliss was pretty sure that Red had no idea of her connection with Connor, so as long as she didn't accidentally over hear any details of their hook up, Bliss figured she'd be okay. She brought in the computer and server, attached a small antenna with a magnet to the pole of the tent, put in an ear piece that was plugged into the audio port and then covered the computer with her jacket so no one would see it. This little set up of hers allowed for her to still monitor the computer, and if it didn't ping with a message, she usually got a pretty good night's sleep.

Bliss fell asleep quickly and without running into Red again, and although her dreams were marred with images of Connor walking out the mess tent door with Red, she felt physically well rested when she woke up.

The next morning she changed into her workout clothes and went to the gym, which, of course, was just another tent. Bliss missed working out when they were on the road. Bo would have never let her go for runs and she would never have asked either.

Whenever they were on a base or at a camp with a decent gym she worked out.

When she got to the gym, she saw a few men and even some women were scattered about, pumping weights, hitting bags, and she noticed there was a boxing ring set up in the middle of the small space. What surprised her more than seeing the ring was the fact that Bo was in the ring with a man larger than himself. This was rather startling to Bliss since Bo was easily 6'5" and must have weighed 280 pounds. The other man had at least two inches on Bo and he was huge. She thought the man had to weigh over 300 pounds. He wasn't a sloppy fat big guy, but as she watched them, she realized Bo was better on his feet than the other man. She watched Bo as he maneuvered around his opponent, jabbing with his non-dominant hand, hoping to open a space for his dominant hand to land a blow. Neither man was wearing a shirt, but they both had on their fatigues and combat boots.

Bliss noticed Bo's torso was all well-defined muscle. He had a great body and Bliss could see the power he possessed. The match was gaining attention and soon most of the people in the gym had stopped to watch. The larger man was throwing hard punches that Bo was blocking. Bliss knew that still had to hurt. She watched as Bo skillfully moved his opponent in a circle, throwing punches that kept the big man off balance. Then the big man threw a combination; a left followed by a right, and Bo had his opening. He side stepped the left punch so that it landed on his shoulder and he blocked the right-hand punch with his left forearm, at the same time he threw a wicked punch over the man's extended left arm. Bo connected solidly with the man's jaw and Bliss saw him stagger. Bo stepped back but kept his hands up in a boxer's stance. He was breathing heavily and sweat slid down his chest making his body look sexy, all slicked up. Damn, Bliss thought, he looked so alpha male hot. The big man shook his head no and then stuck out both his gloves, which Bo tapped gently with his own. The people that were standing around the ring clapped enthusiastically.

Bo saw Bliss watching him from a distance and he gave her a wink. Bliss laughed; he was such a kidder. She was glad she had confided in him. She needed a friend. Bliss wrapped her hands with hand wrap and then found a large bag and started punching. She went through her warm-up moves, interchanging punches and combinations before adding knee and shin kicks. After a good ten minutes she stopped and bent over placing her hands on her knees. She needed that physical exertion, working out always made her feel better. Sweat was pouring off her and she stood up and saw Bo watching her. He had put his shirt on, and he walked over to her.

"You're a good boxer." She told him earnestly.

"Thanks. After I blew out my shoulder, I dabbled a bit." He was smiling and inside he was practically dancing a jig that she had walked into the gym when she did.

"He was a bit bigger than you." She teased him.

"Yeah, and he moves pretty well for a big man." Bo admitted.

"Uh, Bo you're not exactly Tiny Tim, you know?" She joked.

Bo laughed loudly, and Bliss grinned at her own silly joke.

"Okay, well, I'm done." Bo told her.

"I'm just getting started." Bliss replied.

"After breakfast I'm going to check in with Paine. He wants a full briefing on those days in the blizzard." Bliss nodded solemnly, just remembering those days was a buzz kill. "Okay, well, see you later then."

Two hours later Bliss was in the mess tent sitting with Harry and Phil. Thankfully the video from the party wasn't playing anymore. Harry was all smiles and she knew he must have gotten lucky last night because when she sat down the two men stopped talking.

"Oh, please guys don't let me stop you." She chuckled.

Harry began talking about his night with a gorgeous redhead and young Phil was practically drooling.

"A nurse?" Bliss asked.

"Yeah, she's beautiful and she's a nurse here. Teresa is her name. You know her?" Bliss shook her head, "Nope." Bliss was thinking there couldn't be more than one beautiful redhead nurse in Bagram, could there? Well, she thought moodily, it doesn't matter anyway. Connor was out of her life romantically anyway. She knew she'd see him because he was a Doherty and she was practically a Doherty, but for right now he was nothing but a sorry waste of time. Bliss didn't want to hear about Harry's conquest and she wasn't thinking too highly of Red, the nurse either. The one consolation was that Connor and Red must not be in a solid relationship if she had been with Connor one night and Harry a few nights later. Bliss took her tray and told the two Marines she was going to check on Mike. She had transferred the computer and server back to the truck before she had worked out so Mike could oversee it.

Bliss put the tray back on the rack and carried her egg sandwich and container of juice to the truck.

She climbed in the back and Mike greeted her. He was sitting in a chair reading from an e-reader.

"Yes," he said as she climbed in. "You have perfect timing. I have to use the can."

Bliss settled into the chair that Mike vacated and watched him jog off.

Two minutes later the computer dinged alerting her that they had received a message. Bliss opened the email using the password that was changed every other day.

The email contained a series of letters and numbers that to a layperson would make no sense, but to Bliss, who had the code memorized, she was able to quickly translate the array of symbols. The word 'Normandy' was in the subject heading and that meant the message was to be delivered in person ASAP and NTK. Bliss read to whom she was to deliver the message to and put her head out the canvas opening. Thankfully, Bo was walking up to the truck

"Bo we've got to go," she said quickly.

"Where are we headed?"

"Kandahar."

"Really?"

"Yup, I have to see General Jones."

"Wow, he's the highest ranking Officer over here. He works with North Atlantic Treaty Organization (NATO). He coordinates everything."

It made sense to Bliss now why the message was to

go to General Jones. What Bliss had read and memorized, before scrubbing it was a list of all the men working for NATO that were secretly embedded within the Taliban.

The word 'Normandy' in the subject meant 'Need-to-Know' (NTK) and the message was to be delivered ASAP and was code that Mike and Bliss could only give the information to the designated person in the message. The reason she had learned they used the word Normandy was because during the Invasion of Normandy in 1944 there had been a Need-to-Know offensive. It was one of the largest operations ever, utilizing thousands of men, yet it had been planned and put into action by a few deemed NTK (Need to Know.)

"It's a pretty important message." Bliss confided in him.

"Okay, stay put, I'll get the guys."

Bliss remained in the truck and Harry got to her first.

"Loo, Bo said to tell you he was grabbing some supplies and then we'll take off."

"Got it thanks."

Kandahar was a good day's ride from Bagram. They would be able to travel the main roads and they would pass through Ghazni and Qalat-e Gilzay, both considered friendly towns, but Bliss knew that the road between Ghazni and Qalat-e Gilzay had been the site of many recent airstrikes, sniper attacks and small group attacks. They would have to be on high alert. Mike came back, and Bliss told him they had a message that had to be delivered to General Jones in Kandahar. She told him it was 'Normandy' status, so he didn't even ask what the message contained.

Bo came back with Phil and Billy, all three were carrying items. Bliss knew at least one of the boxes contained provisions. She saw that Billy was lugging two plastic containers of gas for the generator and vehicles and Bo had a sack with him that he put in the back of the Jeep.

Bo got into the driver's seat of the Jeep, Billy was in the front passenger seat and Bliss got into the back seat. Mike, Phil, and Harry got into the truck. Mike still had to monitor the computer even though they were on the road.

Chapter 11

Bliss watched the countryside as they drove towards Kandahar. She was hyper alert because Bo had secured a rifle to the side of his seat, which was out of the norm. He asked if she had her vest on and she told him she did.

She looked behind them at the truck and saw that Phil was holding his sniper rifle out the window and he would periodically look down the scope.

Bo looked into the rearview mirror and saw Bliss looking at him.

"We'll be okay." He said trying to reassure her.

"You want to tell me what's going on?" She said realizing that he knew something and hadn't shared it with her.

"There's been a little unrest. We need to take a back road. It might get dicey."

He watched her face as she took in the information.

"Do the guys in the truck know?"

"Yeah, General Paine told me when I told him we were heading out."

"Is this unrest unusual?"

"A little, there has been some skirmishes along this route. Whatever is happening up ahead is bad enough that the General told me we needed to take the back roads."

"Will it take us longer than a day?"

"No, but it will take longer. The General was radioing a few battalions he knows that are sequestered nearby to let them know that we may be passing by."

Bliss nodded feeling better that troops would be near

them as they traveled. She was always vigilant and ready for anything, but the ominous feeling she had as they traveled on the bumpy roadway had the hairs on the back of her neck standing up.

Two hours into the drive Bo turned down a road that was more like a dirt trail. Bliss was being knocked around in the back seat and she looked behind them, at the truck and noted that it had to slow down significantly because of the terrain.

A whistling sound followed by a loud, quaking boom shook the Jeep and Bliss heard Bo swear as he skillfully got control of the wheel. They were taking fire and it wasn't from any sniper bullets, it was something much bigger and more devastating. Bliss looked behind her and saw the truck take a direct hit to its back tire. The truck flipped and Bliss watched in horror as the three men inside flailed trying to remain balanced. The truck landed on its side and Bo slammed on the brakes and jumped out while Billy had his rifle on his shoulder ready to fire.

"Left." Yelled Billy as gunfire pelted the Jeep. Bliss jumped out and took cover. Bo was trying to extract the men from the truck. She could hear one of them moaning in pain. Bliss ran to the back of the overturned truck and felt sand spray her pants as bullets fell just short of clipping her. She smelled the gasoline that they had packed and knew she had to help get the guys out of the truck. She jumped into the back and walked along the canvas side. She tore the canvas separating the cab from the back part.

The men were on their sides and stacked on one another. Mike was in the middle of the two men. He had cracked his head on the dash and blood was pouring down his face. Phil was holding his gun and his arm protectively to his side. Bliss could see his arm was fractured. He was gritting his teeth and she knew the poor kid was in terrible pain. When she saw Harry, her heart lurched. He wasn't moving or making any sound. Harry was at the bottom of the pile and Bliss knew he was hurt the worst.

She saw Bo through the window, which was above her and he motioned for her to help
the other two guys out. She could hear bullets hitting the metal of the truck and Billy must have been returning fire because she heard a gun go off close by. Bliss grabbed Mike by the shoulders since he was the one she could most easily extract first and yelled at him to use his legs to help her. She managed to pull him into the bed of the truck, and she pointed to the back gesturing that he needed to get out of the truck. She could see smoke starting to billow in the corner and she knew she didn't have much time.

Next, she helped Phil out. He refused to let go of his rifle, but she helped him to climb through to the back. She yelled for him to get out of the truck, which was now filled with dark smoke making her cough.

Bo must have started firing at the insurgents because there was a steady barrage of gunfire. Bliss had to climb into the cab to get to Harry who was still not moving. She tugged and tried to wake him, but it was useless. She reached to find a pulse and when she couldn't find one, she took a second to look at his face. It was then that she saw the bullet hole that had entered a few centimeters from his temple. Blood was running from the wound and down the side of his neck and even though Bliss knew he was dead, she put her hand under his vest and on his chest hoping she'd feel his heart beating. Outside she heard Bo yelling for her and she knew she needed to get out of the truck. She jumped back through the opening and out the back onto the snow-covered ground. The other four men were hunkered down behind the Jeep. Bliss stayed by the trucks under carriage, but she saw Mike wave at her frantically seeing the flames were precariously close to her.

Bliss ran towards the men and felt a sting in her thigh. A grenade was thrown under the Jeep and the team of five dove away from it. Bliss felt the heat as the Jeep erupted into a mass of flames.

The gas in the truck exploded a few seconds later and Bliss' cars ached from the deafening noise. Metal pieces flew through the air and Bliss lay flat on the cold ground praying nothing would land on her.

Bo got to his knees and Bliss watched in horror as a bullet tore through the part of his shoulder not protected by the vest. He grunted in pain and fell back to the ground. Phil was holding his arm and she imagined the look of fear that she saw on his face was reflected on hers as well. Billy rolled towards her and told her to crawl towards the burning truck. She knew he was hoping she could hide somewhere in the remnants of the mangled burning shell of the vehicle. Bliss heard a vehicle approaching them, so she army crawled towards the truck.

Smoke and debris swirled around them as bullets continued to pepper the ground around them. She pulled herself so she was near one of the over turned tires and she tried to hide herself by pressing up against it. The metal burnt her hip and she cried out in pain as she jumped away. She rolled onto her side and fell silent as she watched boots jumping out of a truck that had rolled to a stop behind the truck.

The insurgents were yelling, and she heard Bo grunt in pain as one of the boots came in contact with his wounded shoulder. From her position she saw Mike, Phil, and Billy who were on their knees, raise their hands in the I surrender gesture and she heard a man yell out a few words in Pashto. Bliss understood one of the words, ssedze which meant woman. Fear spiked in Bliss; they were looking for her. How did they know about her?

Boots crunched against the snow packed road as men came towards the truck and one man bent down and pointed at her. Two other men crawled in after her. Bliss started kicking at them and she knocked one of them across the chin. He pulled out his gun and leveled it at her and she heard Bo yell, "No!"

Two things happened at once. Bo had leapt to his feet and was trying to get to her, and she watched in horror as he was shot again and fell to the ground. It was only a second after watching Bo fall that she heard a shot go off near her and the burning pain of a bullet burst through her upper thigh. Bliss looked down as blood soaked her leg, she could see Phil, Mike and Billy were yelling, but all sound was blotted out by the searing pain Bliss felt. She looked back at her wound and was momentarily relieved that it hadn't hit her femoral artery and then the burn started, and she cried out in anguish.

The two men dragged her out from beneath the truck and held her between them. She couldn't put any weight on her leg, and she looked around wildly and saw that Mike, Phil, and Billy were all lying face down with rifle nozzles touching the back their heads. One of the men had their gun trained on Bo too, but he wasn't moving.

Bliss was tossed into the back of the truck and the men followed her inside. They didn't even like touching her, so they gave her berth. The insurgents used their feet to kick her so she would move to the back in the truck bed. She was panicking and was waiting to hear gunshots broadcasting the killing of her team. She heard a scuffle and a grunt from outside the truck and one of the men barked out in a commanding tone. A few seconds later Bliss watched in fear, but also relief as Bo was lifted by three men and roughly tossed into the truck. His face was covered in blood and she saw the jagged gash on his forehead. He was breathing, but unmoving. One of the men grabbed her wrists to secure her hands with a plastic zip tie and she struggled with him, lashing out with her hands and one good leg. She managed to land a solid hit against the one man's chin, and she heard him grunt. The man spat at her; his eyes were wild; he was seething that she had touched his skin. He quickly gripped her right wrist, fisted her two middle fingers, and then he pulled them back so hard and so quickly that the bones snapped. Bliss cried out in pain and passed out.

Chapter 12

She woke up because she was shivering from the cold. Slowly she opened her eyes and knew she was in a dark cold place. She realized she had been stripped completely naked and she was able to see her surroundings only because a sliver of light was filtering from down a hallway off to her left. A guard was positioned just outside her cell door, but he did not even glance in her direction. She knew that according to Ihtiyat Wajib, a man is not allowed to look at those parts of a woman's body that are normally covered. She found it strange that the men holding her captive would strip her naked if they weren't allowed to look at her.

Her prison was a small cell built into the corner of the room. The back and one sidewall were made of stone, the other was made of thick boards, and the front of her cell was metal bars with a traditional cell door secured with an oversized lock.

Outside her cell where the guard stood was a large wooden crate. It was rigged with a rope running through a hook attached to a pulley that was fixed to a beam on the ceiling. Sometimes the guards would sit on the crate, so Bliss figured they had it in there to use as a seat. It wasn't until she watched one of the guards flip the crate a few times and heard something large inside the wooden crate being tossed roughly about, that she felt true terror realizing that Bo might be in the crate. She didn't hear him at all, not a cough, a moan, nothing. She hoped Bo wasn't in the four by four crate because the guards enjoyed flipping it. They would turn it over and then listen. If Bo was in there, he was either dead or close to it because she couldn't believe he wasn't even grunting from the harsh battering the crate was taking.

Bliss had no idea how many days had passed. She was given a bowl of water on what she figured was her third day and after she dipped her finger in it to taste it, she discovered it tasted fine and she gulped it down. She saw the guards open a small hatch in the crate and put a bowl of water inside. She knew then that there was definitely a person in the crate and part of her prayed it was Bo because that meant the guards thought whoever was inside was still alive, and part of her prayed that he was being held someplace other than the crate, that had become a form of cruel entertainment to the guards.

The guards changed duty every few hours and Bliss had tried to communicate with them, but none of them acknowledged her. After a few days she gave up trying to communicate. She had lost track of time and she was seriously afraid that she would fall asleep and not wake up because of hypothermia. She was getting weaker each day. She tried to keep her mind occupied. She silently recited everything she could think of. She wrote letters in her head to the Doherty's, Caitlyn, Collin, and even Connor. She even ran to the park and exercised on the fitness trail in her mind, anything to keep awake and alert.

Bliss awoke with a start. Her leg throbbed from the unexpected movement, and it jarred her hand with the two broken fingers causing her to gasp from the sharp pain. She realized she was soaking wet, the freezing water that had been thrown onto her scorched her skin painfully. Her hair on one side of her head was plastered to her face and the cold water sluiced off her naked body onto the cold dirt floor of the cell.

A man she hadn't seen before stood above her holding a bucket that she realized had held the water that had been thrown on her. She sat up quickly sending more pain radiating through her leg as she tried to cover her nakedness. It struck her that the man holding the bucket had no problem looking at her, but the man outside the cell was still following his religious rules. The man tossed the empty metal bucket into a corner and spoke to her harshly in very broken English. Bliss could not understand what he was saying.

She was having trouble focusing. His accent was thick, and she was so cold she was shaking uncontrollably. Her teeth were chattering so hard that she could hardly hear him. The man picked up another bucket that was near him and Bliss instinctively tossed her hands out defensively thinking he was going to throw the bucket at her. Instead he threw more ice-cold water at her.

Bliss yelped as the freezing water hit her, and then groaned because she had jostled the wound in her leg. She heard a weak, "Leave her alone." Coming from a small wooden crate with no openings, and a tiny spark of hope fueled her knowing Bo was alive.

The man standing guard pulled the rope and Bo's crate was turned upside down. Bliss heard Bo groan as the wooden crate slammed to the ground, and the eerie quiet that followed was frightening.

Once again, the man in her cell spoke. Although she could hardly distinguish his words,
she finally understood that he wanted information. Bliss shook her head pretending to not understand him. She had understood him though. He wanted to know about her last email. She heard him say General Jones. Bliss was shocked. How the heck did he know about that? Her mind was sorting through how this man could know about the email, and she wished that her brain wasn't feeling so sluggish. Now, she had to out think this man, handle the pain she was in, and deal with being very cold. Forget the fact that she was stark naked in front of a stranger, that barely registered on the fear trip she was currently riding. Bliss knew there was no way she could tell him about the last correspondence. It would be a death sentence to countless men.

The man stepped towards her and knelt down grabbing her hand with the two broken fingers. He laid it on the ground, stepped on her wrist, and then he drew his gun, and shot a hole into her hand. Bliss screamed as the burning heat of the bullet punctured the muscle and bones. She snatched her bloody hand to her chest when he stepped off of it, and hugged it protectively to her chest, not caring that blood streamed from the circular open wound sliding down her arm and chest to puddle into the creases of her one leg that was pulled as tight as possible to her torso. Tears clouded her vision. She was in so much pain that she was nauseous, and the harsh reality that she was as good as dead, seared into her foggy consciousness.

Bliss could barely make out what the man was saying as he yelled at her. Spittle was flying out of his mouth and the sneer on his face was filled with hatred. He grabbed her feet and straightened her legs by pulling them towards him and trapping them under his arm. She tried to kick out, but her one leg wasn't functioning and the other leg he held in a vice like grip. She watched in horror, while she tried in vain to twist out of his grip, as he produced a knife from beneath his robe. Spitting at her and muttering what sounded like a prayer, he viciously slashed the bottom of her feet, two on one sole and three on the other. Her feet stung from the quick slices that he had delivered and once again, he yelled at her to tell him what her last email had contained. Bliss was not going to give him the satisfaction of crying out in pain, and she bit her tongue hard enough that she felt the metallic taste of her own blood as she held it in. She looked back at him defiantly. She was in more pain than she had ever felt before, yet something had snapped inside her. She glared at the man feeling an unwarranted resolve, knowing that no matter what he did to her, she would not give in to him. He grinned seeing the determined look mask her face, and then he smiled sickly before delivering kick her to her ribs that caused her to lose her breath and literally to see stars.

"Dareezzem!" She heard someone yell. Bliss had memorized words in the Pashto language that she had read off Afghanland.com on the internet. She couldn't pronounce them properly, but her gift of memory helped her to pick out a few words when she heard them. Dareezzem meant stop, and the crazed man stopped; mid a second kick. The two men spoke too quickly for her to comprehend what they were saying. It didn't help that she was in such agony that her cell was spinning. The man that had just entered the small space seemed to be infuriated with the man who had been hurting her. The new man pointed at her hands and feet that were bleeding profusely, and he yelled at her tormentor. He then pointed at the door and yelled, "Preezzdem." Which Bliss knew meant leave.

The man angrily skulked away, and Bliss knew he had been chastised, but with her brain barely functioning she couldn't understand why. She forced herself to sit up, still attempting to keep her private parts hidden and scooted back towards the wall as best

she could use the heels of her feet and her one uninjured hand.

The new man said something to the man standing guard outside the door and he left too.

Bliss looked warily at this new man. He wore the traditional robes that men in Afghanistan wore, plus his face was completely covered, except for his eyes. His eyes peered out at her and she noticed how blue they were. This man was not originally from Afghanistan and hope rose inside of her.

He spoke gently to her with an English accent.

"You must tell them what they want to know."

"I don't know anything." She mirrored his hushed tone.

The man shook his head and clucked his tongue.

"You are being foolish. They will release you if you tell them."

"Where are my friends?" She asked thinking of Phil,

Mike, and Billy.

"Dead, I am sure," he said with no emotion.

Bliss' heart ached thinking about the men she had been whisked away from, but she too knew they were most likely dead. Now she had to save herself and hopefully Bo too. "What do they think I know?"

"Of spies."

"I don't know anything about spies." She countered. "Why would I know about spies? I keep track of food and supplies coming over." She had been told if she was ever captured that she should use that lie.

"You were sent information last week that we want. Do not be a fool."

"Yes, I was, and I was on my way to tell the General what supplies he will be receiving." The man chuckled, "You are a good little liar, but we have a very reliable source that told us you received information about the spies that are embedded inside the Taliban. We want that information and we will get it."

"Really, I can't help you. You're informant was wrong."

"Enough!" he yelled, causing Bliss to jump.

"I will come back tomorrow morning and if you refuse to talk, I will let Zarghun make you talk, using his methods."

Bliss stared at him and blinked back tears. She was shivering from the cold and her entire body ached. Her fortitude was crumbling knowing she was in dire straits.

"Do you know what Zarghun means?" He asked with a snicker.

Bliss shook her head no.

"It means 'little heart'. He changed his name when his entire family of five were killed by an airstrike; an airstrike by Americans. He will love hurting you. Think about that, maybe it will loosen your tongue." The man then left her cell and Bliss crumbled to the dirt floor, hugging her cold body as best she could with her damaged hand. No one came back to her cell, not even the guard and Bliss lay on the cold floor thinking about the Doherty's and how distraught they would be. She thought about Connor and that only caused her more pain. She knew he'd be upset too, and she wished she could talk to him one last time simply for closure. Bliss knew Jax would probably beat himself up for not spending more time with her. Then she thought of her team. She knew Harry was gone and she prayed for him and his wife and family that would be receiving the grim news. She thought of Phil and how young he was, and about Mike, who had been so much better accepting his role on the team, and then about Billy, and how his fiancé would soon be grieving for him. Then

she thought about Bo. She called to him and when he didn't answer she prayed he was still alive; Bo, who had bravely tried to save her, even though he'd already been shot. She sent a prayer to God that if Bo was with him, that he would get a special spot in heaven because he was a great guy.

Bliss wiped the tears from her eyes with her thumb and saw that she was still wearing her mom's bracelet with the fake medic tag. She thought about her mom and knew she would soon be with her and that thought was what broke her. Bliss rolled into a ball and cried herself to sleep.

A vibration from the floor jostled Bliss back to consciousness and she slowly sat up holding her damaged hand to her bare chest. She heard a thud coming from down the hall that she couldn't see down but knew that's where the men who had visited her had come from. Then she heard pings followed by a grunt and then another thud. A man wearing an American Flag on the shoulder of white coveralls, night vision goggles over a white full-face covering, knit ski mask, and armed with a gun; kicked in her shabby cell door. Another soldier came into view dressed exactly the same as the first. She thought she must be hallucinating. Could she really be being rescued? How could have anyone had found her? Bliss saw smoke billowing from the hall and the second man produced a gas mask and tossed it to the first man who knelt in front of her and strapped the mask onto her face. He grabbed her hand to lift her from the ground and she yelped in pain, that's when he saw her condition. He then quickly lifted her off the floor and placed her good arm around his shoulder.

He started out the cell door and Bliss knocked on the man's shoulder and pointed at the wooden crate, "Bo. Bo's in there."

She heard the other man say shit and look towards the man holding her. Bliss saw him nod and then the second man used his gun on the lock. A soft ping sounded when the bullet hit the metal lock, which successfully splintered it, but it made a loud sound. The soldier moved quickly from the room holding her naked body against his chest.

The hallway was obscured with a thick cloud of

smoke. Bliss could hear the other soldier that was getting Bo, moving behind them. They stealthily moved down the hallway that led into a larger room and Bliss saw two men in robes lay dead against the wall, their crimson blood pooling around them and soaking into their thick robes. She spitefully hoped one of them was Zarghun. They quickly went through a door leading outdoors and into a snow-covered area. Now she understood why they were wearing all white. Bliss saw two more huts were nearby; one had a light illuminating a small window. It was about 50 yards away from where they were. In the distance Bliss saw a helicopter. The blades were churning noiselessly as the snow around it swirled wildly whipped up by the blades.

When they emerged from the hut, two other men covered in white appeared. The man holding her turned his head swiftly back towards the hut and Bliss watched as one of the men ran into the hut. The other man covered their six as they ran towards the chopper. The man holding her had a death grip on her and she knew he was not going to drop her. Her naked body was freezing, but there was so much adrenaline surging through her, she felt warm. Gunshots rang out from behind them and Bliss turned to look over the big man's shoulder, but he slammed her head down so it was protected by his body. One of the

men behind them must have been hit because she heard someone yell that Ralph was down. Another man jumped from the choppers open door and ran past them, Bliss assumed to help Ralph. The guy holding her kept running. When they were about twenty yards from the helicopter Bliss saw another man kneeling near the chopper and he was firing an automatic, spraying cover fire.

There was a short lull of gunfire from behind them, but then it started up again and Bliss could tell that at least one of the men chasing them also had automatic weapons that scattered bullets all around them. Bliss felt three burning stings in her arm and the soldier holding her grunted and staggered a bit, but he righted himself and kept moving. Bliss knew she'd been shot again. She couldn't hold her arm up that had been clutching her savior's shoulder and it dangled precariously behind him. She could feel the warmth of her blood as it ran off her arm and drop into the white snow below.

When they reached the helicopter, she was literally thrown inside. She tried to cushion the new wounds to her arm, but the pain was significant, and she grunted loudly. A man stationed inside the chopper pushed her roughly to the back as he helped the other men to climb in. Her heart thudded wildly watching two men heaving Bo into the chopper. Another man was carrying the man who must have been Ralph handed him off and jumped inside. Bliss flattened herself to the choppers floor as men dressed in dark pants and shirts ran towards the helicopter, firing their weapons; their bullets dinged off the choppers hull. Everyone was inside the small craft now, and before they even shut the door the chopper rose quickly and banked sharply away from the gunfire.

Bliss' body rolled roughly against the metal wall. She could feel the warmth of her blood as it ran down her body. She held her arm gingerly against her stomach.

When the chopper leveled off, she sat up as best she could and looked around. Her eyes slowly adjusted to the darkness. Although it was painful, she used her one forearm to push the gas mask off her face. A blanket was tossed towards her landing on her legs. Somehow, she managed to maneuver it over her private parts.

Bliss watched the silent activity of the masked men in the helicopter. If not for the American flag patch she would have had no idea who these men were. She still had no idea who they were. She just knew they had rescued her, and they were American; they were the good guys. Some of the soldiers were securing their guns. Others sat silently against the wall. One of the men lay on his stomach and Bliss could make out that the lower back of his white coverall was soaked in blood. Another man was slicing the thin fabric away to attend the wound. One of the men was leaning over Bo. Bliss dragged herself and her blanket to where Bo was lying motionless on his side.

"Bo." She whispered. "Bo, please be okay." She laid her forehead on his cheek. He was so cold. Was he dead?

The man kneeling by Bo pushed her gently aside and she saw that he had a medic bag at his side. She wanted to remain near Bo, but as the agony from her new wounds began to permeate her adrenalin rush, she willed herself not to faint, as she returned to slump against the wall. Her blood pooled around her. She thought it was strange that no one spoke. She watched as the soldier hooked up a plasma drip for Bo and then covered him with a silver blanket. Even without any light Bliss could see that Bo was pale and sweating even though it was freezing inside the chopper. The man that had been helping Bo moved to his teammate and nodded at the other soldier that had been helping him. Satisfied that the man administering first aid to their teammate was doing a good job of applying pressure to the wound, he moved back to Bo.

Bliss was nauseous from the pain, but she finally got up the nerve to look down at her arm that was hidden by the blanket and saw three bullet holes, two of which had passed completely through her arm. The other bullet had lodged in her forearm and she knew it had broken a bone because she could see splinters of bone poking through the bloody gash. Bliss felt light headed and her head spun as the pain began to intensify. She laid her head back on the choppers cool metal wall hoping she would not throw up. She couldn't believe they had been rescued. How was that possible?

The helicopter was now whizzing through the dark sky. The men inside were not talking, and she realized they still hadn't removed their masks. She looked around at the men who had rescued them. The one soldier still knelt alongside the soldier that had been hit, the wound was just below his Kevlar vest and another remained near Bo, continuing to check his vitals and occasionally pressing on his stomach. The men not involved with caring for the wounded were sitting stoically, almost eerily, quietly looking at her. The man nearest the one who had carried her noticed the bloody mess around her and swore as he crawled towards her.

"She's been hit." He whispered above the resonating

drone of the helicopter. He gently lifted her arm to show the medic. Bliss tried being brave, but the pain was excruciating, and she whimpered loudly.

"Throw me the pack." He yelled to the man near Bo. "Shit, she's really been peppered." He said looking at the man who had carried her from her hell.

Another soldier grabbed the med pack and knelt near her. Black spots clouded her vision. She looked at the man who had carried her and even as she was fighting to remain conscious, she realized that if two of the bullets had passed through her then they had to have hit him. The large man was sitting motionless against the wall. His head hung limply with his chin resting on his chest. Using every ounce of available energy she had, she gestured with her chin to the man slumped against the wall and weakly slurred, "He's been shot." That's the last thing Bliss remembered as she once again blacked out.

Chapter 13

Bliss regained consciousness as she was placed on a gurney. She was aware that the chopper had taken off again, but she couldn't see the small black silent chopper in the dark sky as it sped away. Bo must have been on a gurney that was ahead of her because she could hear wheels clacking noisily over the pavement ahead of her. She wished she could cover her eyes as she was pushed through double doors into a brightly lit corridor. Her vision blurred and it reminded her of times before her vision operation when she had tried to see without having her glasses on. She felt someone push a needle into her arm and she drifted off to sleep again.

The next time Bliss awoke she was in a bed with monitors beeping loudly nearby. Her one arm was in a cloth sling, suspended by pulleys attached to her bed frame, so that it was even with her chest. She saw sutures holding together her skin where the bullets that had broken her arm had entered. Her feet were bandaged and slightly elevated and her other hand was in a short cast. She knew her burnt hip had been attended to and her ribs were bound. Remarkably she only felt a dull ache of pain.

Bliss looked around the large open room and one of the nurses saw that she was awake and hurried to her. "You're awake. We were starting to worry."

Bliss didn't answer. If the medical staff was worried; maybe she was hurt worse than she thought.

The nurse, whose name plate read Lt. Chan took a

little plastic cup and poured water into it, then inserted a straw and held it so Bliss could reach it with her lips. Bliss sucked down the cool water feeling it slide down her parched throat.

"Yeah, I bet that feels good." The nurse said with a grin.

Bliss finished the cups contents and while the nurse refilled the cup, Bliss managed to croak, "Where am I?"

"Bagram." The Lt. Chan answered as she put the cup back up to her lips.

Bliss took another long sip and then thanked her. Lt. Chan put the cup down and reached for Bliss' neck to take her pulse.

"Where are the men that brought me in? Two of them were hurt. Where's Lt. Pike?" The nurse looked around and then leaned in close.

"No one knows who brought you in."

Bliss looked at her wondering how that could be. The nurse shrugged her shoulders. Bliss didn't know what to make of that.

"No one knows who they are?"

"No, looks like you had some guardian angels though."

Bliss thought about the other members of her team. "And Lt. Pike?"

The nurse hesitated before answering " He's in ICU." He was alive, was Bliss' first thought, but then she saw Lt. Chan's face and knew Bo was not doing well.

"Can I see him?"

"Lt." Lt. Chan said with a slight frown. "You need to worry about taking care of yourself." "I need to talk to General Paine." Bliss told the nurse. She would have to report what happened.

There was commotion at the doorway and Bliss saw Phil and Mike trying to get through. She couldn't believe her eyes. They were alive. Phil's arm was in a sling and Mike had a bandage across his forehead. They almost pushed the little nurse over trying to get to her. Bliss started crying, she was so happy to see them. She couldn't believe they had made it.

"How?" Was all she could say.

Phil started talking animatedly. "After they threw you in the truck, Bo tried to go after you, and they clocked him in the head and threw him in the truck you were in. We thought we were done for, but some English-speaking guy yelled something that made them leave without hurting us."

Bliss was stunned. Her sharp mind, although still sluggish, was telling her this had not been a Taliban ambush/kidnapping.

"How did you know he was English?" Bliss asked her mind buzzing with the information.

Mike piped in," He told us we were free to go, in English."

"Free to go?"

"Yeah, weird, right?"

"What happened to you? Where did they take you? What did they want? How did you get away?"

Bliss smiled at Phil's exuberance.

"First, tell me where Billy is?"

"He's here in the hospital. He was shot in the shoulder, he'll be fine." Mike told her calmly. "After they left, we started walking, and a group of Marines found us."

Mike interjected. "We think Bo somehow radioed for

help before we were overtaken." Mike continued, "They called for a chopper and we were brought here."

"Have you seen Bo?"

Both men shook their heads. "No, we know he's bad though."

A cloud of worry blanketed her happiness that she had been just been feeling upon seeing Mike and Phil.

A loud "At ease," was heard and Bliss saw that General Paine had walked in. He headed immediately to Bliss' bed, his lips were set in a tight line, and she could see tension lines formed thin groves across his brow.

"Lt. glad you're awake."

"Yes, Sir," she answered.

"Men, I need to talk to your Lt. alone."

Both men responded, "Yes, Sir." Giving Bliss concerned looks before they left.

"What happened? Who took you? Do you know why? And who the hell rescued you?" "Sir, I don't know exactly who took me. I heard Pashto being spoken and the men I saw wore the traditional robes, not military clothes." She paused, "Except for when we were fleeing and then the men chasing us wore black military clothes."

"Do you know why you were taken?"

"Yes Sir, they wanted the information from the last email I was holding and still need to deliver to General Jones."

The General paused taking in the vital details.

"Do you know how they even knew about it?"

"No Sir, and Sir, there was a man there, dressed in robes with his face covered, but he spoke English and had an English accent."

"Anything else?"

"One of the men is named Zarghun. He was the one that tortured me."

"Who rescued you?"

"I have no idea, Sir. I don't even know how they found me. They wore masks and barely spoke. They found me in my cell, and rescued Lt. Pike and we left in a chopper." "And you have no idea who they were?"

"No Sir. Don't you?"

The General looked uncomfortable. "No, the Marines that found your team searched for you and Lt. Pike. After a two-day search, we classified you both as MIA."

"Shit." Bliss swore softly. "My family was notified?" The General nodded. "As protocol dictates."

Bliss thought about the Doherty's and how upset they had undoubtedly been.

"Have they been called back?"

"I made the call myself. They are expecting a Skype from you ASAP."

"Yes, Sir."

"Lt. the chopper that brought you and Lt. Pike in was a Sikorsky UH-60 Black Hawk." Bliss didn't know much about helicopters, so she remained quiet and let the General continue.

"We didn't even know it had landed. It made it through our airspace undetected, dropped you and Pike off on the roof of the hospital, which set off an alarm and then it took off. The only reason I know what kind of chopper it was is because a nurse was on the roof when it landed, restocking the medical

cabinet there, and she was able to describe it."
The General stopped talking and Bliss knew he was
hoping she could shed more light on her rescuers.
"Sir, I'm sorry. I have no idea who they are. I passed
out pretty much right away."
The General stood and patted her arm in a fatherly
way letting out a frustrated sigh. "Okay, Lt. I'll send
in a computer and a tech so you can Skype with your
family." He looked at his watch. "It's almost 10:00
pm on the East coast, but I guarantee they are waiting
for your call."
"Yes, Sir." Bliss remembered she still needed to talk
to General Jones. "Sir, I really need to deliver my
message to General Jones. It's an NTK status and it's
very important that I see him."
"I'll see what I can do. Get some rest soldier."
A half hour later and after help using a bed pan and
some more water, Bliss was in front of a computer
screen held by a tech officer. Rose's face was the first
to come into focus on the laptop screen.
"Bliss, oh my heaven's, Sweetheart, it is so good to
see you." Rose had tears in her eyes. "How are you
feeling?"
Bliss watched as the General moved his face near the
camera so that he could see her. "I'm good, really."
Bliss said to her surrogate parents. A lump had
formed in her throat and she didn't want to get
emotional in front of them.
"We were so worried." Rose told her.
"I know. I'm sorry, but I'm fine. I promise."
"You're coming home soon." Rose said happily,
"General Paine told us when he called yesterday."
This was news to Bliss and the look on her face

prompted the General to take over the conversation. "Bliss, what are your injuries?"

"General, I'm pretty good. I..."

"Report Bliss." The General interrupted using his no-nonsense tone. Bliss sighed; she had hoped to keep her injuries from them, knowing that upon hearing them they would be upset.

"Yes, Sir. Well, I took a bullet to my thigh. My one hand has a through and through, plus two fingers on that hand have been broken. On my other arm, I have a through and through in the arm and hand, and my radius was hit, but it's been pinned back together. My feet have some cuts on them, I have a few broken ribs, and my hip has a small burn on it."

Bliss could see that Rose was visibly shaken. "I'm good. I promise." She added.

"Are you in pain, Sweetie?"

"A little, I'm more concerned for Lt. Pike who was also taken hostage and rescued. He's in ICU."

Bliss saw the General nodded thoughtfully; poor Rose had been stunned into silence. "General, Rose, I'm so sorry you were worried. Does anyone else know?" Bliss was wondering if Connor knew.

The General answered, "Yes, Caitlyn and Collin know, and I sent word to Jax."

"Have you heard from Connor?" Bliss asked.

The General remained quiet as Rose spoke, "We haven't heard from him Bliss. He usually checks in every couple of weeks, but we haven't heard from him recently." "Now Rose," The General interjected, "he's busy or someplace he can't call. I'm sure he's fine."

A different nurse approached her bed holding a food

tray and Bliss felt her stomach rumble.

"My food tray is here." Bliss told them giving them the best smile she could muster. "Okay Honey, you eat. You get strong. We can't wait to see you." Rose was back to being her normal chipper self.

"Okay, take care."

"We love you Honey." Rose said waving at the screen, prompting Bliss to once again remember how lucky she was that the Doherty's had made a place in their family for her.

Chapter 14

Two days later Bliss was feeling much better. She still hadn't been allowed to walk anywhere, she knew her feet were bad, and they hurt. She had cut back on the prescription pain medications to just taking Tylenol, so now her brain was starting to function without the haze of drugs making her sluggish.

"At ease," once again sounded through the hospital room causing everyone to look up to the door. General Paine had walked through and another General with two stars on his lapel followed behind him. They walked to her bed.

"Lt. Allen this is General Jones." General Paine said. "I'm going to leave you two alone." He walked off stopping to talk to one of the nurses, who Bliss saw look at her and then nod at the General.

General Jones sat down.

"Lt. I've been expecting a classified document for a few weeks now. I'm guessing you're going to give it to me?"

"Yes, Sir, but I didn't print it out."

He looked at her skeptically.

"Sir, I have a pretty good memory and when a message of this magnitude is sent to me, after I decode it, I memorize it before I scrub it. This time I am very glad I did."

The General nodded. He took out a small pad and pen from his jacket. Bliss looked at the pen ready to write down the information she had guarded with her life and frowned. The General noticed her apprehensive

expression. "My memory isn't as good as yours, Lt."
"Yes, Sir. Sorry."
Bliss recited the names of the men and places they were embedded and when she finished, she felt the burden of holding that information in lift from her shoulders. The General turned his paper towards Bliss so she could see what he had written down and to her amazement he had written what she had said down in an unrecognizable code. The General smiled gently, seeing her face.

"Lt. I know how important what you just told me is," he said with a chuckle. "I've learned a few things and one of those things is that I don't write anything down that could be
damning to others. I made up this code about ten years ago." "Sir, that's smart, Sir." Bliss said with a genuine smile on her face. The General stood up, wished her a speedy recovery and left.

Bliss was bored out of her mind. She'd been in bed for a week now. She couldn't walk yet, and she was sick and tired of using the bedpan, it was embarrassing. She had seen Red a couple of times, but she had been nothing but nice.

A Psychiatrist had been to see her a few times, checking her for any signs of lingering distress. She seemed satisfied that Bliss was mentally sound but warned her that she would probably experience nightmares. Bliss had already had a few, but she hadn't shared that with the good Doctor.

Mike and Phil visited daily. Billy had visited her once and then she learned that he had been shipped home to recuperate. Mike told her they were giving him a team so they could carry on with their information sharing. He wasn't bragging or trying to make her feel bad and she was happy for him. She knew he would be upgraded to full Lt. and with the experience he now had, she was sure he'd be good at his new position. Bo was still in ICU, and she was told he was starting to show signs of improvement, which Bliss thanked God for.

A week later Bliss along with five other wounded soldiers, including Bo were loaded on to a C-17 rigged to transfer wounded back to the states. A doctor accompanied them plus three nurses. Bliss was surprised to see that Red was one of the nurses. When she was rolled up the back ramp, she asked that her bed be put near Bo's, so they strapped her gurney across from Bo's. Bo was awake and when he saw her, he got the biggest smile on his face. He had lost weight and she could see his face was strained with the pain he was still feeling. Bliss discovered that Red was his nurse and had been the entire time in Bagram. They were both careful not to talk about anything regarding their time that they had been held hostage or about their rescuers. Instead Bo talked about heading home and recuperating. He told Bliss that Teresa, Red, lived in the County next to his and Bliss could see he was smitten with her. She was always at his side and Bliss noticed the way her hand lingered on his arm and that sometimes when she talked to him, she would lean down to his ear and whisper something to him making him smile. At first Bliss felt like he was a traitor. After all he was totally aware of the fact that Connor had broken her heart twice with Red.

During a quiet time on the plane, when everyone

including the medical staff was asleep or out of ear shot, Bliss heard Bo calling her name. Bliss looked over at him.

"Bliss after we recover, we need to talk about what happened."

Bliss nodded.

"Do you know who rescued us?" he asked.

Bliss shook her head. "No, do you?"

"I have an idea."

"Really?"

That piqued her curiosity.

"Listen, I probably won't be able to talk to you alone again." He paused. "I just want you to know it was an honor serving with you."

Bliss felt a small lump form in her throat. "You too Bo."

"And Bliss," she waited for him to continue. "You need to talk to your Green Beret. Let him explain."

"Bo, come on," she said irritated with his advice. A nurse walked past them indicating they needed to be quiet.

When the nurse had moved far enough away, Bo whispered to her again. "You're one terrific person Bliss. This guy is no dummy. You need to talk to him."

"Bo. I..."

"Shhhh." The nurse chastised them again.

Bo whispered, "Sorry" to the nurse and then winked at Bliss. The wink brought back the memory of him winking at her after his boxing match in Bagram. Bliss had thought maybe he was interested in her and she remembered thinking, if anyone could erase

Connor from her soul, it could be Bo. Bliss turned towards the wall feeling so alone at that moment. When the plane landed in Charlotte, the patients were rolled off the large plane and wheeled in different directions. Bo had been whisked off in an ambulance and Bliss noticed how Red had gotten in the ambulance with him. He had given Bliss a thumbs up sign before the ambulance doors closed. She wondered sadly if she would ever see him again. Bliss was placed in another ambulance and no nurse from the plane got in with her. She knew she was the least injured of all the service persons that had been flown home, and she reasoned the nurses and doctors had most likely gone with them others. Bliss was placed in a bed in the back of an ambulance and her head was raised comfortably and she was surprised to see that she could see out a small window that was right near her. A male nurse introduced himself to her.

"Lt. Allen, I'm Second Lt. Roger Benjamin, we have a good drive ahead of us, so you just let me know if you need anything." Then pressed an intercom button and told whoever was driving they could leave.

"Where are we going?" Bliss asked. She had assumed she would be going to the base in Charlotte.

"We got a directive that you are to be delivered to Fort Dix."

That got a smile out of Bliss. The General had called her home. Bliss settled down for the drive, which Roger told her would take about nine hours. The ride wasn't bad. Bliss had been given a sandwich and she was able to sleep. The only awkward moment came when she needed to relieve herself, but Second Lt.

Benjamin was the consummate professional. He aided her discreetly and made sure she was covered at all times. He even pretended to be busy while she peed into the plastic basin.

Nine hours later Bliss saw the familiar brick pillars outside the Fort Dix entrance. She thought of her mother, who had once worked there and felt slightly emotional. She regrouped quickly because she did not want to appear unstable. The ambulance pulled up to the small on-site medical building and as she was pulled from the back of the ambulance, Bliss saw the General and Rose were waiting for her.

Second Lt. Rogers opened the back door and he and the driver unloaded Bliss' bed from the back. The wheels to her gurney were barely on the ground when Rose flew to her bedside and wrapped her in a much-needed hug. The General gave her a hug also and Bliss felt the sting of tears in her eyes

"Happy tears, happy tears." Bliss quickly told Rose who was immediately alarmed. "We're taking you home Bliss." The General told her.

"But Sir I..." She never even finished her sentence. He gave her the sweetest, the gentlest look that she had ever seen on his face, then he patted her arm and said, "Don't bother arguing Honey, we got this." Rose was smiling happily so Bliss shrugged her shoulders and muttered a happy, "Okay."

When they got home, Bliss saw that a ramp had been placed at the front door and the General helped her out of the car and into the wheelchair that he had rented. They rolled up the front walkway and when she was pushed inside, she heard, "Surprise!" Collin and Caitlyn stood side by side just inside the door.

Collin was holding flowers and Caitlyn had the most adorable stuffed bear wearing Army fatigues.

The reunion was heartfelt and just what Bliss needed. Leaving behind her new friends in Afghanistan had been very difficult. She felt like she was letting them down by coming home. Seeing Bo leave in the ambulance was heart wrenching. The fact that he had been with Red had not helped either. Bliss didn't resent that he seemed happy. She just couldn't wrap her head around the fact that he had found that happiness with Red, her rival, the same woman who Connor had slept with not once, but twice.

Bliss soaked in the love her family was giving her. Collin wheeled her around and she saw that they had rented a hospital bed and that it was set up in the Generals office. They had hooked up a television for her and Bliss learned that a nurse would come in daily to help her bathe. She also was told that a Physical Therapist and an Occupational Therapist would be coming to the house on alternate days to rehab her hands.

That night, after a wonderful dinner, Caitlyn and Rose had helped Bliss change and get ready for bed, the General shooed the two women from her new room and sat down at the end of her bed.

"How are you really, Bliss?" He asked.

She sighed and looked away for a second to compose herself.

"I feel odd General. I can't really describe it. I feel like I shouldn't be here. I feel guilty for being here."

The General patted her lower leg.

"That's a normal reaction Bliss. Soldiers that come home have to adjust to life back here. They feel guilty for leaving their buddies. You have to work through that."

Bliss nodded.

"General, any word from Connor?" The Generals lips thinned.

"No, it's been a month. I'm a little worried."

The fact that the General was worried wasn't a good sign.

"Honey, I know you were tortured over there. If you ever need to talk, I'm here. I can also send for someone."

"Thank you. I'm handling that better than the guilt, believe it or not."

The General smiled. "You're so much like my Connor." He said giving her a sad smile. "So empathetic; almost to a fault."

"I'll pray for him General." Bliss said seeing the concern for his son etched on his face. "Thank you."

The General stood. "If you need anything, use that bell." He said pointing at a little bell that sat on a table to her right.

"Thanks again General."

He bent down and kissed her forehead. "We are so glad you are safe Bliss, so glad."

After the General left her alone Bliss prayed for Connor's safety and for all her friends she had left and then she added a prayer for all Military personnel. As she drifted off to sleep her final thoughts were of Connor, unfortunately, they were of him leaving the mess hall with Red.

One week later two things happened; Bliss was allowed to walk short distances, and Connor had emailed his father. All the General revealed was that

Connor was okay, and that he would be coming home next week. The family was overjoyed, and Bliss was happy too, but she had a doom and gloom feeling that was poking away at her. She was worried how Connor would act around her. She knew she would have to try to forget their stolen kisses, and his claims to care for her. She had to act as normal as possible for him so he wouldn't be uncomfortable in his own home.

The General's office once again became his office and Bliss settled into her room upstairs. She had cabin fever so badly that the General arranged for her to do her PT and OT on the base and Rose happily drove her there and back daily.

Bliss was feeling stronger every day. She couldn't walk far or fast, and her hands were slowly gaining strength. She still couldn't hold anything, button, zip, or even pull up things, so her clothes consisted of yoga pants and tee shirts. Rose happily helped her and not once did Bliss ever feel like she was a burden. She still had the cast on her one arm that covered her from elbow to palm. Her other hand which had the short cast on it was now thickly bandaged.

A week later Connor called his dad telling him he had landed. The family was waiting anxiously in the living room for him to get home. Caitlyn had helped Bliss to put on actual clothes, she had been living in sweat pants and tee shirts, Caitlyn dressed her in a cute skirt and a top with the sleeves that miraculously had fit over her cast. The skirts hem sat right at the angry red pucker mark on her thigh that the bullet had left behind, but Caitlyn assured Bliss she looked great. She had even done Bliss' hair and make-up.

Rose made Connor's favorite supper and it sat warming in the oven as they waited.

The family was even going to sit at the dining room table normally reserved for Holidays. Bliss hoped she wouldn't embarrass herself by dropping any food on the shirt Caitlyn had found for her. She still couldn't handle silverware very well yet. Although they were talking animatedly, every person in the room was eagerly waiting for the sound of Connor's rental car. Just as Jeopardy ended, headlights swung through the living room window and they heard an engine shut down and a door close. The entire family, except Bliss, ran outside to greet him. Bliss used that time to fortify herself. She plastered a smile on her face as the front door swung open. The family re-entered, everyone smiling and talking at once, Connor was surrounded in the center of his happy, wonderful family.

When Connor got inside, he saw Bliss sitting on the sofa. Whatever his family was saying to him took on a hum as his total focus was on Bliss as she smiled at him. He saw that the smile didn't reach her eyes and his heart lurched a little. He heard his mom tell Caitlyn to help her get the dinner out, and Collin grabbed his duffel bag and told him that he was taking it to his room. The General went into the kitchen to get him a beer leaving them alone. Connor walked to Bliss who was sitting so still, it frightened him.

"Hey," he said kneeling down next to her.

"Hey," she answered. He was so handsome, but she could see he had lost some weight. "We were worried about you." She told him.

"I know. I couldn't get internet where I was."

They were inches apart and Bliss saw him look over her body at her injuries. His face registered concern. "Are you okay?"

"I will be. Your family has been great."

"Our family." He said quietly, causing her to nod. The General came back in and handed him a beer and Collin came back downstairs and sat down on the sofa near her.

The men talked about sports and local news. Bliss saw that Connor would sneak glances at her and she worried that he was feeling awkward. Rose called everyone to dinner and when Bliss went to stand, Connor watched as Collin helped Bliss to her feet and then remained by her side as she slowly walked to the table. He gave his father a questioning look.

"She was hurt pretty bad, son."

"But she'd going to be all right?"

"Yes, she's feeling guilty for leaving her team behind in Bagram."

Connor nodded, he knew all too well what she was feeling.

"I'll talk to her." Connor said. The General put his arm on Connor's arm. "You need to tell her son." Connor knew what he was talking about and nodded. He knew that was going to be a difficult conversation.

The dinner was a happy affair. Bliss was seated next to Rose and Caitlyn and they helped her by putting the spoon in her hand and when the food fell from it, they didn't bat an eye before reloading it for her. Connor was aware of the difficulty she was having, and it broke his heart. She was still gorgeous and although she was putting on a brave front, he could see how frustrated she was that people had to help her.

After dinner the family sat watching a game and just chatting. Caitlyn was in her glory telling the family all about her trip to Paris, which had come to a close a month earlier. She had found a job in New York City working for Macy's, and she was blissfully happy. Collin was up for partnership in his firm, and Caitlyn was currently crashing on his couch until she found a place to live.

Caitlyn asked Bliss what her plans were, and Bliss told the family that as soon as she was able, she was going to ask to go back to Afghanistan. The family was stunned into silence.

"You want to go back?" Caitlyn asked.

"I do. I liked what I was doing. I think I was making a difference."

The General came to the rescue. "I'm sure you were great at your job Bliss. Let's get you healed up first though okay?" He said with a chuckle and the family relaxed. Connor was looking at her, but not like he was shocked, almost like he was proud of her. Well, Bliss thought, if anyone understood, it would be Connor.

The family talked until the 11:00 news ended and then they all walked upstairs together. Collin had swept Bliss up and carried her up the steps and Bliss was laughing, slapping gently at his shoulder telling him she could walk. Collin laughed and teased her by saying that by the time she got up the steps, it would be time to come down for breakfast, which got a laugh out of everyone, including Bliss.

Caitlyn helped Bliss to brush her teeth and then she helped her put on a pair of short, hot pink boy shorts and a light pink and very sheer baby doll pajama top. Bliss was giggling. "You know when I get the use of my hands back, you're not going to be able to play dress up with me anymore." Caitlyn laughed out loud. "Yeah, but maybe by that time I'll have triggered your feminine fashion sense and you'll dress like this all the time."

"I doubt it." Bliss was chuckling.

Bliss fell asleep quickly considering her mind was overrun by of how wonderful Connor had looked. She was pulled from her sleep when she felt a hand gently covering her mouth and a soft whisper in her ear. "It's me."

Bliss turned to see Connor kneeling by her bed.

"Can we talk?" He asked her.

Bliss nodded and when she slowly pulled back the covers, Connor saw her outfit and gave her a small grin before lifting her from the bed and walking out of the bedroom. As they descended into the living room hall Bliss had de ja vu, remembering when she had been carried from her cell. It was the way Connor was carrying her now. She thought it odd that when Collin had carried her earlier it hadn't triggered that memory.

Bliss was reminded how her rescuers arms had lifted her quickly and protectively against his body, and how his gloved hands had felt warm against her icy skin. Her left arm was around Connor's upper back and her hand rested on Connor's right shoulder, just like it had been around the service man that had rescued her. Her hand was in the cast, but her fingers were able to feel Connor's muscled shoulders, shoulder's just like her rescuers, and that's when she knew.

Connor heard her breath hitch as she dragged her fingers up the short sleeve of his shirt until she found what she was looking for.

"Connor?" She whispered in a tone so full of surprise that Connor stopped walking. He gazed down at her and her beautiful blue eyes gazed at him in wonder and he knew that she knew.

"Shush, we'll talk in a second."

Connor turned into the kitchen and then took her down the steps into the basement. He placed her gently on the couch.

"Connor, take off your shirt." Bliss said almost tersely.

"Bliss, can we?" He wanted to explain everything to her first.

Bliss impatiently interrupted him. " Now Connor." She already knew what she would see. Connor drew his shirt over his head and Bliss placed her hand on his hip and nudged him gently, indicating to him that she wanted him to turn around. He turned around, then she tugged on his pants so he would sit on the couch next to her. With is back to her she ran her fingers along his shoulder and then up high on his back. She grazed the two puckered welts, one in his shoulder and one on the left side of back just where his back met the top of his shoulders.

"It was you," she said softly, tears filled her eyes. She had thought, at first, it might have been him, but when he never got in touch with her afterwards, she thought maybe it wasn't.

"How? Why? I don't understand."

Connor turned and slipped his shirt back on over his head.

"God, I have so much I want to tell you," he said watching her face intensely. "How did you find us? Why didn't you talk to me?"

Connor reached for her hand and fingered her mom's bracelet. It fell above the bandaged palm. "This led me to you," he said softly as he kissed the bracelet.

Bliss looked at him incredulously.

"Bliss, your dad gave this bracelet to your mom because he was worried about her." "Connor how can you know this?" Bliss stared at him skeptically.

Connor blew out a large breath. "Let me explain, okay? Everything."

Bliss nodded and waited.

"Your father worked for the CIA. It's why your mom always worked on Army bases. Your dad knew if her days were spent on a base that she'd at least be safe for half of her day. "

Bliss drew her fingers to her mouth astonished that Connor knew all this about her parents.

"Your dad was always concerned about her safety. It's why he left. Things were getting dicey and he worried about all of you. He was concerned that someone may try to get to him by hurting his family."

"Oh my God." Bliss whispered.

"Your dad had this bracelet made after you were born. It contains a GPS tracking chip. He thought if your mom was ever kidnapped, he would be able to find her."

"She never took it off." Bliss whispered reverently.

"When your mom was killed my dad was given a

letter, from her attorney explaining all of this and more. The letter said that if she died that he was to make sure you wore the bracelet."

Bliss fiddled with the small chain. "That's why your dad gave me the fake medic tag?" "Yes."

"So you've known about this?"

"No, not until later when I was able to talk to my dad. After you were listed as MIA, Dad checked the coordinates on the bracelet. He knew where you were, well, where the bracelet was so he got in touch with me. We were holed up in Pakistan. Dad pulled major strings to reach me. We did not have internet access and we had only two radios, one of them I carried, and the other was on the Black Hawk. Dad was able to connect to my radio. He was only on the airwaves for a few seconds. We know someone picked up the transmission, but there is no way they know what was said or can even pinpoint the origin or destination."

"How can you be so sure?"

"Dad radioed me from Ohio, he drove there using a rental car. A buddy from Vietnam gave him radio access. Then dad used a code when I answered the transmission. He only said a few words; well actually names, and then he disconnected."

"I don't understand?"

"Dad spoke the names of a few pro baseball and football players, and the name of the street we used to live on. I had no idea what was going on, I just knew if my dad had radioed me that it had to be something pretty significant. The names he had given me have a number connection. You know like Jeter wore number 2? So, I was able to get coordinates from that. I had no idea you were MIA. It wasn't until I saw you in the cell that I knew it was you."

"Why didn't he just tell the Army where I was?"

"Because he knew that I was your best chance of coming out of it alive." Connor didn't say it with any cockiness in his voice; it was just an honest answer. "Bliss, the army would have had to verify the information, even coming from my dad. It would have taken days for them to organize your rescue. This is what my team and I do. The General knew this. The Army waits a few days before notifying next of kin when their loved ones are MIA, it's protocol. The General knew that meant you'd probably been missing a week."

Connor sat quietly, letting Bliss absorb everything he had told her.

"It was awful Connor." She admitted quietly. "Thank you for saving me." Her hands were laying on her lap and her head was bent to avoid Connor's gaze. If she looked at him, she knew she would cry. She didn't want to cry.

Bliss finally composed herself. "You were shot. Are you okay?"

Connor nodded. "I am now." She could tell he was troubled about something, so she waited for him to continue. "I wish I had known sooner. I wish I could have come before that man hurt you." Bliss could hear the anger in his voice. She looked up to find him staring at her with a sad look on his face.

"You did get there in time Connor. I'm alive. Bo's alive."

Upon hearing Bo's name Connor stilled and then rubbed the back of his neck. "Your friend Bo was hurt pretty bad."

"Yes, he was, but he's better. He flew stateside with me. He's going to the VA Hospital near his home in Mississippi."

Connor looked away uncomfortably. He then turned back to her, "Do you love him?" Bliss cocked her head and looked at Connor thoughtfully.

"Connor, I love him like you love your men. We became close over there, yes."

"I saw how you were looking at him in the chopper."

"Connor, why didn't you tell me it was you?"

"I couldn't. We stole the Black Hawk."

"What? You didn't?"

"Well, actually we borrowed it. I asked Andy, the pilot to help me after I figured out that my dad had given me coordinates. I figured it was a rescue mission. Andy's my best friend. I was going to go alone, but I needed him to fly the chopper. He told the guys and they all volunteered. Thank God, because we needed every one of them."

"Are you in trouble?"

"Don't know, maybe. The Army knows it was a Black Hawk that rescued you and your Lt., and they also know that the one my team had access to has a few extra miles on it." "Oh Connor no."

"I think we'll be okay. I actually flew home to talk to the General about it."

"Oh."

Bliss realized he hadn't said he also had wanted to see her and it stung.

"Bliss I'm sorry I couldn't tell you, we all swore to keep it a Dark Op. It was for your own protection, too. I wouldn't want to drag you into anything that could hurt your career." "I'm in the clear now, so you decided to tell me?" She said still hurt.

"Well, yes, and the General said to tell you. He said you should know about the bracelet and your father. He also said that if it ever came out, you know, about the unauthorized rescue, he wanted you to be prepared to defend yourself against any slanderous accusations."

"That you came for me? I don't understand. How could it be spun to make either of us look bad? Well, except the unauthorized part."

"Bliss, it's why the Military frowns on spouses serving together. We'd do anything for the ones we love."

"Connor, we aren't married, and you certainly don't love me. I don't see..."

"Don't love you?" Connor's voice bristled, cutting her off mid-sentence.

"Bliss, I loved you with every fiber in my body. Didn't you get my letter?" He looked at her wrist and saw that the bracelet he had given her wasn't there.

"Did you take it off? Or did someone else?" He said heatedly, pointing at her wrist.

"I did." Bliss said fuming that he had just professed to love her. "I took it off the day I saw you leave the mess hall tent with Red, back in Bagram, during the party!" Bliss' voice was shaking she was so mad. She was more annoyed that Connor had the nerve to look shocked.

"Yeah, Connor I know all about that little rendezvous. You can't imagine my surprise when I saw the man I cared so much for, up on the large screen, chatting it up with Miss Perfect Nurse, and then watching them leave the party together. It was a real treat!" Connor was staring at her opened mouth. "That was on a video?"

"Yes, Captain," she said using his rank, "they video all their parties."

"Shit."

"Yeah, that's what I said."

Bliss stood up shakily from the couch. She couldn't deal with him right now. He had just thrown her so much information and now he was trying to tell her that that he loved her. Well, she wasn't going to listen to him lie anymore.

"Sit down Bliss, we need to talk."

"I'm done Connor. I can't do this."

"You can, and you will." He said with a little harshness in his tone.

He took hold of her wrist, but it was a gentle hold.

"Please Bliss, sit down." He said using a gentler manner.

Bliss sat and crossed her injured hands over her chest.

"So, let's clear up some things, okay?" He said.

Bliss nodded.

"You saw me on the video, in Bagram talking to Red, I mean Teresa, and you thought I hooked up with her again?"

"It sure wasn't a stretch to reach that conclusion, Connor," she said vehemently.

"Let me ask you something?"

"Okay."

"Did you hook up with your Lt. after that?"

"You have a hell of a lot of nerve," she spat back.

"Answer please."

"No, Connor I never hooked up with Bo or anyone else over there, all right? Are you happy now?"

Connor put his hand on her cheek tenderly. "Yes, Baby, I'm very happy."

Bliss shook his hand off of her face.

"You are a jerk, you know that?"

Connor was grinning at her. "Stay here." He jumped over the back of the couch. "What?"

"Stay right there." He said as left her, taking the steps two at a time.

Bliss was thoroughly confused. He said he loved her, yet he hooked up with Red? He was angry that she may have been with Bo. She didn't get it, and if this was what lay ahead of her in the world of dating, well, she may end up a lonely old cat woman. Connor flew back down the steps and jumped back over the back of the couch and landed by her side. He took her hand in his and straightened her fingers. Then he laid a beautiful silver necklace on her white bandage. A heart shaped charm was affixed to a chain and inside the heart was a small blue tourmaline gem. Bliss was speechless. "Say something." Connor said anxiously.

"I don't understand?"

"Bliss, I love you. I was never with Teresa. I took her outside to show her this necklace. I bought it for you about a month after I left you in Kabul, and I've had had it in my pocket the whole time. I'll admit that she had hoped to get together with me again, but I told her I had a girl. Someone I loved, someone who had made me want things I never thought I'd want. She was happy for me. I told her I had bought you a necklace and she asked to see it. I didn't want my guys to see it, so we went outside."

"You left the party to show her this necklace?" Bliss'

whispered still stunned.

"Yes, I told you on the plane ride over that you I cared for you. What I hadn't said was that I love you. I gave you that leather strand, tied with a 'love knot' because I was just too scared to say it then. When I was over there, I thought about you all the time. We completed our first mission and it was pretty hairy. It made me think about what if something happened to one of us, and I hadn't told you how I felt? I knew I had to tell you, but I wanted it to be in person. I left you that letter."

"Connor after seeing you leave the party with Red, and then reading the letter. I honestly thought it was a Dear John letter. Bo did too."

"You let Bo read it?"

"Connor, I was devastated. He was a good friend."

"He cares for you, doesn't he?"

"Honestly, I thought he did, but you want hear something weird, full circle weird?" Connor nodded. "He's smitten with Red now."

"What?"

"Red took care of him in the hospital and she came home on the transport plane with us. She lives near him and I think he likes her, and she looked like she liked him too." "Well I'll be damned." Connor said grinning. He looked down at the necklace still perched on her hand.

Connor took the necklace and placed it around her neck. He leaned down and sealed it with a kiss like he had the leather bracelet. "The stone reminded me of your beautiful eyes. I saw those eyes every night before I fell asleep. When things got crazy, I prayed to God to let me see them again."

"Connor." Bliss said his name softly, tears glistened in her eyes.

He leaned down and nuzzled her cheek and wiped the tears away with his thumbs. "I love you Bliss," he whispered.

"I love you so much and I love this, thank you. It's beautiful. I wish I still had that leather bracelet now," Bliss said wistfully.

"What, you don't like this?" He said grinning.

"I love this. It's just that the bracelet had actually gotten me through some lonely nights in Afghanistan. You know the guys told me it was tied with a 'love knot'. I had no idea." "I'll make you another one." Connor said kissing his way over her injured arm. "God I
hate thinking of you being hurt."

"I don't like that you were hurt either."

"I guess we need to talk about that night, but not now."

Connor sat back against the couches back and lifted her onto his lap so she was straddling him.

"Did I tell you that you look seriously sexy in these pajamas?" He said as he ran his fingers under the hem of her top, just grazing her soft skin. She felt her nipples pebble in anticipation against the gauzy top material.

A blush stole over Bliss with the intimacy of their body position. Connor cupped her neck and back with his hands and pulled her close as he leaned down, brushing his lips against hers. He gently slid his tongue tip across her lips, and she opened for him. Their kiss deepened as their tongues mated erotically. Bliss felt him harden beneath her. She wanted, so desperately, to touch him, but she knew she would not be able to satisfy him at all with the constraints on her hands. Bliss pulled back from the kiss and cocked her head. "Is this really happening?"

"Yeah, it is long overdue." His voice was husky, and his eyes were smoldering making her private parts warm and wet.

Bliss laid her arms carefully over his shoulders, not wanting to scratch him with her cast. "Connor, I can't even touch you. I really want to touch you." Her voice was syrupy, and Connor reached between them to adjust his growing length. The back of his hand brushed softly against her sex.

"But I can touch you, and that's all I've thought about since leaving you in Kabul."

"Even when you thought I was with Bo?"

"That almost did me in. Seeing you look at him like he was your everything when we were on the chopper. When you whispered to him to be okay, that killed me. My team was looking at you and noticed how much you cared for the Lt., and then they had look at me, knowing I had to sit there quietly, enduring it. Ralph and I were wounded and when we got back to our little village in Pakistan, the guys had to take the bullets out of us themselves and stitch us up. Luckily Tippy is an EMT. We couldn't go to a hospital. No one could know. I told Andy that as soon as I was healed, I was going to find your Lt. Pike and beat the shit out of him." Bliss giggled at his machismo.

"I wish I had known it was you Connor." She said again.

"But then when you were asked who rescued you,

you would have had to lie. No, it was better this way."

"I'm worried Connor. Please let me know what's happening with this, okay?" "Sweetheart, I'll tell you everything, no more secrets, promise. We're a team."

"Are we going to tell your parents about this team?" She teased gently.

"Dad knows how I feel about you. I bet mom does too."

"Really? Do they approve?"

"I'm sure they will love it." Connor started kissing her again.

"Connor wait," Bliss said pushing away from his warm kiss. Connor actually groaned with the loss of contact.

"When do you go back?"

"Two weeks."

"You know I want to go back."

"Can we talk about that later?"

"Connor really?"

"Bliss, can we just enjoy this moment? You and I are finally on the same page. We will get no privacy when we tell the family. Can we just, you know, love each other for the next few hours?"

"Connor we are in your parent's basement."

"Yes, I'm aware of that." He said working his lips over her sensitive neck. "We are going to have to be really quiet."

Chapter 15

Connor kissed her ardently and Bliss felt sexual heat surge through her. She placed her elbows on Connor's shoulders, crossing her forearms behind his head and pressed against his solid chest. Her inexperience made her apprehensive and she was wondering what she should be doing to please him. Should she be moving? Her self-doubt manifested in her body becoming ridged.

"What's wrong?" Connor asked breathlessly laying his forehead against hers. Bliss colored with embarrassment.

"Tell me," he asked softly.

"I'm not very experienced," she admitted quietly. Connor paused before talking. He wanted her to feel comfortable with him.

"Do you like kissing me?" Connor asked almost nervously.

Bliss gave him a huge smile and whispered, "I love kissing you, Connor."

Connor smiled back. "Okay, that's good, I love kissing you, too. I want you to be comfortable with me; completely at ease. Trust me, Babe, I'm not going to stop loving you because you are inexperienced, it's actually a turn on. If you have a question, ask it."

"Okay honesty it is." She said still grinning. "I want to move on you." She rocked her hips so that her female lips traveled up and down his erect shaft. "Like this."

Connor groaned and placed his hands on her hips to encourage her to keep moving. "That feels so good." Bliss nodded and looked between their bodies as she rode him. Connor helped her and then slipped his hands under her top sliding them up to her breasts. He cupped them softly and his thumbs grazed back and forth over her sensitive nipples.

"Oh God." Bliss moaned leaning her head back. Connor took advantage of that position and fastened his lips to her neck, sucking gently so as not to leave a mark. Connor felt Bliss pressing against him harder and working her hips faster, and he knew she was going to come. He was holding fast, praying she would come soon, because he was close to blowing like a teenager in his pajama pants.

"Connor," she pleaded, unsure what she was asking for. "Connor, Oh God, please."

"I got you." Connor reached between them and used a thumb to rub her engorged nub. "Ohhhhhh. Ohhhhhhhh, yes, yes, yessss." Bliss hushed out huskily as the orgasm shuddered through her.

Connor rubbed her until he was satisfied that he had completely wrung every orgasmic tremor from her. Connor took his fingers from her boy shorts and tasted her essence. "Oh man, I knew you would taste great." He said looking at her with a sexy grin on his face.

Bliss was still reeling from the body shattering orgasm he had just pulled from her, but when he tasted his fingers her face displayed shock and she turned crimson, making
Connor chuckle.

"Sweetheart hasn't anyone... Haven't you ever?"

Bliss shook her head no. "No, if what I'm thinking you are asking is, then no."

Connor smiled, "Good, I'm going to love being your first."

He made Bliss feel so comfortable that she snuggled into his chest, careful to not scrape him with her cast. "What about sex?" Connor asked.

Bliss sat up looking uncomfortable. "Well, I've had it, once, but it wasn't enjoyable." "One time?" Connor was astonished.

"My Junior year in college there was a guy who was nice, really nice. He was in my Computer Club. So, one night I decided to join everyone else after our meeting for a drink. He was flirting with me and well I guess I just wanted to see what all the fuss was about."

"Oh baby," Connor said sadly.

"Yeah, more like dumb-ass," she smirked. "He did me doggie style and it hurt. He laughed saying how he had popped my cherry and that I'd always remember him."

"I'm sorry Bliss, he was a jerk."

"My girlfriend told me he bragged about it the next day and what's even more embarrassing, was that he bragged that he didn't even have to look at my Magoo face." "That bastard," Connor said heatedly.

"So that's the extent of my experience." Bliss bent her head feeling the pain of that awful memory all over again.

"He was a jerk Bliss."

"I know. I'm madder at myself." She peered up at him and her heart slammed into her chest seeing how gorgeous he was and how affectionately he was looking at her. "Connor, I can't help but think of you and Red and all your other girls. I'm not like them. I don't know anything."

"I love you because you aren't like them." He kissed her forehead and then her eyes and settled gently on her lips. Their kiss was so sweet and warm, and Bliss melted all over again. She felt Connor's steely length beneath her, and she moved on him again, forcing a groan from Connor.

"I want to be good for you, Connor."

"You are good for me, baby." He said suckling her neck.

"I mean sexually."

Connor held her cheeks in his hands. "We are going to be great together, Bliss. We're already great."

Bliss kissed him on his cheeks and nose and worked her way to his ear. She realized he liked his ears being kissed and she put that tidbit of information away. She kissed his neck trying to emulate what she'd read in some of her romance novels. She kissed and nibbled and even gently bit her way down his neck. She used her one hand without the cast and pulled up his tee shirt and Connor helped her by pulling it completely over his head.

His cock was thick beneath her and she continued to stroke it using her moist female bits. She kissed her way down his chest and sucked around his nipples. She noticed that his were erect, too and he moaned appreciatively as she suckled them gently. Connor was aroused and that only stirred her passion more. She sunk to her knees on the floor and Connor cocked his head unsure of what she

wanted. "Pants, Connor, off please." She said huskily.
"Baby, you don't have to."
"I want to. I've never done it before, but I've heard the guys talk about it. If I do something wrong, tell me. I want to be good for you Connor. I want to love you right." Connor lifted his rear from the couch and pulled down his thin PJ bottoms. His cock stood straight up when released from the confines of the material.

Bliss looked at his cock, standing strong, with a thick vein running down the underside and in the center of the purple colored plum shaped dome sat a small white pearl sized drop. Bliss decided to start there. She licked his head savoring the salty taste and then proceeded to lick around his head, paying special attention to the small rim under the dome.

She kissed and licked her way to the base and glanced up to Connor, who was watching her with a look she wished she could capture and keep with her forever. Bliss kissed her way back up to the head and now she opened wide and took in as much of him as she could. She bobbed up and down letting her saliva lubricate his shaft and she could hear him moaning softly, "yes, yes, just like that."

Bliss was so turned on, she knew she could come again, and she decided she was going to. She continued to love Connor with her mouth while she took two fingers that were functioning and slipped them down her shorts. She couldn't believe how wet she was. She started strumming her sensitive pearl and moaned sending rich vibrations around Connor's sensitive cock.

"Oh God, Bliss are you touching yourself? Oh man,

that is so hot." His voice cracked a little. "Baby, I'm going to come, I'm going to come." Bliss took in as much of him as she could and felt his cock throb. She was so turned on that an orgasm blasted through her making her shake and moan.

"Oh. God. Yes," Connor groaned. Bliss felt him tremble just before salty sweetness coated her throat. Bliss peered up at Conner as she continued to lick his essence; his eyes never left hers. A few seconds later he lifted Bliss back on to his lap. "If that was your first time Angel, I am a lucky man." He said depositing tender kisses all over her face.

Bliss was smiling so that Connor hugged her to him happily. "Good enough?"

"Better than good. Freaking awesome!"

Connor slipped his shirt back on and pulled his pants up. Bliss snuggled back into his strong arms. Connor was content just holding her close. He felt her breathing even out and realized she was falling asleep. He rubbed her back gently and thought about how things were going to be for them. He hated to think of her going back to Afghanistan. He wouldn't be able to focus knowing she was in danger and he knew she'd be thinking of him as well.

The first thing he needed to do was tell his family. He thought his parents would be fine. He was a little worried about Collin, and he hoped Caitlyn was good with it. If she weren't, Bliss would be devastated.

Bliss was now sound asleep against his chest. He kissed her head. "Baby I'm taking you to bed, okay?"

"Mine or yours?" She mumbled.

Connor smiled, "Yours, unfortunately."

He picked her up and snuck her back into her bed.

Before he left, she motioned for him to lean closer to her. "Connor?" Bliss whispered.

"Ummm?"

"Thank you for rescuing me and Bo and thank you for tonight." She said sleepily.

"I love you woman." He said kissing her forehead. "And we will remedy this sleeping situation soon okay?"

"I think I'm going to like sleeping with you."

"Me too, sleeping and not sleeping," he murmured.

She was already asleep again.

Chapter 16

Bliss slept soundly for the first time in weeks. She woke up to Caitlyn attempting to tip toe around the room as she rummaged through a drawer to find pants.

"Hey, good morning." Bliss remained laying down but stretched contently.

"Hey, I was trying not to wake you." Caitlyn answered.

"What time is it?"

"9 AM"

Bliss sat up quickly. She never slept this late. She remembered why she probably had slept later than usual, and a smile formed on her lips.

"What are you thinking about?" Caitlyn said giggling at Bliss' dreamy expression.

"Just thinking about something." Bliss couldn't keep the silly grin from her lips.

"Care to share?"

Bliss thought about it and then decided she should be the one to tell Caitlyn that she loved Connor. If Caitlyn heard it from anyone else, she'd probably get upset. Bliss patted her bed and Caitlyn sat with a bounce and a giggle.

"We used to sit like this a lot." Caitlyn remarked. "I'd come home from a date and need advice and you'd pat the bed; like you just did, and we would talk for hours."

Bliss smiled remembering those nights.

"So spill Bliss. What's up?"

"I don't want you to be upset."

"Upset about what?"

"What I'm about to tell you."

"Bliss, you're like my sister, come on." Caitlyn said with mock annoyance in her tone. "Okay, here goes. I'm head over heels in love with someone."

Caitlyn clapped and hugged her. "I knew it. I knew it!"

"There's more."

"Are you engaged? Are you moving in together?" Caitlyn saw the necklace around her neck and gently grasped it. "Oh my gosh, did he give you this? It's gorgeous."

Bliss grinned at Caitlyn's exuberance. "I'm not engaged. We aren't moving in together, and yes, he did give this to me."

"Do I know him?"

"Yes," Bliss said slowly.

Caitlyn paused. Bliss could see she was thinking of all the men she knew.

"I give up. Who?"

"Promise you'll talk to me if you're unhappy."

"Bliss, come on!" Caitlyn was not a patient person.

"Connor."

Caitlyn was stunned into silence and Bliss watched a myriad of emotions cross her friends face.

"My brother Connor?"

Bliss nodded.

"You love Connor?"

Bliss grinned, "Yes."

"Does he know? I mean does he love you?"

Bliss chuckled," he says he loves me too."

Caitlyn was quiet for all of three seconds before she pounced into Bliss' arms squealing happily.

"Oh my gosh. We can be family for real!"

Bliss laughed, "Caitlyn slow down. We aren't there yet. I don't even know if he wants that. Right now, we just know that we care for each other. We get each other."

Caitlyn nodded still smiling.

"Does anyone else know?"

Bliss shook her head, "No, I think Connor's going to tell them. Is this weird? Please tell me it's not weird."

"Honestly, you two are so much alike. It's a wonder I didn't try to set the two of you up before this."

"Will your parents mind?"

"No, no way. They love you. They will just want you and Connor to be happy."

"I hope so."

Bliss got out from under the covers and slowly got to her feet. "Bathroom and shower." She said throwing on a robe and heading down the hall.

When Bliss got back to the room, Caitlyn helped her put on a pair of sweatpants and a tee shirt. She then brushed her hair for her. Bliss had physical therapy that morning and for the first time, she wanted to blow it off so she could be with Connor.

Caitlyn scampered down the stairs ahead of her and Bliss slowly followed her using the wall and stair handrail to support her. Her feet were feeling better and they didn't hurt as much as they had. She couldn't wait until she could run again. She missed working out. The most her PT would let her do was ride the stationary bike, which Bliss rode until sweat poured off her and the PT made her quit.

Bliss could hear the family talking and the wonderful aroma of coffee wafted to her as she made her way downstairs. When she reached the kitchen the first person she saw was Connor. He was standing by the counter wearing what he had worn last night. She fought the blush creeping up her face as she remembered him dropping those pants. "Morning, here sit-down sweetie." Rose said guiding her to the counter and looking to Collin to aide her.

The counter seats were high, and Bliss hadn't tried to get up on tone yet. Her feet were tender to push off of and her hands had been almost useless.

Collin stood from his stool to help her, but before he even took his second step Connor stepped between them. He lifted her at the waist and gently placed her down on the curved stool. His eyes were twinkling mischievously.

Bliss was bright red now. She was so unused to attention. "Thank you." She said as his one hand lingered on her waist. He didn't step back from her and she knew he was about to announce that they were dating.

Collin was still standing nearby looking annoyed that Connor had just stepped in front of him. Caitlyn was smirking behind her cup of coffee. She was totally aware of what was about to happen, and the General and Rose were looking to each other and Connor and Bliss.

The General laid his paper down on the counter and waited. Connor knew he had everyone's attention. He remained next to Bliss and placed his hand proprietarily on her back. Connor looked down at Bliss and gave her an adorable wink and then looked around the kitchen at his family.

"Bliss and I, well, we're dating. We've cared about each other for a while now and last night we had a long talk," Connor looked at his dad and smiled, "and we just wanted you guys to know."

Rose smiled and got up and hugged Bliss and then kissed Connor. The General remained in his seat but nodded approvingly. Caitlyn was all smiles and hugged both Connor and Bliss. Collin was the only hold out.

Connor looked at him with a questioning glare. Collin shrugged his shoulders. "I guess if you're both happy, that's great. I just want to go on record here." He said sounding so much like the lawyer that he was. "That if this dating," his fingers made air quotations as he said dating, "goes south, things might get awkward around here."

Connor turned to face Collin; he had known Collin would have reservations. "Collin, I love her. She loves me. We are so in sync with each other. We know we face some difficulties. Heck, just being in the Military creates an entire set of problems, but I want this to work out. I need my family to accept this. We need your support."

Bliss sat quietly taking in the expressions on everyone's faces. Connor had said he loved her to his family. She knew he was going to tell them they were dating, but that they were in love? She peered around Connor and Collin caught her eyes.

"Bliss this isn't anything against you. I'm actually more concerned because of you." Connor put his hand on Bliss' shoulder. She loved how his touch felt. Somehow it gave her courage just knowing how much he cared for her.

"Collin we didn't plan to fall in love. It just happened. We spent time playing online video games and connected with that. We are both Military, so we connected that way. We know how awkward it will be if we break up."

"But we won't." Connor said quickly making Bliss smile.

"Please be okay with this." She finished.

Collin finally grinned. "Okay, you have my blessing, but," he looked at Connor, "if you hurt her you will answer to me."

Connor chuckled, "and what of she hurts me?"

"I'll deal with her then!" Caitlyn quipped happily.

Connor bent down and gave Bliss a tender and short kiss.

"Oh no, I am not watching my big brother and almost sister have PDA, no way." Everyone was laughing, but Bliss noticed that Rose gave the General a look and she wondered what that was about.

While the family ate breakfast she and Connor suffered through a few gentle teases, but all in all she felt it went well. The Doherty's still treated her the same and she was still feeling the love that they had an abundance of. Bliss still thought Collin held reservations; he didn't look happy and that worried her.

"So, I have PT and then a doctor's appointment on the base today. General, can I ride with you?" Bliss asked sliding gently from the stool.

"Actually Rose is taking you today, Honey. Connor and I have some things to discuss."

Bliss looked at Connor who didn't seem unnerved, so she figured it didn't have anything to do with her.

"I'm going to pick you up." Connor told her.

"Great, thanks. Rose I'm just going to brush my teeth and I'll be right down."

Bliss turned and left the kitchen and Connor followed her into the foyer. "That went well," he said.

"Umm, I think so, too."

Connor picked Bliss up and carried her up the steps.

"Connor, I can walk. I'm feeling better"

"Oh Babe, can you pretend you're still hurting please? This may be the only way I get to hold you while we are here." He said kissing her on her neck as he walked.

Bliss playful slapped at his shoulder. When he reached her bedroom door, he didn't release her. Bliss leaned back against his shoulder and gazed up at him. "We need to carve out some time for us. Alone, no one around, and not in this house, kind of time." He said nuzzling her neck.

"Ummmm, yes please." She murmured as a warm amorous feeling made her tingle in her woman parts.

"The sooner the better." She whispered in his ear.

Connor's grin was flat out sexy, "We are so good together."

He lowered Bliss to the floor and followed her into the bathroom. "What are you doing?" "I'm going to help you brush your teeth."

"Oh, I don't..." She started.

"Bliss I know it's difficult for you to hold the brush. I want to help you."

"But..."

"Which toothbrush is yours?" He said ignoring her.

Bliss decided to just go with it and within minutes he was carrying her back downstairs. Rose was waiting by the door and she gave Connor a raised eyebrow seeing him carrying Bliss.

"Son, she can walk."

"Thank you." Bliss agreed.

"Yeah but carrying her is so much more fun." He said mischievously.

Rose laughed and held open the front door for them. Connor carried her down the walk sneaking kisses before lowering her into the car. Before he shut her door, he leaned in and gave her a kiss that made Bliss' head spin.

"What was that for?" She whispered as Rose got in the driver's seat.

"I just want you to think about me."

Bliss smiled and nodded. She then mouthed, "Always." She then fingered the necklace he gave her, and Connor gave her a huge smile.

Bliss waved at Connor standing in the driveway as they pulled away and as she settled back in her seat, she saw Rose had a silly smile on her face.

"What?" Bliss asked Rose.

Rose glanced at her, but kept her attention focused on driving. "Bliss, you know I think of you as if you are my own daughter, right?"

"Yes, you and the General have been and are the best thing that ever happened to me." "Can I ask you something personal then?"

"Of course."

"How do you know you are in love with Connor?"

"Oh." Bliss said slightly taken back with the question. "Well, I guess that's a fair question. He is your son and you want to protect him."

"And you, I want to protect you, too."

"Thank you." Bliss said really meaning it. "Okay, well I really haven't ever had a boyfriend and I have only been on a few dates, so yes, my experience is very limited. Connor and I have been playing video games together for years. Even when I was still in high school there was something different about how he treated me. He saw past my ugly glasses. He accepted me for me. When we talked online and even when we emailed each other our conversations just flowed. He gets me and I think I get him, too. Last Thanksgiving things took a turn. We started to think of each other as more than friends. It just happened. It was so natural. Gosh, this is hard to explain." She said throwing her hands up.

Rose looked to her, "You're doing fine, Honey."

"So, I guess, to answer your question, I love Connor because he is a good man, a good person. I love how smart he is. He's sensible. I like sensible. He's ridiculously handsome." Bliss giggled. "He makes me feel special. I can talk to him about anything. Anything! We have so much in common. He works out like I workout. He's 100% male wrapped in a blanket of sweetness. Gosh, I don't think I'm explaining this well." Bliss' voice conveyed her exasperation.

Rose patted her hand and gestured for her to continue.

"Rose, he makes my heart pound. Should I even be telling his mother this?" Bliss asked anxiously.

Rose laughed, "That's how the General makes me feel. To this day, when I see him my heart seems to swell inside my chest."

"Yes!" Bliss said enthusiastically. "That's it!"

Rose was smiling. "So, I guess you do know what love is."

"I know I loved my mother, and I love Jax, and your family, but my feelings for Connor transcend those in different ways. He makes me happy. Jeez, he makes me so happy." Bliss smiled fingering her necklace.

"Did he give you that?"

"Yes, I love it. It's perfect."

Rose pulled out a necklace from her blouse holding it away from her neck and towards Bliss. "The General gave me this when we were dating. I never take it off."

Bliss looked to see that her necklace had two hearts entwined. Rose always wore it; Bliss had just never thought about it before that moment.

"It's beautiful."

"It is."

The two women shared a comfortable silence as Rose drove them towards Fort Dix. While Bliss reminisced about her night with Connor, from her side mirror, she noticed a beige sedan following them. It had made two turns tasty with them already. Yesterday, she had noticed what looked like the same car. The windows were heavily tinted, and the plates on the car were from Florida. In New Jersey tinted windows were illegal. Bliss couldn't see the person or persons inside the car. A few minutes later they turned into the Fort Dix entrance and Bliss watched as the sedan following them remained on the road bypassing the entrance. A tingle of apprehension crept up her spine. Rose pulled up to the medical building and Bliss thanked Rose and politely declined her offer to help

her inside. Once inside, she walked slowly using the railings that bracketed
each wall. Bliss was pleased that her feet were feeling better and she couldn't wait to show the doctor the progress she had made. Maybe she would let her add something to her normal workout routine.

Her first stop was to the Physical Therapist. Her therapist was a nice civilian man, Hank. He was in his 50's and the perfect therapist for her. He worked her hard and wasn't all chatty like some of the other Physical Therapists. He recognized that Bliss wanted to get better as fast as possible and that she wasn't much for casual conversation. The two of them struck up an easy relationship and Bliss enjoyed the innovative ways he challenged her physically.

An hour later, bathed in sweat, and wonderfully sore from her workout, Bliss walked gingerly to the Doctors office, which was just down the hall. Her Doctors name was Dr. Tanner and she was hard core military. She had served three tours overseas and had also put in time on bases in Africa and Germany. She had a great bedside manner and Bliss liked that she was no nonsense, yet kind.

While Dr. Tanner checked Bliss' vitals, they chatted amicably. Bliss answered all the Doctors questions regarding pain level, mobility, hand strength, and even her mental state. Dr. Tanner examined her hip, thigh, ribs, arms and finally her hands. She took the bandage off the hand with the broken fingers and the one bullet hole and turned it over and over in her hand scrutinizing it.

"This looks good Bliss. I think we can keep the bandages off now. Make sure you are flexing these fingers out and you can start with the ball exercises we talked about last week."

Bliss was all smiles, "Great."

"Now let's see what's under this cast okay?"

Bliss had been hoping the doctor would take it off. Her skin was itching like crazy and she wanted to see what her arm looked like.

The doctor cut through the plaster and gently pried the white protective cast back from her skin. Bliss saw the two angry red bullet marks that pulled her skin into ugly welts. Where her arm had been broken from the bullet hitting her radius there was a thin red line about two inches long where the doctors in Bagram had surgically fit the bone back together with pins.

"This looks good, too. I'm pleased that your muscles haven't atrophied too much."

"I've been working out."

The doctor smiled at her kindly. "Probably more than you should. Am I right?"

Bliss grinned, "Can you ever workout too much Doc? Come on."

The doctor chuckled. "I only wish every patient had your determination Bliss."

The doctor turned the arm over and over and looked at the wound on her hand. "I think I'm just going to give you a brace for this arm now. I want you to start moving your wrist more okay?"

"Yes, Sir!" Bliss said happily.

"Okay Lt. Let's see those feet."

Bliss took off her sneakers and socks and the doctor ran her finger over the hard welts. "How's the pain?"

"It's actually starting to feel better."

"I'm worried that there isn't much I can do for them. Operating would only give you another wound to deal with. You're lucky that bastard used a straight edge. Otherwise you may have never been able to walk without pain."

The doctor was frowning as she ran her finger across Bliss toes watching for signs that Bliss could feel her touch. "You can feel my fingers Bliss, right?"

"Yes."

"That's good."

The doctor straightened up and wrote a few things down on a clipboard. "Well, you're ahead of schedule recovery wise."

"When can I go back?" Bliss asked anxiously.

"Whoa, Lt! Hold your horses." The doctor chuckled. "I know you want to get back there, and I admire you for it. However, I will not sign off on you until I know you can run, jump, climb, shoot, basically pass the whole boot camp test again."

Bliss groaned, which made the doctor laugh.

"Lt. take a vacation. You need to get away, relax. I'll put a note in your file. As long as you're on vacation somewhere near a base and you can check in once a week, you will be listed as on medical R and R. I'll sanction it."

Bliss thought that taking a vacation would be wonderful, but she wasn't going anywhere as long as Connor was in town. They had only spent a few incredible hours together and Bliss hoped they could find that alone time Connor had referred too. It made her tingly just thinking about it.

Bliss thanked the doctor and they walked into the waiting room to find Connor sitting in a chair waiting for her.

"Captain." The doctor said.

"Doc. How's the patient?" Bliss wasn't surprised they knew each other. His father worked on the base, and he was Army, after all.

"She's good. I recommend a vacation. A medical R and R. Can you tell the General for me?"

Connor chuckled, "You got it Doc."

Connor opened the door for Bliss as they left the office.

"No cast?"

"Nope."

They turned a corner and Connor stopped and took her cast free arm in his hands turning it over gently, perusing her ashy arm. He noted the indented marks and the raised red scar, and she could see he was distraught.

Bliss threaded her fingers through his short hair. "I'm good Connor. I'm alive, thanks to you." She said softly.

Connor tenderly kissed her wounds on that arm and then placed his hand at the small of her back guiding her out the door. His hand remained there as they walked down the corridor and Bliss enjoyed the feeling of a man caring for her.

"My car is in the lot, wait here okay?"

Bliss grabbed his arm before he turned from her. "Connor, I need to start walking more. I have to toughen my feet up, get back in shape. I'm starting that right now. We'll both get the car, okay?"

Connor looked around to make sure no one was looking at them and then he quickly kissed her on her lips.

"And that is just one of the many reasons why I love you." He said grinning.

Bliss walked as fast as she could to the car. Connor was watching her closely, so she was careful not to let the burning pain, that the simple movement of walking, show on her face.

"I can tell you're hurting." Connor said to her. His lips were pressed tightly together, and she could feel his anger.

She shrugged her shoulders nonchalantly reaching the car. "Yes, it hurts, but they're going to. I just have to toughen them up."

Connor opened the door for her and leaned in as she settled into the seat. "I get that. I just hate it." He told her honestly.

Bliss touched his cheek with her now freed fingers and ran her tips down to his chin, which she gently tapped twice. "There are cameras in this lot Connor. I want to kiss you. Get in the car and get us out of here." Her voice was syrupy, and Connor felt himself thicken as he watched her lips part and unconsciously but very sexily touched her upper lip with her tongue. Connor drove them off the base and pulled down a side street before pulling into a walking trails empty dirt lot. He unhooked his seatbelt and turned to her and Bliss unbuckled her belt and met him half way as their lips collided in a fury of sexual need. The console prevented their bodies from meeting, but Bliss took advantage of her freed fingers and ran her fingers through his short hair and around his strong neck.

They breathlessly pulled back from each other and their foreheads rested against each other as their hearts pounded.

"We have to get away." Connor said thickly.

"Soon." Bliss agreed.

Connor's thumb rubbed her cheek tenderly. "Feel like talking?"

Bliss chuckled, "Now?"

"I need a few minutes to, umm, calm down." He said glancing at the bulge behind the zipper in his pants.

Bliss' eyes had followed his gaze and a small sense of satisfaction ran through her knowing that she affected him the same way he affected her.

"Sure," she said sitting back so her shoulders rested on the seats back. Connor was twisted similarly, but the cars steering wheel prevented him from turning completely. Connor took her hand in his. "Tell me what happened."

Bliss didn't bother playing coy. She knew exactly what he wanted to know.

"I got an email that was very sensitive in nature. It was coded, of course. We were in Bagram and the message called for me to take it to General Jones in Kandahar. General Paine told Bo there had been some activity along the main route, so he suggested we take an alternate route, which we did. We were ambushed. Harry was killed. Bo and I were taken hostage. I thought Phil, Billy, and Mike had been killed, too, because the last I saw them there were rifles pointed at their head." Bliss sighed heavily; her eyes were shut as she remembered that awful moment. Connor squeezed her hand gently bringing her back to the present.

"So, I passed out when they broke my fingers and regained consciousness in the cell you found me in. A man with blue eyes wanted me to tell him what the email I had received said. I played dumb. He sent in another man named Zarghun who started to hurt me." Bliss' words were barely discernible. She hated talking about her kidnapping. It was still such a raw memory that the just thinking about it was agonizing. She peered at Connor who remained stoic but kept his eyes on her. Bliss knew he wanted details, and she found that she wanted him to know everything.

"Honey, it may help you to tell someone what you went through. I want to be that person for you. I can't take any the hurt from you, God knows I would, but if you let me in, maybe, just maybe it will help you to heal.

Bliss nodded, "I want you to know what happened Connor. I trust that you won't share what I say."

"I won't." He grazed his finger along her cheek tenderly. "I love you Bliss."

"I love you too."

Bliss took a deep breath and unloaded all the awful memories she had about her kidnapping. She almost broke down when she told Connor when she came to realized Bo was in the crate.

Connor's face was frozen in a practiced look. It was his eyes that gave away how upset he was. "The man that told Zarghun to leave, tell me about him."

"He was dressed in typical Pashtun dress; a khet partug and pakul on his head, but he hid his face behind a piece of cloth attached to the pakul. I could only see his eyes, they were blue, and he had an English accent. I don't think he was disguising his voice. He seemed mad that Zarghun had hurt me, but he was serious that if I didn't talk, he would allow

Zarghun to torture the information out of me."
Bliss gulped back the sickening memory. A tear slid
down her cheek that Connor wiped away with his
thumb.

"I'm sorry, Baby. That had to be awful." Bliss just
nodded numbly. She hadn't told anyone else the
specifics of time in captivity, and voicing her ordeal
scraped up the terrible memory. She watched
Connor's face and knew he was deep in thought.

"Tell me what you're thinking."

"Okay, first of all I'm wondering how they knew
where you were? How did they know you had the
information you did?"

"I've been wondering that, too."

"Secondly, the fact that you were naked is odd."
Bliss nodded.

"Then, of course, the man that was English, with blue
eyes, makes me think that this wasn't strictly an Al
Qaida mission."

"I've thought about all of that."

"Did you ever deliver the message?"

"Yes, General Jones came to Bagram and I told him
what it said."

"Let me ask you this." He paused. "Is this
information, now that it's in the Generals hands,
something that is no longer dangerous knowledge for
you to possess?"

Bliss turned her head to look out the front window
and then looked back to Connor who was patiently
waiting for her answer.

"I can only suppose that it's still relevant."

"Shit." Connor said softly banging his hand against
the wheel of the car. "Bliss I don't like this. You

could still be in danger."

Bliss thought about the car that she thought had followed her and Rose this morning, but she didn't want to stress Connor out any more than he already was.

"This transmission was Normandy status, Connor. I've received others like this. Why this one?"

"I don't know. You can't tell me what was in the email, right?"

"No, sorry."

"I figured. Do any of your team know the specifics of the email?"

"No, none of them."

"It's amazing that they weren't killed."

"I know. It's so out of character with the Taliban."

"You know why they kept Bo don't you?" Connor asked her with a slightly crisp tone. Bliss nodded, "They were going to use him against me to make me talk."

"Yeah, he must have done something to indicate your relationship was more than..." Bliss put her hand over Connor's that was resting on her thigh. "He tried to save me, Connor. He was wounded and as injured as he was, he still rushed them when they took me. I honestly don't know how he even stood up."

Connor nodded, "He really cares for you."

"Yes, we've talked about this Connor." She said tenderly.

"I know."

At that moment Bliss' stomach growled loudly, and Connor chuckled. "Time to feed my girl." He said as he turned back to the steering wheel and put his seat belt back on. Bliss followed his lead.

"Diner?" Connor asked.

"Yes, love the diner."

They finished eating and Bliss was delighted that she could now feed herself without the cumbersome cast and heavy bandage. Connor had watched the joy spread over Bliss' face as she carefully picked up her cheeseburger and bit into it. Connor's cell rang as they were getting back into the car and Bliss knew it was work related by the number of, "Yes, Sir's." that Connor's said.

"Well?" Bliss asked anxiously.

"I have to go to Fort Bragg. Andy's flown in."

"Crap."

"I have to make sure Andy doesn't get into trouble. He's our pilot. He would have been the only one able to fly the Black Hawk. Shit."

They drove home in silence. Bliss noticed a beige car sitting on the corner, but she remained quiet. There was no way she could tell Connor about her suspicions now. He had enough to worry about. When they got home Connor went into the study with his dad and when they came out, he gave Bliss a small smile and ran upstairs to grab his duffel.

Rose was looking at the General. "Where's he going?" The General put his arm around his wife. "He has to go to Fort Bragg. It's routine." Rose slapped at the Generals hand. "You're an awful liar." She said, but Bliss could see that she appreciated her husband's attempt to not worry her.

"He'll be okay." The General told her.

Connor returned dressed in his regulation uniform.

"Where's Collin and Caitlyn?" Connor asked.

"Shopping," Bliss said, repeating what Rose had just

told her.

Connor hugged his mom and shook the Generals hand, and then took Bliss by her hand and they walked outside to his rental car.

"I hate that I have to leave." Bliss leaned into his arm and gave it a little playful nudge. "I know. Do you think you'll be able to come back before your leave is over?"

"Unless I'm in the brig, I will be back." He said jokingly. He turned to Bliss and wrapped her in a strong embrace, giving her a sizzling kiss.

"That wasn't a good joke, Connor." Bliss said breathlessly after they separated.

Connor grinned, "Yeah, but that was a good kiss." He grinned cockily.

Bliss grinned, "Yes, that was a good kiss."

"Stay safe Sweetheart. I'll call as soon as I know anything."

"I love you Connor." She whispered into his ear.

"I love you too. Be cautious, okay?"

"Promise." A small niggle of unfaithfulness slid up her spine knowing she was keeping a secret from him. Bliss watched as the car drove away and she felt a heavy weight fill her chest. She sent a prayer to God that Connor came out of this okay. It would kill her if he lost his Military career because of her.

Chapter 17

The next day Caitlyn and Collin insisted that Bliss come back into the city with them. Collin's roommate was away for a week and he had a king-sized bed that Caitlyn and Bliss would share. The General had called Dr. Tanner and told her that Bliss was taking her up on her medical R and R and Bliss had called her Physical Therapist canceling her upcoming appointments.

Caitlyn was ecstatic that she had someone to play with, as she called it. She had the week planned; they were going shopping, having a spa day, going to a play, and going dancing. Bliss groaned when she said they were going dancing.

When they got into the city Collin parked in his apartment's parking garage and they took the elevator to the first floor. They got off and he took Bliss to the front desk where a security man was sitting.

"Howard, this is Bliss. She's going to be staying with me for a week. Can you cut her a card please?"

The security man took Bliss' picture and within a minute she had a card with her face on it. He handed it to Bliss. "This card will give you access to the front door, back door and garage door. It's good for one week. If you're here longer, come back with Mr. Doherty and I'll reprogram it. If you lose it, please tell Mr. Doherty immediately."

Bliss took the card from the man and noticed there was no address on the card. It just had her face and a series of random numbers. She thanked him and then tucked the card into her wallet.

They took the elevator to the tenth floor. Bliss hadn't been in Collins apartment before and when he opened the door Bliss gasped.

"Collin it's beautiful." She said running to the window to look out onto the street below. Collin was grinning and Caitlyn giggled. "It seems my brother has very good taste." She said.

"Did you decorate it yourself?" Bliss asked looking around at the large living area. "Pretty much. Caitlyn helped with some of the furniture. I picked out the colors though." He said proud of himself.

The room was well lit and had large ceiling to floor windows. Bliss could see there was a sliding door that led out to a small balcony. A dining area was set up next to an open kitchen. Everything was done in beige, browns, blues and greens.

"Is this your roommates' stuff, too?"

"No, he's renting the room from me. I own the apartment."

"Well it's fantastic; no wonder you can't get rid of Caitlyn." Bliss teased.

"Hey!" Caitlyn laughed.

Bliss and Caitlyn headed out as soon as they got settled. Caitlyn was determined to get Bliss some clothes that weren't camouflaged colored, sweats, or had ARMY written across the chest. Bliss knew she couldn't argue. It wasn't like she didn't have money either. She had only spent a small amount of what her mom had left her and that was on the eye surgery. Bliss decided a shopping spree might be the perfect distraction for her and she needed the distraction. She already was missing Connor.

Three hours later Bliss was exhausted. Caitlyn had taken her for a manicure, pedicure, and facial, and then they had hit the shops. Bliss thought back to when the salon worker had seen the bottom of her feet and had actually cringed. Bliss told her she'd been in a car accident and then she lifted her soft brace up hoping to add credence to the lie. The salon worker bought Bliss' story and began telling Bliss about a car accident her brother had been in. The young girl did a wonderful job and gave Bliss a primo pedicure. She had spent more than average time gently massaging the angry lines on Bliss' feet. After stopping in countless stores, Bliss couldn't hold any more bags in her hands. Her weakened muscles were getting a better work out today, shopping, than anything Hank, her PT, could have made her do. Luckily, they had taken a cab everywhere they had gone, and the pedicure had been wonderful so Bliss' feet felt great. Caitlyn was jabbering away about the restaurant that Collin was taking them to that evening. It had been featured on a morning show that Caitlyn had seen, and she was sure that they would see at least one television star.

As they turned the corner onto the block that Collins apartment was on Bliss' phone rang. She looked at her screen and saw Connor's name on the screen. She quickly shoved her bags into Caitlyn's hands and answered it.

"Hey."

"Hey yourself. You sound breathless. Are you working out?"

Bliss laughed. "Kind of. I'm shopping with your sister."

She heard Connor chuckle. "So they talked you into going to the city?"

"Yeah, how did you know?"

"Dad told me they were going to try, when we talked before I left."

"So, how's it going?"

"I'm waiting for Andy to get out of his meeting. Then I go in."

"Oh Connor. I'm so sorry about this."

"Don't you worry, Honey. Oh wait, here they come now. I'll call you later." He then hung up.

Caitlyn handed Bliss back some of her bags keeping a few to help carry. "So, what's my awesome big brother up to?"

"He's getting ready to go into a meeting. He'll call later." Bliss told her, silently praying that the next time they talked she hoped it would include him telling her he wasn't in trouble.

They walked towards the large glass doors of Collins apartment building. The sidewalks were busy with people hurrying home from work and the weather was turning colder. It was March and the wind in New York City was whipping around the tall buildings, making people duck their faces into the cover of their coats.

Bliss dropped one of the smaller bags she was clutching in her stiffening fingers and when she turned to retrieve it, she saw a man quickly step into a doorway behind her. His face was lowered into his coat and he had on a black felt fedora hat that he was holding to his head. It was just how he moved into the doorway and when, that set Bliss' Spidey senses into overdrive.

She quickly stomped on the escaped bags handle before it skittered down the sidewalk and when she bent to pick it up, she covertly looked towards the doorway again. Seeing nothing out of the ordinary, she felt silly thinking that someone may be following her. The sidewalks were jam packed with people and it wasn't unusual to be jostled by a passerby. Bliss wasn't a city person. She craved open spaces and walking right next to persons she didn't know had her in a hyper aware state. When they reached the apartments' front doors the doorman recognized Caitlyn and opened the door for them. As soon as they were inside, off of the hectic New York City sidewalk, Bliss was able to relax.

The two women unpacked their purchases and waited for Collin to come home from the office. Bliss had bought two dresses and a pair of wedge black patent leathers that remarkably did not hurt her feet. She had purchased some new makeup, and in Victoria's Secret she bought new under garments and a teddy that she couldn't wait to wear for Connor. Connor had still not called back, and although Bliss was becoming anxious, she was determined to enjoy her mini vacation, so she vowed to only think good thoughts. A long bubble bath and a glass of wine helped to put Bliss in a more relaxed mood.

Bliss had chosen to wear one of her new dresses. A bright red wrap around that clung to her curves. It wasn't provocative, at least it hadn't been on the mannequin, but the way the silky material clung to her, accentuated her body in a very sexy way. When she had looked in the mirror, before they had left, she had almost taken it off thinking the dress was too showy, but Caitlyn had told her that she looked wonderful, and to stop being silly.

Bliss still had her one arm wrapped in a soft cast and her hands had small flesh colored bandages on them, but the long sleeves of the dress hid the cast, and the bandages were hardly noticeable. Caitlyn had done her makeup and her hair and Bliss noticed how her eyes popped with just the small application of eyeliner Caitlyn had used. Bliss kept sneaking peeks at herself in the mirror. It was still so foreign to her to look good, and she realized that she looked good.

Two hours and quick cab ride later they arrived at Carina's. The place was packed, there was standing room only at the small bar and every table appeared full. Carina's was dimly lit and each centerpiece containing beautiful Lily's which were wrapped in strands of tiny white lights. Caitlyn was appropriately stunned into silence, which Bliss found amusing. The place was oozing with sophistication. They checked their coats at the door and Bliss noticed, as she and Caitlyn made their way to their table, that men were openly stared at them. At first Bliss thought they were just looking at Caitlyn, she was the beauty, but as they made their way towards a table near a large window Bliss saw that the men's eyes were following her as well. Garnering positive attention was still such a novelty to her that she felt like checking to make sure she wasn't unzipped or dragging toilet paper under her heels. Half way to their table she relaxed and delighted in the fact that she did look good and these men were simply appreciating that.

The Maître de seated them immediately at a very prominent table near a window and Bliss noticed that

there were three more place settings. She looked to
Collin who smiled sheepishly, "I invited a few
friends."
"Oh good," squealed Caitlyn, "the more the merrier."
Bliss instantly became uncomfortable. She wasn't
comfortable around people she didn't
know and she was miffed that Collin hadn't told her.
He knew that she was shy. He leaned into her, "Come
on Bliss. It will be fun. You'll like my friends."
"I don't know. I"
She was interrupted by a man saying, "Great table!"
Bliss turned, as did Collin to see two men and a
woman approaching the table.
Collin shook the hands of the men and deposited a
small kiss to the cheek of the woman. The men were
grinning as they looked at her and Caitlyn and Bliss
couldn't help but feel they were about to Rock, Paper,
Scissors each other to see who got which girl.
"Caitlyn, Bliss, these are my friends from work; Greg,
David, and Lisa. Caitlyn, I think you've met Lisa
before, right?"
Caitlyn shook Lisa's hand and said yes, and the men
and Lisa all said hello to Bliss. The six of them settled
into the table and Bliss found herself sitting between
David and Greg. Dinner conversation ranged from the
Knicks, the upcoming Presidential election and
grievances about their jobs or the people they worked
with. Bliss remained quiet during much of the
conversation. She was content listening to the lively
group of five. Hearing them complain about a late
subway train or how a co-worker had not made
another pot of coffee after pouring the last cup made
Bliss realize that her priorities were very different

from theirs, and she was once again grateful that she had connected with Connor, who was so much like her. She didn't begrudge them their life choices, but she also didn't envy them either. Her life was perfect for her. She loved the regimentation of being in the Army, and the fact that she was doing something that she considered necessary for her country. Her fellow soldiers were her friends and family. Hearing Caitlyn laugh out loud brought Bliss back from day dreaming. The meal was fantastic, and except for the fact that Bliss was somewhat uneasy because Greg was seriously flirting with her, she would have actually enjoyed herself. Bliss unconsciously fingered her necklace, wishing Caitlyn would stop flirting with David and talk to her. David kept looking past Caitlyn to her and it made Bliss feel uncomfortable.

"What did you do to your arm?" Greg asked trying to pour more wine into her glass. Bliss placed her hand over the goblet indicating she did not want any more and told him that she had been in a car accident. She decided the fabrication had worked once, perhaps it would work again.

"So tell me what you do for a living." Greg asked hoping to draw Bliss into conversation.

Bliss didn't want to tell them that she was in the Army, not unless she had too. She knew from experience that it would lead to more questions, ones, she did not want to answer, not with civilians. "I work with computers." She told him.

Bliss asked him what he did, and he told her he was a lawyer and he worked for the city. He was an Assistant District Attorney. Bliss used that bit of info to ask him questions and to keep him from delving any further into her life.

"So do you have a boyfriend?" Greg asked giving her a sexy grin.

"Yes, I do." She realized that Greg wasn't expecting that answer and she saw him look to Collin who had also heard her answer. Collin frowned and shrugged his shoulders. He then looked to Bliss who gave him a 'what's up?' look.

The waiter came to the table with the check, which Collin paid.

"Hey, I'm having way too much fun. How about we hit another bar?" Lisa said speaking to the table but looking at Collin with a sexy little pout on her perfect lips.

Everyone readily agreed, except for Bliss who was really starting to worry because Connor had not called her back yet.

"Bliss?" Collin asked. She realized everyone was staring at her and she felt her face become heated with an embarrassed blush.

"I, um, well I guess if everyone wants..." She couldn't even finish her sentence before Caitlyn began animatedly discussing where they should go. Bliss sat back in her chair exasperated. Her hands hurt and her feet ached. She'd done more walking today, than she had in a week back in Jersey. She should have said no, but she didn't feel like dealing with the guilt crap she knew Caitlyn and Collin would lay on her. Bliss decided that she would go for one drink and then beg to leave, claiming she had a headache. She had to give Greg some credit. He knew she wasn't happy about extending her night out and he discreetly offered to take her home. His car was valet parked.

He whispered that if she really wanted to go that he would drop the others off at the bar and then take her back to Collins.

Bliss told him that she appreciated the offer, but she'd go for a drink. She just hoped that wherever they went it wasn't too far from Collins apartment.

The group settled on a club that was right around the corner from where Collin lived. Bliss hadn't realized how late it was until they got inside the club and she looked at her phone hoping to see that Connor had texted. He hadn't, and that's when she noticed that it was after 11:00pm. Bliss couldn't imagine what was keeping him from calling her. He knew that she was worried.

The group found a table off to the side and ordered drinks. The DJ was spinning terrific music and Caitlyn and Lisa finally cajoled Bliss into joining them on the dance floor. Bliss was starting to enjoy herself. Her feet felt pretty good and she loved dancing, what harm could one dance do, she thought? Both Caitlyn and Lisa complimented her, saying they wish they could move the way she did, which bolstered Bliss' confidence. The three women were facing each other in a small circle when Bliss felt hands grasp her hips and pull her backwards into a gyrating pelvis of a male. Bliss turned to look over her shoulder as she grabbed the man's hands quickly taking them off of her. It was David. He was laughing and he tried again to attach himself to Bliss' backside. Bliss stepped away from him, she was furious. He was lucky she hadn't knocked his dumb ass to the floor. Caitlyn was looking at him with a shocked expression on her face and Bliss knew that she was upset because she had been hoping David liked her. Bliss left the dance floor followed by Caitlyn. Lisa and David stayed, and Bliss breathed a sigh of relief that he wasn't following her. Before they got to the table, Bliss caught Caitlyn by her arm.

"Caitlyn, I'm sorry. He's a douche. I wasn't flirting with him."

Caitlyn smiled, but Bliss could see she was hurt. "I know. I heard you tell Greg you had a boyfriend. I always pick the wrong guys." She said with a dejected smirk.

"Greg's actually very nice. You should talk to him." Caitlyn said that she would, and they headed for the table. When they got there Collin was putting his phone away and Greg stood up like a gentleman and waited until they sat back down before he did.

"See." Bliss whispered to Caitlyn, "and he's a gentleman. Rose would love him." Bliss giggled causing Caitlyn to give her playful nudge with her elbow.

They each had another drink, except Greg, who was being a responsible designated driver. An hour after they had arrived, they left the bar. Everyone except David piled into Greg's car. David lived in the opposite direction and he was getting a cab. Both Bliss and Caitlyn were relieved that they would not have to feign polite conversation with him.

Greg left Collin, Bliss, and Caitlyn off at their door setting off a chorus of 'thank you" to Collin for dinner, and pleasant, 'it was nice meeting you' goodbyes. All in all, it wasn't a bad night Bliss thought as they rode the elevator to Collins floor.

Dinner had been good, really good actually. Greg turned out to be a nice guy and once she had told him she had a boyfriend he had completely backed off with the flirting, which Bliss totally appreciated. The only blemish on the otherwise fun evening was David pawing her on the dance floor. That unwelcomed moment was something she definitely hadn't appreciated. Bliss once again checked her phone and saw that Connor still hadn't called. She was so worried.

When she got into the apartment, Bliss headed for the bathroom in the hallway and when she came out Caitlyn was yelling at Collin. Collin was shaking his head, and Bliss could see that Caitlyn was infuriated with him.

"Tell her!" Caitlyn said to Collin, pointing at Bliss. Collin froze noticing Bliss was standing in the opening of the living area. "Tell her right now Collin or I swear..."

"Tell me what?"

Caitlyn crossed her arms and came to stand by Bliss. Whatever was going on was not the usual brother sister squabble. This involved her.

"Caitlyn." Collin whispered completely embarrassed by whatever he was supposed to show her.

He was holding his phone in his hand and Caitlyn swiped it from him.

"No!" He yelled trying to get it back.

"Collin sent a picture of you to Connor." Caitlyn blurted out.

Bliss looked to Collin still not understanding why that might be a bad thing.

"Look." Caitlyn said holding the phone up for Bliss to

see.

Collin had taken a picture of the exact moment that David had chosen to rub up against her. She was looking over her shoulder at him and it appeared as if they were dancing together in a very suggestive way. Bliss gasped, and Caitlyn tossed the phone back to Collin. "You're an ass!" Caitlyn spat at her brother. "Why?" Was all Bliss could choke out. A mix of emotions flooded her; betrayal, sadness, hurt, and most prevalent was how mad she was.

Collin looked upset, but Bliss could see that he wasn't sorry he had sent the picture. He was just sorry he'd been caught. He knew how that picture would appear to Connor, and he knew his brother would lose it. He had done it on purpose, hoping to drive them apart. He never answered her. Bliss turned from them and headed into the bedroom. She immediately started packing her small duffel. Caitlyn followed her in. "Where are you going?" Caitlyn asked clearly upset. "Don't know yet." She answered briskly. Then Bliss remembered that Caitlyn was just as mad as she was at Collin. "Thank you, Caitlyn, for telling me."

"I don't get it Bliss. That was just mean."

Bliss nodded. Someone she cared for, like a brother, had just sabotaged the one thing she cared the most about, her and Connor's new relationship.

"Bliss, please sleep here tonight. We will iron it out in the morning." Bliss looked at the clock.

"Caitlyn, I love you and your family. You guys saved me, and you have no idea how much I appreciate that. Collin must be pretty dead set against Connor and I being together for him to do something so cruel. I won't come between members of your family. I love

Connor, but I won't hurt your family. Plus, he hasn't called me back. Now I know why. He's probably seen the picture and I'm sure he's off having a good time."

Caitlyn was flabbergasted, "Wait, that's it! You aren't even going to talk to him? Fight for him?"

Bliss sat down on the bed her shoulders sagged defeated. "I would die for him Caitlyn. He's everything to me, but so is your family. If Connor saw that picture and thought I was with someone, he will be really hurt. If he is with another woman because of that picture, I won't be able to take it."

"Listen to yourself. You're full of what ifs. Bliss, call Connor, you know him better than anyone. He's not going to take that picture at face value. Call him!"

Bliss sighed heavily maybe she should call him. She picked up her phone and put it on speaker. She knew it was late, but she did want to know what happened at the meeting, and she wanted a chance to explain about the picture.

The phone was ringing and when it was answered, Bliss' heart thumped happily. "Hello." A sultry female voice answered. Caitlyn looked as shocked as Bliss. "Um, hi, I'm looking for Connor."

"This is his phone sugar." Bliss heard the woman giggling, "but he's currently occupied." The woman hung up after another rush of giggles.

Bliss looked up to Caitlyn. Her heart was splintering into a million pieces and Caitlyn, who was normally a chatterbox, stood next to her with an expression that Bliss could only describe as pity.

Bliss stood up from the bed and started shoveling the remaining clothes in her bag. She grabbed her coat and gave Caitlyn a hug.

"I love you, Caitlyn."

"Bliss, please don't leave."

"Caitlyn I'm so mad at Collin, I'm afraid I'll dismantle him." This caused Caitlyn to smile. "You could too." She said.

"I need to think things out. I'll be in touch okay?"

"What about Connor?"

"What about him?"

"He loves you Bliss; I know he does."

Bliss shook her head. "I thought so, too. No, I know he does, but that picture may have done too much damage."

"I'm going to beat Collin up myself." Caitlyn said tersely.

Bliss drew the strap of the duffel over her shoulder and walked into the living room where Collin was standing, staring out the large glass window.

"Where are you going?" He said moving towards her. Bliss didn't answer.

"She's not staying here with you. You idiot!" Caitlyn lambasted him.

Bliss opened the front door and let herself out. She could hear Caitlyn starting in on Collin again and she had a moment of regret that she had caused a rift in the wonderful family that had taken her in.

Bliss handed her ID badge to the doorman and he followed her outside.

"Cab, miss?"

"Yes, please."

He hailed a taxi and Bliss asked to be taken to Grand Central Station. She had no idea where she was going to go. She wasn't going back to Jersey, that was about the only thing she did know.

Chapter 18

Inside Grand Central Station it was relatively quiet
compared to the other times Bliss had been inside the
beautiful and expansive train hub. Bliss knew it was
because there were very few trains running at that late
hour. The first thing Bliss did was to seek out a
restroom change into a pair of jeans, a tee shirt, her
worn gray Army sweatshirt, and sneakers.

She then left the restroom and found a coffee shop
that was still open. She sat at the counter and
protectively tucked her duffel between her legs and
the counter. A half hour later Bliss was feeling the
welcomed buzz of the caffeine, so feeling fortified,
she paid and headed down the long corridor towards
the large area that housed the overhead departure and
arrival information.

There were very few people waiting and a quick
check to her watch told her it was almost midnight.
She noticed that one of the AMTRAK trains was
departing for North Carolina in an hour. She wanted
to hop that train and find Connor, but she was
apprehensive. She couldn't believe that he could toss
away their new relationship because of a photo.
Maybe, his meeting had gone badly, and he blamed
her? No, Caitlyn was right, it wasn't like him. Yet,
that photo Collin sent could have pushed him to do
something he had done before; he may have found
another 'Red' to ease his pain. Somehow Bliss didn't
think so though. She had no idea who the woman was
that had answered Connor's phone, but Connor was a

good guy. She trusted him, hell she loved him, and he had said he loved her. No, she needed to talk to him. If they were through, then she needed the closure that only talking to him in person would bring.

Bliss hurried to the ticket counter and purchased a seat in the car that had internet. She didn't have her computer, but she had her iPad. The train left Grand Central heading for Fayetteville. It was scheduled to arrive in twelve hours, at 1:00 AM.

Bliss settled into a window seat and sat back watching the landscape change from city to country. She thought about trying to sleep, but between the coffee she had and thinking about Connor, she was too wired. She pulled up the tray attached to her seat so she could place her iPad on it. She was going to email Connor, let him know she was coming and that she hoped they could talk. As she reached into her duffel, she glimpsed a man, wearing a black fedora hat, sitting a few rows back from where she was. She couldn't see the man's face and she didn't want to be caught staring. She pulled her iPad up onto the lap table and sat back trying to reign in the ominous feeling that was surging through her.

Bliss needed to think logically and not let her imagination cloud her normally good judgment. The beige car she knew had been following her. There was no way that was a coincidence, and now a man wearing a black fedora had popped up twice in one day. She tried to argue with herself that fedoras were in style, and surely there were many men wearing them, yet Bliss couldn't shake the apprehension building in her gut, and Bliss had learned to trust her gut.

Bliss forgot about emailing Connor. She had to find out for sure if she was being followed and then she had to figure out why. She used her iPad to look up the AMTRAK stops between New York and Fayetteville and saw they would stop in Washington DC.

It was five hours away and she knew the city. Bliss then reserved a rental car. A flicker on her screen drew her attention and it was then that she realized that her iPad activity might be being monitored. She knew there were a few good Apps available, such as mSpy, but Bliss being a computer geek herself, regularly checked her iPad for spyware. If she was being monitored it wasn't through any store-bought software. If her iPad had been hacked it had to be FBI/CIA caliber spyware. Bliss canceled the reservation for the car and shut down her iPad. She turned off her phone as well.

Bliss decided to get off the train in Alexandria. If her iPad was being monitored someone could have seen that she had rented a car in D.C., alerting them to the fact that she would be getting off there. She decided that if the man in the fedora followed her off the train in Alexandria, she would try at least one more furtive move, just to be sure. If he continued to dog her, then she knew she was in trouble. She had no idea who might be following her and Connor's intuition, that she could still be in danger, knowing the information she still possessed was still viable, sent a prickly sliver of fear through her.

Bliss couldn't risk turning her iPhone or iPad back on, and she also realized that she needed to ditch them in case a tracking signal had been embedded on them.

She placed them under her sweatshirt and stood up, and then using a loud whisper, asked the woman sitting across from her to watch her bag while she went to the restroom. Normally, Bliss would never leave her bag unattended, but she wanted to appear relaxed and naive. Bliss walked towards the restroom, past the man who had now taken his fedora off. She wanted a glimpse of his face, but it was conveniently obscured behind a newspaper. She did see that he had a black coat folded on the seat next to him and a pair of brown leather gloves lay on top of that. Just like what the man in the city had on.

Bliss walked through the next car scrutinizing the faces of everyone she saw, but no one looked familiar or showed any interest in her. In the restroom, Bliss turned the water on and sunk her iPhone and iPad into the small sink. She hoped she had gotten them wet enough to disable them, but she wasn't done yet. On her way back to her seat, she stopped before she entered her car, and wedged the iPhone and the iPad into the skinny garbage chute next to the door. If there was a GPS attached to either device it would still show, to whomever may be monitoring her, that she was still on the train. Bliss returned to her seat and thanked the woman for watching her duffel. She then pulled the duffel up onto her lap and pretending to use it as a pillow to sleep. She arranged her body so that her back was blocking any views from the large mirrors near the doors. Bliss reached into her duffel and surreptitiously took out her wallet, squirreling it away into the large front pocket of her sweatshirt. She hated that she was going to leave her duffel bag that had all her new clothes behind, but they could all be replaced. She wasn't even going to take her coat. She also realized that everything she was doing could be for naught, but her gut told her differently. The car, the black fedora, and now the small blip on her iPad could all be coincidence. Bliss decided it was better to play it safe. She needed to find out for sure if she was being tracked.

Four and a half hours later the scratchy voice of the conductor came over the loud speaker alerting the riders that the next station was Alexandria. The train stopped and

Bliss pretended to sleep while a few passengers shuffled off the train and a few came on. When Bliss saw that the conductor was about to close the doors she bolted from her seat and into the small exit/entrance area. She jumped from the top step and instantly regretted the move as pain resonated from her feet causing her to yelp. Pushing the pain aside, Bliss quickly jogged to the side of the well-lit station building and down the stairs to the parking lot. She ran to a car parked at the edge of the lot where she could see anyone coming from the station and ducked behind it and waited.

Less than a minute later the man carrying his coat, gloves and fedora jogged down the steps. She watched as he looked around the lot and then to Bliss' surprise, the woman that had been sitting across from her joined him. They spoke for a few moments, the man seemed agitated with the woman, and then Bliss saw the man use his cell phone. The woman spoke to him and Bliss saw him pointing at the train that was pulling away from the station. Bliss knew that he had just checked where her iPhone and iPad were. Well, that answers that, Bliss thought mordantly, she was definitely being followed. Bliss remained hidden behind the car. She still had to lose them, and she had no idea if anyone else had been on the train with her that hadn't shown themselves yet.

Bliss took in her surroundings and realized she was probably on camera in the small car lot. She had to make a move, so she simply stood up and walked towards the exit. She knew she was exposing herself, but she needed to get someplace safe as fast as possible. Bliss hurried towards the small booth that housed the parking lot attendant. An older man inside the booth saw her and gave her a big toothy smile.

"You need a taxi?" He asked from the warmth of his small glass booth.

"I do."

"Wait right there." The elderly man said giving her a grand grin. The older man was putting on a coat and saying something to another man in the booth. Bliss looked around anxiously. She saw that the man and woman were now jogging towards her and for a brief moment Bliss didn't know whether she should confront them, or she should run.

The younger man affectionately slapped the older man on the shoulder as he left the booth. The older man motioned for Bliss to follow him. In a parking space right next to the booth was a black sedan. The man pointed at it and then put on a ball cap that said Pap's Taxi.

"It's my day time job." He said chuckling.

Bliss jumped into the back seat and from the safety of the car watched as the man and woman slow their pace to a walk. The man was talking on his phone again and she knew he was reciting the license plate of the car that she was in to whomever he was talking to.

The taxi driver introduced himself as he turned out of the lot; his name was Pap's, of course.

"So, where can I take you little lady?"

Bliss didn't want to be in the car for too long. She didn't want to risk it for her sake or Pap's. She had enough cash to get a room and whichever hotel she chose needed to have guest computers. She still needed to make sure she had lost her tail.

Bliss asked Pap's to drop her off at the Alexandria bus terminal. It took them twenty minutes. Bliss paid for the cab ride in cash and tipped Pap's well. She told Pap's if anyone asked about her that he was not to lie, just tell the truth. Pap's gave her a questioning look and then nodded.

He handed her his business card, in case she needed another ride, but Bliss would never call him. It was too chancy.

At the bus terminal Bliss bought a one-way ticket to New Mexico, because it was the next bus leaving the station. She waited in the line of passengers boarding, being careful to keep her head down. The bus driver, who was moving down the line of wiring to board passengers, was collecting tickets. He took hers and she stepped towards the bus door, but then she pretended she had dropped something. Bliss stealthily moved out of the line, successfully slipping behind another bus to hide. She then reentered the terminal, using a different door, hidden amongst a group of passengers that had disembarked from another bus.

She stayed near the small group, pretending to be with them and exited the terminal.

Bliss walked a block away from the terminal before hailing a taxi, which she took to a hotel off 495. She went into the hotel, stopping at the desk for appearance purposes only, asking a benign question, and then she exited from a different door. She walked to the large fast food restaurant next door and after using the restroom, she left the restaurant and headed to yet another hotel, that was on the other side of the restaurant. The entire time Bliss was on high alert. She figured if they had sophisticated enough spyware to hack into her iPhone then they could certainly hack cameras around the city to look and monitor her.

Bliss walked to the front desk, pretending that she was a registered guest and asked them to call a cab for her. The persons at the desk were polite and asked if she needed to settle her bill, but Bliss told them she was staying with them for a few days and that satisfied them.

Bliss took the cab that arrived for her and had the driver drop her between four prominent downtown hotels, one of them being a Marriott, which she knew had a free buffet breakfast, and more importantly guest computers, so that's where she was headed. Inside the hotel she paid for a room on the first floor with cash and immediately went to the breakfast buffet. It was after 11:00am and she made it to breakfast just as the staff began to clear it. Bliss was aware of everyone she saw. She kept her head down when she passed people and hurriedly packed her plate with eggs and a bagel.

Bliss carried her breakfast to her room and double

locked her room with the chain and dead bolt after attaching the do not disturb sign on her door handle. She wolfed down her breakfast, showered, and got into the bed. She thought that she'd crash the second her head hit her pillow, but her mind was replaying, revisiting everything that had happened in the last twelve hours, and worst of all, was that she kept hearing the woman's voice telling her that Connor was occupied. Finally, she fell into a restless sleep. When Bliss awoke, she saw that it was almost 4:00 in the afternoon. She had to make some decisions and luckily the few hours of sleep that she had were enough for her to feel rejuvenated and that allowed her to think rationally.

She couldn't run for the rest of her life. Hell, if she didn't check in with someone this week, she'd be considered AWOL. She also had no idea what she was up against, who these people were or even what they wanted. Bliss came to the common-sense decision that she needed to get in touch with Connor. Even if Connor thought she had hooked up with someone, even if he had hooked up with someone, the one thing Bliss was sure of was that Connor would help her. He was the one person she unequivocally trusted.

Bliss decided that she would email him. It needed to be a coded message but appear like a normal email. She had to let him know where she was going and hoped he would be able to meet her. She still had no idea what had transpired at his meeting and hoped he was able to get his emails. She thought about how to make the email seem commonplace. Something that no one would think out of the ordinary.

Bliss knew once she sent the email, she was going to have to leave the hotel quickly and she had to get some more cash to hold her over until she was safe again. Most ATM's only allowed for a five-hundred-dollar withdrawal limit, so Bliss decided she would hit three ATM's as fast as she could, hopefully staying a step ahead of whoever was tracking her. She knew, without a doubt, that her credit card was being monitored. Once that pinged, they would know exactly where she was.

Bliss formulated a plan, one she prayed would work. She showered again and then left her room to find the computers for hotel guests. First Bliss had to create an email address that hopefully Connor would recognize, and if his email was being monitored, it had to look as if it was coming from someone other than herself. Bliss invented Magoo815@gmail.com. Magoo, of course, was the name she'd been called for years before her operation and 815 was the date she and Connor had flown to Afghanistan together. Next, she found the coordinates for Manchester, Vermont. Bliss had been to Manchester a few times. It was one of her favorite places. Her mom had taken her and Jax there when they were younger. She'd learned to ski on Bromley, a small mountain between Manchester and Londonderry. She loved the area; it was serene and beautiful no matter what the season.

Lastly, Bliss Googled pro baseball players attempting to find players with the numbers that matched the map coordinates to Manchester. It wasn't easy, and she tried to stick with Mets and Yankee players, but she couldn't do that either. Finally, she was ready to email Connor.

The subject line was from Magoo

Dear C.,

I just wanted to write and tell you that I had a wonderful time on our date last night. I know you won't be Stateside for much longer, but I really hope to see you before you go. It was great talking sports with you. Most men don't like it when woman know sports, so I was excited when we were able to discuss my upcoming Fantasy baseball picks. I'm going to add Addison Reed, Starlin Castro, and Mason Williams, who is a reverse hitter to my roster. Then I'm thinking of Gary Sanchez, Ryan Braun, and I wish Brian Wilson still played because I'd totally pick him. That song from Annie you were singing on the way home last night has been stuck in my head all day. Thanks a lot. Oh, and next time we go for a late night, post drinking meal, no jelly for you, you'll never get that stain out. Thanks again, Your Magoo

Bliss hit send and then headed for the front desk. She had until tomorrow to get to Manchester, Vermont, and she prayed that Connor would meet her at The Jelly Mill, a well-known tourist stop.

Chapter 19

Bliss called the front desk and asked them to call her cab. Her bill was paid so she did not need to stop when she checked out. While she waited for the cab outside, away from any hotel cameras, she took off her Army sweatshirt, turning it inside out, and put it back on. The cab came and she had the driver stop at three stores that advertised having ATM's. With a sufficient supply of cash and what she hoped was a solid game plan, Bliss felt like she had taken some control back. She had the driver drop her a block away from the same bus station she'd been at earlier. As she walked to the terminal she stopped at a small store. Bliss bought travel snacks, a Raven's knit hat, gloves, sunglasses, a magazine, and a book. She put on the gloves, sunglasses, and hat, stuffing her blond curls completely into the cap and donned the large sunglasses. Inside the terminal, Bliss purchased three, one-way tickets, one to Manchester, one to New York City, and one to Fayetteville, North Carolina. If these people were somehow still tracking her, she knew that they would think that she would go to North Carolina. There was no doubt in her mind that there were people, in the terminal watching for her, or even scarier, that they had hacked into the terminal's security footage, giving them views of everything including arrivals and departures.

Bliss took off her cap and sweatshirt in a bathroom and held her head up giving cameras a good view of her. She once again pretended to board a bus; this one was the one headed to Fayetteville. Using the same fake drop and dodge routine that she had used earlier, she ducked behind columns and buses, carefully avoiding the security cameras. She quickly put the cap and sunglasses back on, and boarded her bus bound for Vermont.

Bliss settled into a seat in the last row. Her heart was racing as she looked around suspiciously. Satisfied that she had made it aboard the North bound bus without a tail she rolled her sweatshirt up in a ball and rested her head against it. She had an eleven-hour bus ride ahead of her.

She was too amped up to sleep, even though she had only slept a few hours. She kept thinking about Connor and wondered what he had thought when he had seen the picture. She thought about Collin and was immediately saddened by the thought that he didn't think she and Connor were good for each other. She smiled remembering how Caitlyn had lit into him. Lastly, she thought about the man and woman, and God knows who else that was following her. She couldn't help but wonder if her kidnapping in Afghanistan was somehow connected to all this. Connor had said he didn't like that she had been stripped naked. Al Qaeda deplored female's showing any skin. She thought about the man with the blue eyes and wondered how he played into her kidnapping.

The only thing that made sense was if someone still wanted the information, she had given General Jones, just like Connor had said. Bliss slowly sifted through all the Normandy status emails she had delivered while in Afghanistan.

Bliss had memorized so much intel, that if what she

knew were to fall into enemy hands, it could be potentially dangerous. She knew locations of munitions, and where certain Battalions would be on specific dates. She knew information regarding drone reconnaissance, and even personal information, such as names of soldiers and where they were assigned. What scared her the most was the fact that Zarghun and Blue Eyes seemed to know that she could recite the information that they wanted. There were very few people that knew about her gift.

The bus drove up Route 95 stopping in Philly, and Trenton. Then it turned on to 84 where they stopped in Harrisburg, and Albany, New York. The ride was long and whenever the bus had stopped everyone would get off, except her. She pretended to be sleeping, but she was just being vigilant watching for any new persons boarding. After Albany, the bus got on Route 7A and Bliss tried to relax by watching the snow-covered mountains and quaint barns along the route. She knew they were getting close to Manchester when they passed Basketville, a shop that her mom had loved that specializing in every kind, size, and shape of baskets.

Bliss couldn't believe how nervous she was. What if Connor never saw her email? What if it had gone to his spam box? She was trying to calculate how long it would take him to get to Manchester from North Carolina, but the ways he could get there were numerous, so she just gave up. The bus was due to arrive in Manchester at 9:00 AM. Bliss looked at her watch which read that it was almost 8:50 AM. Bliss put her sweatshirt back on, making sure it was still inside out and stuffed her hair underneath the black and purple Raven's cap.

The bus drove past The Jelly Mill and Bliss saw that the parking lot only had a few cars in it, most likely employees, because the sign out front announced it opened at 10:00 AM. The bus came to a stop just past the center of Manchester's main intersection. Bliss noticed that the town was just waking up. A few shopkeepers were shoveling the inch of snow they must have gotten the night before and Bliss watched as they smiled and chatted with persons walking past them. This was life in a small town. Not that Manchester was really small, but it was intimate enough where everyone knew everyone.

Bliss put on her sunglasses and along with a mother carrying a child got off the bus. Bliss watched as a man greeted the mother and child and immediately engulfed them in a loving embrace. The sweet family reunion triggered an unexpected feeling of sorrow in Bliss that hit her like she'd been sucker punched. She felt the loneliness of having no family, except for Jax, who was never around, and basically unreachable. Bliss fought back the despondency she was feeling. She had to remain focused.

Bliss walked down the street and realized she was not dressed for the cold Vermont weather. She did not want to attract any attention being so abysmally dressed, so she slipped into a coffee shop and waited until the clothing store that was next door opened. At exactly 10:00 AM Bliss entered the small shop and purchased a warm ski coat. She also bought a pair of boots and a knit cap. She told the shop owner she was going to be wearing her purchases and the nice woman cut off all the tags.

Bliss asked if there was a restroom she could use, and the woman let her use the employee one in the back of the shop. Bliss freshened up as best she could, threw the Raven's cap into the trash can, and after thanking the clerk she left the shop and headed towards The Jelly Mill that was on the other side of town.

It took Bliss 15 minutes to get to The Jelly Mill. The Jelly Mill was a large shop featuring country crafts and Vermont made items. It was a huge stop for most tourists. It had a cafe on the top floor that used local produce, meats, and cheeses, and boasted a large window that visitors loved to sit near. Bliss wasn't sure where she should go. If Connor never came, she would be sitting there the entire day, and then the local sheriff would probably be notified, and she did not want to deal with that.

Bliss decided she would first browse the shop slowly, and then get something to eat, then browse the shop again. She knew she'd have to leave at some point, so as not to draw attention to herself, but for now that was all the game plan she could muster. She was tired and worried; her body ached from sitting for so long on the bus. She was relieved that her feet were not hurting her and even her arm and hands felt better. Bliss walked through the large parking lot towards the entrance trying to keep her head down. She heard the gravel crunch behind her but moved too slowly as a large hand grasped her shoulder tightly. Bliss whirled, dislodging the hand, ready to fight, but her eyes landed on Connor. He looked exhausted, his eyes were darker than usual, and he looked pissed. Bliss stood there waiting for some sort of reaction from him. She was thrilled that he was there, and wanted to jump into his arms, but the look on his face unnerved her.

"Where the hell have you been?" He finally said, his voice was shaking. He then clutched her shoulders and pulled her into his chest.

Bliss melted into his arms as tears blurred her vision. She wiped her eyes quickly as Connor pulled back; she didn't want him to see that she was an emotional mess.

"I have been out of my mind; I've been so worried." He said his tone gentler.

Bliss was too choked up to answer at first. "You came." Was all she could spit out. Connor looked at her as what she said sank in. "Of course, I came." He immediately understood that she had no way to be certain that he would come, and the realization of how alone she must have felt hit him hard.

"Shit, we need to talk. You look about as tired as I am."

Bliss nodded. He took her by the arm and led her to a Jeep Cherokee that was backed into a spot on the edge of the lot. He opened the door for her and then got in the driver side.

Connor began driving and the entire time he kept glancing nervously at her. Neither one of them talked. Bliss kept looking in the side mirror to see if they were being followed.

"No one's following us," he said noticing what she was doing.

"Are you sure?" She asked and then immediately regretted questioning him.

"I'm sure," he said calmly.

Connor drove through Manchester and pulled into a motel just outside of town. "Wait here," he told her. Bliss nodded numbly.

Bliss watched as he got out of the Jeep and went into the office. She couldn't hold back the tears any longer. The burden of being alone was lifting and in its wake, it left her feeling emotional. She couldn't believe he was actually here, with her. He had gotten her email and decoded it. He cared enough to come. Connor came out of the office and got back into the car. He looked at Bliss, who had placed her hand on her forehead basically hiding half her face from him. He drove to a corner unit and parked in front of it, then opened the back door and pulled out a small black bag. He walked around to the front of the car just as Bliss was shutting her door. He put his hand on the small of her back and guided her to their door. After unlocking it, they both stepped inside. Connor immediately locked the door behind them and then wedged a chair under the handle. He tossed his bag onto the table and then walked around the unit checking the windows. Bliss remained standing near the door.

The room was an efficiency. It had two double beds, a table with four chairs, a television, and a built-in dresser. Along one of the walls, furthest from the bed, there

was a sink, a stovetop, a microwave, and coffee maker all on a 1950's green Formica counter. Alongside of the counter was a mid- sized refrigerator. There was a closet in the back of the room and across from that, a door leading to a bathroom.

Bliss took off her coat and hat laying them on one of the chairs. She was disconcertingly quiet as Connor watched her from across the room.

"Bliss you're scaring me," he said quietly.

Bliss hung her head. She couldn't believe how raw she felt. He came. She wasn't alone. Her attempt to maintain her composure was lost as a wave of emotion crashed through her.

Bliss sat down on the nearby bed and buried her face in her hands. Connor was at her side immediately. His arms wrapped around her as he pulled her protectively against his chest. Bliss wept openly burying her face in his chest. Bliss rarely cried, even at her mother's funeral she had not wept openly. He patiently waited for her to regain control; all the while he comforted her by rubbing her back. It may have appeared as if he was consoling her, but simply touching her was comforting him.

He had never been more worried in his life, when he couldn't reach Bliss. The fact that he had found her, and she was now in his arms took a momentous weight off his shoulders. He still didn't know what was going on, and he knew they had to talk, but for now, he was happy to just be holding her.

He could tell she was getting herself together. Her hand left his chest to rub her face before she looked up.

"Feel better?" His voice was tender and reassuring.

Bliss graced him with a small smile. "Yes, thank you. I'm sorry. It's just, it's just been a tough couple of days."

"I'll say."

"What happened, Connor? What happened in your

meeting?"

He thought, how like her that on top of whatever she was dealing with, that she was still concerned about him. He kissed the top of her head affectionately. "Why don't I start at the beginning okay? First though, are you okay?"

"I'm physically fine, emotional drained, exhausted, and really worried, but yes I'm okay." Connor took his boots off and Bliss did too. He sat back against the bed headboard and motioned for her to join him. He still needed to touch her. The contact was the only thing holding him together. She settled naturally under his arm and he held both her hands with his one.

"I need to hold you, Honey."

His statement gave her the first hopeful feeling that she had, and she needed to be held.

"So, Andy came out of his meeting and before we could talk I was called in. There were three Officer's in the room, two General's and one Major. They were seated behind a long table and it was all pretty official. My story was that we had been training. I didn't want Andy to get into trouble, and I was emphatic that he flew where I told him to fly. When I was dismissed from the meeting, I saw that it was after 11:00 PM. When I walked out of the room, Ralph, the soldier that had been shot was waiting to go in. I had no idea where Andy was. I was told to wait, so I did. Ralph came out and hour later and I couldn't read him. He is the newest member of our team. We all knew what we were to say if asked. We were keeping it simple and as close to the truth as possible without lying. I knew Andy wouldn't deviate, but I was a little concerned about

Ralph. I don't know him as well as my other men."

"Oh Connor, I can't imagine what you were thinking."

"I was thinking I was going to have to find a job in the Private Sector, and I was debating whether to go State Police or Private Investigator." He admitted with a chuckle. Bliss squeezed his hands in hers.

"Then I was called back in. It was after midnight and I have to tell you I was expecting the worse."

"But?" She asked cautiously.

"But the panel got a call from General Paine telling them that he had authorized the mission to rescue a MIA Marine and an Analyst. From what I understand the Review Board got the call from him while they were questioning Ralph. General Paine told them he got the coordinates from Marines that were in the area. He explained that he knew we were in the area and issued the order for the rescue mission. He also told them it was a Normandy status, Dark Op and should not be discussed further."

"General Paine?"

"Yeah, I guess he had heard that my team was on the hot seat and he decided to bail us out."

"Wow, that's incredible. So, you're not in trouble?"

"No, in fact we might get a commendation." Connor was grinning ear to ear.

"That's fantastic."

"So let's talk about the elephant in the room." Connor said gently planting a kiss on her temple.

"A woman answered your phone." Bliss blurted out, "and I was not dancing with that guy."

Connor put his hand on her arm to calm her. "I

know."

"You know?"

"Caitlyn called me and told me everything. I'm going to beat my brother's ass for that stunt."

"It was pretty mean," she paused. "Connor, if you're going to tell me that you had another 'Red' indiscretion, I don't know if I can take it," she said quietly, her eyes studying his face.

He recognized that she was anxious about what he was going to tell her, so he pulled her in even closer to his side.

"Here's what happened. When I left the base, it was about 1:00 AM. I went to a bar that my team hangs at when we are Stateside. I wanted to find Ralph and Andy to tell them the good news. I also wanted to call you, but it was so late. I was going to text you, but I was driving. I wanted to get to the bar before it closed. I get there and thankfully they were both there. They were over the top happy. We had time for one drink before last call. Andy picked up a girl who had been coming onto him all night, but he had been so worried that he had been rejecting her advances. He rectified that as soon as he heard we were not in trouble. Ralph and I were heading back to my apartment. Ralph was going to stay with me since Andy was going home with the girl. I had my cell on the bar and Andy picked it up by mistake. Ours are identical; we got a two for one deal a ways back."

"But I asked for you by name," Bliss said slowly.

"Yeah, well Andy has this annoying habit of using my name when he picks up chicks.

He told the girl his name was Connor, and when you called, she thought you wanted to speak to Andy thinking his name was Connor. The only reason I know this is because Andy heard what she said and then he realized he had my phone and that she must have been talking to you. He told me the next morning. I was pissed. When he gave me my phone back, I saw the picture Collin had sent. That threw me, and I also saw that you had called; I assumed it had been you that Andy's girl had spoken to. I also had a ton of missed calls from Caitlyn, and she also texted me that I had to call her ASAP. I called her first because honestly, I thought something had happened to one of my parents.

Bliss, there were so many scenarios running through my head. I was thinking about the picture, that another man was touching you, man, that was not a good feeling. I was so upset knowing what you must have thought when Andy's girl had insinuated that she was with me. Shit, my head was spinning. So, I reached Caitlyn first and she told me what happened on the dance floor and explained what Collin had done, and then how you had left the apartment. I hung up with her and started calling your phone right away. It kept going to voice mail. I had a bad feeling something was wrong. I've been a mess not knowing where you were. I had a feeling that you might have thought I had seen the picture of you with that dick head and gone off with another woman."

"I did think that, but Caitlyn said there was no way you would do that, and a part of me couldn't believe it either."

Connor kissed her ardently threading his hands through her curls. "So, we're good. No man was grinding on my girl and you know there was no other woman for me."

"We're good, maybe." She added.

"I guess now you should tell me what's going on."

"Don't get mad, okay?"

"I won't. I'm too damn happy to be holding you. So, talk, woman."

Bliss started from the beginning telling him about the car in New Jersey and then the man and woman that followed her. She told him everything she had done since leaving Collins apartment, and when she finished Connor was looking at her with astonishment. "Jeez, you have been through a lot. I wish you had told me about the car in Jersey though."

Bliss nodded. "I just wasn't positive and you were dealing with your own stuff."

"Yeah, I get that."

"I was so worried you wouldn't get the email, that it might go to spam."

"I saw the subject line and knew it was from you. By then you'd been missing for most of the night and the next day, so I was actually relieved to get it. I'm impressed that you used our code. I liked the reverse hitting reference. Wait until I tell dad." He said chuckling.

"I couldn't find anyone with the number 08, so I just used the word reverse instead of switch hitter and hoped you would understand. I was kind of winging it."

"It was brilliant. I had to look up the songs from Annie, and when I saw the one called Tomorrow, I knew that was a clue. Then, when I figured out where you wanted me to go, I Googled Manchester and found The Jelly Mill."

"I knew you'd figure it out. I just wasn't sure if you'd see the email. I'm so glad you're here."

"Me too baby, me too."

Connor kissed her softly and Bliss sighed happily before ending the contact.

"How did you get here? You couldn't have driven all this way."

"No, I flew into Albany and rented a car. I have been sitting in that Jelly Mill parking lot since dawn.

Bliss kissed his cheek. "Thank you, Connor."

"Sweetheart I love you. I'll always come for you."

Connor could feel Bliss' body relax into his own.

"Why don't we get some sleep and then we will figure out who the hell is following my girl?"

"Oh yes, please," Bliss responded wearily.

They both stripped down to their under clothes and Connor gave Bliss one of his tee shirts so she could take off her bra. Bliss unfastened and took off her soft brace and laid it on the nightstand. They sought out each other under the covers and all thoughts of sleep were obliterated when their bodies came together. Connor gathered her against him and bracketed her face in his hands as he kissed her passionately. He ended the kiss but remained holding her closely.

"I know you're tired, but there is no way I will be able to sleep now that I have you in my arms. We are finally alone, and damn, I want to strip you naked and make love to you forever."

Bliss cradled his strong neck in her hands and pulled him towards her.

"If you're asking if I want to make love with you, or sleep, the answer is make love with you; and for the

record, it will always be to make love with you."
Bliss was lying on her back, her hand was resting on
his bicep, and Connor was on his side gazing down at
her. She was stunning. He felt a lump form in his
throat remembering how panicked he had been not
knowing where she was or if she was okay. He pulled
the tee shirt she wore over her head and tossed it to
the floor. Bliss watched his face as he looked upon
her nearly naked body.

"You're so damn beautiful." He whispered, kissing
her gently before uttering each word. Connor's hand
moved slowly up her soft stomach until he reached
her breast. His thumb grazed the sensitive underside
and then flicked quickly across her taut nipples
eliciting a hushed throaty moan from Bliss.

He captured her tight beaded nipple in his lips and
grazed his teeth over the sensitive skin. Bliss held the
back of his head with one hand, holding his exquisite
lips to her responsive flesh, as her other hand roamed
his back. She could feel warm wetness between her
legs and the wonderful ache of a pre-orgasm
bloomed. Bliss slid her hand between their bodies and
pushed his boxer briefs down. Connor lifted his hips
and pulled off his briefs. Before he settled himself
next to Bliss, he slipped his fingers under the sides of
her thong and pulled them off.

Bliss took in Connor's all male body. He was firm and
muscled and his cock stood straight up against his
hard abdomen. Bliss wiped the pearly pre-cum from
his satiny dome with her fingertip and lifted the liquid
bead to her mouth causing Connor to groan. Connor
was using his eyes and hands to commit Bliss'
beautiful bare body to memory. "When I go back,"

He told her. "This moment, right now, the first time seeing you in your glory, and you are glorious, Darling, this moment, is going to help me through some long lonely nights."

Bliss reached for him not wanting to hear any more of him leaving her. She pulled him gently, so he covered her body with his own. She opened for him placing her calves across his backside. She wanted him and she wanted him now. She was practically vibrating with need.

Connor felt her molten heat as his thickness slid through her female lips.

Bliss moved her hips to match Connor's seductive pace. He held his weight off of her and Bliss saw him look between them to watch their lower halves dance erotically. His strokes teased her clit and she felt a tightening in her core that she knew would unfurl into an epic climax. Her soft whimpers stoked Connor's desire further and he rolled off of her to find his pants. He needed a condom; fast.

"Connor, no. No condom."

"Honey, it's for your protection."

Bliss was momentarily hurt. Had he been with so many women that he was afraid he would give her a STD? Connor saw her pained expression.

"No, Bliss. I know what you're thinking. I just don't want to get you pregnant." Somehow that didn't make Bliss feel any better.

"Bliss, look at me." He forced her eyes to his. "I love you. I respect that you want a career in the Army. I'd be the happiest man in the world if you were pregnant with my kid, but I want time with you alone first. Do you understand?"

"I do. I'm sorry, I did I think it was because of you being with other women. I want time with you too; just you and me. I'm on the pill. I'm clean. Right now, I need to feel you Connor, all of you."

Connor rolled back to her and took her face in his hands.

"Oh God, you are so made for me." He whispered, struck by the sheer love he heard in her voice. "I'm clean too, no condom, Honey."

Bliss pressed against him and he moved to her opening. "I love you Bliss." He said as he pressed inside of her. They didn't kiss as he worked his way in. They stared at each other, each passionately. Their souls were physically connecting, and the special moment felt as if it was a long-awaited homecoming. Connor felt her sheath tighten the further he thrust inside of her. He didn't want to hurt her. He pressed in and then retreated, then he pressed in further and retreated again. He did this for a minute and Bliss was delirious as her arousal spiraled tighter. She knew he was taking care to not hurt her but all she wanted was him; all of him, inside of her.

She quickly rolled him over onto his back and before he knew what she was doing, she sank down on him with a hearty groan. He was fully seated inside her, and his cock throbbed impatiently. He had almost cum, and he had bit his tongue to hold back the pressing orgasm.

"Finally," she said, resting her forehead against his. "My baby is not patient." Connor said with a grin after he fought off the impending urge. "Not when it comes to having you like this. I've thought about this, about loving you like this, for so long."

"Me too."

Connor rolled her back, so he was once again on top of her. He took her hands in his and pushed them above her head, claiming her lips as he began to work in and out of her primed core. Their bodies fused, moving as one, in a sensual ballet that created such heat their skin glistened with a mist of sweat. Their tongues played erotically as their love making grew more ardent.

Connor felt his balls tightening and a pre-orgasmic tingle in the base of his spine flared as he drove into her intimate channel. There was no way he would come without her. He took his hand from hers and pushed up on his forearms allowing for space to come between their joined bodies. The separation severed their kiss, but their eyes connected. Connor reached between them and found her swollen pink nub. Bliss moaned and looked down between their moist bodies.

"Look at me Bliss," Connor whispered as he strummed her clit and move in and out of her It took less than three seconds for Bliss to shatter. Connor felt her tightened and spasm around his cock triggering his own earth-shattering release.

Their bodies continued to shudder as their orgasms slowly subsided. Connor stroked Bliss gently and when he heard her whimper, he knew he could pull another climax from her. He rolled to his side, his softening cock sliding out of her heat. Conner added more pressure as he massaged her responsive clit. He nuzzled her neck watching her body react to his touch.

"Connor," Bliss choked out.

"I want to see you come again." He told her as he

drew a hardened nipple into his warm mouth.

"Oh God. Yes, yes, yesss." She uttered as her hips followed the rhythm of his hand. Bliss felt the out of control synapses begin in breast and shoot through her like a runaway train. She convulsed as an incredible orgasm consumed her entire body, making her back bow off the bed. Warm liquid gushed from her channel as Connor continued to rub her.

"Stop, stop," Bliss choked out, pushing his hand away. She couldn't physically handle. Her clit was vibrating it was so sensitive. "No more, no more," she whispered for mercy. Connor chuckled. His male ego soared, knowing that he had given his woman two very powerful orgasms.

He leaned over and kissed her tenderly. "I love watching you come." He told her after the kiss ended.

"I love you making me come." She answered breathlessly.

Connor lay back on the bed and Bliss settled her head on his chest. Connor held her to him possessively.

"Connor?"

"Ummm?"

Bliss leaned up so she could see his face. "You know how I'm not very experienced with all of this?" She said gesturing to the two of them in bed.

"Yes," he said cautiously, not knowing where she was going with the conversation.

"I just want you to know that I'm willing to do anything with you, and for you; I just need you to tell me. Teach me. Is that a turn off?"

Connor grinned, "No, Honey, if anything, it's a turn on. I want you to be honest with me, too, okay?"

"Of course. Like what though?"

"Tell me what you like when I'm doing it, or if you don't like something. It will make me a better lover for you."

"Well, so far, I like everything," she said giggling.

"Yeah, me too," he paused, "I knew making love with you would be the best."

"Connor, you've been with women way more experienced than me." She hated bringing that up, but she didn't want any hollow compliments. She really did want to please him sexually.

"Yes, but when you love someone it's the best, and I love you." He kissed her nose playfully.

Bliss settled back into the groove of his shoulder and sighed happily. "Connor?"

"Ummm?"

"Want to move to the other bed? This one's wet."

Connor laughed out loud and pulled the covers back as they left the one bed for the other.

Chapter 20

They slept solidly until late afternoon. A car pulling up outside woke them at the same time. Connor slipped from the bed not even bothering to hide the hard on he had woken up with. He walked to the window and peered out the drawn drapes.

"Anything?" Bliss asked anxiously sitting up.

"No, looks like skiers coming for the weekend." Connor got back in bed and drew her to him. "Why don't we use the next few days for that R and R you're supposed to be on?"

"Oh, yes, I'd like that."

"I need to call home. I'm sure the family's pretty worried about you."

"They don't think I'm still in New York with Caitlyn?"

"No, Caitlyn took the train home the next day. She was livid with Collin. I called my dad before I left. I told him I was going to find you."

"You didn't tell him where you were headed did you?" Bliss asked instantly worried that her whereabouts', that she had so carefully covered, might be revealed.

"No, I'll email him if we can find a public computer and tell him we are together. I know he just wants to make sure you're okay. He doesn't know about you being followed, of course."

"I don't want your family involved Connor. I have no idea who's after me, but your family needs to be cautious."

"Yeah, I'll figure out a way to tell him that in the email."

Bliss pulled back the covers and walked to the bathroom. She didn't bother trying to cover herself and Connor liked how comfortable she was around him.

"I'm going to take a shower." She said as she disappeared around the doorframe. She poked her head back out, "Want to come scrub my back?" She grinned playfully.

"Hell yeah." Connor said scrambling from beneath the covers.

The shower was in a tub and there was a curtain to keep the water from spraying onto the floor. Bliss had already turned on the shower and was testing it with her hand when Connor walked in. The smile on his face was so sexy. He had a day's growth of beard on his face and it only enhanced his handsome features. Satisfied that the water temperature was good, Bliss pulled the curtain back, stepped in and held it for Connor. It was a tight fit, but neither minded. Their bodies came together like a magnet and steel; their mouths met feverishly. The water sluiced down Bliss' back and when she tipped her head back to get her hair wet, Connor took advantage of the provocative position to feast upon her slim neck.

Bliss was instantly aroused, and her nipples pebbled with need. She wrapped her arms over Connor's shoulders, and he lifted her easily, placing his forearms under her rear. Bliss wrapped her legs around his trim hips and Connor turned them, so she was against the tiled side wall.

Bliss could feel his cock poised at her entrance and she and Connor stared into each other's eyes as he slowly lowered her onto his hardness.

"Oh, God," Bliss whispered. "So damn good."

Connor pulled out and Bliss pulled him back using her knees and hips. Connor groaned as her heat and her desire to hold him inside of her engulfed him. Connor drove into her further, his love for her fueling his passion. She sucked on his neck and then remembered that he had liked it when she licked the shell of his ear. As Bliss softly tongued the rim of his ear, she heard what resonated as a growl come from his throat. Connor lost control and hammered into her. She clung to him with her hands and legs bolstered from the tiled wall behind her. Connor rested his forehead against her shoulder and resituated his hands so that they gripped her round globes, spreading her soft cheeks. The new position set off tingly sensations in her female parts. Connor surged deeper and his cock rubbed a place inside of her that had Bliss reeling.

Bliss used her legs to aid Connor as best she could. She had no idea if she was doing the whole sex standing up bit correctly, but it sure felt good. Her body began to shake from Connor's cock massaging her g spot and she whimpered blissfully as an orgasm tore through her. Connor felt and heard her as she shuddered uncontrollably in his arms, his balls tightened, and he felt the heat uncoil through his shaft as he pushed into her one final time.

Connor held her until his cock softened and their breathing returned to normal, then he gently lowered her, so she was standing. He loved how she continued to cling to him. Connor placed his hands on the wall behind her, caging her in while Bliss kept her hands on his hips for balance.

"So damn good." Connor said depositing a sweet kiss on her lips before resting his forehead against hers.

"Ditto," she replied breathlessly.

They regained the use of their arms and legs and began the original chore of washing up. Bliss ran her hands over Connor's sculpted torso and then ran her hands over his back and hips. She could see his cock stir and she slowly washed towards it, but Connor caught her hand with his.

"Sweetheart, I am sure we could spend a week in this shower pleasing each other, but we're going to run out of hot water soon and I'm hungry."

Bliss pretended to pout and he tickled her smile back, grinning at her playful nature that was emerging.

"I'm hungry, too. Plus, I need a tooth brush and some clothes."

"Okay let's get dressed, find a place to eat, and then find you some clothes, not too many though. I like seeing you naked," he teased.

It was dusk when they came out of their little efficiency and both glance around the lot guardedly before moving to the Jeep. They turned towards Manchester and found The Double Hex Restaurant. Connor asked for a table in the back that they could see people entering the parking lot and the front door. Bliss was once again so grateful that he was with her.

"What?" Connor asked seeing her expression.

"I'm just so happy you're here."

Connor grinned. Because we make good love together?"

"No. I mean yes, that too, but it is such a relief knowing you're here. That I'm not alone." Connor took her hand in his. "I know that must have been awful. I wish I could erase
the last few days for you. I'm feeling the same way."
"Connor, you're never alone," she teased.
"When I didn't know where you were, I've never felt more alone."
"You came though. I keep thanking God for that. You came for me." Her voice hitched slightly so Connor folded her hands within his affectionately.
They both ordered cheeseburgers and when they finished Connor asked the waitress where the best place was to buy clothes. She told him that the outlets stayed open until 9:00pm every night so that's where they headed.
On their way to the center of Manchester, Bliss saw a drug store and asked Connor to stop. She ran in and bought deodorant, shampoo, conditioner, body soap, a toothbrush, toothpaste, a disposable razor, and mascara. She came out in less than ten minutes and Connor joked that he never had a woman shop that fast before. The second he said it, he wished he could have taken it back. He saw Bliss momentarily freeze, the smile on her face remained, but her eyes betrayed her.
"I'm sorry. It was a dumb joke."
"I know," Bliss said with a sigh. "You shouldn't have to be worried about watching every word you say around me Connor. I'm the one that's sorry. This is all so new for me. I admit that I get jealous thinking about you and other women."
"If you didn't get jealous, I'd be worried. Shit, you

know I lost it when I thought you were with your Bo, and that damn picture still haunts me, but I'm with you Bliss. No other woman compares to how I feel about you. Okay?"

"Okay." She answered; comforted that he truly understood her. She did not want to appear clingy or needy, so she vowed to herself to stop acting so insecure.

"Now, let's go buy me some clothes. Ugh, I can't believe I'm even saying that! Caitlyn, on the other hand, would love it." She laughed leaning over to kiss Connor on the cheek.

Connor laughed. "She sure would."

They parked in a pubic lot that was close to all the shops and headed to the Bass outlet first. Bliss loved that Connor held her hand as they walked. It was the most wonderful feeling to have someone care for her the way Connor did. She loved being part of a couple, and the simple gestures, like holding hands. It was so normal, yet something she had never experienced.

They were in their fourth store, and she had already bought a pair of jeans, four tops, under garments, socks, boots, a long sleeve tee shirt, and two sweaters. Connor was carrying all the bags and Bliss thought he looked adorable.

He never left her side, or complained, and she became aware that he was actually guarding her. She teased him about it, and he chuckled. "Just being vigilant," he replied giving her a delightful wink.

Wherever they went woman openly ogled him and Bliss felt her jealous feelings subside as they were replaced with happy contentment. She was with him, they were a couple, and he had no desire to be with anyone but her. In fact, she saw that he had no idea that women were openly staring at him. The stupid grin she had on her face drew Connor to her.

"What the heck are you grinning about?" He teased her sweetly.

Bliss motioned for him to look at the two women standing in the shoe section. The two women were gawking at Connor and when he turned towards them, they quickly turned

away and giggled. Bliss whispered to him when he turned back to her.

"You have no idea how handsome you are, do you?" Connor shrugged his shoulders and pulled her to him so he could whisper to her.

"You know I could say the same about you?" He motioned for her to look over his shoulder where a man wearing a black fedora was staring at her.

Bliss froze and Connor knew immediately that something was wrong.

"Babe?"

"That's the man from the train."

Connor turned towards the man who was slowly walking towards them. Bliss put her hand on Connor's arm.

"He can't hurt us in here. There are too many people. Let's hear what he has to say." "Feeling brave?"

Connor muttered, as he dropped the bags to the floor. Bliss actually smiled and squeezed his arm. "We got this." She looked around the store and recognized the woman who had also been on the train, approaching them from behind.

"6," Bliss said quietly.

Connor nodded letting her know that he understood

that they were being approached from behind. Bliss turned letting the woman know that she saw her. Connor remained watching the man.

The man reached them first. He stopped a yard away from Connor, out of Connor's immediate reach. Connor would not have let him come closer anyway. The woman reached them, and she moved to stand at the man's side, so Bliss turned facing them. The woman was staring at Connor and Bliss watched as a small, almost cocky smile appeared on her face. Connor's stance was practiced; he was ready for anything. Bliss readied herself as well by standing with her left side slightly forward. She had learned this defensive move back in Afghanistan from Bo. He showed her that by standing the way that she was, if the person in front of her pulled a gun, her full torso was not exposed.

"You're a pretty elusive young lady." The man said stoically.

"Why are you following her?" Connor countered.

The man nodded and began to put his hands in his pocket.

"Keep your hands where they are." Connor said harshly.

"I'm just getting my ID."

"I'll get it for you." Bliss said looking at Connor who nodded.

Bliss reached into the man's over coat and pulled out his billfold. She quickly stepped back and opened the leather holder. Inside was a gold badge and a very official looking CIA ID with the man's picture in the corner.

"CIA?" She said in disbelief.

Connor took the billfold from her and perused it quickly. Bliss had already memorized everything that was on the ID, including the series of random numbers and letters printed across the top. Connor tossed the badge back. He was not letting his guard down.

"Why don't we go someplace we can chat?" The woman said overtly winking at Connor and using a flirty voice. She nodded towards a few persons that were shopping nearby. "I don't think so." Connor replied quickly, barely looking at the woman. Bliss was fuming seeing the woman's blatant gesture.

"I think you'll want to hear what we have to say." The man said looking at Bliss.

Bliss remained quiet. The woman was frowning now, and she sighed and looked at the man who nodded.

"We have information regarding your kidnapping, and it involves your father."

Bliss felt like her gut had been sucker punched. All the air whooshed out of her lungs and Connor knew that they had effectively shaken Bliss. If they chose to attack them at that moment, she would get hurt.

Bliss' mind was reeling and Connor nudged her with his arm, hoping to refocus her.

"I don't understand?" Bliss said quietly.

"We have to talk." The woman said obviously pleased that she'd shocked Bliss, "And it would be better if we went someplace less public."

"And where I could get a damn cup of coffee. It's too damn cold in this state." The man said attempting to ease the tense atmosphere with a joke.

Connor looked around and realized there were too

many innocents in the store, including parents with children. Connor looked to Bliss and nodded.

"Okay, there's a dessert bar across the street. We can go there." Bliss said hoping Connor was okay with that.

Connor stooped to pick up the bags and Bliss tapped his arm and told him she'd carry them. He knew Bliss was focused again. It was smarter that his hands remain free and ready. They walked out of the store, Connor gesturing that the couple should walk ahead of them.

Inside the small dessert bar, they took a table near the back. Bliss put the bags on the ground against the wall so they would not impede a speedy get away should they need to run. A young waitress came to their table and pointed at the desserts that were written in chalk on a board shaped like a barn hanging on the wall.

She took their orders for four coffees. The man dismissed her by saying they would perhaps order dessert later. No one spoke while their order was being filled. Bliss saw that Connor was looking at the woman and she saw a flicker of discernment in his eyes that set off an ominous feeling in her gut. The woman was staring at Connor and she too had seen the minuscule change in his expression causing her to smirk. It was all very unsettling. Bliss felt Connor's leg move to lean against hers and the warning bells going off in her head were muffled by the comforting gesture. She was once again feeling so grateful that he was with her.

The waitress returned and placed their coffees on the table along with a variety of flavored creamers.

"How do we know you're really CIA?" Bliss asked when the waitress left.

The man smiled. "We heard you were smart." He reached into his coat again and Connor tensed.

"Relax," He said looking at Connor. "I'm pulling a card out." The man pulled out a business card and a pen from his coat pocket. He wrote a number on the back of the card before handing it to Bliss. "You can check us out by calling him."

The number on the card was to Jax's liaison.

"Who is it?" Connor asked. He thought the man would answer but Bliss did instead. "It's the number I use to getting touch with my brother."

"Are you sure?"

"Yes, I'm sure." Bliss said pocketing the card.

"What are your names?" Connor asked.

"Special Agent Jake Hammond and Special Agent Britney Sparrow." The man told them.

"Special Agents? Isn't that FBI?" Bliss asked.

"Yes, and CIA Operatives as well," Agent Hammond acknowledged. Bliss took a sip of her coffee and saw that Connor had a small frown on his face. He still wasn't comfortable.

Bliss saw that Connor was again looking at the woman. She hated that her spicy senses were kicking in. "Connor, do you want me to call the number?"

"We will, later. Let's hear what they have to say first."

Bliss returned her attention to the Agents.

"You really had us running back in Alexandria." The woman said looking at Bliss.

"You were in New York, weren't you?" Bliss said ignoring SA Sparrow, looking at SA Hammond.

"I was."

"And Pemberton?"

SA Hammond nodded.

"If you just wanted to talk to her, why didn't you just talk to her? Why all the cloak and dagger?" Connor asked.

The question clearly made the two Special Agents uncomfortable and Bliss knew they weren't going to like the answer.

"We were going to borrow you." Hammond said looking at Bliss.

"Borrow her?" Connor's tone was incredulous.

"We needed to talk to her with no distractions," he said looking directly at Connor, "alone."

Bliss looked to Connor still not really understanding, but Connor obviously did.

"You were going to fucking kidnap her? An American Agency was going to kidnap a United States Military Officer?"

Bliss gasped.

"Well, technically borrow her, like I said."

"Why?" Bliss asked.

"We were made privy to your report regarding your kidnapping in Afghanistan. We have always had you on our radar, but."

"Why have you had her on your radar?" Connor interrupted becoming agitated.

Sparrow sighed dramatically. "We know about your gift," she told Bliss.

Bliss froze, and Connor was now staring at her in disbelief. "What gift?" He asked with a growl like tone.

Bliss glared at Sparrow, pissed that her small secret

was now out in the open. Connor looked like he was mad as well. She remembered him saying, 'no secrets', and she knew he was thinking the same thing.

"Oh, dear," Sparrow said sarcastically, "I see you haven't told the boyfriend, "sorry about that."

"Fuck you," Bliss spat out. She realized that Sparrow was purposely trying to drive a wedge between her and Connor, she just didn't know why.

"Now ladies," Hammond said looking around the bar, hoping to defuse the situation before it got out of hand.

Connor sat back and crossed his arms over his chest and Bliss gave him a look that she hoped portrayed that she was sorry.

"What gift?" He repeated.

Hammond didn't want to add fuel to the already hostile atmosphere, so he answered him honestly.

"Bliss here has inherited her father's gift of memory." Connor looked at Bliss for clarification. "My dad had this gift; it's what my mother called it."

Bliss placed her hand on Connor's thigh needing to touch him and she felt him stiffen. She withdrew her hand, but before she could place it back on her lap Connor grasped it and placed it back on his thigh. She looked at him with so much relief on her face that he draped his arm over the back of her chair to further convey his support. Bliss continued. "It was genetically passed to me. I have this ability to commit a vast amount of information to memory."

Connor nodded, and she felt his thumb rub her shoulder. She could tell he was processing this new information by the way his forehead had a deep line running across it.

"So you were kidnapped in Afghanistan by someone wanting information that you have locked in your head?"

Bliss nodded and looked to Hammond who acknowledged him. "Exactly."

"What does this have to do with my dad? Why do you want to borrow me? I still don't get it?"

"Like I said, we read your report after you were taken. We knew you had this gift." "How did you know?" She asked interrupting him again.

"Your father told us." Sparrow said delighted that she could throw Bliss off balance again.

"You need to knock it off, or we're out of here." Connor told Sparrow coming to Bliss' defense.

Hammond was frowning at Sparrow and he must have given her some signal to behave because she wiped her smirk from her face and sat back looking annoyed.

"Bliss, your father was a CIA Agent for years. He is semi-retired now, but he has been taken hostage by a group in England who sympathize with Al Qaeda."

"My fathers in England?"

"Yes."

The smirk was back on the woman's face and Bliss wished she could smack it off her. "Bliss your father was taken by this group after you were rescued. They want the information they know you have locked in that head of yours."

"Shit," Connor swore softly.

"But I didn't even know my father was alive. How were they going to do that?"

The table was quiet and it finally dawned on Bliss that whoever had her father was going to try to barter with her using her father's life for the information. "So, is he still alive?"

"Last we heard he was."

Bliss' heart lurched inside her chest. "What can I do?"

"Bliss," Connor said hoping to stave off the inevitable. "They'll figure out a way to get him without you getting involved."

"Well, actually we were hoping to persuade you," Hammond said looking at Bliss, "to come to England and help us."

"No way!" Connor said heatedly.

"Connor." Her voice was soft, and her hand squeezed his thigh gently. He knew he had already lost the battle. "How do you know what was in the message I decoded?" Bliss

asked them.

"We don't."

"How do they know I can give them this information? It's not something normal people could remember."

"When you submitted your report, after you were rescued, you described a man named Zarghun. He works for a man that used to be your fathers partner years ago."

"Blue eyes?" Bliss said.

"Well, yes, he has blue eyes. His name is Tobias Conti. He was your father's partner and best friend I might add. His wife was killed in a car accident and two years later the CIA lost contact with him. Your brother Jax actually remembers him."

"You've talked to Jax?"

"He knows we wanted to talk to you."

"Not kidnap her," Connor said bitterly.

"No, we were hoping to persuade her to help us after she heard about her father."

"And if she didn't?"

"I don't think we have to worry about that anymore, do we?" Sparrow said mockingly. "You didn't answer my question. What does she need to do?"

"That is something we can only discuss with Bliss." Bliss felt Connor's muscles tense under her hand. "If you had kidnapped her, she would have been AWOL and that would have killed her career."

"She can always find another career." Sparrow said tersely.

"I'll explain everything to you in more detail when we are in a more private setting." Hammond told her obviously annoyed.

Not knowing if he wanted a more private place to talk or to simply be rid of Connor, Bliss replied, "Anything you have to say to me you can in front of Connor."

"Sorry sweetie, your ears only. Normandy actually," Sparrow said staring at Connor. "What is your problem?" Bliss asked weary of the game this woman was playing. Hammond waved his hand as if waving off the question.

"We are all tired. You know what we know Bliss. Call the number I gave you. Check us out. Then call the number on the front of the card. We'll be waiting to hear from you. We need to leave the day after tomorrow."

Hammond stood up and Sparrow followed. He tossed a few dollars onto the table and put his fedora back on. Then he looked at Bliss. "We really need your help. These people are bad and they're going to kill your father. He's a good man Bliss. I hope you think about this with a clear mind."

Sparrow was heading away from the table and before Hammond turned Connor stopped him with a questioning look.

Hammond smiled almost fatherly like.

"You recognize her now?" Hammond said looking at Sparrow who was almost at the door.

"Yes, but I don't know where from."

Hammond chuckled, "New Orleans."

Bliss heard Connor mutter, "Fuck me," under his breath and the uneasy feeling that she had earlier returned tenfold.

Hammond tipped his hat to them and followed Sparrow out the door.

Bliss turned her body completely towards Connor, who was leaning back in his chair.

He closed his eyes and then opened them knowing that Bliss was staring at him, waiting for an explanation.

"I fucked her in New Orleans." He said quickly with no buffer or apology.

Bliss visibly blanched and then sat back in her chair absorbing his revelation.

Connor put his hand on her knee waiting for her to look at him again.

"Bliss, it was years ago. I don't even remember. I was so drunk."

"It's okay," she interrupted him." You don't need to apologize."

"She was being a bitch."

"I think she was mad that you didn't remember her."

"Yeah, but she shouldn't have taken it out on you. That wasn't professional."

"I guess you just leave a lasting impression Doherty." She teased him then nudged him with her shoulder. Connor shook his head and grinned at her. "You're sure you're okay?"

"Yeah, I'm good. We're good."

Connor leaned over and kissed her lips. "Love you," he said softly.

"Love you back."

Chapter 21

They left the dessert bar and headed for the car. "I guess we don't have to hide anymore." Bliss said bumping his arm playfully.

"Good point. Let's call my dad so they know where we are and that you're safe." Back in the motel Bliss used the bathroom as Connor used his cell to call his parents. When she came out, she sat next to him on the bed.

"Were okay dad. She's fine." Bliss listened to the one-sided conversation. "Manchester, Vermont," he paused, "it's a pretty long story and I can't go into it on the phone." He paused again. "Can you get me some information on a Special Agent Hammond and Special Agent Sparrow? Both CIA." He listened to his dad and smiled reassuringly at Bliss. "You can call me back at this number." Bliss heard the General tell Connor to stay safe and Connor replied, "always," before disconnecting.

Connor turned towards Bliss. "They were understandably happy to hear that we are together."

"Good, I'd hate to cause them to worry."

Connor kissed the top of her head and as Bliss melted into his embrace, his lips moved slowly down her cheek and settled on her mouth. The kiss was warm and tender and so sensuous that she whimpered softly. Bliss separated from him just enough, so that she could take off her soft brace, which she lay on the table.

Connor took her arm in his hand and kissed her scars

sweetly. He placed a final kiss on her palm before
taking her hands in his helping her to stand with him.
He lifted her shirt over her head and tossed it on the
nearby chair. Bliss unbuttoned his shirt and slid it off
his shoulders. She took her time, slowly pressing
warm kisses to his chest as she slid the sleeves down
his arms.

Connor was grinning, and Bliss loved the sexy
twinkle that brightened his eyes as he watched her.
When she tossed his short to the chair he sat on the
bed and took off his boots and socks and Bliss sat in
the chair and did the same. He stood and unbuckled
his belt and then unbuttoned and unzipped his jeans.
Bliss followed his lead, undoing her own jeans. They
pushed them to the floor simultaneously.

Sexual energy swirled between them as they
completed the stimulating foreplay of
discarding their clothes. The bedside light glowed
softly outlining their naked bodies in the otherwise
dark room. Connor stared at Bliss and her heart pitty
pattered watching his arousal grow. Her tongue
unconsciously slipped out to dampen her lips and
Connor's gaze moved to her mouth. Bliss stepped to
him, wanting to feel his sculpted body against hers
and Connor welcomed her within his strong arms.
Their lips met and their tongues gently played.

Connor picked Bliss up and settled her on the bed. He
looked down at her pink, just kissed lips and traced
them with his index finger. Bliss sucked his finger
into her warm mouth. Connor slipped his finger from
her mouth and traced it slowly down her front to her
moist feminine lips, provoking another whimper from
Bliss.

"You know when we're done here; we are going to talk, right?" He told her as he ran his finger back up her torso, circling her tight nipples.

Bliss nodded quickly. He already had her so primed she could barely think. "Later." "Later." Connor repeated as he lightly moved his finger back down to her swelling clitoris.

Connor continued watching her face as his finger drew a line from one sensitive place on her curvy soft body to another. One finger had her quivering. She moaned as he expertly navigated her sensitive clit again. It was too much, her skin prickled waiting for a release. Bliss was on the brink of a tsunami of an orgasm. She clamped down on his hand, holding it to her wet heat as she ground herself unabashedly against his fingers. Her body detonated. Her orgasm raced through her so unchecked that she screamed. Her pelvis twerked uncontrollably as Connor continued to manipulate her until every last tremor had been wrung from Bliss' body.

Bliss opened her eyes to find Connor smiling down at her. "You're so beautiful when you come."

Bliss blushed. "One finger Connor. You did that with one finger."

Connor grinned and kissed her gently. He rolled to his back and Bliss moved to straddle him. Her hands rested on his shoulders and she bent and swept her tongue over his nipples and then worked her way up his neck to his sensitive ear. His cock was thick and long and rock hard between her still sensitive folds. Bliss moved over his length, her wet heat stimulating him further.

"Teach me," she whispered as she blew softly into his ear.

She felt his cock grow even harder. Connor reached between them and guided his granite hard shaft to her entrance. Bliss slid down upon his steely rod, watching his face as she did so. When she had taken him fully inside her, she watched as his eyes shut, for just a moment, and grinned seeing the look of pure contentment that was etched on his face.

"Move up and down on me." He said, showing her how by guiding her hips with his hands.

"Ohhhhh, that feels so good," she whispered. She rode him slowly, at first, savoring the contact, the connection. This new position was so deliciously stimulating that she picked up the unhurried pace to hasten the heady sensations that were building.

Connor was pressing deep inside of her, using his heels for leverage. Her tight channel gloved him intimately. Her breasts bounced alluringly, and he felt his balls tighten, signaling his nearing release. Wanting her to come again, he sought out her pearly bit of flesh and using his thumb pressed on it using a circular motion.

"Oh God, yes, yes," she moaned. Bliss' head fell back as she worked her hips provocatively as the avalanche-like orgasm roared through her body. Connor groaned loudly as he exploded simultaneously, his cock shuddered deep within her undulating core. He held her down on his cock, grinding into her tight channel.

"Yes," he growled as his hot seed shot into her rippling channel.

Bliss collapsed against his heaving chest and he wrapped his arms around her tightly, burying his face into her neck. For minutes they lay sated and still. Their bodies began to cool, and Bliss reached down to pull the covers up. The movement dislodging his cock from inside of her and she frowned with the loss. Connor fingered a cork screwed piece of her hair that had fallen in front of her face.

"It just gets better each time." He told her lovingly. Bliss kissed his chin and tucked herself against his side. "That was unbelievable," she agreed.

Connor stroked her arm and Bliss traced her fingers across his chest. They were each lost in their own private thoughts, dreading the conversation that loomed ahead of them. Bliss broke the quiet first, "you know I have to do this right?"

Connor tipped her chin up with his finger, so they were looking at each other. "Would it make any difference if I told you I didn't want you to?"

"Of course, your opinion matters to me, but Connor, it's my dad." "Someone who has chosen to remain out of your life."

"To keep me safe," she replied quickly.

"Tell me about this gift?"

"I first knew I had something special, something other kids didn't, when I discovered that memorizing things like spelling lists, multiplication facts, geography, and things like that were easy. If I saw it, I remembered it. My mom figured it out pretty early on and explained that my dad could do what I did. She said it was a gift that I needed to protect. I wasn't allowed to tell anyone about it. Jax knew, of course. He was mad he didn't have it. When we were little, he'd run these little tests on me, like show me a map and then ask me questions about it. He actually helped me to hone it."

"Was it hard to keep it hidden?"

"Sometimes, my mom told me to mess up on tests once in a while just so no one would notice."

"Smart woman."

"She was." Bliss's voice softened. "I can't believe my father's alive. You know I always felt that my parents had remained in touch with each other. Once in a while my mom would get a call and go to another room to talk. Afterwards, she was always distant; sometimes I think she'd go into her room and cry."

"I can't imagine knowing the love of your life was out there and you couldn't be with them."

"It must have been awful."

"She did it to keep you safe, Honey."

"I know."

"I won't tell you not to go with them Bliss, but I don't like it. I have to go back in less than a week. I can't be AWOL."

"Connor, I would never ask you to do anything that would jeopardize your career. I know you have to go. You know this time is going to be much harder when I say good- bye to you. I already ache."

Connor nuzzled the side of her face and they clung to each other.

"Can we talk about some details regarding this rescue operation?" "Of course."

"First of all, my guess is they are going to use you as bait."

"That's what I think too."

"Keep that bracelet with you." Connor said rubbing his finger across her fake medical tag.

"I will."

"I also want you to make sure someone in the Army knows what you are doing, and who you are with. Tell Hammond you won't do it unless your Commanding Officer knows, okay?"

"That makes sense."

"I want you to be prepared that this thing with your dad may be a ploy to get you to England."

"Understood."

"We are going to use every resource we have to make sure Hammond and Sparrow are legit before you leave with them."

"I'm already thinking about that. I'm going to work some computer magic and dig up their files."

"Good."

"Connor, do you think they would just hand me over to, you know, to get my father back?"

"I thought about that too. If he has the same gift as you, he may have some useful information. My guts says they still want that information. The CIA is just dangling you to get your dad back. I don't think they want you to be taken again and risk that you would giving up that intel."

"Then why pretend to?"

"I don't know. Maybe their agenda is to bring down the group, or at least part of it." "Connor was Sparrow CIA when you were with her?"

"Why?"

"It's such a coincidence you know?"

"Yeah it is. Honestly, I don't remember if she was or if she even told me what she did for a living. We had just flown home after a failed rescue mission. Andy and I were together at a bar. I was trashed Bliss. It's all a blur. I do remember waking up with her in a hotel room and all I wanted was for her to leave. Finally, I told her I had to meet with my CO, and I pretended to take her number. I was so hung over and pissed about the f'd up mission. She just wouldn't leave."

"Ugh, I can't stand that she's had you; Red and now her. This better not be a regular occurrence Doherty." Bliss told him part jokingly, but part seriously.

"I hear you loud and clear." He said rolling her onto her back and giving her a ferocious and awesome kiss.

"And this is the most important thing of all." He said lifting from her delectable lips. "Please stay safe. I want more nights like this with you, lots more. I love you."

Tears rimmed Bliss' eyes and she buried her face in his chest hugging him tightly. "You need to stay safe, too Connor. Please stay safe."

Connor rubbed her back as they lay together. His mind was running over everything he had learned today. He knew Bliss was probably doing the same thing. Thank goodness Bliss had handled his drunken hook up with Sparrow. He had thought she had looked

familiar, and when she had winked at him in the store, it had sent warning vibes skittering up his spine. He felt Bliss' breathing even out and knew she had fallen asleep.

He was normally in control of everything including his emotions. He made life and death decisions all the time. He was cool under pressure and his logical thinking had saved his team's ass more than once on a mission. Yet, holding Bliss and knowing that she was going to be leaving for England, with two CIA Agents that had admitted they were going to kidnap her if she refused to go with them, made him uncharacteristically emotional. He couldn't lose her now. She was all he'd ever dreamt of in a woman, a partner. She had to stay safe and he had to get his shit together or he wouldn't be a good leader for his team. A feeling of helplessness overwhelmed him.

Connor fought back the lump in his throat and rested his chin on Bliss' head, tucking her against him. He heard her mumble and he kissed her face tenderly.

"Ummm," She murmured stirring. "Are you okay?"

He didn't answer, and she looked up at him. He gave her a weak smile and she knew he wasn't.

"Make love to me Connor." She said moving against him seductively.

Connor rolled her to her back and penetrated her warm wet sheath in one long thrust. "I love you, so much," he said as he rocked into her.

The emotion in Connor's voice almost undid her as she uttered the same words back to him.

They made love slowly. Their bodies pressed against each other; fighting to get closer. Bliss wrapped her legs over his hips and urged him on with her own movements. She knew he needed this closeness.

"Yes, Connor, right there." She said breathlessly as his hard cock stroked over her sweet spot. "Yes, baby right there. Oh, God." She reached underneath them and gently massaged his heavy sacks.

"Blisssss," Connor choked out as he came hard. Bliss

moved her hand from his balls to her clit. Connor looked between them and watched. A sexy, but sad smile drew his lips up. "That's so hot, Bliss." He drew her nipple into his mouth and sucked hard. Bliss exploded, riding her fingers as she held Connor's length inside of her using her core muscles.

"Don't pull out." She said keeping her legs wrapped around him. "Don't ever leave me," she uttered quietly.

"Never." He kissed her tenderly and she felt wetness on her cheek. She didn't know if they were her tears or Connor's.

They didn't sleep much that night. They made love and talked, neither wanting the night to end. They eventually succumbed to sleep, wrapped in each other's arms, and when they did wake, it was noon. Bliss headed towards the shower and Connor followed her. They washed each other tenderly, pleasuring each other with their hands until their skin wrinkled, and the water cooled.

As they were dressing, Bliss told Connor she wanted to find a computer to check in with her Commanding Officer in San Francisco, and to also call Jax's liaison. Connor said he had to check in with Andy and make sure the team had checked in. They were to meet back in Kabul in five days. That meant Connor needed to be on the base and ready to go in four days, and that was even pushing it. Bliss sat on the bed and dialed the number on the back of the card.

"Yes?" A man on the other end answered.

"04211958" Bliss told the man.

"Please hold."

Bliss waited, and another man answered.

"Hi, everything okay?" Bliss recognized Drew Tellers voice.

"Yes, I just need to check on something."

"Shoot."

"SA Hammond and SA Sparrow."

"Hammond spoke with your brother a couple days ago."

"Do you know what he wanted?"

"Yes, he told Jax to verify that they were CIA if you should ever call."

"That's it?"

"That's it."

"Okay, thanks."

They disconnected.

Connor sat next to her and took the phone from her to call Andy. The conversation was brief, and Andy was relieved that Connor had found Bliss and he said for Connor to tell Bliss again that he was sorry for what the woman had said to her.

"Well, now we have to find a computer." Bliss told Connor.

"Any thoughts?"

"Usually hotels have a few that their guests can use" Connor got out the phone book and found a Hotel near Stratton Mountain. He called the hotel and asked for directions since neither of them had cell phones to access GPS. As they headed for the hotel, Connor was a little subdued and it worried Bliss. She knew he had a lot on his mind, but a niggle of fear that he was rethinking their whole relationship surfaced.

"Are you okay?"

Connor glanced at her and smiled. "Yes and no," he admitted honestly.

"Want to share?"

"I'm concerned about you, and I'm thinking maybe I should put in for an extended leave so I can come with you."

Bliss paused debating the best way to answer him.

"What are you thinking?" He asked her.

"I don't think it's in your best interest career wise, to take a leave Connor."

"But wanting you safe is more important."

Bliss turned in her seat and placed her hand on his forearm.

"I love that you want me safe Connor. I want you to be safe, too. We aren't exactly in a 'safe' line of work, and we have known this since the start."

"In Afghanistan I thought about you all the time." He told her. "It was hell not knowing if you were okay."

"I felt the same way."

"I don't know. I was just thinking about it."

"I love you too." She said leaning over and kissing his cheek, which got her a smile. They found the hotel and Connor had to run interference at the front desk, while she located the computers. It took her a few minutes to find what she was looking for. Hammond and Sparrow were looking pretty good on paper. She traced them both
through their military background. Then Hammond was recruited to the CIA in 2000 and Sparrow in 2011. Their records appear unblemished. Hammond had some financial problems, but her digging hadn't turned up why he was in debt. Sparrow, on the other hand, was squeaky clean. Neither of them was married and they both had commendations in their files.

Next, Bliss emailed her Commanding Officer, Colonel Francis Otterman. She explained that she had been contacted directly by Hammond and Sparrow, and that they wanted her to accompany them to England to help with a case. She asked what the protocol was for this inter-agency situation. She explained to Otterman that she had lost her cell phone but would check her email later for his answer. She also explained that she was still technically on the R and R leave, that Dr. Tanner had prescribed and that she was currently in Manchester, Vermont.

Bliss slipped back out to the front foyer and saw that Connor had the women at the front desk totally enthralled. They were absolutely smitten with her man and Bliss chuckled seeing the hopeful looks on the two young ladies faces as they gazed at him. She sauntered up to the desk and placed her arm through his possessively, she just couldn't resist.

"Ready Sweetheart?"

Connor leaned into her and gave her a quick kiss.

"Sure am." He said giving the two ladies a wink before leaving.

"Connor you are so bad." Bliss chastised him playfully as they left the hotel.

"You mean so good."

"Those poor women, I don't even want to know what lines you were feeding them." Connor laughed and wrapped his arm over her shoulder.

They spent the rest of the day visiting the quaint shops in Weston, a small town north of Manchester. They walked hand in hand everywhere they went, and Bliss loved how Connor would randomly wrap his arms around her and nuzzle her neck. He had often slowed his pace and even had stopped a few times to make sure Bliss' feet were okay. She happily told him that they were not hurting her at all.

They took the scenic road back to Manchester and stopped at a Tavern in Londonderry to eat. Neither brought up what tomorrow would bring. They traded stories from their youth, high school, and even from Afghanistan. They told each other dreams they had for their future and Connor smiled when Bliss said she hoped she could be the kind of mother Rose was. Bliss wasn't just saying that either. Rose was kind, but tough. She had endured the General being overseas for long periods of time and she had done just fine raising Connor, Collin, and Caitlyn.

Connor was pleased that she wanted to settle down someday and have children. He'd been slightly worried that she wouldn't be happy being a mom, especially being career Army.

When they finished dinner they headed back to the motel and stopped at a Pub near their motel. A band was playing country music band and when Connor saw that she was tapping her foot to the music, he took her hand and led her onto the small dance floor. Connor looked so sexy as he moved to the music. Bliss saw woman glancing his way, so she proprietarily played her hands over his chest as she gyrated rhythmically against him. A slow tempo song played next and Connor crushed her against him and kissed her hard, leaving her breathless.

"What was that for?" She asked when the kiss ended.

"That was me, showing you, how I feel right now."

Bliss grinned up at him mischievously, she could feel his arousal.

"Ready to leave?" She asked keeping her lower half fused with his.

"Hell yeah," he said giving her a peck on her lips before leading her outside.

They drove the short distance to their motel but to their dismay discovered Hammond and Sparrow waiting for them in a car near their door.

Connor's heart pitched as a foreboding premonition assaulted him. All four waited while Connor silently opened the door. He held it open, even though every fiber in his body was telling him to shut them out. After taking off their coats they sat at the small round table.

"You do know what time it is?" Connor said sourly pointing to the digital clock which read 2:00am.

"Have you decided to help us?" Hammond asked Bliss, ignored Connor's question. "Only if my CO gives me the okay. I'm supposed to be on R and R."

"He has."

"Given me permission?"

Hammond handed her two pieces of paper. One was an email addressed to Hammond from Otterman stating that as long as she was physically able, that she was on loan to the CIA for an undisclosed operation that involved National Security. The other piece of paper was the formal paperwork making Hammond her new CO until further notice. Connor had been looking at Bliss' face while she had read through each paper and he knew, whatever it was, was official. Bliss handed Connor the papers and looked to Hammond.

"So, what's next?"

"What's next is you come with us." Sparrow said

smugly.

"When?" Bliss refused to look at Sparrow.

"Now."

Connor stood quickly, "No fucking way. You said tomorrow."

"It is tomorrow." Sparrow said pleased to have set Connor off.

Bliss put her hand on Connor's arm effectively mollifying him against any more outbursts.

"Why the sudden change?" Bliss asked.

"We thought they were holding your dad in England. We just got word that he's somewhere in New York State."

"How did they get him here?"

"No idea and it doesn't matter. We don't have much time." Hammond said seriously. "So, what's the plan?" She asked.

Hammond looked at Connor and then back to Bliss. "I'll tell you when we are on the way."

Connor leaned towards Bliss. "I don't like this."

"What can I do? I have an order from Otterman." She said tapping the paper he was still holding.

Hammond stood up putting on his coat looking at Bliss. "Listen, these people are terrorists. The information they want must be pretty damning to the US if it gets out. If they don't use your father against you, they'll use someone else you are close too."

"Shit." Connor muttered thinking of his family.

Bliss touched Connor's arm. "Connor you have to tell the General."

Connor nodded. Hammond looked to Connor. "We already have someone watching your parent's house."

"Thanks." He couldn't believe this was happening. He

couldn't think of any loophole to keep Bliss with him. His hands were basically tied, and he was beyond pissed that Hammond and Sparrow were whisking her away in the middle of night.

"Gather your clothes and kiss handsome here good bye. I'm done with this Podunk hamlet." Sparrow said standing up. She walked out the door and Hammond followed, telling Bliss she had five minutes.

As soon as they left, Bliss started throwing her clothes into one of the large plastic bags from one of the stores she had bought clothes from. She retrieved her toothbrush and hairbrush from the bathroom and when she came back out Connor was standing near the bed still holding the papers. Bliss walked to him and wrapped her arms around him, burying her face into his chest. They stood quietly for a minute relishing what they knew would be the last time they would probably see each other for a while.

"Connor, I don't have a phone, but I'll try to call you. Also, I'll use the Magoo email if I can."

"Bliss, I don't want you to go with them. I'm worried."

"I am too honestly. My mother would flip out if she knew I was with the CIA."

Connor had to chuckle at that. "Well, she wouldn't be alone, wait till I tell dad." "You have to make sure they stay safe Connor."

"I will. Dad will probably move everyone onto the base."

"That would be smart."

Connor threaded his fingers through Bliss' curly strands pulling her closer and fused his mouth with hers. It was a kiss that would have to hold each of them until they saw each other again. It was warm, sweet, and desperate all wrapped into a brief, all consuming, moment of splendor.

Connor lifted from her mouth and held her tightly placing his chin on her head. "I love you. Be safe and don't take any shit from Sparrow."

Bliss chuckled. "I won't and you stay safe, too. I love you Connor Doherty."

Connor walked her outside and gave her another quick kiss before watching her settle into the black sedan. He heard Sparrow mutter, 'How sweet.' And he wished he knew why she was being such a bitch. He'd have to ask Andy when he got home. Andy had been with her friend that night.

Connor watched the sedan drive away and he had to physically remind himself to breathe his chest hurt so.

Chapter 22

As Hammond drove the sedan tout of the motel lot,
although Bliss was grief stricken having to leave
Connor, she observed two cars turn into the stony lot.
She watched as the drivers spun their tires recklessly,
sending the gravel flying, and an ominous feeling
permeated her.

"Wait." She said. "I forgot something back in the
room." Hammond made the turn onto Route 7.

"Sorry, no can do." Bliss saw Sparrow shoot
Hammond a perplexed look. "What did you forget?"
Sparrow asked her civilly.

"Uh, my brush."

"I'll get you another one." She said turning back
around.

Bliss sagged back in her seat. Her imagination was
probably just in overdrive she decided as she sat back
in her seat.

"So, what's the plan?"

"We get you to a safe spot and send out a message
that we have what they want."

"So, I'm bait?"

"Yes, but we won't let them get to you."

"Can you give me any details?" Bliss asked
exasperated.

Sparrow turned around, seemingly just as exasperated
as Bliss was.

"No, we don't have the details. They will contact us
when they know we have you." "Why do they think
you'll hand me over? It doesn't make sense."

Hammond looked at her through the rear-view mirror. "They don't know, that we know, you have the gift. They think, that we think, we are just handing over an Analyst that can just break codes."

"So, how do you know about my gift?"

"Jax, of course."

"What? He'd never tell anyone."

"He told us, because he knew if we went in this blind, that we could not only lose you and your dad, but a shit load of information."

"I still don't know why he'd trust you?"

Sparrow turned around in her seat. "Oh dear, seems like our little Lt. here doesn't know that her own brother is CIA."

"No way."

"Way," said Sparrow mocking her.

Bliss folded her arms across her chest and leaned her back on the headrest. This was surreal. Her father was alive, Jax was CIA. What the hell was she going to learn next? Bliss heard Sparrow muttered to Hammond, "Well, that shut her up."

It was still dark when Hammond drove them into Troy, where he stopped at a gas station mini-mart. Hammond got out and inserted a credit card to pump gas. Sparrow also got out and headed inside, Bliss took out her small fabric billfold from her plastic bag and followed her.

Sparrow entered the ladies' room and Bliss quickly went to the counter and bought a cheap disposable phone and a phone card. She then purchased a water and trail mix. She had just put the phone in her coat pocket when Sparrow appeared at her side. Bliss held up the water and trail mix giving Sparrow a syrupy f -

you smile. She pushed the billfold back into her rear pocket and gathered her water and trail mix.

Bliss headed for the rest room. Inside, she quickly opened the phones packaging, downloaded the minutes from the card onto it and called the number in their motel room. When Connor didn't answer, her gut pinched apprehensively. She reasoned he could have left already, but she couldn't get those damn cars that had blown into the parking lot just as they were exiting, out of her mind. Bliss called the number of Jax's liaison next.

"04211958"

"Hold please." Came the familiar response.

"Bliss, twice in one day, what's up?"

"Drew, I really need to speak to Jax."

"Well, I can tell him to call you."

"Drew, tell him I'm with Hammond and Sparrow."

Drew was quiet for a second.

"Why are you with them Bliss?"

"It's a long story and I can't explain it now. Connor Doherty, the Generals son, knows what's going on. I left him at the Bugle Motel in Manchester, Vermont. Can you tell Jax to call Connor please? It's important."

"Where are you now?"

"In Troy, NY."

"What the hell are you doing in there?" Sparrow yelled pounding on the door.

Bliss did not want to risk Sparrow hear her, so she closed the small cell and stuffed it in her coat pocket. Bliss opened the door. "Sheesh, can't I even pee in private?" She pretended to be pissed, as she mulled over what Drew had told her. He did not seem happy that she was with Hammond and Sparrow. If there was anything remotely hinky going on though, why would her CO tell her she was on loan to the CIA? There were too many questions that needed answering and Bliss knew then, that she couldn't trust anyone. She followed Sparrow to the car and Hammond pocketed his cell that he had been talking on when he saw them, and grumbled about women taking so long, which made Bliss remember Connor, who had basically said the same thing when she'd come out of the drug store. Bliss was worried about Connor. She would have to call the General and Rose to make sure Connor had made it home.

"Who were you talking too?" Sparrow asked Hammond as they all got into the car. "Cooper." Hammond told her. Then he glanced back at Bliss, silently gesturing to Sparrow not to ask any more questions in front of her.

An hour later, heading south on 84, Hammond turned off the highway at the Kingston exit heading west on 28.

Bliss saw Sparrow raise her eyebrow questioning Hammond and then Hammond glanced at her in the rear view mirror, again thwarting any more questions from Sparrow. Bliss didn't like the fact that Sparrow didn't seem to know what was going. That could only mean that there had been some change in the actual game plan. She reasoned that Hammond was probably being extra cautious by not giving Sparrow any advanced information considering the way she had been openly aggressive towards her.

Twenty minutes later Hammond pulled into a closed Minnewaska State Park.

"What are we doing here?" Sparrow asked.

Hammond didn't answer her and Bliss' spicy senses kicked into overdrive.

He drove through the park, and Bliss noticed that there were trails that were used for cross country skiing in the winter and hiking in the warmer months, but the park was currently deserted. Bliss, who was sitting behind Sparrow, saw a small black object appear between the door and the seat. It was a gun. Sparrow was handing her a gun? Bliss knew that things were about to go south. The problem was she didn't know if Sparrow was giving her the gun so that she could shoot her and claim it was self- defense, or if Hammond was dirty and Sparrow had just figured it out.

Bliss cautiously took the gun from Sparrow and put it in her pocket.

Hammond turned down a small road that had a layer of snow still on it. He was taking them someplace that was remote. "Is it happening here?" Bliss asked hoping he would
reveal the plan.

He looked back at her through the rear-view mirror and didn't answer her question, instead asking one of his own. "So, Bliss, I see that you wear a medical bracelet.
What's it for?"

"Oh, I'm just allergic to some meds." She lied hoping she didn't sound as nervous as she felt.

Hammond nodded. Bliss thought it odd that he would notice it.

Hammond turned down a road that had big orange cones placed to keep out cars. "Where are we going?"

Bliss asked nervously.

"We are actually here." Hammond said pulling into a small, very dark lot. As the car's lights swept the lot, Bliss could make out a porta- potty and a metal garden shed sitting on the edge of the parking area. He stopped the car and got out. Sparrow got out as well, and Bliss could tell she was not happy. Bliss remained in the car. Hammond walked around the car, past Sparrow and opened her door but Bliss remained in the car.

"Please don't be difficult. Get out." Bliss got out of the car nervously looking around. "Hammond what's going on?" Sparrow said glancing around the obscure wooded area. Hammond turned towards Sparrow and with one quick movement bashed a gun on the side of her head. Sparrow grunted and collapsed unconscious onto the ground. Bliss tried to move out of Hammonds reach, but she was caged between her open door and his body. The gun that had smashed Sparrow in the head was now pointing at her. Bliss saw movement behind Hammond, and she watched as a man step out from behind the shed and crunch through the crisp snow towards them.

"Well done." He told Hammond. Bliss shivered instantaneously hearing the familiar British accent. The man moved closer and Bliss saw the blue eyes that had been haunting her dreams; the same eyes that she had seen in Afghanistan. Her heart was beating so fast that she thought she might hyperventilate, and she looked down at Sparrow desperately, but saw that her injury had been so damaging that the snow around her head was turning pink with blood. She wasn't moving at all and Bliss could not even tell if she was breathing.

"The money better be in my account." Hammond said to Blue Eyes, who she now knew was Conti.

"It is, check it."

Hammond took out his phone and after a few clicks smiled. "Good."

Conti now had a gun pointed at Bliss as well.

"I don't think your boyfriend will be able to help you out of this one." Conti said to her with almost a bored tone in his voice. Why had he said that? Bliss was sweating nervously even though it was freezing out.

"I'm out of here." Hammond said walking to the front of the car. He got in and Conti pulled Bliss from the door well and before he shut it, he told Hammond to ditch the car as soon as possible.

Hammond drove off barely missing Sparrows foot that remained unmoving on the cold ground.

Conti pushed Bliss towards the shed and when they rounded the corner she saw a truck with tinted windows parked behind it. Bliss froze and when Conti tried to shove her towards it, she resisted.

"Come on, get in."

"No." Bliss said.

"Sweetheart, you do realize I have a gun pointed at you."

"Yes, and I also realize that I have information that you need so you won't kill me."

The truck door swung open and Bliss' knees wobbled as Zarghun emerged. Hammond laughed seeing the expression on Bliss' face.

"I see you recognize my friend."

Bliss didn't answer. Her mind brought up the memories of him slashing her feet and she shuddered.

She shook her head back and forth clearing her mind from that awful memory. She had to focus. She had a gun and a phone and that meant she had a chance. There was no way she could take both men on, and she was sure Zarghun probably had a gun as well. She had to think.

Zarghun reached into the truck and pulled out bolt cutters, which he used on the lock of the shed's door. The heavy lock fell open, banging on the metal frame and with the solitude of the woods surrounding them it sounded much louder than it actually was. Bliss jammed her hands in her coat pocket grasping the gun. She couldn't risk being inside the enclosed shed's space with these men. It was too small and even if she got off a clean shot on one of the men, the other would be close enough to overtake her. Bliss held the gun inside her pocket with her finger ready on the trigger; she felt for the safety and pushed it off. Zarghun opened the creaky door giving Bliss the opportunity she needed. Bliss turned towards Conti and without even taking the gun from her pocket sent three quick rounds flying towards his torso. The bang from the gun echoed loudly and Conti fell with a grunt to the ground, clutching his stomach. Blood poured from his stomach; she had hit him at least once, Zarghun whirled on her and launched himself at her, knocking what he thought was her gun away, but Bliss had traded the gun for the phone. Zarghun sent her careening into the hard-shed wall, delivering a painful punch to her cheek. Bliss grasped the gun again, leaving it in her now tattered pocket and sent two shots towards him, but they missed wide. He deftly rolled to his side landing on one knee. The anger on his face was terrifying. Bliss tried to distance herself, hoping to get off a better shot, but he launched himself at her like a crazed animal. She tried to pull the gun from her pocket, but it caught on her shredded coat. She managed to squeeze off a couple of shots, but again, she missed him completely. Zarghun pinned her against the shed with his large body and wretched her hand from the inside her coat before twisting her right arm behind her back so violently that black spots swam in front of her eyes. He flung her to the ground, her face slamming against the cold snow packed ground. He placed his knee in the middle of her back, holding her arms behind her, rendering her immobile.

Bliss was gulping for air, the throw to the ground had knocked the wind out of her and with his full weight on top of her and with his knee pressing down on her lungs, she couldn't draw in a breath.

She continued to struggle beneath him hoping to dislodge his large body from hers.

She was suffocating, and as she tried one last time to move him off of her back, she heard a sickening pop and her last conscious though was of the unbearable pain in her shoulder.

Chapter 23

A consuming pain wracked Bliss' body as she was thrown against something hard and cold. Her first thought was that she no longer had her coat on because she was freezing and there was no buffer between her shirt and whatever she was laying on. Although she thought her eyes were open, she saw nothing but blackness. She realized she was blindfolded and gagged. She discovered that her hands were bound behind her back with a plastic zip tie and her right shoulder was throbbing with white, hot pain. Bliss moved so that her weight was off of her hurt shoulder and she took a few focusing breathes through her nose, as the pain in her shoulder subsided slightly. She pulled her legs up to her chest and rubbed the side of cloth that was over her eyes against her knee until she had it moved to her forehead. This was another thing Bo had taught her. When attempting to pull a blindfold downwards, the nose would hold it in place. However, a blindfold, if pushed up, could effectively be moved. Once again Bo's advice came in handy as she slowly pushed the cloth from her eyes. Her vision became accustomed to the dark and she saw a very thin line of light that stretched around her. Bliss realized that it was daytime.

Next, she rubbed her gag on her knee and managed to dislodge that as well. Bliss took in deep breaths, relishing the cool air that she sucked deep into her lungs.

She heard a motor and from the way she was being tossed around she realized she was in the back of the truck. Her back ached where his knee had been, but as she took stock of the rest of her body, she realized he had not done anything else to her, except tear her arm from the shoulder socket. Moving pained her, so she wedged herself against the truck bed wall and used her feet against what was either the top of the bed or the tailgate to stop from rolling whenever the truck took a turn.

She no longer had her coat on. Bliss used her fingers to feel for her bracelet and when she did not feel it, she knew he must have removed it. Zarghun wouldn't be stupid enough to bring it with him, but she hoped that he had left it near where she had been taken from in case Sparrow was still alive.

Bliss was freezing and she tried to curl up hoping to warm herself. Her teeth were chattering, and her cheek was tender where she had hit the ground. The only positive thing was that the cold had numbed her shoulder enough that the pain was becoming bearable. Bliss remained in a curled position for what seemed like a very long time and she wondered where he was taking her. She rubbed the blindfold against the trucks lining and was successful in totally removing it from her head. Bliss determined which end of the truck was near the front end, so she squirmed towards it, gritting her teeth as the pain from her shoulder resurfaced. She placed her ear against the cold metal and heard voices. Her heart dropped realizing that Conti was still alive. Their voices weren't tangible, so she repositioned herself and was able to make out a few words.

Conti, with his unmistakable British accent, was telling Zarghan, that he needed a doctor.

Zarghan said something, but she couldn't understand him, and she remembered that she had difficulty understanding him in Afghanistan, even without the hum of the engine and the metal barrier now between them. The only word she was able to understand came from Conti; Doctor.

Where were they taking her? Was her father there? Now that they had her, maybe they didn't need him, and they would kill him? Bliss realized that was probably the plan all along since Hammond had obviously been paid well to deliver her. Maybe they never had her father. Bliss lay her head down against the truck bed floor as a wretched feeling of despair settled over her. This was not good, and unlike when she was in Afghanistan, she had no idea when anyone would realize she was missing, and now without her bracelet, how would anyone find her?

Bliss had no idea how much time had passed but she felt the truck turn sharply and she bounced against the wall biting her tongue, so she didn't cry out loud in pain. The truck slowed and she heard two doors open. Without the noise of the engine she could hear Zarghun and Conti much clearer now.

She was able to piece together enough of the conversation to understand that they were at a doctor's office. Both doors slammed shut and Bliss knew she had been left alone. They must have felt pretty confident that she was not a threat; maybe they thought she was still passed out? After all, she had been blindfolded and gagged. Bliss shimmied to the tailgate and tried wedging her good shoulder against the bed's cover. She couldn't believe her luck that there was actually some give to it. Bliss realized that the trucks bed cover must be like the one Connor had on his truck. Bliss had helped him install it when he had been home on leave one Christmas. She pulled up the schematics from her memory bank. Even if it wasn't exactly like Connor's, she still had some insight. The problem was that she couldn't use her hands and her one shoulder was dead weight.

Bliss used the back of her head to feel where the small latch was. Normally, to open the truck bed's cover the tailgate needed to be open, but Bliss realized if she could unlatch the cover from the inside that she might be able to push the back section of the cover up. If she could, unlatch it.

She felt the small metal bolt and quickly lay on her back toeing off her one boot. Using her toes, she worked the latch, and finally she was able to wiggle it enough that when she pressed her feet against the cover, she saw it give.

Bliss quickly moved to the other side and repeated the process. Just as she was about to kick up against the cover, she heard a door slam. She knew if it was Zarghun coming back to the truck, she knew would not get very far if she tried to escape at that moment. She deduced that Conti had to be with the doctor. She knew she had hit him, and she reasoned that given the placement of her shot, he would need treatment for longer than the amount of time they had been parked for.

Bliss heard one of the truck doors open and the engine restart. Knowing that she had successfully unlatched the back piece of the truck bed cover, a glimmer of hope sliced through her. She had a chance now, a fighting chance, she just had to execute her escape so that Zarghun couldn't recapture her.

Bliss shoved her foot back into her boot and wiggled back up towards the truck's cab, hoping to gather any useful information.

Unfortunately, all was quiet, not even the radio played. She'd been hoping that she might hear something that would tell her where she was. She thought perhaps she'd hear a radio commercial, but Zarghun, if it were Zarghun driving, she really couldn't be positive about that either, drove in silence.

Bliss slid back down towards the tailgate wanting to be ready, praying she would recognize an opportunity to initiate her escape. She knew she would have to kick up and back on the cover. Hopefully it would open enough for her to get out. She positioned her head against the tailgate so her kick would send the cover up and

towards the cab of the truck. Hopefully.

Her next problem would be navigating out of the bed without the use of her hands. Bliss shut her eyes and envisioned exactly what she would do, and she replayed it and replayed it in her mind while remaining ready.

The truck had slowed, and she could tell they were in traffic. She didn't want to try her escape only to be hit by another car, so she knew timing and opportunity would be crucial. Bliss held the cover up an inch catching a glimpse of the sky and listening intently for what was around her.

The truck came to a full stop and Bliss could hear a

bell sounding; ding, ding, ding.

Bliss realized they were stopped at a train track crossing. Now or never she said to herself as she kicked up hard on the folding bed cover. The black cover folded back like Bliss had hoped it would. She quickly rolled to her knees, popped up, placed her ass on the side wall of the truck bed on the passenger side, and slid to the street on her feet. Zarghun was already out of the truck heading towards her. There were a few cars in front of her waiting for the train to pass and another car was behind them. Bliss sprinted towards the tracks and saw the train was fast approaching. She was doing her best to stay ahead of Zarghun when a man got out of his car. Bliss yelled for him to call the police.

The Good Samaritan realized that something sinister was happening. He saw that Zarghun was chasing her, so he stepped in front of him, effectively slowing him down. Bliss heard a gun fire, but she didn't stop running. She prayed the man wasn't hurt.

She ducked under the tracks warning barricades and sprinted over the tracks a few seconds ahead of the train. She kept running but looked down the track to see how long the train was. She knew she had about 30 seconds before Zarghun would be able to see her. Luckily, she was in an area with buildings nearby. Bliss ran up the road ducking into the second building, which was a storefront. She ran through the store and out the back without anyone seeing her. She was in a back ally and her eyes locked on a door in that ally that was being held open with a small plastic crate. She jogged across the ally and through that door. She was in a back-hallway foyer and she pressed herself against a wall to remain concealed. After taking a few seconds to catch her breath she glanced down the hall and saw that it led to a kitchen for a restaurant.

Bliss quietly moved the crate that was holding the door open with her foot causing the door to close. She leaned back against the wall, her chest was heaving, and her legs wobbled uncontrollably. She'd made it. She couldn't believe that she had gotten out of the truck. Racing the train to cross the tracks had been way to close and she sent a quick prayer to God thanking him for keeping her safe.

Hiding in the small foyer she could hear the people in the kitchen talking and she honed in on the peoples voices hoping none would come down the hall. She thought of asking them for help, but something held her back from doing that. Her reasoning was if Conti felt safe enough to seek medical help around there, it stood to reason that others may be supporting his cause.

As Bliss looked around the vestibule she saw, a snow shovel, a large bag of salt, a crate of lettuce, flattened boxes and two unopened boxes that were stacked on top of each other and tied with string. Hanging near those boxes was a pair of scissors, a box cutter, and a large metal hook.

She took a quick step across the small room and turned her back so her fingers could
grasp the box cutter. Thankfully she was able to grip it and she used her thumb to expose the sharp razor. Bliss carefully sawed off the plastic zip tie at her wrist and when the plastic severed, and her hands fell apart she groaned out loud as her injured arm sagged

uselessly to her side. The pain that pummeled her made her physically ill. She did not have time to dwell on how much she was hurting because she heard footsteps coming down the hall. She put the box cutter in her front pocket, opened the door and ran out to the ally, she could hear who ever had been in the hallway yell, "Hey!" before the door closed behind her.

Bliss looked down the ally and saw another door; this one had a sign next to it reading Roses' Hair Salon. Hoping it was Divine intervention she quickly opened the door and stepped inside. The door closed loudly behind her and Bliss remained in the dimly lit hallway gathering herself.

She was again in a small vestibule that held a shovel, a bucket of salt, and a couple of winter coats hanging on a wooden coat rack.

A cheery voice called to her, "Welcome to Rose's."

Bliss watched as a short rotund woman approach her with a huge smile on her face.

Bliss held herself as normal as possible, she knew she had to look a mess and the one side of her body was tilted awkwardly.

"Oh, dear, Honey are you all right?"

"I, uh, slipped out back there and I hurt my shoulder."

"Why the heck didn't you use the front door?" The woman asked with a hint of annoyance in her voice.

"I didn't want anyone to see me." Bliss said pointing to her swollen face. As she spoke Bliss noticed dried blood on her shirt. She touched her face gingerly but didn't feel any wound. She figured the blood was probably from Conti.

The woman instantly softened. "Aw that is nasty. I've

been in one of those relationships before." Rose said assuming a significant other had hit her. "Get out now, Honey.

They never end well.

Bliss nodded, and the woman stepped closer to her. "How bad's the arm?"

"I think it's dislocated."

"Looks painful."

"It is." Bliss told her honestly realizing the battered woman lie was a terrific cover.

"Well, I assume you came in to fix that hair of yours, but I suppose you better get that arm fixed first."

"Yes, is there a 24-hour Urgent Care or someplace like that close by?"

"Yup, four blocks down and two over. You can't drive, can you?"

"No, I walked here."

"Well, one of my girls, Hallie is just getting ready to leave. She goes that way. Let me see if she can drop you. There's no way you can walk that far."

Bliss faltered quickly, "I really don't want to put anyone out."

Rose looked at her and smiled gently. "He's looking for you, right?"

Bliss nodded and pretended to look embarrassed. A younger woman walked into the small hallway, eyeing Bliss suspiciously.

"Hallie, this here is?" Rose said needing Bliss' name.

"Caitlyn." Bliss said quickly, it was the first name that came to mind.

"Caitlyn here needs a ride to Omni-Med and she needs to get there without someone seeing her, if you get my drift?" Rose said championing her.

"Oh, hell, damn men!" Hallie said tersely. Bliss realized she'd found another sympathizer. "You wait right here, sister, I'll pull up and beep."

Bliss smiled weakly, grateful she had walked into the salon. "Thank you, thank you both."

Rose waited with Bliss and when they heard the horn, Rose popped her head out of the door to make sure no one was in the ally. She fully opened the door and Bliss thanked her again and hurried into a little compact car. She had to reach across her body to shut the door and the movement jostling her shoulder proved excruciating.

Hallie had backed into the ally so when Bliss shut the door she took off. Bliss slumped down in her seat. Hallie recognized that Bliss was attempting to stay out of sight from her presumably woman bashing boyfriend.

"Are you married, Hun?"

"No." Bliss answered quietly.

"Good, won't have to deal with any lawyers when you leave that bastard of a boyfriend." Bliss smiled weakly. "Yeah, I'm out of here." Bliss replied and she saw that her response made Hallie smile.

Hallie pulled into an Omni-Med and Bliss scanned the parking lot and nearby street for any sign of the truck.

"Here," Hallie said reaching into the back seat and placing a sweatshirt and a knit hat on Bliss' lap. "This should help."

"Really, I'm okay." Bliss told her trying to give it back.

"No, you take it and keep hidden until you're out of here. You got family you can go to?" "Yes."
"You got a phone?"
"I ran out without it." Bliss told her.
"Here, use mine." Hallie handed her an iPhone.
Bliss called the Doherty's house number, but no one answered. "Can I try another number?" she asked Hallie, who said yes immediately. Bliss called Caitlyn cell. After the fourth ring she picked up.
"Hi, it's me." Bliss said, relieved she had reached someone.
"Do you have any idea what you've done?" Caitlyn hissed so vehemently that Bliss almost didn't recognize her voice.
"I" Bliss stuttered. "What?"
"Connor's been beaten up. He's in ICU fighting for his life."
"Oh my God!"
"You stay the hell away from us!" Caitlyn spat out before cutting the connection.
Bliss was visibly shaken, and Hallie patted her back.
"Don't you worry. Some people think you need to stand by your man no matter what."
Bliss realized that Hallie thought the person she had called had given her hell for leaving her boyfriend.
Bliss nodded; she was numb. The irony was she had left her boyfriend and he had been hurt because she had left him. Once again, the feeling of being alone pummeled her. Her heart ached thinking that Connor was hurt. She frantically tried to reign in the panic that threatened to render her immobile.
A slow count to ten and a few deep breaths thwarted the debilitating panic attack. Bliss thanked Hallie and

turned all the way in her seat to open the door, since she could not
use her left arm.

Before she shut it, she once again thanked Hallie.

Bliss walked into the Omni-Med scanning the waiting room from the doorway. She signed in and produced her medical card. The doctor was able to see her right away and Bliss was relieved when she was taken into one of the back rooms. The nurse asked her a ton of questions and Bliss answered them all, except when she asked how she had been hurt, Bliss refused to answer. The nurse tried a few times to get her to open up, but Bliss shook her head and remained quiet.

The doctor came in and gave her shoulder a few shots to numb it. He told Bliss to count to 3, but when she reached 1, he yanked on her arm and Bliss heard the pop as it went back into the socket. The doctor also tried to get Bliss to tell him what happened, but she insisted it was too personal. The entire time in the doctor's office Bliss was thinking about Connor. She wondered where he was, and she knew she had to see him despite what Caitlyn had said.

The doctor cleaned Bliss' cheek and applied a steri-strip to a small cut over her eye. Now she knew where the blood from her shirt was from. Bliss had no idea what she looked like, but she knew it had to be pretty bad. When the doctor finished, he handed her a card with the number of a hot line for battered woman. Bliss took the card and slowly got down from the examining table. Her right arm was in a sling and the shots had numbed it sufficiently that she was not in any pain.

She thanked the doctor and left the office. Outside,

she put the sweatshirt on as best she could with one hand, her one arm was being held against her chest by the sling, so one sweatshirt sleeve hung loose. She then put on the cap, stuffing as much of her underneath it as possible. Bliss began walking towards the town's center that Hallie had passed. She kept her head down and ducked into doorways keeping her eyes peeled for any sign of Zarghun and the truck.

Bliss came to a large shopping mall plaza and saw a Wal-Mart. Perfect she thought. Inside the Wal-Mart she went to the rest room first and was shocked at how disheveled and pathetic she looked. Pieces of her hair were streaked with blood; her shirt was torn, and she had lost one of her earrings. Instinctively she reached for the necklace Connor had given her and almost wept with joy when she felt the delicate piece of jewelry. After cleaning the blood out of her hair Bliss shopped. She bought a new shirt, a pair of jeans, a winter jacket, a thick scarf, and a prepaid cell. The Walmart had an attached hair salon. Bliss needed to blend in, and new clothes would help, but her wild hair and battered face was noteworthy. Bliss walked in and was able to get her hair washed and braided. Before she paid, she asked if she could use the bathroom to put on her new clothes. They must have taken pity on her because the woman even cut the tags off for her.

After leaving Wal-Mart, Bliss walked to the Friendly's Restaurant next door. She sat in a back booth so she could see the door and ordered a coffee and scrambled eggs. Her jaw was still tender from the hit she had taken, and she didn't think she could chew on anything.

Bliss dialed Drew Tellers number and after saying the code numbers Drew answered. "Where are you?"

"I have no idea." She told him wearily.

"Bliss, Connor's been hurt."

"I know."

"How?"

"Caitlyn told me."

"He's bad Bliss; some guys did a number on him."

Bliss did not answer right away. A horrifying feeling of dread had come over her.

"Will he, will he make it?"

"He's in ICU."

"Where?"

"Bennington, Vermont at the VA Hospital, but you can't go there Bliss."

Bliss had barely heard what he said and then it registered. "Why not Drew?" She was so afraid he would reinforce what Caitlyn had said, that the family did not want her near Connor.

"Bliss, we found Sparrow, she was hurt bad and she's a wreck knowing you were taken by Hammond. We can't go into this on the phone. We have to bring you in."

"Bring me in? To the CIA you mean?" She replied starchily.

"You know?"

"Yes, it's been a delightful twenty- four hours." She spat out.

"Well, you were going to be told soon anyway. Jax just wanted to do it in person.

Listen, tell me where you are, we'll send someone for you."

"First I need to see Connor."

"No, you need to come in where we can protect you."

"Tell Jax to meet me at the VA in Bennington. I'll be there." Bliss disconnected.

Her mind was whirling, and she was afraid to eat the eggs because she knew she'd throw it up. Bliss was fighting back tears. She had never felt so alone and so disconnected in her life. Even when her mom had died the Doherty's had rallied around her. Now she had no one. No Doherty's, Connor could be dead for all she knew, Jax had betrayed her telling her he was DEA when all along he had been CIA, even her own CO had set her up with a dirty Special Agent. As Bliss hung her head, she noticed the paper placemats on the table and discovered that she was in Troy, NY. She was an hour from Connor and that's where she was headed. She had to see him, if only for a minute. Bliss paid her bill and saw that a bus was just pulling up to a weather protected bus stop. She jogged to it feeling the pain in her shoulder again. She knew the numbing shots the doctor had administered were wearing off.

Bliss hopped on the bus and was delighted that it was heading north to Hoosick Falls. She asked the driver if another bus would be coming that could take her to Bennington from there and he told her there was, but she'd have to wait for it.

After talking to the bus driver Bliss sat in the back of the bus and tried to calm herself, but it was impossible. What if Connor dies and it was all her fault? The guilt that assaulted her took her breath away. She thought of Connor and the wonderful night that they had had together. She could not imagine life without him, but it appeared that even if he were to pull through, that his family would never allow for them to be together now. The crushing pain of knowing her and Connor were never going to be together again broke her and she sobbed silently into her forearm.

The Hoosick Falls bus station was a small one room, one-bathroom building. The next bus to Bennington was at 6:00pm, that was five hours away. She thought about hitch hiking, but if Zarghun were to drive past her she'd be as good as dead. Bennington was only twenty minutes away by car.

There was a newsstand inside the small bus depot and Bliss bought water and a packet of Advil. She took the Advil immediately, not because of her shoulder, which did hurt, but because she had a whopper of a headache. Unfortunately, taking the Advil on an almost empty stomach made her so nauseous that she had to sprint to the bathroom where she vomited up the coffee that she had earlier. Bliss cleaned up and washed her face. Her eyelid was purple, and her cheek was puffy and red. Her jaw was also turning a sickening shade of battered blue. She returned to the newsstand and bought peanut butter crackers and another packet of Advil and after eating the crackers she took the Advil, which thankfully stayed down.

Waiting for the bus to Bennington was one of the hardest things Bliss ever had to do. She was so close to Connor, yet she couldn't get to him. She had no idea how she would get in to see him, once she got there, she assumed his family was with him. Finally, the bus came. Bliss gave the driver her ticket and sat in the back again, still being vigilant. They arrived in Bennington at 6:25pm. Bliss got off the bus and asked the bus attendant where the VA Hospital was. She was relieved that it was on the main road and only a half mile from the bus stop. Bliss started walking. It was dark and cold and except for watching for Zarghun's truck, the only thing on Bliss' mind was Connor. She walked up the front steps of the small hospital and asked where ICU was. The nurse pointed out a hallway but told her only family was allowed in there. Bliss did not want to run into any of the Doherty's, so she headed in the opposite direction. Hoping to get in another way.

A nurse asked if she could help her after she noticed her bruised face and arm in the sling, so Bliss decide that might be a good way into the ICU area. Bliss told the nurse she was supposed to be seen but she couldn't remember which doctor she had an appointment with. She handed the nurse her Army ID, which was thankfully in her wallet. The nurse must have not had thought this was out of the ordinary, because she took Bliss name and escorted her to a waiting room telling her to sit tight. She even brought Bliss a cup of water.

Bliss waited patiently and a young doctor appeared in the doorway and gestured for her to follow him.

"I'm Dr. Porter. We didn't have your name in the system, but I'm between patients, let me take a look okay." He was soft spoken and had the kindest eyes she ever saw. They were close to Connor's eye color and she felt tears dampen her cheeks.

"You're going to be fine Lt."

Bliss wiped her eyes quickly. She recognized this

could be an opportunity to find out about Connor. "I know." She told the doctor. "I'm just worried about my friend that was brought in here. He was beaten up."

"Captain Doherty?" The doctor said as he manipulated her shoulder slightly.

"Yes, is he, is he going to be okay?" The fear in her voice did not need to be faked. "He's going to recover. We just moved him out of ICU a couple of hours ago. His family is here."

"Yes, I know I spoke with Caitlyn, his sister." She told him adding some validity to her story without even lying.

"They were pretty upset, but now that he's been downgraded, they went to find a hotel room."

"They are a wonderful family." She said sadly.

"Well, everything looks good. I changed the bandage and you should get some ice on those bruises. You didn't tell me how you got hurt."

"Oh, it's a long story I'd rather not go into right now." She said softly, to Bliss' surprise the doctor did not try to needle her further.

Bliss thanked him, and she left the room. She turned away from the exit and walked down a series of hallways. There were signs indicating x-ray, neurology and Bliss kept walking until she found a floor that appeared to be for patients.

She walked down the hall pretending to know where she was going and after her third turn saw a nurse's station.

"I'm looking for Connor Doherty."

"Visiting hours are almost over and I know he's asleep." The nurse told her.

"Yes, I know," she lied. "I was just with Doctor Porter and he told me if I hurried, I could just peek in on him."

"Oh, well if Dr. Porter said it was okay, I guess it's okay." She said cheerily.

The nurse pointed to a room close to the station and Bliss thanked her. Before she walked in, she peeked inside to make sure none of the Doherty's were inside. Relieved he was alone she walked in.

Connor was lying in the bed and she gasped when she saw him, he was unrecognizable. His one eye was swollen shut and the other was covered with a thick white bandage. He had a broken arm, broken leg, and his lip was stitched. He did not have a gown covering his torso and she could see he had deep gashes that had been closed with sutures all over his chest. Large bruises covered him, and she knew he had been kicked violently. Bliss reached for his chart at the end of the bed and quickly read through his list of injuries. He also had suffered a bruised lung. Bliss' heart broke. She really had almost gotten him killed. Collin had been right all along. They were not good for each other.

Bliss walked to the side of the bed and was relieved that he seemed to be breathing normally and on his own. A small clear tube ran into his nose and he was hooked up to a blue monitor. A bag of clear liquid ran into his arm. She could hear that his breathing was more of a wheeze and that scared her.

She laid her hand on his and leaned into his face placing her cheek against his so she could whisper in his ear. "I am so sorry Connor. I never meant for you to get hurt. If I could take back that email, I sent you,

I would. Please get better." Tears fell from her cheeks wetting his cheeks. Bliss shut her eyes and silently prayed for Connor to recover.

She kissed his cheek then stood up. With a hard jerk on the silver necklace Connor had given her, she broke the dainty chain. She slopped the small charm off the chain and placed it in Connor's hand, folding his fingers over it so it remained in his palm. She tossed the broken chain in the nearby garbage can. "I will always you Connor Doherty." She said gently touching his forehead. She kissed his lips softly, "good bye."

Bliss turned and left the room. Her stomach was churning, and breathing was difficult because of the pain crushing her chest. She left the hospital using the front door making sure that she did not inadvertently run into the Doherty's.

Bliss did not have any idea as to what to do next. Her thoughts were consumed with self-pity knowing just left the one man she knew she would always love and self-loathing that she had gotten him hurt. She walked down the small drive past the little pond and as she reached the street a car swerved to the curb to stop next to her. They had found her! Bliss started to run. "Bliss! Stop!" Jax? It sounded like Jax. Bliss turned back to the car and standing on the sidewalk was Jax. She slowly walked back towards the car and Jax met her halfway. Bliss walked into his arms and Jax hugged his sister who started to sob. Jax immediately knew this wasn't good, Bliss never cried. Even as a kid, she had held back her tears until she was alone. He gently helped her into the back of the car and followed her inside before the car pulled away from the curb. It took a minute, but she finally pulled herself together enough to realize someone else must be with them if Jax was in the back seat with her. Jax was worried; he had never seen Bliss so distraught.

"Is he? Connor, did he?" He couldn't even finish his sentence it was so awful.

"No, no, he's going to be okay, but Jax he was really beaten badly."

"I don't understand then, why are you so upset?"

Bliss did not want to deal with that question so she asked him one of her own.

"You're CIA? What the hell Jax?"

"Oh boy. Drew told me you knew."

Bliss looked at the driver of the car to see a very handsome man smiling at her through the rear-view mirror.

"Drew?"

"That's me, nice to finally meet you in person." He said giving her a charming smile. "We have a lot to talk about." Jax said to Bliss.

"Yes, where are we headed?"

"Fairfax Virginia. CIA Headquarters."

"Bringing me in?" She said sarcastically.

"Yes and debriefing you on the way. You look exhausted. What the hell happened? Are you okay?"

"Yeah, my face got dinged up and my arm was dislocated, but I've been seen by a doctor." She managed a weak smile, "Two, actually."

Drew passed back a bottle of water. "Here."

Bliss took it and thanked him.

"So, Sparrow is okay?"

"Yeah, she got clocked on the head and took twenty stitches."

"Yeah, I saw the hit, it was brutal."

"She's been a mess; she's so worried about you."

"You're friends?"

"We've worked together."

Bliss nodded. Her breath hitched unevenly as her chest felt as if it was being constricted. She swallowed uneasily trying to cover the actual sickness she felt swelling inside of her knowing that Connor could date her or anyone else that he chose too now; if he recovered. Jax was looking at her with a worried expression on his face.

"Are you sick?"

Bliss didn't answer right away and Jax took her hand in his. She saw him glance at Drew and she saw Drew frown.

"Bliss do you want me to pull over?" Drew asked.

"I'm sorry, no, I'll be fine. I'm just tired."

Jax accepted her answer and looked somewhat relieved, but Bliss saw that Drew wasn't buying it. He kept looking at her in the rear-view mirror and the concern on his face was obvious.

They had been in the car for four hours as they turned onto 287 South in New Jersey. Bliss was leaning on the door with her head resting against the cool glass. She had tried to sleep, but every time she had shut her eyes, she saw Connor looking so battered and broken. The pain he must have endured must have been horrific and Bliss felt guilt consume her once again.

"We need gas." Drew told them.

Jax checked an App on his iPhone and told Drew that ten miles ahead there was a gas station just off the highway. Ten minutes later they pulled into a station and all of them got out to stretch their legs.

Jax went inside to buy some snacks while Drew stretched his legs. Bliss walked a little way from the car, her hands were stuffed in her pocket and her head was bowed. She had so many thoughts pounding through her that her head ached fiercely. She still wasn't safe. Zarghun and Conti were still out there hunting her. Well, maybe not Conti; physically. She had limited his activity. He could and probably was still pulling strings from wherever he was recovering. Bliss also wanted to know how Jax had gotten involved with the CIA. She needed to check in with Otterman, her CO. She had no idea if he knew that he had basically handed her over to a dirty Special Agent. She had so many questions, she rubbed her face unconsciously, hoping to wipe the hammering in her head away.

"Bliss?" Bliss turned to find Drew standing behind her. "I know you're not okay."

Bliss smiled at him weakly. "Busted." She tried to joke.

"Just tell me this, okay? Are you physically hurting? I mean, from your injuries?"

She sighed and headed back towards the car. Drew fell in step with her. "I'm okay Drew. Thank you."

"I have Advil." he offered.

"Um, might have to take you up on that."

"Eat something first, okay?"

Bliss smiled gently at him, he was being so kind. She thought about all the times they had spoken on the phone and she had never wondered what he had looked like, how old he was, nothing but business. Jax came out from the mini-mart and tossed Drew a coke and two packs of peanut butter crackers and he handed Bliss a Fresca. Just seeing the Fresca almost undid her, so Bliss quickly opened it and took a few sips hoping to cover her raw emotions. Jax got into the driver side and Drew got into the back with her. "Drew, you can sit in the front. I'm not going to jump out or anything."

Drew chuckled, "Maybe I want to sit back here with you, okay?"

Bliss shrugged her shoulders. She was too tired to argue and too busy beating herself up. The most important, toughest, kindest, and most caring person she had ever known had been almost beaten to death because of her, and she knew she would never see him again. The thought crushed her. He probably never wanted to lay eyes on her again. He had told her not to go. Why hadn't she listened to him?

A half a can of Fresca, a sleeve of Drew's peanut butter crackers, and three Advil later Bliss needed some answers.

"Jax, when did you become CIA?"

"You're ready to do this now?" He asked, pointing at her then to him and back to her; indicating that these questions were going to be two way.

"Might as well." She answered wearily.

"I was DEA, and then I met Drew." Bliss looked at Drew who had a small grin on his face.

"Drew and I met on an undercover operation two years ago. Neither of us knew the other was under. I was trying to gather evidence to convict this outlaw motorcycle gang for drugs and Drew was gathering intel about a Syrian connection to the same gang. One night we were drinking, and things started to get dicey. There was a gun fight and during it we both noticed that neither of us was aiming to kill."

"I called my Supervisor." Drew added, "and asked if there was another Agency involved with the gang that could have someone undercover. He got back to me a couple days later saying there was. I knew it was Jax."

"Yeah, and I'd done the same thing and got the same answer. I knew it was Drew."

"We were both brought in and we combined our operation." Drew said.

"After we closed our case, Drew and I became friends. He told me about some of the cases he had been on, so I decided to apply to the CIA. He helped me with the application and putting our fathers name on the resume helped."

"I thought CIA only worked abroad?"

"They work on cases that are important to National Security and sometimes those keep us in the states." Drew told her.

"Is he alive Jax? Dad? Hammond said he was."

"I've heard conflicting reports. I heard he was living in England and I thought about looking him up, but honestly I was afraid what I'd find."

"Like what?"

"Like if he had another family."

"Ouch, that never even crossed my mind."

"So, I was interviewed and passed all the tests and I've been CIA ever since. I was going to tell you, but I wanted to tell you face to face."

Drew handed Bliss another pack of crackers and she took them, peeling the cellophane and stuffing a whole one in her mouth. She then realized Jax had bought him only two packs and she'd already eaten one of them. She held the open pack out to him, slightly embarrassed.

Drew shook his head, "Jax said they're your favorites. I asked him to get them for you." Bliss blushed, self-conscious with his display of kindheartedness. His thoughtfulness reminded her of Connor; it was something he would have done, and she felt an emotional tug, sucking her downward.

Drew pushed the crackers back to her watching her closely. He had seen pictures of Bliss from Jax, and even with her thick glasses on Drew had seen that she was beautiful. How smart she was only served to make her more attractive. Jax was always talking about his little sister and all her accomplishments, and Drew felt like he already knew her. When they had started talking on the phone, being Jax's liaison, they had always spent a few minutes chatting amicably. Jax told him when they had been driving to Bennington that he thought Bliss was involved with Doherty and all Drew had thought was that the guy was a lucky bastard.

Seeing how Bliss had come out of the VA hospital, both he and Jax thought Doherty had died. Neither of them expected her to say he was alive and then fall apart the way she had. Even Drew knew that Bliss held her emotions in.

"Okay," Jax said, "Your turn. What the hell happened?"

Drew laughed out loud and even Bliss had to smile at his simple, but direct question. Bliss recount what had happened starting with being followed in Pemberton. She was once again reminded of when she had told Connor the exact same story not so long ago. She once again envisioned Connor laying in the hospital bed and she didn't realize it, but she had stopped talking.

"Bliss?" Jax coaxed her gently.

Bliss finished her story and fell back into the seat physically and emotionally drained. "Holy mackerel, Bliss. Why didn't you tell me?" Jax chastised her.

"I wanted too! You're not exactly easy to reach!"

"Fuck me," Jax said slapping the steering wheel.

"So tell me what you know?" Bliss said.

Bliss saw Jax nod at Drew. "We got a call from Hammond that came through departmental channels. He said he was working on a case that involved terrorist activity, and that it was connected to your kidnapping in Afghanistan. Hammond told me that he wanted to have a face to face with you and needed Jax to vouch for him being CIA. I told Jax when he called in and Jax told me to tell you what Hammond had requested, which was to verify that he was CIA."

"So why do I think you knew he was sketchy."

"I told you she was smart." Jax said to Drew proudly.

Drew continued. "I talked to Jax after I spoke with Hammond and Jax asked me to do some digging. I discovered that he had big debt, and that he had paid some of it off, not just a little payment, but a huge payment. It set off a red flag. I called Jax in because I thought there may be a problem."

"We tried to get in touch with you. This was yesterday." Jax continued. "I called the General and he said that he had no idea where you were, but that Connor had been badly beaten and the last he had heard you had been with him. He said he was heading to Bennington."

"He didn't say anything else?" Bliss asked hoping for something that would ease her conscious.

"No, he was really worried about Connor. He said he hoped you were okay, if that makes you feel better kid?" Jax answered gently.

"I want these guys." Bliss told the men, her steely determination evident in her voice and body language.

"Let's get you someplace safe first." Jax said not looking at Bliss, but to Drew.

"Don't even think of going after them without me."

"Bliss," Drew said quietly. "Now that we know Hammond is dirty, the CIA is all over this."

"When we left, they were already putting a team together." Jax added.

"I want to be on the team." She said quickly.

Jax sighed. "Let's get to HQ. Maybe you can help by working the computers."

Bliss was pacified for the time being. She knew with her right arm in a sling that field work could be a problem, especially if she had to do hand to hand, but working a computer, that she could do.

"Jax, my CO, General Otterman sent Hammond paperwork that gave me permission to work for the CIA with Hammond being my direct CO."

"Drew contacted him while we were driving to Bennington."

Bliss turned to Drew. "What did he say?"

"He had also checked out Hammond and he even spoke with his Superior. Hammond checked out on paper Bliss, no one knew he was compromised. Otterman wants you to check in with him when you get to Fairfax."

"Well at least my career in the Army is still in-tack." Bliss muttered wearily.

"Last question." Bliss said. "Did you tell Hammond about my gift?"

Jax looked back at her perplexed. "No."

Somehow Bliss wasn't surprised by his answer.

They were still four hours from Fairfax, Virginia and the toll of what she had been through and heartache of seeing and leaving Connor finally overtook Bliss. Her eyes closed as she rested her cheek on the cars seat back. She protectively cradled her elbow that was in the sling with her left hand and fell into a deep sleep.

Bliss slowly started to come awake. Her first conscious thought was that she was warm. Her second was confusion. Her body jerked uneasily, and she heard Drew say, "You're safe Bliss." She felt his hand resting on her arm and thankfully he had pressed against it or it would have hurt from the quick jolt. Her head was cradled on his lap and he had taken his suit jacket off and laid it over her.

She sat up quickly and the coat slipped from her body causing her to shiver. Jax was looking at her in the rear-view mirror and Drew watched her with a concerned look on his face. She ran her fingers through her curly mop that had fallen across her face and took a calming breath, embarrassed that she had been asleep on Drew's lap.

"Sorry about that." She said to Drew.

"For falling asleep?" He grinned.

Bliss blushed, "No for, you know, falling asleep on you."

Jax laughed from the front seat. "Bliss, you were exhausted."

She handed Drew back his coat and rubbed her face gently, hoping she hadn't drooled on him. Drew took his coat and laid it across his lap. "I didn't mind." He said softly.

"I'm sorry if that made you uncomfortable."

Bliss appreciated that he wasn't the kind of man that joked all the time, or even worse used sarcasm.

"Well, thank you." She said softly looking out the window. "Where are we?"

"We just got into Virginia. We'll be at HQ shortly."

"What's going to happen when we get there?"

"You'll be vetted by Special Agent Rosco Gonzalez; he is the one heading this new task force. He'll decide if you can come home with Drew and me, or if he wants you to go to a safe house."

"Is he the one I have to convince to let me help?"

"Yes, he'll make that call, too."

"Jax, is there someplace I can shower first?"

"Drew can you call ahead and ask Gonzalez? Get her some clothes too."

Drew pulled out his cell and Bliss heard him get the okay that she could shower first.

He disconnected and told Bliss that she could shower in the woman's locker room and that he would dig her up some clean clothes.

Jax drove them through the front gates where both he and Drew had to show ID and then Bliss showed her Army ID before the armed guards allowed them through. Jax parked in a side lot and when they entered the building, they once again showed their ID's and Bliss was asked to lay her palm on a screen that scanned her palm. The guard confirmed that she was who her ID said she was.

"Pretty high tech." Bliss whispered to Drew and Jax. She had a small smile on her face and Jax grinned, loving that his sister was a geek at heart.

They both walked Bliss to the locker room and outside of the door stood Sparrow. Bliss froze in the hallway.

"It's Sparrow, you know her." Jax said confused as to why Sparrows appearance would have shaken Bliss.

"I, yes, I do." Drew didn't like how Bliss was looking at Sparrow.

He took Bliss by the elbow and steered her away from Sparrow. Jax remained where he was, and Sparrow walked to him.

"Spill Bliss." The last time anyone had told Bliss to 'spill' information had been Connor and she had to suck in a breath to make her mind move on from that sweet moment with him.

"I'm fine Drew." She said more confident than she actually felt.

"Do you think Sparrow was working with Hammond?" He whispered to her.

Bliss looked over his broad shoulders to where Jax and Sparrow stood talking.

"I don't think so. If she hadn't slipped me the gun, I'm sure I'd be dead right now." Bliss replied cautiously.

"Then what is it? Why did you freeze when you saw her?"

"It's nothing really."

"Bliss," he said frustrated, running his hand through his blond hair.

"It's dumb," she admitted. "She slept with Connor and was pretty nasty to me when we met."

Drew let out a deep breath. "Connor, huh?"

"Yeah."

"The whole woman scorned thing?" Drew said, immediately understanding.

Bliss shrugged her shoulders. "I guess. Maybe she just doesn't like me."

Drew scoffed loudly, "No, I guarantee it was because of Connor."

"You know her well?"

"No, just heard rumors. Jax knows her."

"Well, I need that shower." Bliss said fortifying herself from whatever Sparrow may dish out.

They walked the few yards back to Sparrow and Jax.

"I'm glad you're okay." Sparrow said sincerely.

"I wouldn't have been if you hadn't given me that gun. How did you know?"

"He'd been acting weird for a couple of days. We were supposed to bring you in, one way or another. No one was supposed to know that we were bringing you in, so when he said he was talking to Cooper back at the gas station that set off a red flag. Then when he turned off 87, I got a bad feeling. I knew you were unarmed."

"Why the lie about my dad? It was a lie, right?"

"It was. That was Hammond's idea. I was only supposed to use it if we needed to." "And it did, work, I mean."

"Yeah, it did." Sparrow looked uncomfortable.

"Connor, was he hurt badly?"

Jax interrupted. "I told her." He explained.

"Yes, very."

Sparrow looked away from her to Jax. "I have a towel and spare clothes in the locker room." She looked

back to Bliss. "I have to stay with you since you're technically a
visitor here."

Bliss groaned inwardly hoping that she wouldn't have to endure any snide comments regarding Connor. She didn't want her to know that he was available. Bliss wasn't ready for that. It was such an agonizing thought that her face registered pain and Drew touched her arm concerned.

Sparrow turned to the locker room and gestured for Bliss to follow her.

"Bring her to my office when you're done." Bliss heard Jax say as they passed through the door.

Bliss followed Sparrow into the large locker room. On a bench near the individual shower stalls sat two towels and a washcloth.

"Each shower has shampoo, conditioner, and body wash dispensers."

"Okay, thanks. You look pretty good for just getting clocked in the head."

Sparrow grunted with a grin. "Yeah, that was not fun. I still have a headache but don't tell anyone."

"You look like you've been roughed up too."

Sparrow said gesturing to Bliss' face.

"Yeah, but I'm good."

Bliss started to take off her sling and Sparrow stepped to her side. "May I?"

Bliss nodded slightly thrown by her kindness.

"Bliss."

Bliss thought, oh boy, here it comes.

"I never slept with Connor."

Bliss looked at her surprised. Sparrow continued to gently remove the sling off of her arm.

"I wanted to, trust me, but he was really drunk, and he passed out. I stayed the night hoping to get lucky in the morning, but he didn't want any part of it."

"Why all the shit then?"

"I was jealous. Connor's special. Before he was drunk, we were getting along really well. I knew he was upset about something. My friend, who was with Connor's friend, told me that they were just back from a mission. I really liked him. It just brought up some harsh feelings. I never choose the right guys." She admitted candidly. It reminded Bliss of Caitlyn who had told her the same thing.

"Well, as long as we are being honest." Bliss said hating what she was about to tell her. "Connor and I are over."

It took a second for Sparrow to get over her initial shock. "How can you be over? You were fine when you left with us and I know he's been in a hospital?"

"I don't want to get into it." Bliss said hurriedly. Sparrow stared at her with a puzzled expression on her face. The sling was now off, and Bliss gingerly moved her arm, relieved that it felt stiff, but not painful. She walked towards the shower stalls with the towels.

Bliss took a long shower and like in Afghanistan she allowed the tears to fall unchecked. She felt so lonesome, even though she was with Jax now. She hated that the Doherty's were out of her life, and even worse, she knew she would never get over Connor. Sparrow was correct, Connor was special. By the time she had finished washing she had gotten herself together. She was able to move her arm enough to wrap one of the towels around her hair and then she wrapped the other towel around her body.

When she walked out of the shower, Sparrow was sitting quietly on the bench. "Here are some clothes." She said pointing at a pair of black pants, a white blouse, a black

blazer, and a bra and underwear.

"I had to guess your size." Sparrow admitted meekly.

"If they're really big on me, I'll beat your ass." Bliss said extending Sparrow an olive branch in the form of a friendly joke.

Sparrow's mouth dropped open and then she burst out laughing.

Bliss did not put the sling back on, even though Sparrow offered to help her with it. They left the locker room and even though the void, Bliss felt still threatening to devour her, was building inside of her and tried to focus on what lay ahead.

They walked into a large room with cubicles and then Sparrow turned into a corner office, which held two desks and a long couch. Jax sat behind one desk and Drew sat behind the other. Both men stood when they entered the room.

"You look very official." Jax said looking at her outfit.

"Yes, very CIA-ish." Drew confirmed with a smile.

"What's next?" She said ready to get going.

"Gonzalez is waiting for you."

Jax thanked Sparrow and Bliss did too. Drew was watching her wondering what had happened in the locker room. As they walked down the hallway, Drew whispered to her. "You okay?"

"Yeah, she never slept with him and she apologized."

"Whoa, that's good, right?"

Bliss sighed sadly, "It really doesn't matter anymore, does it?" She replied softly hoping she didn't sound like a bitch.

Jax knocked on a door and was told to enter. He opened the door and Bliss saw four men sitting at a table.

He introduced her. "Bliss this is Special Agent Gonzalez, the head of this task force, Special Agent Phil Price, Special Agent Darren Hayes, and Special Agent Griff Deal." Bliss shook hands with each one of the men hoping they didn't jar her arm too hard. "Have a seat," Gonzalez motioned to a chair near him. Bliss sat down and Jax and Drew did too.

"I know you've been through a lot and Jax has already told me what you shared with him on the ride here. Would you mind retelling your story to the group? It would save time and I'd rather they hear it from you, so all the facts are correct."

Bliss launched into her story again, beginning with getting the email in Afghanistan, her kidnapping, her rescue and everything that ensued. She finished with how she had escaped Zarghun. The room was silent, the men were looking at her with mixed emotions. Gonzalez appeared impressed, Price was empathetic, and Hayes and Deal looked appropriately shocked.

"You are amazing Lt." Gonzalez told her confirming that he was impressed with her. "Quick thinking, smart, it's amazing to hear what you have been through and yet you appear to be remarkable collected."

Bliss' immediate thought that if he knew how she was really feeling, he would probably change his opinion. Bliss felt anything but collected. She was hanging on by a virtual thread. She needed to keep working and that would help her not fall into the abyss she felt clawing at her.

"Please call me Bliss." She told the men. "So how do we get these guys?" She asked leaning her arms on the table.

Gonzalez chuckled. "And spirit to boot." He added.

"I want to help."

"We know you're a whiz on computers. We need to track down Conti, he's the key." "Conti is the same man from Afghanistan, right? Blue eyes?"

"Yeah, Hammond didn't lie about that fact. Conti was a friend of your dad's and he is ex-CIA."

"And Zarghun?"

"We have no idea how he got into the country and that's scary."

"So, what do you want me to do?"

Again Gonzalez chuckled. "Bliss we appreciate your enthusiasm, but it's 10:00pm.

How about we pick this up in the morning?"

"But we know where they are, or where they were. I think we need to use that to our advantage."

"Bliss," Jax tried to placate her.

"No, she's right." Price said. "We have the benefit of Bliss' information now. Why don't she and I stay here and work the computers? Maybe we'll have something for you guys in the morning and we can move on it."

Gonzalez nodded with a smile towards Price. "He's our computer guy."

Knowing she had just met a kindred geek, Bliss smiled.

"Aren't you tired?" Jax asked her.

Bliss blushed, "I had a nap." She said glancing uneasily at Drew.

"Well, okay, everyone get some sleep. Price and Bliss, you do your thing."

The men stood, and Bliss followed their lead. Jax moved to her side. "If you get tired tell Price to call me, okay?"

"I'll stay here with her." Drew told him as he came to stand by them. Jax gave him a questioning look.

Bliss turned to Drew. "I'll be fine Drew. You have to be tired, go get some sleep."

"I'll sleep in the office." He said turning from them and walking out the door.

"He doesn't have to do that Jax."

"Yeah, and it should be me staying." Jax admitted honestly annoyed that he hadn't offered first.

Price walked up to them. "Ready," he said smiling happily. Bliss almost giggled at her fellow geek's enthusiasm.

Jax gave Bliss a peck on the cheek. "Call me if you need anything."

"I got her." Price assured him.

Jax chuckled. "No funny business Price, work only." Bliss realized that Jax thought Price was going to hit on her and it made her uncomfortably aware how very naive she was when it came to men.

Price escorted Bliss down yet another hallway and stopped at a door with beveled glass. He placed his palm on a black screen on the wall near the door and his print was scanned and they were buzzed in.

The CIA computer room was, to Bliss, the equivalent of what a toy store was to a child. Bliss stood wide-eyed looking at the rows of servers and felt instantly at home.

Price chuckled seeing her face. "Let's get started." He led her to a laptop workspace where the very latest laptops available sat ready for them to use.

"This is incredible." Bliss said still in awe.

"Yeah, I love it in here. We have access to so much information that we don't even have to get past firewalls to hack into whatever we need."

Bliss sat down at the first laptop and opened the sleek silver top.

"Any thoughts as to where we should start?" Price asked.

Bliss had been mulling this over and she knew exactly where to start.

"Yes, I have a couple of ideas. I shot Conti in the stomach. We know I escaped in Troy. My guess is that Conti sought out a Doctor in either Troy or Albany or a town near there. I think we need to do a search of doctors in that area, earmarking any with ties to terrorists, or other known groups that could support them. We also should look for any old contacts of Conti's in the area, any doctors with a lot of debt, and lastly doctors with home offices."

Price looked at her to explain the last one.

"When I was in the back of the truck they stopped someplace where he could get medical treatment. The area we stopped at was quiet. It wasn't at a hospital or even a clinic, it seemed more residential."

"That's good," Price said as he opened his computer. "Anything else?"

After we stopped, I was in the truck for about a half hour before I escaped." Bliss pulled up a map of Troy and found 'Rose's Hair Salon'. "I think the doctor's office is in this radius." Bliss drew a circle around Rose's that was equivalent to a half hour radius by car.

"Those are great places to start." Price sat down and began tapping away at the keyboard.

There had been something Bliss thought she had been overlooking and it had been needling her, but she just hadn't been able to grasp it yet. Her brain held so much information that she sometimes felt like it all sloshed together and the only way she could access the information that she needed was when she conjured up the image.

"I know I'm missing something, but I'm hoping that working will help me remember." She told price as her fingers flew across the keyboard.

Three hours later she and Price had put together a list of five potential doctors that fit all their criteria. Price sat back and stretched his arms over his head.

"You're good." He complimented her.

"I like this." She said shyly.

"Time for a break, okay?" Soda?"

"Yes, I'd love one." She knew, without even asking that they couldn't bring the soda into the computer room.

They left the room and as they walked past Jax and Drew's office she popped her head in. Drew was lying on the couch with his arms behind his head. He turned to her the moment she opened the door and then quickly sat up.

"Oh sorry, I didn't mean to wake you."

"You didn't. How's it going?"

Price stuck his head over her shoulder. "I'm getting sodas want one?" He offered.

"No, I'm good, thanks."

"Bliss if you want to stay here, I'll be right back."

"Thanks," she agreed.

"You're not tired?" Drew asked her. "It's almost 2:00am."

"No, actually the opposite. I'm anxious to keep going. We've narrowed down the list of doctors Conti may have gone too."

"Wow, that's great."

"Will we have to drive back up there tomorrow, well today?" She corrected.

Drew grinned. "No, we'll take the jet."

"Oh good, that was a long drive."

"Uh, Bliss, you need to be prepared that you may not be allowed to go."

Bliss frown, "I want to be there."

"I know you do," he said chuckling.

Price returned and sat down on a chair. He handed Bliss her Coke.

"Do you mind if we drink these in here? Can't take them to the computer room." Price said smiling.

"No, it's fine."

Five minutes later they had finished their sodas and Bliss popped up looking at Price.

"I guess you're ready," he laughed.

Bliss waved to Drew as they left the office and Drew smiled at her gently. He was a nice guy. She wondered why he didn't have a girlfriend or wasn't married. Maybe he did have a girlfriend. She had been so wrapped up in her own drama; she never asked him anything about himself. She used to be more thoughtful. It dawned on her that she needed to get herself together. A life that included Connor was over and as much as it pained her to think that way, she had to stop dwelling on how lost she felt and concentrate on finding these dangerous men. Constantly thinking about Connor and what might have been only continued to make her feel miserable. The problem was, she knew she would never stop thinking about him.

Back in the computer room, Bliss shut her eyes trying to recall any information that might help them. She started from the moment Hammond and Sparrow had picked her up. Price wisely did not interrupt her.

She recalled everything, including kissing Connor good-bye, so much for trying not to think about him, she thought, annoyed at herself. Bliss remembered leaving and then seeing the cars rush into the lot. The cars!

"Oh my God, the cars!" She said out loud.

Bliss began typing on the computer keys as Price watched her.

"The cars," she once again said out loud. "The cars that drove into the motels lot when we were leaving. The men that beat up Connor, they were in those cars. I memorized the plates!"

Bliss hit return and two names with pictures and other personal information popped onto the screen.

Bliss read the names "Fathi Homsi and Obed Akbari"

"Holy shit!" Price said, becoming excited. "They're on a watch list."

"A watch list? You guys know they are here?"

"Yeah, they're here legally. We basically just watch them."

"Well shit. You haven't been watching them too well!"

Bliss hit print and all the information regarding the two men printed onto a piece of paper.

Bliss pulled up the address of the men and found that one of them lived next door to one of the doctors they had narrowed it down too.

She scrolled through three more pages of information committing it all to memory.

"We have to go." Bliss said standing up. "We need to go there now."

"Bliss, it's early in the morning. We'll get there. Let me text Gonzalez, okay?"

"Hurry," she pleaded.

Price texted Gonzalez and Gonzalez told him to get the team together, that they were

leaving in 45 minutes. Bliss was pleased that he didn't want to wait until morning to leave.

The team assembled back in the room where Bliss and Price told them what they had discovered. "It was all Bliss." Price said giving her the kudos.

"Great job," Gonzalez told her.

"Everyone ready?" All the men were all dressed similarly wearing black pants, white button shirts, black ties, and black jackets. Bliss almost giggled thinking of all the B spy movies she had seen. The wardrobe persons had nailed it, seeing their almost matching attire.

"What about me?" Bliss asked as they filed out of the room.

"We'll keep you posted." Gonzalez said turning from her.

"No, I want in!"

"Bliss." Jax said once again trying to calm her.

"No, Rosco, she should be there." Drew told the

group.

Gonzalez looked annoyed but told her to grab a vest. "Yes!" Bliss said with a little fist bump in the air, then she mouthed a thank you to Drew who gave her an adorable wink.

Jax looked pissed and he was staring daggers at Drew.

Bliss grabbed a vest from a hook in a closet that Drew opened and followed the men down a flight of steps and into a waiting car. The car drove them to a hanger where a small jet was already warming up. It looked like the one the characters on the show Criminal Minds flew in. Bliss was once again impressed.

She settled into a seat and Jax and Price dropped across from her and Drew sat next to her.

Gonzalez announced that they would be there in an hour and twenty minutes. A car would be waiting for them. He had already spoken with the FBI in the area who was coordinating with the local police department. Bliss estimated that they would land around 5:00am. Her excitement showed on her face and Price was smiling with her. Gonzalez got off the phone and used a remote to pull down a screen. He handed Bliss a laptop and told her to pull up the two houses plus the doctor's residence.

Bliss' fingers tapped away as she brought up a map of the area. All three homes were located within the same neighborhood.

"Here is the home of Obed Akbari, and right here," Bliss used the arrow to show the house on the right, "is Doctor Muhammad Aziz house. Fathi Homsi lives over here." She said moving the arrow.

Bliss had an idea. "Do we have access to internet?"

She asked Gonzalez.

"Yes."

"May I?"

Gonzalez nodded so Bliss pulled up sheets of information that slid across the screen. Information that she quickly scanned. She clicked on one of the sheets and enlarged it. "Yes!" She said with a little fist pump. "The man I know as Zarghun is a cousin to Obed Akbari!"

"I don't even know how you got that!" Price exclaimed excitedly.

"It was right in the papers that." She let her voice trail off. "I have a good memory."

She finished abruptly.

"What's the plan?" Deal asked.

"Who lives in the homes?" Gonzalez asked looking to Price and Bliss.

"I need to check the." Price began, but Bliss interrupted.

"Akbari has two children, a wife and a mother in his home. Homsi lives with two men. The doctor, Aziz is alone. He has two kids in Ivy League Schools and his American ex-wife has him paying major alimony after she caught him in bed with another woman. Aziz has a girlfriend that often spends the night, a Christy Wiggins. There are no red flags with her. She works at Albany Medical with the doctor.

"Holy shit!" muttered Price.

Bliss smiled feeling confident, "It's a gift." She explained.

"Good thing we brought you with us." Gonzalez said seriously. He then shot Price a look who sheepishly shrugged.

Chapter 24

The jet landed and the team got into a black suburban with tinted out windows. Gonzalez had gone over the plan on the jet with them. The neighborhood was close knit so setting up blockades could set off an alert to the house members of the homes they were about to enter, to they opted for the hit them fast plan. Gonzalez didn't want any casualties and they hoped to take the two men who owned the cars and the doctor alive. That was step one. The next step was to get these men to give up the location of Conti and Zarghun.

The Suburban drove through the quiet neighborhood. It was a Saturday morning and the only person they passed was in a car tossing newspapers out an open window onto driveways. Drew was driving the Suburban, Bliss had pulled up the addresses on an iPad Gonzalez had given her and she had directed Drew through Albany and into the small Troy neighborhood. He dropped off Price and Deal, a block away from Homsi's home, where they were meeting up with other law enforcement members.

Drew parked the Suburban around the corner from the doctor's house. Everyone was outfitted with ear pieces and bulletproof vests. Bliss reminded them of the house numbers and told them which rooms were bedrooms and which ones probably contained the children and the mother. She jogged along behind the men and ducked behind a bush where they were met by two FBI agents, a man and a woman. "Everyone know what to do?" Gonzalez asked.

They all nodded.

Bliss peered through the bushes and couldn't believe it when she saw Zarghun's truck in the driveway of his brother's house. She ducked down quickly.

"Zarghun's truck is here." Bliss pointed to it.

"No way," Jax answered shocked. Gonzalez cracked a grin hearing the news. "Everyone on my go." Gonzalez whispered.

Gonzalez had Bliss watching the front of the two houses. Bliss didn't mind not being included in the actual raid. She knew she had done her part and she was happy that they had allowed her to come along. She watched the FBI Agents peel off and go with two Troy Law Enforcement Officers to cover the back of the homes. Jax and Gonzalez went to one front door and Drew and another officer went to the Doctors home. Two loud pops resonated, and Bliss knew the homes had been breached. She heard Gonzalez talking through her ear piece and she could hear footsteps on the floors and screams coming from within the homes. The men were yelling "Get down." And Bliss waited nervously hoping not to hear any gun
fire.

A window opened on the east side of the one house and Bliss saw Zarghun jumping from it. Bliss stood and began running after him. She spoke into her mic to alert the team.

"Zarghun's on the run. He's moving north through the yards. I'm in pursuit." She heard Jax and Drew say, 'shit' at the same time.

Bliss pursued Zarghun as he ran across the street,

jumping a small hedge, and through another yard. Bliss kept up with him. She was thinking of nothing except catching the man who had tortured her and had a hand in beating Connor. She flew through the small snow-covered yards and saw him trip over a dog chain, hidden under the snow. As he scrambled to his feet, she jumped on top of him using her hands to push his head back onto the frozen ground. The hit was unexpected and hard, and she knew she had dazed him a little.

Zarghun didn't hesitate and was able to roll onto his back. He placed his fingers on her injured shoulder, pressing them into her joint, hoping to dislodge it again. Bliss cried out in pain and jammed the heel of her hand into his chin. Blood spurt from his mouth and she pressed down on him frantically trying to keep him underneath her smaller body. Just when she knew he was about to throw her, she heard Jax yell for him to 'Freeze,' and four hands grabbed him. She quickly rolled to give them better access and watched as Jax and Drew put Zarghun in cuffs and yanked him to his feet.

Zarghun was yelling in Pashto and Bliss was able to decipher a few of the words. Jax looked at her and she grinned, "you don't want to know."

"You understand him?" Drew asked.

"A few words," she admitted.

They walked Zarghun back to the houses where Bliss saw that two men and one woman were in handcuffs, the children were standing on the front steps crying, and an older woman was yelling. Gonzalez was questioning the doctor asking about Conti and the doctor kept shaking his head. She saw the police officer and the female FBI Agent come out of the doctor's house and walk towards them.

"Nothing?" Drew asked.

"No."

Bliss was disappointed, she really had hoped that Conti would be recuperating in the doctor's house. She knew she had hit him with at least two bullets. He wouldn't be very mobile.

Zarghun was placed in a car and the two men and one woman were placed in separate vehicles. Children services came to check on the kids and when the old lady assaulted the government worker, she too was taken into custody and the children were taken away in a van.

The neighbors were standing behind caution tape that the police had set up and Price and Deal had joined them. They had arrested four men and they had found Connor's driver's license on a dresser. Bliss' heart squeezed painfully hearing his name.

"Let's check out these homes." Gonzalez told his team, "Maybe we can get a clue as to where Conti went."

Bliss followed Drew and Gonzalez into the Doctors home. She went immediately to the basement where the doctor's home office was located. She could hear Gonzalez walking around upstairs; Drew had followed her downstairs. Bliss stood in the area that must have been used as a patient waiting area before she opened the doctors
examining room. Something was off. She walked back to the waiting area and then back to the examining room.

"What?" Drew asked.

"This doesn't match the floor plan." She told him looking around the examining room. "It's off, it should be bigger."

Bliss walked to the wall and Drew called Gonzalez down from the upstairs. Bliss was tapping on the wall and listening to the sound her taps made. She knocked on an area behind a small cabinet and looked back to Drew and Gonzalez, pointing at the wall. Drew motioned for her to get back as he took out his gun. Gonzalez did the same. Drew pointed at the faint outline that he could now make out in the pine paneling of the wall. Gonzalez found a small button in a groove that would open the hidden door. Gonzalez used his fingers to signal 3, 2, 1 and then he pressed the button, opened the door and Drew stepped in gun ready. Shots pinged into the now open doorway, just missing Bliss, as she dove to the floor. She heard a grunt knowing someone was hit. She peeked over the chair she had dove behind and saw the men in a scuffle with Conti. He was on a hospital bed and he had tubes running into his arm.

Gonzalez disarmed him quickly and Drew kicked the gun away from the bed and handed Gonzalez his cuffs.

Jax, Price, and Deal ran down the basement steps, they had heard the gunshots. Bliss saw Jax relax seeing that she was okay. She pointed into the room, "We got Conti." She couldn't keep the smile off her face.

Two hours later they were back on the jet. Homeland Security had taken the men to a Federal maximum holding area. The woman, Akbari's wife and mother, were taken to a county lock up. Gonzalez said that both women probably knew about the illegal activity and they would use the children's welfare, as a bargaining chip to garner more information. It had been a good raid. Drew suffered a grazing wound to his bicep and had refused treatment from the local EMT's. Price had wrapped it with gauze. It didn't need stitches and Bliss was thankful that his injury hadn't been worse.

Gonzalez told his team that they would have access to the men next week, after Homeland questioned them. The men were fine with that. This wasn't a departmental pissing match. The bad guys were off the streets.

Gonzalez turned to Bliss. "Bliss you really were the catalyst driving this bust. Thank you."

"Thank you for bringing me." She was grinning and Jax realized it was the first real happiness she had displayed since they had picked her up in Bennington. He chuckled knowing his sister was in her element.

"Let's talk, okay? The team has a week off, so come in next week. I'll talk to Otterman, so he knows where you are."

Bliss nodded. The adrenaline rush was ebbing and the team relaxed, chatting amicably with each other in hushed tones.

Jax leaned to Bliss. "You're going to sleep at our house tonight. Then we'll figure out what's next."

"What's next? What's next big brother is that I go back to work." She told him affectionately.

Bliss spent a peaceful week with Jax and Drew. She tried to keep busy in an effort to
not to think about Connor. She was still concerned about him. Jax told her that the General had been told

that Conti and Zarghun had been captured, so the threat to his family was over. She didn't ask who had told him, and it was clear that they did not care about her, because no one from the family had tried to get in touch with her. She wasn't even sure if they knew where she was.

The first day she spent with Jax and Drew they had taken her clothes shopping. She joked with them that the last two times she had bought clothes had been a precursor to her having misfortunate adventures. Jax assured her they would not be letting anything happen to her, and she was reminded of how Connor and Collin brotherly safeguarded Caitlyn.

They ate out every night. Bliss learned that they rarely ate at home, and she teased them regarding how many of the wait staff at the places they ate at knew them by name. Bliss finally purchased a new phone and a new iPad. When she had down time, she downloaded Apps and music onto them. There wasn't much free time though. The men always had something planned, which Bliss was grateful for. She learned that the guys weren't much for sitting around either and she appreciated staying busy. They went to a paintball park, the movies, a bar where they played darts, and at night Drew and Jax challenged her to video game matches. Neither of them was as good as Connor and she won easily every time.

Bliss had also started working out again. Jax and Drew took her to the CIA's gym every morning, where all three of them worked out. Bliss ran, lifted, and swam. Her shoulder felt great, her feet were toughening up, and she didn't have to wear her brace or the bandages on her hands anymore. She realized that except for the ever- present emptiness she felt; she was physically in the best condition since her kidnapping in Afghanistan.

The next Friday afternoon Bliss entered Gonzalez office and he ushered her to a chair in front of his desk. Jax and Drew had returned to work and Bliss was getting antsy sitting at home. She was thinking of heading back to San Francisco.

"I spoke with Otterman this morning." He told her.

"Did he say when I was expected back?"

Gonzalez chuckled. "No, you're technically still on R and R?"

"Yeah, I know. I'm not much for sitting around though."

Gonzalez chuckled again. "So, I noticed. He did tell me that your enlistment is up in one year and two months.

"Yes." She confirmed.

"I expressed an interest, well more than an interest; I told him that I want to buy out your contract."

"What?"

"I want to buy out your remaining time with the Army and have you come work for the CIA."

"You can do that?"

"Of course, we're CIA." He said, causing Bliss to laugh. "So, do you think you might like to work for us?"

Bliss thought about it and knew it was too important of a decision to make right then. "Can I have a few days to think about it?"

"Of course. Otterman wants to talk to you at some point. I think he's feeling guilty that he almost got you killed."

"Ya think?" She joked, prompting Gonzalez to laugh out loud.

"Can we meet on Tuesday, 9:00am?" Gonzalez said after checking his calendar on his computer.

Bliss replied that would not be a problem and they both stood and shook hands ending the meeting.

Bliss left the office with a huge grin on her face. The CIA wanted her! She was reminded of the time when she had told Connor that her mother would have flipped knowing she was aiding them, now she may be working for them! She felt a moment of sadness wishing she could talk to Connor about this possible career change. Thinking about Connor caused her heart to feel as if it was being squeezed in a vise. She wondered if the ache she felt would ever go away.

Bliss walked towards the exit where Jax was supposed to be waiting for her and Price almost ran her over with his nose buried in a laptop.

"Hey."

"Hey yourself." She answered. Thinking about Connor had her wondering how he was doing, and she decided to take advantage of the CIA's computer room again to find out. "Uh, Phil could you help me with a little favor?"

"Does it involve a computer?" He asked with a knowing grin.

"Why yes it does," she giggled.

"Do we need to go to the computer room?"

"Umm, yes please."

Price turned towards the computer room and Bliss fell into step with him. After his palm was scanned, they were buzzed inside.

"How long do you need?" He asked.

"One minute, tops."

Bliss opened a laptop and her fingers danced over the keys pulling up the information that she wanted.

Price looked over her shoulder. "Doherty's medical records?"

"I just want to make sure he's still doing okay."

"No problem, my lips are sealed."

Bliss pulled up Connor's current medical records from Bennington and saw that he had been discharged just that morning. She quickly read through his chart and was relieved to see that he was not going to lose the vision in the one eye, that his lung was almost fully healed, and she also read that he had been given a prescription to begin Physical Therapy. At the bottom of his chart she read that his prognosis was considered excellent and that the doctor treating him had already sent off a letter to his CO, stating that he estimated that Connor could return to active duty in two months, pending a full physical. Bliss blew out a sigh of relief. She had been so worried that his injuries might have ended his career, and she hated herself knowing she would have been the cause. She shut the laptop. "Thanks, I owe you." She told Price.

"I accept beer." He told her with a wink.

Bliss walked with Price as he led her outside where they met Jax who was waiting at his car.

"Everything okay?" Jax asked.

"Yeah, but I need a drink. You game?" She asked Jax.

"I'm always up for a drink," he answered.

Bliss looked at Price, "You, too." Price smiled and jumped into the back seat happy to be included. Jax knew Bliss was not a big drinker and he realized something was bouncing around in his little sister's brilliant mind for her to want to have drink, especially this early in the day. On the way to the bar Jax called Drew to tell him where they were headed, and he told Drew to call Deal. Jax then looked to Bliss.

"Can we invite Sparrow, too?"

"Sure, why not?" She said hoping Sparrow wouldn't want to talk about Connor. Bliss couldn't handle that. Ten minutes later Bliss, Jax and Price were sitting in a bar, in the middle of a Friday afternoon. They took a table near the back and Jax order wings, Price ordered nachos, and Bliss ordered a pitcher of Budweiser.

Drew walked in as the beer was being placed on the table. "Are we celebrating something?"

"Just having a drink with new friends." Bliss said clinking glasses with everyone. "Where's Deal and Sparrow?" She asked.

"Deal's a family man." Drew told her taking a seat next to her. "Sparrow may come by later."

Bliss actually had a motive for getting the team together and she had wished Sparrow would join them. She was going to pick their brains about being in the CIA without letting them know that she had been offered a job. She'd listen to them and take what they said into account and make her decision based on that.

The group emptied two pitchers and as Bliss discreetly pumped them for information, she discovered that they all loved their jobs. Price especially loved the work he did with the computers coupled with the field work. Bliss knew she would like that too. She asked if any of them had girlfriends and Price and Drew shook their heads no.

"Can I ask why?"

They didn't answer her at first and Bliss hoped she hadn't crossed any proverbial line. "It's probably different for all of us Bliss." Jax told his sister.

"Oh, so tell me then." She said looking to Price first. "I actually date a lot; I'm not ready to settle down yet."

She looked to Jax. "I don't know if I want to ever get married, and anything other than a few dates with the same girl tends to mislead them. Been there, done that." He replied honestly, which Bliss thought was sad. "I'm not a monk though." He chuckled, hoping she'd let it drop.

"And you?" She said looking at Drew.

He chugged the rest of his beer. "I'm just waiting for the right girl to realize that I'm the right guy."

Bliss smiled at him. "You'll find her Drew." She said gently. She had no idea that he had meant that she was the right girl, but Jax and Price did.

"So why all the questions?' Price asked.

"I just, well hell, okay I'll tell you." Bliss couldn't keep the small grin from widening into a smile." Gonzalez wants to buy my contract out. He wants me to come to work for the CIA."

The three men's reactions were mixed.

Price said, "That be awesome!"

Jax said, "No fucking way." And Drew was all smiles.

Bliss looked at Drew, "So no comment from you?"

"I'd like for you to be around all the time." He told her honestly and that's when Bliss realized he liked her. She hadn't picked up on it before and she felt a little awkward "You are so not dating my sister!" Jax said a little too seriously.

Drew started laughing, "I think she has a say in who she dates."

"Maybe she'll want to date me." Price piped in making the entire conversation comical. "Uh, guys I'm right here!"

Bliss laughed as the men traded friendly insults. Drew had his arm casually draped over the back of her chair and Jax reached across the table to knock it away. She couldn't help grinning seeing Jax act so brotherly.

Her back was to the front door and she heard Price say, "Oh shit."

Bliss saw that he was looking at something over her shoulder, so she turned. Connor was standing, more like leaning, not more than a yard behind her. She heard Price tell Jax and Drew, "That's Doherty." Quieting the table.

Bliss looked back to Phil raising her eyebrow, but she quickly returned her focus to Connor.

Price shrugged and said loud enough so she could hear him, "What? I Googled him." Knowing she wanted to know how he knew whom Connor was.

"Maybe she won't be dating any of you yahoos." Connor said, his deep voice laced with anger. Bliss cringed hearing his venomous tone. She had never seen him this angry before and it made her nervous. She took in that his bruises were still evident, but not as horrible as the last time she'd seen him in the VA. He had a half cast on his leg, and a half cast on his opposite arm. She had no idea how he was supporting his weight on the crutches that were under each arm. He wasn't wearing the big gauze patch over his eye anymore, but the eye socket was surrounded with deep purple and green coloring. Her gaze ended on his lips, his wonderful, kissable, and now thinned in anger, upper lip. A small fine red line ran through it where it had been split. Most worrisome however, was how furious he looked.

"He's big." Price whispered to her, causing her to kick him under the table. She didn't dare take her eyes from Connor.

Bliss stood up. "Connor, what are you doing here?" Her voice came out shaky.

"What the hell do you think I'm doing here?" He was still intimidating, even as injured as he was.

Jax and Drew quickly stood up, not liking his tone and gently nudged Bliss protectively behind them, causing Connor to look even more cross. She wondered if he had come there to give her hell for what had happened to him and endangering his family. Somehow, she didn't think so, that wasn't Connor.

Connor eyeballed the men surrounding Bliss and recognized one of them as Jax. They were watching him warily. He realized they thought he was a threat to her.

When he had first walked into the bar and he had seen the one man with his arm on the back of Bliss' chair he had wanted to rip the guys arm out of its sockets. As he had made his way towards the table, he saw Jax knock the guys arm away. By then he was close enough to hear that they had been debating who was going to date Bliss. If he hadn't been hampered by his injuries, they would have known exactly who was going to be dating Bliss, and it wasn't any of them. He just hoped that Bliss was on board with that.

Connor got himself under control. "I just want to talk to her." He told the men, his tone not as menacing. His eyes had never left her, and Bliss felt them travel up and down her body and settle back on her face. "You mind giving us a few minutes?" He asked the men but staring at Bliss.

Bliss nodded to Jax, and Jax gestured to Drew and Price to give them some privacy, so the two men moved to another table, not too far away. Jax remained where he was. "Connor, this is my brother Jax." Bliss said introducing them. The men shook hands still sizing each other up.

"I'd like to talk to Bliss alone. " Connor repeated. "You hurt her you'll need a wheelchair to leave." Jax told him without an ounce of jest. Bliss knew Jax wasn't referring to him hurting her physically. Jax knew Connor would never do that. She could tell he wasn't kidding though. Her brother could be a bad ass when he wanted to. To her surprise Connor chuckled. Bliss saw that Collin was standing quietly behind Connor, which made her edgy. She folded her arms across her chest hoping to calm her heart that was thumping wildly. She really had no idea why he was there. Bliss released a breath that she had been holding. She could get through this, she told herself. Connor was watching her face and Bliss' eyes locked on to his. "You were just discharged this morning. Are you okay? You should be resting. How are you even here?" She asked, her voice nervous, but soft with concern.

"Checking up on me?" Connor asked a little too

harshly as he sat down heavily on one of the empty chairs at the table.

"Well, yes." She sat down turning the chair to face him. "I wanted to make sure you were okay." She was not going to let him intimidate her.

Connor leaned towards her and Bliss felt his warm breath on her cheek.

"Okay? Do you have any idea how not okay I have been?" His voice was trembling, and Bliss recognized that Connor was hanging on to his composure by a thread. "Connor..."

He cut her off. "Are you done with me Bliss? Is that why you gave this back to me?" He opened his one palm and Bliss saw her charm sitting in his hand.

"Done with you? Connor, I almost got you killed. I could have cost you your career. Your family hates me."

Connor's eyes softened along with his voice. "You didn't answer my question." "Connor, I don't want to cause you any more pain." She answered so sincerely that it saddened him.

"You came to the hospital." It wasn't a question, but she nodded yes.

"When I found your charm in my hand, I asked my family where you were. No one could answer me." He took a calming breath. "I lost it. I found out what Caitlyn had said to you, and I knew that you had run. Why would you leave me?" The hurt she saw in his eyes undid the bravado attitude she had been trying to pull off.

"I didn't run, exactly. I didn't want to put you or your family in any more danger."

"But you left me Bliss; me."

Bliss paused. "Connor leaving you in that hospital was the hardest thing I've ever done, and I'll admit to being a coward and not wanting to face your family." She gestured to his injuries. "But I also left because I want you to have a good life. You've been hurt twice because of me." There she'd said it. She really thought she was doing what was right for him, even though it was slowly killing her.

Tears welled in Bliss' eyes and Jax stepped towards the table concerned. "Bliss?"

"I'm okay." She said wiping her eyes.

"You sure?"

Connor was mentally and physically drained. Up until a day ago he had no idea where Bliss was, if she was safe, and worse, why she would come to the hospital, leave her charm with him and then take off? It took some time, but he eventually found out what Caitlyn had said to her on the phone. He had been so mad at Caitlyn that he had told her to leave his room. No wonder Bliss had fled. He hoped it was because she thought his family was mad at her and nothing else. Then the General received the call from Jax telling him that the terrorists had been caught and his family was safe. His dad had asked about Bliss, and Jax had said she was fine and that she was staying with him. The General asked where exactly they were at and Jax had told him Fairfax.

Connor had tried to leave the hospital right then, but he could barely move on his own. He endured almost a week of hoping Bliss would come back to him on her own. There was no way to reach her and it drove Connor crazy.

That morning he was done waiting to find out. He had

taken off all the heart monitors and told the doctor he was checking out. His parents weren't happy, and he made Caitlyn go to a store and buy him clothes. She was so happy that Connor was talking to her again she flew from the room eager to help him.

Connor wanted to touch Bliss, hold her hand, but she held herself away from him guardedly. "Listen we're checking into the Sheraton down the street. I'm beat. Will you come with me so we can talk, please?" Bliss could hear the exhaustion in his voice. Jax was still standing next to her. "If you go with him, I can come get you later." He offered.

"Okay. Thanks. Connor really needs to be in bed." She said causing Connor to smile for the first time in days. Her unintended double innuendo put an adorable mischievous grin on Connor's handsome face and her heart pitty pattered vulnerably.

Bliss stood up and Collin came forward and helped Connor to stand. She still couldn't believe Connor was there. She watched as he maneuvered slowly towards the exit. Drew and Price moved quickly to her and Jax.

"You're going with him?' Drew asked. She could see he was troubled.

"Bliss you don't have to go with him, you know?" Jax said.

"I want to talk to him Jax. If it's over between us, then this will give me closure."

"It doesn't sound like it's over to me." Price told her with a smile, and she could see Drew's face drop.

"Bliss, coming?" Connor called to her from the door. She may not have known it, but there was no way Connor was leaving without her. She was his.

Bliss said she would be right there and then she told the guys in a hushed voice not to tell anyone what she had disclosed to them. Price was doing the key and lock thing with his fingers on his lips and it made her smile. If she did take the job, she already knew that she and Phil Price would become great friends.

When she reached the door Connor was struggling to get down the steps. Collin was at his side and Connor grunted as he made it to the sidewalk.

A rental car was parked in a handicapped spot out in front of the bar. Collin helped Connor into the front seat and took his crutches from him. Collin still hadn't said a word

to her and she couldn't help but feel that he didn't want her anywhere near his brother. Bliss got into the back and she saw Connor rest his head wearily against the headrest. Collin had tossed the crutches into the trunk before getting in.

The ride to the hotel was made in complete silence. Bliss felt so awkward that she silently questioned her decision to go with them. When they arrived at the hotel Collin got the crutches and then opened the door for Connor. Bliss got out and stood back uncomfortably, not knowing what to do, if anything. Connor slowly made his way to the hotel lobby and Collin remained diligently by his side the entire time. She could see how unsteady Connor was, and she realized that Collin didn't want to risk Connor falling flat on his face and injuring himself further, so he patiently walked next to him. Bliss followed behind the brothers. She was thinking about what Connor had said to her at the bar. She still wasn't sure why he was there, and she hoped she would be brave enough to handle whatever he intended to verbally dish out to her. She also thought about her job offer. She couldn't help but wonder what Connor would think about it. Watching Connor as he shuffled ahead of her was bittersweet. She was happy he was going to recover, so happy, but seeing the pain he was obviously in and knowing she had caused it was something she didn't know if she could ever forget or forgive herself for. Connor must have sensed her anxiousness because he looked back at her and gave her a sweet small smile. The front desk had everything ready and Collin took the two room key cards from the desk manager and helped Connor to the elevator.

Connor looked dog-tired and Bliss could tell his trip today had taken a major toll on him. She leaned against the wall of the elevator and saw Collin was looking at everything except her. What an ass, she thought. I'm the one who should be mad at him.

"What gives Collin? I'm the one that should be mad at you! The silent treatment is so Junior High." Bliss knew it was a snarky comment, but she was fed up with the charade.

Connor chuckled hearing Bliss lament his brother. "He can't talk." Connor told her. "What? Why not?"

"Because I broke his jaw and it's wired shut."

Collin pressed his lips back and Bliss saw the metal wires holding his mouth almost completely closed.

"I owed him that." Connor said with a tiny grin. "For that picture."

Bliss was staring at Collin who shrugged.

"My mom was mad, but dad said he deserved it." Connor finished as the elevator opened onto their floor.

Luckily their rooms were nearby. Collin open Connor's door and handed Bliss the key card before leaving. Bliss held the door open for Connor as he shuffled inside to the nearest bed. When he sat on it, he let out an agonizing grunt.

Bliss stood inside the door unsure of what to do. Connor tossed his crutches to the ground.

"Will you help me lie down?" He asked her. He watched her intently searching for a clue as to what she was thinking or how she was feeling.

Bliss was relieved to have something to do. First, she helped him take off his jacket. Then she helped him to move back on the bed, so his head lay on the pillow. She placed another pillow under his arm and then took the two pillows off the other bed putting them under his leg. Finally, she untied his boot and placed it on the floor. "Perfect, thanks." He sounded so tired; Bliss wondered if he'd fall asleep. She stood uncertainly next to the bed and then turned to sit in a nearby chair. "Will you lay down by me while we talk?" His voice was gentle as he patted the bed next to him. "Connor, I..."

"Come here Bliss, we both need this." She couldn't argue with that, so she took off her coat and boots and crawled onto the bed, propping herself up on her elbow so that she was looking down at him. She looked at the bruises covering his face and felt a lump form in her throat. She did not want to get emotional. "I'm so sorry Connor. I'm so, so very sorry." She said. Her voice betraying how vulnerable she was feeling. She couldn't stop herself from touching him as she ran her fingers tenderly near his split lips and stitched forehead.

He took her fingers in his hand and held her hand gently. "I knew you would feel guilty about this. Bliss, it's not your fault."

"It is," she said. Her voice cracked, exposing her feelings. "If I hadn't asked you to come to Manchester, you would have been safe."

"And what about you?"

"What about me?"

"Who would've kept you safe?"

She dismissed his question. "I should have never emailed you, Connor. You missed going overseas with your team, didn't you?"

"Yes, Andy's the team leader until I get back."
Bliss smiled sadly.

"What?" Connor asked seeing the tiny smile.

"How like you to be so positive and ready to go back." She said. "Connor, how did you know I was here? Why are you here?"

"The General told me where you were. He talked to Jax last week. Why am I here? I think you know why I'm here."

"Jax didn't tell me he talked to the General." She said wondering why he hadn't.

"What happened Bliss? I don't know anything. No one even knew where you were." "It's a pretty long story. Are you sure you're up to hearing it?"

"I think I deserve to know."

"Yes, you do." She paused, pushing her hair back. "I just want you to know that I saw those cars drive into the motel lot and I knew, damn it, I knew something wasn't right. I tried to get Hammond to turn around. I pretended that I had left something in the room, but Hammond refused to stop. He said we were already late."

"They actually knocked on the door. I thought it might be you. I prayed you'd come back, that you had rethought going with them. I opened the door, there were four of them. I held them off for a few minutes." He said with a little smirk, which had Bliss grinning. "They were dragging me to one of the cars. I'm pretty sure they were taking me to use as leverage against you." He paused, "Bliss, I don't think they ever had your dad."

"No," She agreed softly.

"Anyway, I was barely conscious, but luckily our motel neighbors had heard the ruckus and had called the police. I heard sirens in the distance, and they dropped me and left.

I passed out. The next thing I remember was being transported to an Emergency Room. Once they stabilized me, they sent me to Bennington VA."

"I hate that you were hurt. I hate that I caused it."

"Sweetheart, we are going to have a big problem if you don't stop saying that." He was serious, but he said it so kindly that it made her feel better.

"So tell me what happened? Where did you go after you left the motel? I know Zarghun was captured. It was all over the news. Were you involved?"

Bliss told him everything that had happened after she had left him, and Connor was stunned into silence.

"Say something." She said worried what he could be thinking.

"You are amazing. You have had more excitement in the last few weeks than most people have in a lifetime." He said truly astonished.

"Well, I wouldn't call it exciting, but it's been very

eventful."

Connor touched her cheek tenderly. "That one man back at the bar, he likes you, doesn't he?"

She didn't even try to deny it. "Drew. I actually just figured that out today." She said self-consciously.

"Do you like him?" Connor held his breath.

"No. He's a nice guy, but no, I like him as a friend only."

Connor sighed relieved. Bliss watched his face visibly ease.

"Bliss, you never answered me. Are you done with me? Are you cutting me loose?" "Connor you make it sound like I have a choice?" She said exasperated.

"I'm not the one that left me in the hospital and took off." He said brusquely.

"Connor, your brother sent you a photo hoping to break us up. I got you beaten within an inch of your life, so I know your parents aren't happy with me, and Caitlyn, someone who I have thought of like a sister, told me to stay away from you!"

"Yes, I know all that. My siblings are idiots. I can't undo that hurt that they've caused you. I wish I could. Caitlyn feels horrible and wants to talk to you. Collin charted a plane and came with me today. I know he feels bad about the picture. My parents though, you're wrong about them. They are worried about you and neither of them blame you for what happened."

"Really?" She said meekly.

"Really." He said cradling her face with his hand.

"Connor how did you know we were at the bar?"

"I called Sparrow. Her number was on the card that Hammond gave you. You left it in the room. She said you were at a bar. She gave me the address."

Bliss looked uncomfortable. "Uh, did she say anything else?"

"She actually apologized for acting like a bitch and she said she was sorry that you and I had split up."

"Oh, I..." He didn't let her finish her sentence.

"Are we split up? Are we over?"

"You still want me?" Bliss whispered.

"You're going to have to do something really awful to make me not want you, Honey." Bliss grinned,

"What? Almost killing you wasn't bad enough?" Connor chuckled at her joke. "I love you. I will always love you."

Bliss looked down at Connor and saw the man she knew she would love for the rest of her life staring back at her.

"Maybe I should tell you something first."

Connor became immediately apprehensive. "I'm not going to like this, am I?"

"I don't know?" She admitted.

"Crap, okay, tell me."

"I've been offered a job with the CIA."

Connor was quiet for a few seconds.

"What about your Commission?"

"They want to buy my remaining time from the Army."

"Do you want to take the job?"

"I think I do, but could we talk about it? I really value your opinion."

Connor smiled at her. "I would love to talk about this with you, and for the record, nothing will change how I feel about you." Connor said threading his hand behind her neck.

"Connor." Her voice came out syrupy and sexy and

tears gathered in her eyes.

"I love you Bliss. I want you in my life, no matter what."

"CIA included?"

"Yes, CIA included."

"Now, tell me what I need to hear."

"I love you Connor Doherty."

He pulled her down and tenderly kissed her lips. "Call your brother." He whispered against her softness.

"To pick me up?" She said sitting up quickly.

"Hell no, your sleeping here and I don't want him to worry."

Bliss grinned happily and the heaviness that she had been carrying inside of her dispersed instantaneously. Connor pulled her down to him once again and kissed her with heat. Their mouths fused gently, and their tongues mated erotically. Bliss feathered her hands through his short hair careful not to put any weight on him. The hand not in the cast slid underneath her shirt and skimmed up to her breast.

Connor pulled back from the kiss. "Sweetheart, you have no idea how bad I want you, but I'm a little challenged right now."

Bliss sat up and saw just how much her man did want her. His hardness evident under the loose sweatpants he wore.

"I got this." She said huskily.

Bliss took her time undressing Connor. She touched him lightly, massaged him sweetly, and left wet, warm kisses everywhere on his body. Connor was literally vibrating by the time he was completely naked. She then stood from the bed and quickly took off all of her clothes, never taking her eyes from his.

When she was completely naked, she knelt on the bed, just out of Connor's reach, and let her hands slide over her curvy frame. Connor's cock swelled further causing Bliss' female lips to moisten with want.

He reached for her, but Bliss remained where she was. His eyes locked in on her exquisite breasts with their dusty rose nipples. Bliss cupped them tenderly.

"Is this what you want?" She asked promiscuously. Connor nodded; unconsciously he licked his lips and bit out a hoarse, "Yes."

Bliss swept her thumbs over her taut nipples and moaned seductively.

"Bliss. Come here." Connor choked out as he watched the tantalizing show.

Bliss slowly ran her one hand down her stomach and abdomen to skate seductively through her trimmed curls.

"Bliss, please."

"Or do you want this?" She said huskily sliding her finger through her pinkness.

"Yes, I want to touch you there." His voice was raspy and so sexy. "I want to taste you and touch you."

Bliss continued to pleasure herself wickedly and she could see that Connor was enjoying her stimulating seduction. His cock's large dome glistened with pre-cum and he grasped his thick shaft pumping it unhurriedly.

Bliss crawled to Connor and straddled his hips. She skimmed over his thickness lightly with her female lips and Connor groaned. She leaned forward and her chest met his, her needy clit pressed against his maleness, and she kissed him so ardently that she shuddered as a small orgasm rippled through her.

Connor held her to him surging through her wet lips with his throbbing heat. Bliss raised herself up and guided his firmness to her entrance, and with her hands on his chest and her eyes locked on his, she sank down on him until they were one.

Their groans of satisfaction were simultaneous and the grin on Connor's face matched her own. Bliss rode his steely horse never taking her eyes from his. The carnal sizzle began to unfurl within her, her breasts tingled deliciously, and her core gripped him tightly.

Connor was using his one leg to press up into her and their pace quickened as they reached new heights. Connor thumbed her swollen clit and Bliss careened out of control; the fiery sizzle of a grand orgasm consumed her entire body. Her spasming muscles hugged his length and Connor growled sexily as his release tore through him. Spent and sated Bliss fell against Connor's chest. He clutched her to him nuzzling her neck, relishing their closeness.

"I missed you so much." Bliss whispered into his warm skin.

"I wish you had called me, come back to me."

"I know. I'm sorry Connor. I really did think I was protecting you by letting you go."

"I know your intention was unselfish, but Sweetheart, you leaving me hurt worse than those bullets or that beating."

Bliss kissed his chest tenderly. "I was hurting too, trust me."

Connor rubbed her back lovingly.

"Connor?"

"Ummm?"

"Thank you for coming here; for not letting me throw this away." Connor kissed her head affectionately. "Love you Baby."
"Love you too." She whispered happily.

Chapter 25

The wind mercilessly whipped Bliss' hair as she stood on the open airport tarmac, but she didn't try to hold it back from covering her face. If she did, anyone would be able to see the tears that ran unchecked down her face, and that included Connor, whom she was sure, was watching her from inside the enormous C-17 that was now taxiing to the runway.

The last two months had been the best in Bliss' entire life, and she prayed there would be more. As she watched the plane move further and further away, she thought back on
them.

Bliss had accepted the CIA's offer and was delighted to learn her increase in pay was substantial. Connor had remained in Fairfax with her, neither of them wanting to be apart from each other, and since he was on medical leave it had been a no brainer that he remain with her. Their first full week together, before Bliss started working, was spent shopping. The first thing they did was lease a car and arranged for her old car, that was in San Francisco, to be donated to a charity. Next, they found her a place to live, one she could move into immediately, a two -bedroom townhouse, with a private patio and a garage that was in the same complex as Jax and Drew's place. By the end of that first week, Connor had made the medic at the nearby VA Hospital remove the one cast on his leg and replace it a walking cast so that he could get around better. They spent the next two days shopping for everything she would need; furniture, kitchen items, sheets, towels, televisions, and of course a state-of-the-art gaming unit and console. Many of the items she purchased for the home she bought online, so they did not have to go to the stores, but the furniture they hand-picked from a reputable store and Connor paid extra to have everything delivered and set up the next day.

It was exhausting setting up her home and Bliss marveled that Connor never complained once. He was simply content to be with her. When she asked him if he minded all the shopping, he explained that it was actually nice to do normal couple things. He also confessed that when he went back to Afghanistan, because her home was completely furnished, he would be able to conjure up images of her on her couch, in her kitchen and, he said with a mischievous smile, in the bed. Their first night in the townhouse Connor asked if he could move in with her and Bliss laughed and handed him an envelope with a cute card inside that she had been planning to give him that night. Inside the card she had written that she loved him and, 'My home is your home?' She had taped the spare key to the card. Connor chuckled loving that they were once again proving how in synch they were with each other. So, Bliss' home became their home. Bliss started her CIA training the next week. Unlike when she was in the Army's boot camp her time training with the CIA was spent learning protocol and learning about the various operations that the CIA was involved in around the world. Once again, her gift served her well as she memorized everything put in front of her. She still had to pass a fitness test and she learned that the CIA required their Agents to pass a fitness and shooting test every year.

While she had been training, Connor spent his free time recovering from his injuries and helping to get their new place organized. He had waited for the cable company, hung pictures, bought a small grill, and even a patio set.

Spending time with Connor only solidified what she already knew; they were perfect together. The days flew past and Bliss hated that Connor would be leaving at the end of the next month. Their townhouse was completely set and comfy, but she knew that Connor being in it, with her, was what made it feel like a home.

Bliss loved her training and every day when she came home, she shared what she had learned with Connor. They had been living together for a month now and both his casts had been taken off, and he had started working out again. His bruises had healed, and Bliss could tell he was antsy to get back to work.

Jax and Drew lived in the unit of townhouses that were two away from their place. Bliss learned that Drew was preparing to go undercover and Jax would be remaining at

Headquarters as his liaison. It took some time, but Drew eventually warmed up to Connor. Connor knew if Drew was given the chance, he would still want to date Bliss, but Connor also knew that Bliss had no such designs on Drew. She was his and she let him know how she felt every day. Price and Bliss were becoming closer too. Connor wasn't concerned about him hitting on his girl, he recognized that the two of them were kindred geek spirits and Connor was actually happy that when he was gone Bliss would have a good friend to lean on if she needed too. During the final week of Bliss' formal training Bliss thought that Jax had been acting peculiar. She had hardly talked to him, Drew or Price, not even at work, which was even more strange. That week she had been told that she been partnered with Sparrow, which was a funny twist of fate. Connor was relieved to learn that he had never slept with her and he hoped that Bliss would come to see Sparrow as a friend as well as a partner. She needed female companionship. On her final day of training Bliss was excited to share with Connor that she had passed her physical tests and her shooting qualifier. It was Friday and she and Connor had the entire weekend to relax together. Gonzalez told her she would be working computers for the first two months and then she and Sparrow would be given an assignment.

Bliss walked outside to the parking lot ready to celebrate with her handsome man. Connor always dropped her off and picked her up so he could have the use of the car while she was training. It was one of the nicest parts of her day, seeing him waiting for her at the end of the day. He always had a smile on his face and the delicious butterflies he set off in her chest, when she looked at him, never seemed to lessen. "Hi." He said giving her a little smooch as he opened the door for her.

"Hi yourself. You look nice." Connor had on a pair of nice trousers, a light blue shirt and a blazer. She knew he had to have just purchased the outfit because she hadn't seen it before. They had bought him clothes, but they had consisted of jeans, sweats, shorts, and couple of shirts.

"How did you do?" He asked getting into the car.

"It was great. I passed both tests. You know, I thought I knew so much about computers and coding, but I now know I have so much more to learn. Don't get me wrong, I love it, really love the work, but thank goodness I have a great memory, because it really helps that I don't have to refer to the manuals every second."

Connor turned left instead of right.

"Where are we going?"

"A surprise."

"Oh, you know how I like surprises." She said with a mock chuckle. She figured Connor was taking her to a celebratory dinner.

Connor stole a glance at her and she saw that he looked a little anxious.

"Is everything okay?" She asked him. Her gut began to churn forebodingly.

"Relax, Honey, I think you're going to like this." His smile was sincere so she was slightly comforted.

Connor pulled up to a restaurant that looked a little fancier than where they normally went.

He handed the valet the car keys and Bliss looked down at her simple slacks and blazer outfit hoping she was dressed appropriately.

When they entered the restaurant Connor gave the hostess her last name for the reservation, which she thought was strange, but as they walked through the dining area

Bliss saw that Jax was in the back at a table near the wall, which explained that.

As she neared the table, she saw that there was

another person sitting across from him, a man. Jax stood when they got closer and so did the mystery man. As they approached the man turned around and Bliss froze. The air whooshed from her lungs and she wobbled on her short -heeled shoes. Connor put his arm around her to steady her and she leaned into him grateful for the support. Bliss stared into ha pair of blue eyes, the very same eyes that she had.

"Bliss, this is our dad." Jax told her.

Bliss gasped, her father? Her mouth was slightly open, and all coherent thoughts had fled her.

"Bliss, Honey, are you okay?" Connor asked softly. Her father stood stone still. She could see that he was gauging her reaction.

Bliss recovered from her initial shock. "How?"

"When did you? I don't understand?" "Sit down. Jax will explain everything." Connor told her moving his hand to the small of her back

"You've known?" She looked at Connor a bit perplexed that he would keep a secret of this magnitude from her.

"I only found out today." He reassured her.

Bliss couldn't take her eyes from her father, who seemed as tongue tied as she was. When they were settled around the table her father spoke.

"Bliss, it is so nice to meet you. I know you're a bit shocked to see me. I'm sorry for surprising you. I'm still not out yet, so I needed this to be without fanfare."

"Out?" She asked perplexed.

Jax took Bliss hand. "Bliss I've known dad had been in hiding for a few weeks now. He got in touch with me when he heard your name mentioned in the news after we took down Zarghun and Conti."

"I've been keeping tabs on Conti." Her father added. "Now that you're CIA I thought it prudent to come out of hiding. The CIA has always known where I have been. I'm still considered Active, and I do small operatives when they need me."

"I knew you were alive. I knew mom still talked to you."

"Your mom was the love of my life. I left to keep her and you and Jax safe. Conti knew of my gift. We had actually been close at one time. He also knew that you had inherited it. I figured out that Conti had turned traitor and because I had so many CIA secrets locked away in my head, I became a risk to you, your mom, and Jax. Before Conti completely went dark, I pretended that your mom and I were estranged, that I didn't care about my family, hoping he wouldn't use any of you against me. It was the hardest ruse I ever pulled off. I heard that Conti used me against you anyway. I'm so sorry about that."

Bliss couldn't take her eyes off of him. She had his eyes and maybe his lips, but Jax was one that looked like him.

"You look just like your mom." Her father said softly.

"She said I had your eyes." Bliss replied quietly.

"Bliss, dad reached out to me a few weeks ago. He asked me to set up this dinner so he could meet you. I told Connor about it today."

Bliss felt Connor's hand on her thigh, and she covered it with one of her own hands.

"So you're coming out of hiding now?"

"Yes. Conti had been searching for me for years. I think he had hoped to kidnap you to use against me, but then, from what I understand he intercepted an email and when he saw who was delivering the message, he realized it was you. He knew you had my gift and he realized he could get information from you."

" But he didn't." Bliss said proudly. "Thanks to Connor."

Connor kissed her temple and Bliss reveled in his strong body that was plastered against hers giving her support.

"Do you know how he knew about that email? I've always wondered?"

Jax answered her. "Actually, Price has been working on that. He just found out that Lt. Henry Russ sold code information to Conti. We were able to dig through some emails and it looks like Russ' wife wasn't happy with Army pay. She left him and Russ had hoped that with the money Conti gave him for the codes he could win her back. Russ has been pulled in already."

"That's terrible." Bliss said thinking back to the brief meeting she'd had with him and Brant.

Bliss suddenly remembered something she had always wondered about. "Dad? Wow, that sure sounded strange." She said with an awkward laugh. "Did you send mom money?"

Her father smiled sadly. "I did. Every month, with the help of the CIA, I sent money to your mom's bank account. I hope it helped a little?"

"It did, thank you."

Bliss sat back in her chair and felt as if so many pieces of her life that had been mysteries were now falling into place. The only sad part was that her mother wasn't there for the family reunion.

Her father sensed her thoughts. "I still miss her every day."

Bliss smiled sadly, "Me too."

That evening's dinner went on for hours. He shared stories of some of his CIA exploits and Jax told him how he had gone from DEA to CIA and how mad he was that Bliss wanted to become CIA, only because he was worried about her. Which made Connor laugh out loud before he gave Jax an earful, telling him that Bliss faced danger every day in the Army and that she was probably going to be safer in the CIA, which had her father and her laughing simply because the funny expression on Jax's face. Bliss was delighted to learn that her dad would officially be coming out of hiding within the week and that he hoped to relocate back in Fairfax. He told them that he was getting a little old for field work, but the Agency still hoped to use him to teach new Agents.

The next month flew by bringing Connor's departure date even closer. A week before Connor was to leave Bliss left work excited to share with him that she had asked for the next week, his last week stateside, off. She was thrilled about being able to spend the extra time with him. Connor's departure weighed heavily on her, but she was determined to keep up a brave front. As usual Connor met her and drove her home. Bliss immediately told him that she had a week off and Connor's smile told her everything. He too had been thinking about his upcoming deployment and wishing they had more time together.

She animatedly talked about how they should spend their time. She was still spouting ideas and Connor was grinning at her as she unlocked the front door and pushed inside. She froze completely surprised finding Connor's entire family, Jax, Drew, Price, and her father waiting for them. Her open mouth expression was priceless, seeing everyone she loved in one room, and then Connor dropped to one knee. Bliss was overcome with emotion seeing Connor kneeling before her with a beautiful diamond ring in his fingers.

The room was quiet, and Bliss's eyes connected with Connor's.

"Bliss, I love you. When I'm with you I'm whole. I never expected to want the things I now want, and that's all because of you. I used to laugh when I heard the term better half, but I sure know what that means now. I honestly believe you are my soul mate, and I hope you want to share your life with me, because I want to share my life with you. Please marry me?"

Bliss had tears blurring her vision and she tugged on Connor's shoulders so that he would stand. He was holding the ring in his hand and he watched as she stared at the ring. They had never talked about marriage, was she going to say no?

His voice was low, just a thread above a whisper, and he was aware that everyone in the room was absolutely still, waiting for her answer. Connor knew Bliss though, perhaps better than she knew herself, and he knew she wanted to say something to him. He just hoped whatever she was about to say had a 'yes' somewhere in it.

"Talk to me Baby."

Bliss gave him a tiny nervous grin. If any other man had called her Baby, she'd have them in an arm headlock begging to be released, but not Connor. When Connor called her Baby, it was sexy and sent delicious shivers down her back.

"Connor." She said softly, worried that her thoughts were too personal to share. "You saved me. I'm not just talking about rescuing me in Afghanistan. You always saw the real me and I love you for that. You saved the girl with the thick glasses playing video games, the young lady with no parents who tried to do everything on her own, the female Army Officer determined to prove herself, and the woman who had no idea what real love felt like. You saved me Connor Doherty, and I love you for that and for so many other reasons. I will always love you, and yes, I would love to marry you."

Her hands had been pressed against his chest and Connor grinned down at her and whispered, "Thank you Sweetheart." Then he placed the ring on her finger and kissed it to seal it in its place. Their family and friends began clapping happily and surrounded them giving them heartfelt congratulations.

They were married four days later, two days before Connor was to deploy. Bliss had thought they would wait until Connor returned, so his team could be there, but Connor wouldn't wait. He wanted it legal and binding. Not that he didn't trust her, he did. He simply said it would make him feel better, when he was gone, knowing that they were officially husband and wife, so Bliss agreed.

Her new friends from the CIA came, and Bo and Red flew up from Mississippi. Bliss was delighted to learn that they were engaged. Bo was staying Stateside, and Bliss could see the relief on Red's face when he had told Bliss.

The ceremony was small, but it was everything that Bliss could have hoped for. The ceremony was in a little church on Long Beach Island in New Jersey. The weather had cooperated, and the reception was held on a patio that buffered the beautiful bay. Bliss had found a white dress that hung on her curves perfectly. It was simple yet elegant and Connor looked magnificent in his Green Beret dress attire. They danced and talked and enjoyed the time with their friends and family and kissed a lot. Bliss had danced with the General who had whispered to her that he had always felt that she was part of the family, and that he was even happier now because she had married Connor. He told her that they were a perfect match.

Connor and Bliss left the reception before it ended and drove the 45 minutes to Atlantic City Airport where they took a puddle jumper to Fayetteville, North Carolina. That was where Connor would be catching the plane that would take him to Kabul. They checked into a hotel near the airport and Bliss felt the proverbial clock begin to countdown their last two days together.

Connor had been quieter than usual, and Bliss wasn't sure if it was the stress of getting married or his deployment. She wanted to be a good Army wife and make his departure as easy as possible for him. She had been telling herself that under no circumstances could she cry when she saw him off. Bliss finally got him to open up and he admitted that for the first time in his career he had mixed emotions about going back overseas. When they entered the suite, they had booked Connor dropped his duffel on the floor while Bliss lifted her small bag to the dresser top to unzip it. She felt his hands encircle her waist, so she leaned back into his strong chest. His lips kissed her neck tenderly and not wanting to lose the contact with him she lifted her hands behind his head. "Wife, you're my wife." Connor said softly between kisses.

"I love that I'm your wife." She turned in his arms and stood on her toes to reach his lips with hers, depositing a promising kiss upon them.

Connor picked her up and walked them to the bed. "Are we starting this Honeymoon, husband?"

Connor grinned, "Yes my little Agent, right now." Connor had given her that nickname the week after they had gotten back together, and she had officially taken the job with the CIA.

He stopped short of the bed and put her down only to pull her shirt over her head. Bliss took the hem of his shirt and eased it up his torso and over his head. She trailed kisses over his exposed skin while she lifted the shirt.

She couldn't believe all the horrible gashes and bruises were gone. A few small white welts remained, but the injuries that Connor had sustained were completely healed and most were not even visible anymore.

She kissed his abdomen loving the indented six-pack he sported. His body was magnificent. He was stronger and more physically fit than he had ever been before. His arms were ripped with lean muscle. His legs were powerful, and his chest was strong and solid. His blue eyes latched on to hers as she nibbled her way up his chest. "Baby, I'm not feeling very patient." He told her, his sexy voice husky with need. Bliss stepped away from him, shimmied out of her skirt, her thong, and unhooked her white lacy bra. "Happy Hubby?" She said moving to the bed unabashed with her nakedness.

Connor had a huge smile on his face as he quickly peeled off the rest of his clothes. They made love for the first time as man and wife with a ferocious passion that had them both breathing heavily, after their thundering climaxes. The rest of the night they spent pleasuring each other slowly, deliberately, taking each other to the kind of bliss that only true mates can achieve.

As the plane turned into a mere speck in the sky Bliss touched her lips that Connor had kissed just moments before and prayed for his safe return.

His final words to her were ones she'd always remember.

"Bliss, I'm leaving because I love my country, but I'm going to return home safely because I love you." He kissed her tenderly but with so much passion.

Bliss had choked out her final goodbye. She was trying so hard not get emotional. "Connor, I love you. Stay safe."

Bliss watched until the plane couldn't be seen anymore. She wiped the wet tears from her cheeks, looked to heaven, and prayed for the safe return of all the men and women fighting abroad and especially for her Green Beret.

Epilogue

It had been fourteen months since Bliss had stood on the same tarmac in almost the same spot. She watched the C-17 touch down and roar to slow down. The large plane lumber loudly to a spot where one man holding two orange lights directed it.

To her right, three black hearses from three different Funeral Parlors were waiting. Bliss felt the lump form in her throat again. She had been crying for almost two days now. A Color Guard from Fort Bragg marched to the back of the C-17. Two soldiers rolled out a red carpet that Bliss knew the coffins would be wheeled down. A Priest and a Minister walked out of the terminal towards the plane.

Bliss watched as the back of the plane opened and the three coffins were wheeled down the ramp, between the saluting Color Guard and their flags. The Priest and Minister blessed each casket before they were loaded into the black wagons. Bliss' heart broke watching the pomp and circumstance that accompanied the arrival of deceased soldiers.

The hearses left the tarmac and Bliss watched as the passenger door on the big plane was now opened. Men and woman, all looking exhausted and dressed in fatigues disembarked from the large craft. They knew their plane had carried home three deceased military personnel, so their moods were appropriately sober.

They hurried past Bliss staring into the glass terminal room where their families were gathered. A few of them had looked at her, but she had barely noticed. The first soldier reached the door behind her and when he opened it Bliss could hear the happy shouts and cheers of the persons gathered there. Bliss didn't take her eyes off the doorway. Her stomach was doing flip flops and she couldn't move the tears out of her eyes fast enough for her vision not to be slightly blurred.

Finally, she saw him. Connor stood in the planes doorway and when he saw her, he smiled and waved. He turned towards the two men, who were dressed in formal pilot attire, and shook their hands before securing his pack over one shoulder to walk down the steps. He moved towards her the anxiety that had plagued her since he had left so many months ago lifted. His eyes never left her face.

Bliss made her feet move even though her legs felt like jelly. Connor had a grin that spread wider the closer he got to her and when they were a yard apart, he dropped his pack and she launched herself into his welcoming arms. Bliss sobbed into his neck and Connor held her closely. She felt wetness on his cheeks and knew their reunion affected him as it had her.

Connor gently lowered her to the ground and kissed her passionately. Bliss clung to him and returned the fevered kiss. They were interrupted by a low cough. They broke their kiss and Bliss turned, but Connor kept his arm firmly around her holding her close.

"Cap., it's been an honor, Sir." The soldier said giving Connor a salute. Connor saluted him back. Before Connor could say anything, five other men came back outside from the glass room and repeated what the first soldier had said, all of them saluting Connor.

"It's been a pleasure serving with you men." Connor said.

Another soldier joined the group of seven men. "Bliss this is my team." Connor introduced each one and Bliss shook each man's hand.

"I never did get a chance to thank you." She said sincerely. "Thank you."

Their responses ranged from "Yes, Ma'am's" to "Glad we could help."

Connor picked his pack up and the group walked into the loud room. Each man shook Connor's hand before leaving them to once again be with whoever were waiting for them inside.

One of the men remained next to Connor. "Bliss this is Andy."

"Ah." she said with a little grin. "The famous best friend that uses my husbands' name when he's picking up women."

Andy laughed, "yeah, that's me. It's nice to finally meet you." Andy said with a grin. "The woman who tamed our fearless leader, you must be a very special lady."

Bliss blushed and Connor kissed her temple. "She's everything and more."

Andy turned to face Connor and Bliss saw a sad expression flicker across Andy's face. "You're really doing this?" Andy said.

"I am." Connor answered.

Bliss did not interrupt; she kept her eyes on Connor, hoping to glean whatever they were talking about by watching his demeanor.

"I'll miss you buddy."

"You'll be too busy leading our team to miss me." Connor said giving him a lopsided grin.

A woman squealed, and Andy's name was shouted

towards them.

Andy turned, and Bliss and Connor watched a small woman and large man moving quickly towards them.

"My parents." Andy said as he plastered a huge smile on his face.

Andy turned back to Connor before his parents reached them and Connor released Bliss as the two men hugged.

"Stay in touch." Andy said.

"I will." Connor replied just as Andy was swept up in his parents loving arms.

Connor gathered Bliss again in one arm and grabbed his pack that was on the floor with his other.

Connor was asking Bliss about work and as they walked out of the terminal towards the car that was parked in the lot. When they reached the car, Connor tossed his large bag into back and pulled Bliss back into his arms.

"So, wife I know you're dying to ask." He chuckled nuzzling her neck.

"Yes, but I figured you would tell me when you were ready." She said placing her hands around his neck.

Connor laughed. "Man, just another reason why I love you so much woman." Connor kissed her and while he was kissing her, he took her left hand from around his neck and she felt him slide something over her wrist.

Bliss broke the kiss to look at what he'd put on her. She gasped when she saw a leather strand tied in the 'love knot', just like the one Connor had placed on her nearly two years ago.

"You made me another one?"

"Nope."

"No?"

"No, that's yours. When I got to Bagram, the night before I was to meet up with my team, I stumbled across a little lost and found shelf in the mess hall. It was sitting there. I know it's the one I made you because the leather I used had a small kink in it. See right here." He said using his thumb to tap the spot he was referring to.

Bliss' eyes clouded over again with tears. "Connor." She choked out.

"Baby, what's the matter? I thought you'd be happy?"

Bliss flung her arms back around his neck and cried into his chest. Connor had never seen her come undone before and it scared him.

"Bliss talk to me. What's the matter?"

Bliss got herself together. "I'm sorry. I tried to keep it together. I really did, but you giving me this, well, shit." She said wiping her eyes.

"Tell me?" He encouraged her.

"Connor, I'm so happy you're home. I've been so worried about you. I don't know what's wrong with me. The last two days all I've done is cry."

Connor bracketed her face with his hands. "It's been rough, huh?"

She nodded. "You know how I grew up. The love I have for you is so above anything I've ever known before. I was scared Connor. I was so afraid you would get hurt, or worse. The last two days I've been a wreck."

"I'm home now, Honey."

"I know. I'm so glad. I haven't taken as much as a sick day so I could use every vacation day, sick day that I've accumulated for the last fourteen months, for when you got home."

Connor laughed. "That's my girl, but we have a little problem."

Bliss stared at Connor, her eyes were wide with worry.

"It's not a bad problem, Sweetie, promise."

Bliss remained quiet hoping he'd explain.

"You see I've taken a new Commission."

"What?"

"Bliss when I left you fourteen months ago I knew I'd never be able to, nor want to do that again. I know we got to email and Skype, but Sweetheart, I've missed you and I don't plan on ever having to miss you again. So, we won't have to use all those sick days you've saved up because I have been given a new commission at the Fall Church Base. It's only twenty minutes away from our place."

Bliss was stunned into silence.

"Say something?" He chuckled.

"You want to stay Stateside?"

"Yes, I want to stay Stateside. I'm going to be given a promotion to Major, which is a good pay bump and I've been asked to take over training the men and woman that qualify for Special Ops. I may have to travel once in a while, but unless something big breaks out I won't be going into any war zone."

"Connor, I don't know what to say."

Connor wrapped his arms around her. "Say you're happy that we will finally get to be together, like a husband and wife should be."

"I am very happy about that!" She said kissing him on his lips.

"Say you'll love having me in your bed every night."
"I will love having you back in our bed every night!"
She repeated enthusiastically.
"Say you're ready to start a family with me."
Bliss looked into his eyes making sure she heard him correctly. She stood on her tip toes and kissed him tenderly.
"I am so ready to have your babies, Connor Doherty."
Connor clutched her to him. He had been worried she might balk at what he had just said. She was happy with her job with the CIA and she would not be allowed to work field operations if she was pregnant.
"Connor?"
"Umm", he said still kissing her neck and not quite ready to let her go.
"Can we go get started on that family? I have really missed you!"
Connor laughed, "You are so perfect for me."
Bliss grinned and tossed him the keys knowing he would want to drive.
"Your parents and brother and sister are arriving tomorrow." She told him as she clicked her seatbelt into place.
Connor started the car and turned towards her with a small frown.
"Can I use your phone please?" He asked.
Bliss handed it to him. Her head cocked slightly wondering whom he needed to call. Connor keyed in a number and waited.
"Dad it's me. I just landed." Pause. "Yes, Bliss just told me." Pause. "About that." He paused again and Bliss heard Connor chuckle. "Yeah, thanks, that would be perfect." Pause. "Tell mom I love her."

Then Connor ended the call and looked at Bliss with an adorable little smirk. "They will not be arriving until Thursday." He said smugly. "Thursday?" "Thursday. Babe, I just got home. I don't know what you have planned, but my plans involve you, me and our bed." He gave her a sexy wink as he turned out of the lot. "Connor, that's four days from now." "Exactly." He chuckled.

The End

I hope you enjoyed Saving Bliss. I am a self-published writer and I love sharing my stories. If you have a moment, please share a review on Amazon or Goodreads.

www.zannesweeney.com